THE EMPTY CHAIR

THE EMPTY CHAIR

Baker Street Legacy Book Two

GAIL R. DELANEY

Praise for Gail R. Delaney

I've read both books and am hungry for the next. Gail tells a great story, and I love the premise of Sherlock Holmes having descendants. Highly recommend these books!!

Amazon Review, 5 Stars

Having read and loved "My Dear Branson," I was expecting nothing less than to be swept away into a world of intrigue, danger, and breathtaking romance when I read The Empty Chair. Ms. Delaney not only delivered on my every expectation, but she flew past them with the ease and speed of a bullet, delivering an amazing piece of fiction that gripped me from the very beginning, and made it impossible to put down until I reached the very end. And yet when it was over, I still wanted more — in the best possible way.

Esther Mitchell, author of the Project Prometheus
paranormal romantic suspense series

Copyright © 2016, 2018 by Gail R. Delaney

All rights reserved.

No part of this book may be reproduced in any form or by any electronic or mechanical means, including information storage and retrieval systems, without written permission from the author, except for the use of brief quotations in a book review.

This work of fiction is my own creation. I have never, do not currently, and never will use AI/artificial intelligence to write a book. I have never, do not currently, and never will use AI/artificial intelligence to generate artwork to represent my books. When my books are made into audiobooks, I will not use AI to narrate them. I support artists of all kinds whether they be photographers, cover artists, audiobook narrators, or writers. The creation of art in any form should remain a human endeavor.

I deny <u>any</u> and <u>all</u> permission, whether blatant or implied, for my work to be used by any AI program to "learn" or to produce material. I am the copyright owner and deny any attempts to use, replicate, or manipulate my work via any means not initiated by myself as the copyright owner.

To: Esther Mitchell, once again, for providing me much needed insight. And for letting me borrow her name, her thoughts, and her experiences to create a character I expected a little from, and who gave me a great deal more.

To: David Sookoo. His lovely wife Sandra received a dedication in the first book, but since he made an appearance in this one, he gets a dedication.

To Niall MacDomhnaill ailias MacCuinn, who helped me make Angus "Mac" Hennessey sound Scottish and not just an American trying to sound Scottish. All spelling and word usage came directly from Niall, so no one better say it's wrong. LOL

Book Content Expectations

Due to the nature of the genre and the storyline, please be aware there are instances of terroristic violence that may feel parallel to real-world events, as well as personal danger, violence, and abduction. The characters struggle with PTSD, mental health struggles, grief at the loss of someone close to them, and trauma.

Though in passing, and spoken from the point of view of a non-prominent character, there are themes of ableism against the main character regarding her hearing impairment.

Baker Street Legacy

Baker Street Legacy
Storytelling Style

Baker Street Legacy is a continuous timeline, in which any given book extends the story of the book prior to it and sets up for the next book while also telling its own story. The books must be read in order to have a full understanding of the saga.

This means each book has its own story arc, but also extends the greater story arcs.

There will be cliffhangers, but as the author, I will always provide you with a payoff within the book you're reading. Each book has its own plot, it's own storyline and its own resolutions. Each book (with the exclusion of the final book in the series) will have a setup for the next book. These may or may not be considered cliffhangers by some. But, be aware, they exist.

I hope you enjoy and complete the journey with us.

Baker Street Legacy
Spotify Playlist

Do you like having a soundtrack to the books you read? I've created a playlist for the Baker Street Legacy on Spotify.

You will likely notice Grayson and Kipling are inclined toward the legends of jazz along with some popular contemporary crooners. A little Frank Sinatra and Nat King Cole; a little Michael Bublé and Colbie Calliat.

I hope you enjoy.

Chapter One

"Where is my mobile?"

Grayson forced himself free of the weight of drug-induced sleep. A disconnected part of his brain advised him the words hadn't actually left his lips.

He blinked and looked around the cramped interior of the 2-3-2 seater plane, finally focusing on Mac who sat to his left, chin resting on his chest, eyes closed. Sandra was on his right, and Lynne was across the aisle from Sandra. Grayson had only a foggy recollection of boarding the plane and collapsing into the cramped center seat before they left Helsinki. Before that, there were muted glimpses of a cursory visit with a surgeon who treated him sufficiently to allow him to leave the country.

"Where is my mobile?" he demanded, managing to get the words out of his mouth this time.

Mac snapped up his head with a snort, and rubbed his face, talking into his hand to mumble his words. "In bits, Boss," Mac answered, squinting in apology. "Dinna fret though, I'll get it a' back once we're back in London. I've got it a' in hand."

Grayson cursed and tried to shift his position, hot pain radiating up his side to wrap around his ribs and steal his breath. Perspiration beaded on his brow, running down his temple and he hissed through the burn. At times like this, he would prefer to be shot straight on, even a through-and-through, over the flesh wound on his left side just below his ribs. He'd dodged the shot but fell short by two inches of being unharmed. The bullet had torn through his skin and nicked his external intercostal, which produced a lot of blood and a great deal of pain but would only debilitate him for a few days.

He'd refused strong pain medication until it had been impossible to continue, not wanting to be impaired when closing the details of the investigation. Now he couldn't shake the fog, and at that moment he questioned the intelligence of his decision. He pinched the bridge of his nose, and rubbed at the corner of his eyes in an attempt to break the oppressive fog.

"How long until we land?"

"Nae fur a whiley yet. Aboot an hoor, I'd guess," Mac answered.

Grayson ran the numbers in his head, the pain muddying his thought process. He thought it was a seven-hour difference, maybe eight? Either way, it was mid-afternoon in Boston. Trying again to shift his position and ease the pressure on his side, the movement only resulting in another burst of pain, Grayson clenched his jaw and held out a shaking hand to Mac.

"Give me your mobile."

"We rang Director Cooper," Sandra said from his other side, obvious concern pinching her features. "Lynne gave a preliminary."

She had a mottled bruise at her temple and a swollen lower lip. The Daesch recruiters in Helsinki had put them through their paces, and none came away unscathed save for the three recruiters they left dead. The rest were in custody until it was determined which government had the first right to prosecution.

"Someone give me their bloody phone," Grayson snapped through clenched teeth.

Several passengers around them turned at his barked order,

immediately going back to their own affairs. This time none on his team questioned him, and in moments both Mac and Sandra held out their hands, palms open, with their mobiles ready for him. Grayson reached for Sandra's as being the one closest and requiring the least movement from him.

Of course, he might not be able to get through. He had no idea what type of service, if any, he could manage, but he had to try.

He dialed Kipling's number by memory and swallowed hard against the pain as he brought it to his ear. Grayson wanted to close his eyes, and the demand for sleep was nearly overpowering, but after three weeks of zero communication, he needed to hear her voice far more.

The dial notification sounded four times and he was prepared for the call to go to voicemail when the line connected with a shuffle and rustle. "Sandi?"

He wanted to say something brilliant or light to set her at ease, but all he could manage to say was, "Hello, my darling…"

"Grayson?"

"Yes. Sorry." He managed to break the surface of his fog and blinked to keep awake. Just a few more minutes. "My mobile is apparently…" He lost the thought. "I wanted to hear your voice."

The scrape of a chair across lino carried from the background, and a muffled "Let me out" before she asked, "What's wrong? Are you okay?"

"I'm a good night's sleep away from okay, but I'll be right as rain soon enough," he said, gently cutting her off because he already doubted his faculties would last much longer. "I know you've probably worried, and I wanted…" He lost the thought again, and shook his head, focusing on the core of the truth. "I needed to hear your voice."

She mumbled an "Excuse me" to someone else, and the jangle of a bell preceded the sounds of city life. Cars. Distant conversation. A slight wind brushed her hearing aids, which carried her voice to her phone. She had to be downtown, perhaps at a shop. Even altered, his mind couldn't rest from forming a visual of her standing in the sun, and he wished he could be with her with a heavy ache in his chest.

"I've been half out of my mind. It's been three weeks," she declared, then he heard her low huff. "I'm sorry. Of course, you know how long it's been. I've just been thinking how would I know if anything happened."

"You would know, darling," he tried to assure, knowing his mind and his mouth were not working in accordance with each other, but unable to do much about it. "Were anything to happen to me, my family would be informed, and they have been instructed to contact you immediately."

"I don't know if I feel relief that you thought to plan ahead, or frightened at the idea you felt you needed to."

Grayson smiled and made the mistake of resting his head on the back of the seat, closing his eyes. "It is a temporary solution until I can establish something far more permanent."

"Grayson," she said again, her voice softer still. "Please…are you okay? Tell me honestly."

"I'm sorry, darling. I should have waited until tomorrow. I just needed to hear your voice."

"You've said that. Where are you right now?"

"In the air over Norway." He stuttered over the country name, realizing too late he revealed their location. They weren't home yet, and details of the situation were top secret even though the investigation was effectively over. This was why he made every attempt to avoid mind-altering drugs. "I'll be home with Watson within a few hours."

"Are you safe now?"

"Yes." He licked his lips and swallowed, his throat dry. "Yes, perfectly safe."

"Grayson, listen to me. Okay? I love you but give the phone back to Sandra. I'll talk to you soon. I love you."

"Is everything okay? Oh, who the heck am I kidding? The look on your face while you were on the phone said it all. What's going on?"

Kipling slipped back into the molded plastic chair at the table she'd shared with Mina Russo and John Allen minutes before when her phone rang and her heart started pounding enough to pop out of her chest. She glanced around the small pizzeria for the blond-haired, blue-eyed, linebacker of a man she'd recently become friends with but didn't see him.

"Where's John?"

"Little boy's room, so talk quick. Was that Grayson?"

"Sort of. I mean, it was, but…" Kipling sighed and set her elbow on the table and rested her forehead in her open hand. "He's in a plane *somewhere* on his way back to London. He's been shot." Mina caught her breath, and Kipling dared a glance at her. "Sandi swears it's not bad, called it a flesh wound." She ran her fingers along her side. "Somewhere around here."

Mina sat back and folded her hands in her lap under the table. "Not to make light of a bullet wound, but if he's flying and he was able to talk to you, I'm guessing he's on the sunny side of recovery."

Kipling closed her eyes and shook her head, sitting back with a heavy sigh. Sandi had said not to worry, but it helped to know her physician best friend said something similar. "I thought I could handle this, Mina. I mean, it was one thing when he was here, but now…Three weeks of silence, and then a drugged phone call telling me he's on his way home. Am I crazy?"

Mina snorted a laugh. "You wait until *now* to ask me if you're crazy for dating a spy?"

"He's not technically a spy."

Another snort. "Thin line between definitions, my dear." Mina sat forward and brought her hands up onto the table, pushing aside her paper plate with the crust of her pizza left on it. Most of Kipling's original slice sat on her plate, barely touched. Eating and she had not been friends the last few weeks. "Is being with him really worth being scared all the time?"

Before she could answer, the words already formed solidly in her mind, John snapped out, "The answer is no."

Kipling startled and looked up, taken back by the fire in John's usually calm and relaxed eyes. Realizing the portion of the conversation he'd heard, Kipling shook her head. "John, you don't understand."

"Yeah? Explain it to me, then," he ordered, yanking out the chair beside Mina to sit down hard. John leaned toward both of them, sliding his arm across the table to point at Kip. "But there is *nothing* you can say to convince me being with a man you're scared of is worth it. Not a damn thing."

"I'm not frightened of Grayson," she said, shaking her head.

"Oh, well, at least you're saying his name," he scoffed, sitting back with such force the chair scraped on the floor. "More than you usually do, if you talk about him at all. It's like he's some big damn secret, and now I guess I know why."

Anger flared in her chest, and Kipling pressed her lips together to keep from saying more than she should. Grayson hadn't actually told her not to tell people he was an officer with MI6, but considering the circumstances, she thought the less said the better. Shortly after Grayson had returned to London weeks before, he'd taught her what he called a hole-and-corner; an innocuous phrase that would mean nothing at all to anyone else but would tell her he had to go silent. He wouldn't be able to tell her why, or how long, or where he was going. Just that he would contact her when it was safe again.

Since the night she read "I've been unavoidably detained and will be late for dinner," her heart had been permanently lodged in her throat. Who he was and what he did had never been a mystery, but his ambiguous message had been just one more aspect of this life that drove home the reality.

She could lose him. At any time.

"What the hell has he done to you?" John asked. "Is he the one who left that scar?"

He touched his own forehead near his blond hairline, where it coincided with a small scar Kipling knew was visible near her temple. Where the butt of a gun had knocked her out cold. It wasn't disfiguring, but only weeks had passed since the abduction that still left her unable to sleep some nights, and the scar was still healing on the surface. Kipling instinctively touched the spot, and John's expression tightened. She shook her head.

"No. He didn't."

"No? How'd you get it then?"

"How did you get *your* scars, John?" She'd never so much as implied she'd noticed the small, barely noticeable scars on his neck, near his jawline, and one at his temple.

His expression shifted, but he quickly regained his tense composure. "We're not talking about me."

"You're making wild assumptions, John. What if I assumed something about your scars?"

"Honey, we're not talking—"

"Exactly! It doesn't matter beyond the truth that Grayson didn't hurt me. *Ever.* And he never would." Kipling sat forward to keep the conversation at their table, and not for public consumption by all the patrons in the pizzeria. "You heard part of a conversation. You don't see the whole picture."

"I think I've seen a pretty complete view," he said, shaking his head. John tapped his fingertip on the laminate tabletop with each point he made. "You're jumpy as hell, even worse in the last couple of weeks. You barely eat. I'm willing to bet you barely sleep. You guard information on this guy like it's some government secret. You're taking self-defense classes. Now you're scared of him?"

"I'm not scared *of* him," Kipling snapped. "I'm scared *for* him."

"Why?"

"Just tell him, Kip," Mina said. Kipling shot her best friend a glare, but Mina only arched a dark eyebrow, challenging her. "Did he actually *say* you couldn't?"

"You know why—"

"But I don't." John reached across the table and covered her hand with his much larger one. "Kip, honey, come on. I'm your friend."

"Whom I've only known a few weeks."

"Three whole weeks less than you've known Grayson," Mina pointed out. Kipling stared at her best friend, her chest aching with what felt like betrayal. Mina shrugged. "I love you, sweetie, but you went through hell when he was here, and sometimes I think you're going through a worse hell with him gone. So far, I just don't see him as being worth this much grief. He's eye candy and all, but—"

"You don't know him—"

"Whose fault is that? Kip, nearly every time I had contact with the man was because you'd either been hurt or you were in the hospital."

"That wasn't his fault!"

Several heads turned their way, and Kipling snapped her jaw closed, pressing her lips together to keep from lashing out again. She knew Mina spoke out of love, but as of late her friend's concern had slid more to convincing Kipling to end it with Grayson rather than find a way to make it work. Especially after she heard Kipling's plans later that month.

"No, it only happened *because* of him. From the minute you met Grayson Holmes, you were in danger. You were practically blown up, you were abducted—"

"Stop," Kipling begged, staring wide-eyed at her friend. She didn't dare cast a glance toward John. "Mina, please."

Mina pressed her lips together and shook her head. "I'm only saying this because I love you."

"And I love you, but I also love *him*. Does he not deserve to be loved just because of who and what he's chosen to be?"

"Which is?" John pushed.

"Why do you care?" she snapped, turning on John.

He never flinched, his bright blue eyes leveled on her, unwavering. "Because I care about *you*, Kip. If you are so convinced you could be in love with this guy in so short a time, why is it so hard to believe you and I could be good friends in the same time? Have I ever done anything to make you not trust me?"

Kipling pressed her lips together and sat back, crossing her arms over her body. She felt sick, her insides churning with nerves and the grease from the pizza she'd managed to force down.

"He's an officer for MI6 out of London."

Kipling gasped and stared at her best friend from kindergarten. Mina wouldn't meet her gaze, turning her head to look at John. It didn't go unnoticed how she leaned in until her arm pressed to his. She swallowed, and Kipling stared.

"He's a spy?" John asked, incredulous. "Holy geez, Kip. Did you actually buy that line? How many times has he used that one?"

"No, it's not a line," Mina defended before Kipling tried. "There's pretty much irrefutable evidence that he definitely is MI6. I'll give him that much. He was apparently honest about that from the beginning, though he really didn't have much choice."

Anger seethed under Kipling's skin, and she could only stare until her eyes burned. She pressed her lips together to keep from lashing out and making a bigger scene.

"How did that happen?"

Mina slid a glance toward Kip, but Kipling refused to speak. To either give information or permission for Mina to share. At least Mina had the good sense to look ashamed for what she'd revealed. Mina drew in a slow breath through her nose and let it out before she looked at John again.

"I've said enough already—"

"Too much," Kipling cut in.

"I suppose the circumstances don't matter anymore. Reality is, Kipling loves him and he says he loves her." Mina shrugged. "I doubt anything you or I say will change it, John."

"At least we agree on something," Kipling said in a rough whisper.

"Can't you see why we're worried?" John started to ask.

Before he finished the question, Kipling's phone chimed again and Kipling turned her back on them both, standing again to step away from the table. Any excuse to find some space. The overpowering aromas of marinara and garlic worked on churching her stomach, which had already been rebelling even before John and Mina pushed her so hard, and she welcomed an escape from the clash of chatter and stainless steel being hit by pizza pans in the back of the restaurant. She didn't recognize the number, only that it was international out of the UK, and her heart leaped again. Stepping away from her friends, she tapped the screen to answer. It only took a second for the call to automatically route through her hearing aids.

"Hello?"

"Hello, I'm trying to reach Miss Kipling Branson." The voice was male, with a refined London upper-class accent, a bit rough like he'd spent his life smoking cigars and drinking whiskey. He cleared his throat, ending with a small cough.

"I'm Kipling Branson," she answered, reaching the pizzeria door. She stepped outside to the spring afternoon. "May I help you?"

"I do hope so, Miss Branson. I've stayed up rather past my usual retiring hour to reach you at a reasonable hour in the States." There was a humored lilt to his words that told her he intended to tease rather than scold. "Miss Branson, this is Peter Rathborne. I'm calling from the University of Westminster regarding your credentials."

Chapter Two

London, UK
Two Weeks Later

"You've healed quite well, Grayson. Any lingering pain?"

Grayson picked up his shirt from where he'd draped it at the end of the examination table, and slid his arms into the starched sleeves. "Nothing unusual or troublesome," he answered as he buttoned. "An occasional pull, that sort of thing."

Doctor Tish Shah nodded and took a seat on the swiveling stool near the small cabinet and sink occupying the exam room. "I never know when to believe an SIS agent," she said with a smile. "Either you are well versed in lying, or every one of you has experienced miraculous recoveries."

Grayson chuckled and tucked in his shirttails before draping his tie around the back of his neck to re-knot it beneath his upturned collar. "I assure you of my honesty, Doctor."

Her hummed answer was unconvinced. "You are cleared for any and all duty."

"That is good to hear, and I shall endeavor to do so upon my return to London in a week's time." He finished the tie, and retrieved his jacket, returning himself to a full state of dress.

"Going on holiday?"

Grayson smiled, turning fully to the doctor. "Of a sort. My younger sister is to be married tomorrow, and I'm returning to Sussex for the wedding."

"Oh, cheers. Enjoy yourself, and do try not to think of London while you are gone. It will still be standing when you return."

"I'm counting on it," he said with a smile. Doctor Shah was one of the specially cleared and sanctioned doctors at The Royal London Hospital and had been Grayson's attending physician more times than he cared to list. "Thank you, Doctor."

He had only minor duties to see to in the office before leaving the city, and his cab just made it back to Vauxhall Cross when his mobile buzzed in his breast pocket. Grayson paid the cabbie and shut the vehicle door as he took it from his pocket. The screen indicated it was Director Jeffrey Cooper, and Grayson slid his thumb across the screen to answer.

"I will be in my office within five minutes, sir," he said, bringing the phone to his ear.

"Good. I'll meet you there. Did Shah clear you?"

"Was there any doubt?'

Jeffrey snorted. "Five minutes, Holmes."

He didn't manage to put the phone back in his pocket when it vibrated again. This time he was surprised to see the name of Patrick Flannery, and answered as he stepped into the MI6 building. "I'm not sure if I'm more curious or concerned for the reason you would call after so long," he said, nodding to the security guard stationed near the lift bank.

"Hello to you, too, Holmes."

Grayson chuckled and entered his lift, pushing the button for his office floor. "Hello. What may I do for you, Patrick?"

"Suarez sent over a report this morning, and I figure your people will probably tell you, but I thought it'd be fun to beat them to the punch. What the hell, right?"

"It must be exceptionally interesting news if you prefer to steal their thunder."

"Not really. I want your thoughts before they get filtered and watered down for cross-agency consumption."

Grayson squared his shoulders once the lift doors closed, pushing his free hand into his trouser pockets. "You now have my full attention."

"Isaac Sheldon attempted suicide last night in his cell. They found him hanging from his bed sheet, but cut him down and revived him."

"His failure will not go unnoticed," Grayson said, not allowing any further explanation.

"I kind of figured you'd say that."

"Has the psychological examination been completed?"

"Not yet. It's still morning here, Holmes. The guards found him about…" He paused, and Grayson assumed he might be checking documentation. "Four hours ago. He's been in the psych ward for three. This guy isn't exactly on their short priority list."

"If Sheldon indeed did attempt to kill himself, it was because he was instructed to do so. He would not make the decision to take his own life out of fear of disappointing Howell. He is utterly and completely dedicated to his mission as Howell dictates it." The lift reached his floor, and he exited, heading for his office where Director Cooper likely waited. "Check all records of visitors Sheldon has received in the last forty-eight hours. All phone logs. Any written communications. I assume all visitations and telephone conversations are recorded."

"There are privacy laws—"

"Let's not play into the charade, Agent Flannery," Grayson scoffed. "The order for self-termination will not be blatant. If possible, I would like to see a transcript."

"As far as I know, Stanton plans on asking for your input. He'll probably get clearance."

"I look forward to it; however, Director Cooper is waiting for me."

"Try to act surprised."

Grayson reached his office and pushed against the partially open door he had left unlocked when he left for his appointment, nodding to Jeffrey Cooper where he stood near Grayson's desk, a file in his hand. "Yes. Thank you for your call."

"Yeah, sure. I figure you're pretty well tied into this and should know what the hell is going on, and between you, me, and the fence post I don't have faith in the whole open agency communication crap."

"Unfortunately, on that fact, we can agree. I will speak with you again soon." Sliding his phone back into his pocket, he nodded a greeting to his director and walked past to his desk. He had a single file to see to before leaving the city, and it opened once he tapped in his security code. "What can I do for you, sir?"

"I've just rang off with Director Stanton in Boston. Seems there's been an incident they believed you should be advised of."

"Oh?" Grayson straightened and focused on his superior, his attention more curiosity for the angle Jeffrey would take to the information than what information he would impart. "What did Director Stanton have to say?"

"Seems Sheldon, Howell's sycophant, tried to kill himself this morning."

Grayson arched an eyebrow, simultaneously angling forward to type with one hand to access the system he needed. One more filing, and he would be free to leave. "Is that based on observation or actual investigation of the situation?"

"According to Director Stanton, it was quite obvious Sheldon hung himself by a bed sheet not long before morning check."

Grayson canted his head and made a small "hmm" sound in his throat. "There is nothing more deceptive than an obvious fact, Jeffrey."

Jeffrey huffed and cut his hand through the air. "Save me your ancestral quotes, Grayson." He tossed on the desktop the folder he'd held since Grayson came in. "You may read the rest at your leisure, Holmes," Cooper said, drawing Grayson's attention from his computer screen. "I thought you might wish to know before you leave."

"I will take it with me, and should I find time to review it whilst I am away, I shall."

Jeffrey nodded. "Director Stanton has requested your continued involvement in the investigation, whether that participation be from here or Boston will be determined in the near future. Prior to this turn of events, Sheldon's court date was scheduled for August and your presence would be required."

"Seems the wheels of justice turn no more quickly in the United States than they do here," Grayson said.

"Whether his commitment now changes that timeline we do not know. For now, I have offered no assurances other than your presence here and your assistance as can be warranted." Jeffrey huffed and shook his head. "You made a substantial impression on Director Stanton."

Grayson carefully schooled his expression so as to not seem too enthused at the idea of returning to Boston. "We worked well together." He had not informed Jeffrey of Director Stanton's inquiry into his willingness to "jump ship" and join the FBI office as a permanent transfer. While the instances of a British citizen leaving the Secret Intelligence Service to work with a foreign agency weren't completely unheard of, the instances had been exceptionally rare and only after extreme consideration.

The fact Grayson technically already held dual citizenship was a factor to be considered.

Were it not for Kipling he wouldn't likely consider the option at all.

"Pass my congratulations on to your parents and sister," Jeffrey said over his shoulder as he headed for the open office door.

Jeffrey opened his mouth to say something further, but Grayson's mobile vibrated in his breast pocket. Seeing him go for the mobile, Jeffery pressed his lips together and left Grayson's office, closing the door behind him, which only afforded privacy of sound since the wall was mostly window. Grayson withdrew the phone and smiled to see the name and image on the screen. He slid his thumb across the screen.

"Isn't it rather early for you to be calling? Especially after what I can only assume to be a long evening of celebrating?" he asked as he brought the phone to his ear.

As if inspired by his question, Kipling's long yawn carried through the phone line. "Yes, it's early but I knew you'd be leaving soon for your parents' and I didn't want to call while you were driving. Have you left yet?"

"I will be leaving the office momentarily, then I must pick up Watson and will be on my way." The sound of traffic carried through the phone. "Where are you?"

"Um, just walking down to Dunkin'. It's early, remember?"

"Mmmm, now you have inspired a craving."

"For me? Or for coffee?" The sultry slide of her voice stirred a warm sensation in his chest.

"Both, but if asked to choose, you would definitely win."

"Choosing me over Dunkin'. There is no greater compliment to a Bostonian," she said, and he heard the slow smile in her voice. "How long is your drive?"

"Two and a half hours, roughly, as long as I avoid the worst traffic out of London. I hope to be home by tea. But enough about such boring topics. Tell me, Doctor Branson, how does it feel?"

"Does it make sense to say I feel lighter? But also a bit lost about what to do next. It's been a long time since I didn't have a deadline or a paper or something else due."

"You will find something to occupy your time soon enough, and you will wish for this calm."

"I hope so. The occupying my time part." She sighed. "I miss you, Grayson. I ache with it. Does that sound childish and foolish?"

Grayson bowed his head and closed his eyes, inhaling slowly before he answered. "Not in the least. I ache with it as well." He inhaled and smiled, hoping she would hear it in his voice. "For thy sweet love remembered such wealth brings that then I scorn to change my state with king. Soon, my darling. We need only work out the details."

"Promise?" she asked.

"With all my heart." He pressed his hand over his heart, an impulse even though he logically knew she couldn't see. "Kipling, I am truly sorry I was unable to be there to see your commencement—"

"Stop," she insisted. "Grayson, I know. The timing wasn't in our favor." She laughed, the sound soft, carrying what he recognized as fatigue. "You may be a super secret agent man, but I doubt even 007 could have gotten from London to Boston and back to London and actually be *conscious* for your sister's wedding."

Grayson pressed his lips together, bowing his head. "You are wonderful."

She sighed, and another horn honked. "I'm going to let you go so you can get on the road. Your mother is anxious to see you, I'm sure. I'll send photos so you can see them later." Kipling drew in a slow, deep breath. "I love you, Grayson."

"And I you," he assured. "I will call you once I've arrived."

"Thank you. Talk to you soon."

He disconnected and slid the phone back into his pocket, picking up his satchel, a smile still lingering from the brief conversation with Kipling. Just as quickly, the comfort slid to frustration. Their relationship for the last three and a half months had been reduced to text messages, telephone and Skype calls, and emails. She essentially lived in his phone. When he'd left Boston, he knew it would be a time before either he could return to the States or she would be able to possibly come to Britain, but he had severely miscalculated the difficulty of being apart after only having had her in his life less than a month.

He left Vauxhall Cross and hailed a cab once he reached a main road, walking the short distance in an attempt to clear his thoughts. But they lingered still on Kipling. So much so he barely registered the short drive to Baker Street. As requested, the storage facility where he kept his car had delivered his Bentley Continental during the morning and it sat parked on the curb. He hardly needed a car in the city, so he kept it in a locked facility when not in use. They had polished the deep burgundy finish until it gleamed in the early afternoon sun. Grayson paid his cabbie and then stepped out into the pleasant afternoon sun. A small group of students walked together between him and the door to his flat, their voices heavily laden with German accents and they stared wide-eyed at the museum entrance to his right. Grayson paused, letting them pass as he heard their tour guide begin the story of the Sherlock Holmes Museum and its fictitious address of 221B Baker Street.

Once they cleared the path, Grayson crossed to his door and took his keys from his pocket to let himself into a space the German students would likely find far less interesting — though more authentic — than the museum next door. Halfway up the stairs to the main living level he heard Watson's mewling and looked up to see the tabby peeking at him through the banister railings.

"Yes, Your Highness. I'm coming," he called out, and Watson wailed louder. Grayson chuckled, his phone vibrating in his pocket. It would seem he was quite popular. He held it to his ear as he reached the first-floor landing, nearly tripping over Watson in the kitty's enthusiasm to greet him. "Holmes," he said.

"Official word is you're back on the case," Patrick Flannery said.

"Bad news travels quickly. Especially since my recent conversation with my director left the fact quite unresolved." He turned at the top of the stairs to walk towards the street side to take the next flight to the bedroom level and hopped on one foot to swing his leg over Watson to keep from tumbling. "Watson!" he scolded.

"Who are you talking to?"

"My cat," he admitted. "Yes, his name is Watson. Shall we skip the obvious jokes?"

"Steal all my fun. Anyway, Stanton just pulled us into a wicked quick chat to say you're working with us on this."

"I will be required to take your word for it. As far as the official word here, they are considering my degree of involvement." Despite his ribbing, Grayson smiled. "However, it must wait until my return from holiday."

"Goin' anywhere good?"

"Home," he answered, reaching his bedroom to set his satchel on the bed. His packed luggage already waited by the door, ready to be taken to the car once he changed and wrestled Watson into his carrier. "My sister is getting married."

"Hey, that's great. I didn't even know you had a sister."

"In fact, I have two." Grayson worked his tie loose with his free hand. "In an endeavor not to be rude, Patrick, I am attempting to leave London as soon as possible. Unless there is something specific that requires immediate attention, I intend to study the investigation files upon my return."

"Nah, nothin' specific. We were able to dig up some information on the activities on your Langdon Howell while he was here."

Grayson's hand stilled at his throat. His chest tightened with the anger he harbored for the man. "What did you learn?"

The sound of shuffled papers preceded Agent Flannery's answer. "Langdon Fairfax Howell. British national, born in Oxford. His brother Nelson Howell was one of the most powerful men in European organized crime until last year when he turned up dead."

Grayson's gut clenched. MI6 had successfully managed to exclude his part in Nelson's death, in that he killed the man with his bare hands in a fit of vengeful rage.

"Seems Langdon stepped in where his brother left off but hasn't made himself visible at all until recently. Wicked hard to track him down, the guy practically lives off the grid. We managed to find some photos, but none are great quality. We have a short list of places he visited while here, and some people he talked to. Some photos, but not many, around the university campus."

"You've placed him, then, at the relevant scenes. Any bit of evidence is more than we had, and every bit of truth is better than indefinite doubt."

"Yeah, whatever. The weird thing is in a lot of them, we think we're seein' some other guy. Not every location and we never get a good angle on him, but we're still diggin'. Don't know if it means anything. Hey, you still keep in touch with that lady friend of yours from the bookstore?"

"I assume you refer to Kipling Branson."

"Yeah. I've been tryin' to get ahold of Miss Branson since day before yesterday. We're running through witnesses again, beginning testimony prep, that sort of thing. Haven't been able to reach her, and wondered if you still talked."

"Her commencement ceremony was yesterday for her doctorate degree," Grayson explained. "Likely she has been occupied with family."

"I'll keep tryin'."

"I'd say you are more likely to reach her Monday, but when I speak to her I will inform her you need to speak with her. In the interim, email the photos to me, along with whatever data you have on the man's activities. I wish to review it."

"It can wait until after you get back—"

"No, this cannot," Grayson insisted. "Please send it along to my work email. I will have access while out of the office." He resumed tugging his tie free and tossed it on the bed, Watson immediately batting at it like a toy.

The cat had been different since returning from Boston. Then again, so was Grayson.

"Sure thing, chief. Didn't mean to mess with your vacation."

"Not a problem. I appreciate the call. I will contact you once I've returned, or if I should determine anything worth sharing."

"Got it. Enjoy."

Grayson tossed the phone on the coverlet, and shrugged off his jacket. Uncharacteristically, he tossed his suit and shirt on the bed to be dealt with on his return. He hadn't been back to Sussex since shortly after his return to England in February, and that had only been for a brief visit as an assurance to his mother. His parents had been justifiably upset by the events in Boston and the attempts on Grayson's life, and admittedly, the visit home had soothed his jagged nerves at the time. He found himself now anxious to see the cottage in the spring, eat some of his mother's steam pudding, and laugh with his sisters.

Once changed into jeans and a more casual cotton shirt with his boots, he cajoled and wheedled Watson with bits of cheese into his carrier, and carried his luggage to the car. It took two trips to take the bags, Shirl's wedding gifts, and Watson to the waiting vehicle. He was twenty minutes later than preferred leaving London, but in the end, he was thankful to have heard from Patrick Flannery on the investigation.

He didn't feel he'd quite escaped the city until he reached Kingston Road, heading south. Only then did he take a deep breath and settle back to enjoy the scenery and calm. And only then could he let his mind catalogue and analyze the facts they'd gathered since his return from Boston. Sadly, there weren't many.

Before leaving Boston for London, they had determined the identity of the man behind the bombing at the university to be Langdon Fairfax Howell, brother to Nelson Howell. It seemed Grayson was trapped within the legacy of his family name in ways he had never contemplated growing up with the name Holmes. Nelson and Langdon Howell were descendants of Charles Augustus Howell, a criminal blackmailer in London when Grayson's great-grandfather Sherlock Holmes and his dearest friend John Watson independently solved crimes and investigated cases. Sir Arthur Conan Doyle had made Sherlock both a legend and a fable with his stories, as relayed to him by his cousin John Watson, but the truth ran thick through the fiction, with fiction being the spice to the main course.

In every twist of fiction laid a foundation of truth.

In Conan Doyle's stories, of all the criminals and murderers Sherlock Holmes investigated, Sherlock despised none more than Charles Augustus Howell, calling him "the worst man in London", and said no murderer repulsed him the way Howell did. When Conan Doyle transcribed the adventures of Holmes and Watson, he changed the villain's name to Milverton, but Howell was the cold-blooded, serpentine inspiration.

Grayson was not the only man trapped by the legacy of his name. As much as he followed closely in his great grandfather's foot-steps when he joined MI6, Nelson and Langdon Howell followed in the footsteps of their ancestor in the family business of crime. Inevitably, their paths crossed with death when Nelson Howell held a part in the death of MI6 agent — and Grayson's cousin — Greg McQueen. And Nelson died at the hands of Grayson.

When it became clear that Langdon Howell had focused his

attention on Grayson, and in doing so manipulated lives to attempt to end his, Grayson knew the cycle continued. Only now, Kipling Branson had been drawn into the game.

Watson made a sound somewhere between a meow and a banshee screech, pulling Grayson from his musings. He reached across the car with his left hand and stuck his finger through one of the slots in the carrier. "Sorry, old man," he said to the cat. "Can't have you wandering about in the car. That ended rather badly last time we tried. Not much further now."

His sister Shirley's ringtone chimed briefly from his pocket before the phone connected with the car's hands-free system. Grayson tapped the control on the steering wheel to connect. "I'm on my way," he said.

"I should hope so. Mum is cooking like we're hosting *The Great British Bake Off* this weekend, and if we have to wait much longer than tea to eat it because we're waiting for *you*, none of us will be very happy."

Grayson laughed. "Should I tell you then I've just left Baker Street?"

"You can tell me, but you'd better be lying. Where are you? Really?"

"Piddinghoe Road. I'm not fifteen minutes away. Please try to survive a bit longer."

"I shall try, but Dad is looking a bit wane. You know Mum has had him on a diet, and she's given him leave this weekend. He's ready to get started."

Grayson chuckled, grinning. He pressed his foot a bit heavier to the accelerator, suddenly even more anxious to be home. "I'll be there in ten."

"Good. Love you. See you soon."

The line disconnected, and good to his word, Grayson managed to make it to the cottage in ten minutes, though he did risk a foul glare from Mrs. Gleason in the village. Parking spots were at a premium, with his father's Jeep parked along the road. Johanna and Shirley's tiny cars together took up the space of Grayson's Bentley, but more family would be arriving in the next two days in preparation for Saturday's wedding. He decided to tuck the car behind the house out of the way as best as possible since he had little intention of leaving until it was time.

Once parked, Grayson left most of his bags for later, only retrieving Watson from his spot in the passenger's seat. He paused at the front of the car and looked out over the field behind the house, adjacent to their orchard. The trees were in bloom and the field spattered with various wildflowers. He inhaled, the heady scents of new growth filling his senses, mingled with the savory aromas wafting from the open kitchen windows. The sounds of voices and laughter carried on the breeze, and Grayson smiled.

The kitchen door opened before he reached it, and Shirl flew out. He barely set down Watson before his little sister jumped and he caught her, hugging her tight as she squealed.

"Oh, I've missed you," she declared and pecked his cheek. Her light brown hair, kissed with ginger, caught in the breeze and tickled his nose.

"I couldn't tell," he teased, setting her on her feet again.

By the time he reached for Watson again, the rest of his family had come out of the kitchen or stood in the doorway waiting for him. Perhaps anyone looking on would think he had been away for years, not weeks, but such was always the greeting when a Holmes — whether by name or lineage — came home. He accepted the kisses and embraces of each until he managed to get into the house. Grayson paused and inhaled deeply, closing his eyes as the aromas tantalized him and made his stomach grumble in appreciation.

"Mmmm, I'm not sure what smells more tempting."

He glanced toward his sisters, and immediately the hairs on his arms stood on end. They both stared at him with grins that would put the Cheshire Cat to shame, bright excitement blooming in their cheeks, and Shirl actually bounced on the balls of her feet. Watson protested loudly from his carrier, turning so adamantly in circles within the confines that he made the case shake in Grayson's grip. But Grayson was too interested in the mischief in his sisters' eyes. He glanced at his mother and saw the same shine.

"What are the three of you up to?" he asked, setting down Watson's carrier.

"What makes you think we are up to anything," Annalise Holmes said with a false huff, lifting her chin so she looked down her fine nose at him.

"Mum…" he led, arching an eyebrow. "Would you like a list alphabetically or in order of obviousness?"

Grayson crouched beside the carrier, looking up at his mother and sisters while he noted his father stood to the side as silent as ever, yet sporting an uncharacteristic smile and rosy hue to his weathered cheeks. Something was definitely going on. Watson cried and swatted at Grayson's fingers as he worked the latch, acting desperate for escape. Grayson scowled and looked away from his deceptive family to focus on the latch.

"What on earth has gotten into you, you crazy cat," he scolded, finally opening the gate. Expecting Watson to head for the open door to the backyard, Grayson stood and watched in confusion when the cat bolted instead to the parlor near the front of the cottage.

"It would seem each and every one of you are now possessed and I'm wondering if I've somehow stumbled into the wrong house."

He looked over his shoulder, squinting at his sister. Shirley had her hands clamped over her mouth, her eyes wide, staring at him and absolutely trembling. Grayson pointed at her. "I'm going after that fool cat, and when I get back, you're explaining yourself."

He watched them, walking backward for several steps until he cleared the doorway into the short hall leading to the rooms at the front of the cottage. It wasn't until he turned to pursue his crazy feline that he heard the soft whispers of a feminine voice and his heart stilled.

"You're going to give me away," he heard whispered.

His still heart jumped, making up the lost beats in a thundering race against his ribs and Grayson took three long strides to the wide archway to the receiving room.

And he stopped. Staring. Unable but so willing to believe his eyes.

Crouched in the middle of the room, stroking the gray fur of his cat as Watson frantically tried to brush against her in every possible way at once, was Kipling Branson. Her head turned down, he still knew it was her without question. Long beautiful chestnut hair fell around her shoulders in smooth waves, caressing her bare arms revealed by the yellow sundress she wore.

Grayson sucked in a sharp breath and managed to say, "Kipling…"

She raised her head, her beautiful lips bowed in a smile that made his chest tighten. He couldn't help the quick observations he just as quickly pushed aside. She had lost weight, probably a stone, and it showed in her face. Her eyes were shadowed slightly, and fatigue drew her features. Perhaps fatigue from travel. He didn't care. She was beautiful. So beautiful it stole his breath.

Slowly, she rose to stand, Watson still dancing around her feet. Grayson took a step forward, his only assurance she was not a mirage of the glints of secrecy in his sisters and mother's eyes moments before. Otherwise, he might have thought Kipling a hallucination.

"Hi," she said softly, as if it had not been weeks since he'd seen her. "Are you pleased?"

He crossed the small room in two strides, reaching for her before the space was closed. Grayson took her face in his hands and sucked in a sharp breath before covering her open mouth with his own, diving without hesitation or restraint into a kiss he'd wanted and needed for weeks. Kipling's soft moan against his lips was petrol on open flames.

He was lost. Utterly lost.

Then her arms slid around him, delicate hands pressed to his back, and he never wanted to be found. The memories he'd held firm to since leaving Boston were nothing — pale shadows — in comparison to having her in his arms again, tasting her kiss, and feeling her touch.

"You might want to remember you are in your mother's parlor," came said mother's voice from behind him, and Kipling's fingers curled into his shirt, a soft moan of protest barely passing her lips.

Grayson chuckled, regrettably taking his lips from hers. Still holding her face in his palms, he drew back to look into her shining amber eyes. "I never saw so sweet a face as that I stood before. My heart has left its dwelling place and can return no more." He pressed a kiss to the center of her brow before looking at her again. "Yes," he said.

Kipling smiled, her gaze shifting to study his face. "Yes, what?"

"Yes, I am most assuredly pleased."

Chapter Three

Shirley squealed and jumped up and down, clapping her hands, in the archway to the parlor. Kipling watched her past Grayson's shoulder and laughed. She looked up at Grayson again, and the intensity in his stormy eyes made her skin warm and her heart flutter. He seemed oblivious to his sister's glee, not looking away from Kip. She smiled and sighed, tucking her arms further around his torso until she could press her palms to his back and feel his heartbeat.

She wanted to soak him in, and reacquaint herself with the details of Grayson Holmes. The way his auburn hair waved away from his brow in rebellious curls he'd cursed more than once, with the sharp angles of his face, his cheekbones, his jaw, and his nose, and the unusual mix of blue and green of his eyes. The way his arms felt wrapped around her, and his fingers felt on her face. Every tactile memory she'd held on to for months was immediately over-written by the reality of being with him.

"I'm so happy we surprised you," she said, shaking her head. "I thought for sure you'd figure me out, especially this morning. I was practically holding my breath that you wouldn't hear something around me that said *London* and not Boston."

Grayson chuckled, the deep baritone rumble vibrating against her hands. "I had no idea." He lowered his hands from her cheeks to wrap his arm around her, holding her close while he turned to face his family. "How long have you been planning this?"

"For weeks!" Shirley cried. Kipling had been amazed the young woman hadn't exploded already from her abundance of glee. She wasn't sure if Shirley was more excited about this secret, or that she was getting married in two days. "Ever since you came home and we all saw that sparkle of love in your eyes when you told us of her. Oh, it's been such fun!"

"We haven't surprised Grayson since he was eight years old," Annalise Holmes said, a pleased sparkle in her eyes. "Our only saving grace is he didn't see a one of us face to face."

"Especially Shirl." Grayson chuckled. "I knew something was up the second I saw her. You're all rubbish with secrets." He looked down at her, then canted his head. "How long have you been here?"

"What time is it?" she asked, glancing around the room for a clock. She really had no idea what time it was, her internal clock was completely and quite possibly irreparably out of whack.

"Just past four," Johanna answered from a step behind her mother. She was most definitely the more reserved of the two sisters.

"So, just over three hours. Well," she amended. "I've been in England just over three hours. I've been *here* maybe fifteen minutes longer than you. Haven't even brought in my luggage."

"It was quite the race," Shirley declared, still in absolute glee. "I was afraid we'd be climbing out of the car when you pulled in, and the whole game would have been over."

"I would have been just as pleased." He looked toward Johanna. "Were you in on this, too?"

"They needed someone to drive while Shirl carried on and Kipling tried hard not to fall dead asleep," Johanna said with a very subtle, but completely honest smirk. A smirk that reminded Kipling of one she'd seen Grayson sport more than once. There was far more to Johanna than the reserved, quiet exterior.

Still waters run deep…

Grayson looked at her again, his hand moving up and down her spine in a hypnotic stroke. Before he could say anything, his mother clapped her hands together. "Why don't we have a seat, fill our bellies, and then our dear Kipling can have a lie-down. Twenty minutes until dinner."

"Mmmm, food sounds good," Kipling said, pressing her hand to her empty stomach. The food on the plane had been slightly more than inedible, and she'd managed to grab a snack on her way to baggage claim, but it was hardly enough to hold her for long. Perhaps being with him would allow her stomach to take in a true meal without revolting against her. "It smells amazing, and Grayson has told me how wonderful a cook you are."

"That stands to be proven," his mother said with a wink, and turned to head back to the kitchen, her daughters following. Kipling caught just a glimpse of Grayson's father, who had remained in the background, silent, but his honest yet reserved smile told her he was as pleased with the surprise as the rest.

"I'll take care of our bags," Grayson said, his hand sliding down her back and across her hips until he linked his fingers through hers. "Are Kipling's things in your boot?" he asked of Shirley.

She nodded, already leaving the room, so she spoke over her shoulder. Kipling didn't catch all of it, but enough to know the answer was yes. Grayson looked down at her, and her heart swelled a bit more. Soon it'd be too big for her chest. "Come outside with me."

Kipling nodded and let him lead her back through the cottage, through the kitchen, and out the door she'd come in when she arrived. All she'd seen so far of the house was the kitchen, the parlor, and the downstairs bathroom. There hadn't been enough time for anything else with Shirley terrified he'd somehow gain on them and show up before Kipling made it inside the cottage. As they passed through the kitchen, Annalise glanced over her shoulder and smiled, her eyes misty and happy. She winked and went back to her dinner preparation.

They stepped into the late afternoon sun, and Kipling inhaled deep. The air was fresh and warm and laden with so many wonderful scents she couldn't even begin to categorize them;

wouldn't be able to if she tried. Wonderful reminiscence filled her when she looked out across the field surrounding the cottage, and she was eighteen again, lost in the idyllic landscape. Her feet only kept moving because Grayson drew her along at his side. It wasn't until they went past Shirley's little Mini Cooper that she realized he led her around the side of a small shed. Parked beside it was a rich burgundy, absolutely gorgeous, and clearly late-model Bentley luxury car.

"I'll grab my bags first, then yours," he explained, releasing her hand when they reached the trunk.

Momentum kept her walking, and she went past the car to a worn and grayed split rail fence running along the edge of the lawn separating it from the wild growing field. The beauty was like a magnet, drawing her soul. A gentle breeze made the tall grass and flowers sway, and the soft whisper was a caress. Usually, the wind made her hearing aids whine, or they amplified the sound uncomfortably, but the breeze was so soft and gentle it was a lullaby through the trees. The sky was a beautiful azure behind rolling, drifting clouds, occasionally letting the sun peak through to warm her face and arms. When she reached the fence, she set her hands on the top rail, the tall grass reaching through to brush her ankles, tickling her skin.

She could stay here forever.

"Mum would say you're off with the fairies." Grayson's warm baritone wrapped around her as his hands came to her hips before his arms circled her waist and drew her spine against his chest.

Kipling inhaled and released a sigh, laying her arms over his. "I remember she said that when she found me staring out over your fields the first time. It's so easy to let myself drift away here."

Grayson pressed a kiss to her jaw, then rested his cheek against her temple, his embrace tightening. "Overmorrow I will give you the grand tour of the property."

Kipling tilted her head to look at him. "I don't think I have *ever* heard someone use the word overmorrow in conversation."

Grayson arched a brow, giving her an incredulous look. "I was going to say I might even show you my secret hiding place." He raised his right arm and pointed to the tree line along the back of the field. "It's tucked away in the wood there, so well hidden not even my sisters knew where it was. The only other person who has been inside is Greg, but if you prefer to make commentary on my vocabulary—"

Kipling moaned and nuzzled her nose against his jaw. "The only commentary I ever make about your vocabulary is how sexy I find it." Her heart squeezed, now that she knew the truth of Grayson's lost cousin and how it had devastated him. "You really want to show *me*?" She tilted her head to look up at him.

"You will be the first."

Not that she would have voiced it aloud to anyone, but Kipling had been equally excited and terrified waiting for Grayson to arrive. A small, annoying voice of apprehension had begun whispering from the first day Shirley contacted her with the idea to surprise Grayson. It told her she had read too much into their time together — less than a month, only days when their actual time together was added up — that he wouldn't appreciate having a woman he barely knew show up at his parents' home uninvited *by him*. Even Mina, both gently and not so gently, had pointed out the obvious: if anyone else had told Kipling their plan, she probably would have warned them against it. Mina had even said "Creepy stalker girl-friend much?"

Grayson brought his fingers to her face, stroking her skin from ear to the corner of her lips, his gaze shifting to follow the path and to skim over her features. She hoped she wasn't misinterpreting the warm, happy expression in his stormy eyes.

"You don't know how many times I almost told you," she admitted, and his lips ticked up in a grin that inspired her to smile. "As big a part of me wanted to surprise you as wanted to make sure it'd be okay."

Grayson blinked and ticked his chin. "Why wouldn't it be okay?

Kipling shrugged in his hold. "When looking in from the outside, planning a secret trip to another country to visit a man I barely know — and who barely knows me — might seem strange. Unwelcome."

He was shaking his head before she finished half her statement and turned her in his arms to face him before she said the last word, his lips covering hers before her last syllable. The kiss inside had been a sip of water after a long thirst, something she'd anticipated for weeks. It was a kiss of long absence, but this kiss was one of long need. He held his lips still over hers, possibly just to quiet her unease, but when she opened to him and drew in his breath, stillness turned to frenzy. Kipling couldn't help the low rumble in her throat and raised her arms to lace her fingers into his hair. For three months, her dreams had been filled with the tactile, vivid sensation of his soft curls and his firm kiss when she hadn't been haunted by other, darker images. Grayson curled his fingers into the loose fabric of her dress at her waist, pulling her firm against him.

In a heated flash, Kipling ached for him. So much it nearly brought tears.

Grayson released her dress to take her face in his hands, holding his chin to hers to speak in the space between their open mouths. "If I had just one night to live, I'd live it in your arms, for you hold all my joy, happiness, and desires."

Kipling canted her head to brush her lips to his, smiling. "No fair kissing me like that and following up with a quote like that. You know what it does to me." His rumbling laughter made her laugh with him, and she kissed his smile. "Who said it?"

His tongue skimmed her lip and he kissed again before answering, "I don't know. But the words sing the truth."

She leaned into him, bringing her arms down to wrap around him. When her palms slid across his side, a sudden reminder hit her, and she gasped, pulling back to look into his concerned face.

"What is it?" he asked.

"Grayson, I'm not in any way asking this to be fresh," she said, but couldn't help the tug of her lips into a small smile. "Will you take off your shirt for me?" Kipling tried to keep the request light, but the memory of how she'd felt when she learned he'd been shot pressed on her chest. She tried to maintain her smile, and shook her head, lowering her hands. "It's obvious you're just fine. I'm being silly."

Before she could step back, Grayson reached for her elbow with his left hand and worked open the buttons of his shirt with his right. He held her gaze until he reached the last button, then lowered his chin and with the shirt now open, drew back the open placket and revealed his stomach. His bare torso, defined and taut and definitively male, curled hair the color of his red-tinted waves dusting his chest, was enough to make her skin flush, but the enticement was overshadowed by the choking effect of seeing his two-week-healed wound.

A four-inch red slash marred his side just below his left ribs. There were signs of sutures that had once held closed the wound, but the skin had mended together cleanly. She knew enough to know the injury would have hurt terribly — Mina had explained how sometimes the less life-threatening the wound, the more painful — and her heart ached for the pain he'd gone through. Kipling reached tentatively, glancing to him for approval, which he granted with a small nod, and she laid her hand on his warm skin. She ran her thumb across the raised scar, and his muscle tensed beneath the touch.

"Did that hurt?" she asked, looking up at him.

Grayson's lips tipped in a lopsided grin, and he winked. "Not at all, darling."

"Grayson Oliver!" called his mother from the other side of the shed that shielded them from view. "Dinner!"

Kipling laughed and lowered her hand, chuckling at the mortification in his face. "At least she didn't use the *whole* thing," she offered in consolation.

"No," he admitted, buttoning his shirt. When finished, he slid his arm around her shoulders. "For that, I must be truly naughty."

"I'll remember that." She winked and pulled her lip through her teeth when he looked down at her, loving the heat that darkened his eyes.

"Grayson!" Mrs. Holmes called again.

"Coming!" he called back, and led Kipling back toward the house. After a few steps, he stopped them, turning a few degrees toward her again. "You are wrong on one point," he said, his voice slightly stern.

"What point?"

"You said we barely know each other. Kipling, proximity has little to do with how well I know you. I know a great deal about you, and that which I can only learn in near proximity, well..." He smiled, a slow, sexy curling of his lips that inspired a new flush of heat in her cheeks. "I look forward to the education."

"The sun himself is weak when he first rises, and gathers strength and courage as the day goes on."

Kipling smiled, looking at Grayson's mother. "*The Old Curiosity Shop*. Charles Dickens."

Annalise tipped her head, an impressed curve to her lips. "Very good."

"I've got one," Shirley declared from her seated position on the floor beside her father's easy chair. "I can't go back to yesterday because I was a different person then."

"*Alice in Wonderland*. Lewis Carroll."

"I warned you," Grayson said, his arm around her shoulders drawing her a little closer to his side, and Kipling willingly settled against him on the couch. "She is very good. I doubt you'll stump her. Any of you."

Emerson Holmes cleared his throat, the only indicator he was about to speak. "I've got one," he said with a glint in his eyes.

The transition in the room was fascinating to watch. In an instant, every head turned his way, his inclination toward speaking such a rare thing. Which still made Kipling wonder about the car ride years before when he'd talked the whole drive to the village, and Grayson hadn't quite believed her when she told him. This man was clearly and completely loved and adored by his children, of that there was no doubt, and every softly spoken word a gift.

Kipling sat forward, resting her elbows on her knees in antic-ipation.

"There is," he began, his voice like gravel from the pipe he'd just finished, "though I do not know how there is or why there is, a sense of infinite peace and protection in the glittering hosts of heaven."

Grayson laughed aloud, and Kipling smiled, shaking her head. "Oh, that is a tough one, indeed." She laid her hand on Grayson's knee and shoved him, trying to get him to stop. "But, I've got it. *The Island of Dr. Moreau* by H.G. Wells."

"Sorry, Dad," Grayson said, his hand settling on Kipling's back. "I should have warned you. Kipling's doctoral dissertation was on time and space references in *The Time Machine* and *The Island of Dr. Moreau*."

"Time and space?" Johanna asked, her eyebrows arching. "Sounds like you're a Doctor Who fan."

Kipling raised her hand and tilted her head in concession. "Guilty as charged, all the way back to Tom Baker when it aired on PBS, though I have seen all the Doctors."

Both Shirley and Grayson declared "Whoa…" in unison, Shirley with her hands at her lips, her eyes wide. Grayson leaned forward to look Kipling in the eye, nearly the same smile on his lips as his sister's. "You, darling, have just been challenged."

She looked back to Johanna and looked the younger woman in the eyes. "What are the parameters? Direct Doctor quotes only, or companions as well?"

"Could be either Doctors or companions, classic or revival."

Kipling nodded. "Fair enough. Do you want the episode title?"

"You believe you're that impressive?"

Kipling grinned wider, catching Johanna's subtle ad-lib from a Doctor line of dialogue, and matched her for it. "Oh, I know I'm that impressive."

Shirley glanced from Kipling to Grayson. "She that good?"

Grayson chuckled. "Honestly, I have no idea. This is a side of Kipling Branson I've yet to see."

Johanna straightened and shifted, clearly making herself comfortable with her arms crossed, contemplating. "Okay, here we go. We're falling through space, you and me, clinging to the skin of this tiny little world. And if we let go…that's who I am."

Kipling smiled, loving Grayson's quiet sister more by the moment. Shirley might be the gregarious one, but Johanna was the prize. "Starting with the revival Doctors, okay. Ninth Doctor, depending on your interpretation, Christopher Eccleston. Loved him. Episode title is *Rose*."

"Unexpected as it may be, I do have a mind of my own."

"Kamelion. Companion to the Fifth Doctor."

"I'm not going to make this easy for you," Johanna said, then pursed her lips in thought before trying again. "A straight line may be the shortest distance between two points, but it is by no means the most interesting."

"Third Doctor, Jon Pertwee. Episode *The Time Warrior*. Next?"

"There are worlds out there where the sky is burning and the sea's asleep, and the rivers dream; people made of smoke and cities made of song. Somewhere there's danger, somewhere there's injustice, and somewhere else the tea's getting cold."

Kipling smirked. "Oh, good…that's a good one. Seventh Doctor, Sylvester McCoy. *Survival*."

"I am the Bad Wolf. I create myself. I take the words; I scatter them through time and space — a message to lead myself here."

Kipling sighed. "I thought you were going to make this difficult. Rose Tyler. *Best* companion *ever*. *The Parting of the Ways*."

"Fine. No more easy stuff. But at worst we failed doing the right thing, as opposed to succeeding in doing the wrong."

"Do you prefer I refer to John Hurt as the true Eighth Doctor or the War Doctor?"

Johanna hunkered forward, her eyes pinched. Oh, this would be a good one. Kipling purposefully matched her expression, bringing a laugh from the rest of the family.

"Bingle bongle dingle dangle," Johanna began, saying each word with such gravity one would have thought she quoted the greatest speech ever given. "yickedy do yickedy da, ping pong lippy tappy too tah."

Kipling laughed and sat up, shaking her head. "Oh, that's a low blow, but you're not catching me. Tenth Doctor, David Tennant. And one might argue that wasn't actually *in* an episode, but it was a gag reel from *Blink*."

Johanna raised her hands. "Okay, I concede. You're good."

Kipling sat back again, pressing into the warmth of Grayson's side, and looked up at him. "Here's one for *you*. Not Doctor Who, though." He arched his eyebrows, accepting the challenge. "When we love, we always strive to become better than we are. When we strive to become better than we are, everything around us becomes better too."

Grayson's slow smile flowed into his eyes and warmed her cheeks. "Paulo Coelho. *The Alchemist*." He ended the answer with a kiss on her cheek and held there until she closed her eyes and leaned into him.

"Awww," Shirley gushed. "The two of you are enough to make me jealous, and I'm the one getting married tomorrow."

The vibration of Grayson's phone in the hip pocket pressed to her made her jump, and he chuckled as he shifted to slide his hand between them and take it out, switching the phone to his other hand so he could return his arm around her. He glanced at the screen and scowled.

"Something wrong?" Kipling asked.

He shook his head. "No, just an email I was anticipating. But that was prior to knowing you'd be here." He glanced at her and put the phone in his other pocket. "Sorry, that didn't sound anything like how I intended. It's nothing to worry about."

Kipling nodded and suddenly was hit with a yawn that threatened to crack her jaw. She covered her mouth and tried to laugh through it as she let out air again. "Sorry."

"Poor girl is exhausted," Grayson's mother said, hefting herself from her chair. "Sweetheart, take her bags upstairs to Johanna's room." She headed for the hallway and the staircase leading to the upstairs, then stopped and pointed. "No arguments."

Grayson stood and offered his hand to Kipling to draw her to her feet. "Wouldn't dream of it, Mum." He squeezed Kipling's hand before letting go. "You go on up, and I'll be up shortly with your things."

At the mention of rest, exhaustion landed on Kipling's shoulders like a waterlogged wool blanket. If she really thought about it, she had been awake well over thirty-six hours, part of that being wrapped up in the excitement of her commencement, part in the rush to the airport, and part in the seven-or-so-hour flight from Boston to London. The logical thought process in taking the night-time flight was that she could sleep, and wake in London refreshed and ready to go, but she'd been too self-conscious to sleep on the flight.

It was one thing to wake up alone in her apartment, her throat dry from the cries she thought she might have made, panting for each breath with her heart pounding in her chest like a caged bird; it was another thing altogether to do the same on a plane full of strangers. When Grayson first left Boston, she'd had the dreams nightly, but it had improved. Until Grayson's obscure message weeks before, and his three weeks of silence. Each day that passed without hearing from him had resulted in a more difficult night. Fatigue caused headaches, and worry refused to let her consume anything other than coffee and perhaps a bagel. She'd managed a meal a few times at her parents' encouragement, but it didn't always stay with her. After his call, even though she knew he was safe, the nightmares had grown worse and more frequent. Worrying about the next inci-dent kept her from resting in flight.

Grayson's mother led her up the open staircase, the narrow steps catching her off guard so she had to be more conscious of each step. When they reached the top, Annalise led her toward the back of the house to a closed door.

Annalise stopped at the door, waiting for Kipling to join her before she turned the knob and let her into the bedroom. It was small, and compact, like much of the cottage, but it still caught Kipling's breath. Floral wallpaper on a cream background covered the walls and two twin-sized beds took up much of the floor.

"I hope this will do," Annalise said, going to the window to toss back the curtain, even though it was dark outside. "In the morning you'll have a lovely view of the garden and field."

"It's all perfect," Kipling said, joining her at the window. From here, she saw Grayson at his car removing his bags from the trunk. Her suitcase was already on the ground by his feet. They hadn't managed to claim the bags on their first trip out, too caught up in each other. She turned to face his mother. "Thank you so much for your hospitality, Mrs. Holmes. To open your home to me on the night before your daughter's wedding is so generous of you."

"Please, do call me Annalise. It is our sincere pleasure, Kipling." She smiled and joined her hands together in front of her, regarding Kip. "When Grayson told me months ago he'd met the young girl — now a woman — who had visited here so many years ago, I thought it was the most compelling of coincidences. But, I understand now it was much more." She reached out and laid her hand on Kipling's shoulder, the soft scent of her subtle perfume filling Kipling's senses. "My dear, you are a precious gift from God."

Tears prickled behind Kipling's eyelids and she looked away, back out the window to watch Grayson finagle the bags to return to the house in one trip. "God gave to both of us," she said softly, not trusting her voice to be any stronger. Then she turned her smile to Grayson's mother, swallowing hard. "He told me once he wished he were more like you, but honestly, I see so much of you in him."

His mother waved her hand and mumbled "Pish posh" as Grayson came through the bedroom door carrying Kipling's cases. He set them on the bed closest to the window. "I believe I grabbed it all."

"Looks it," Kipling said, sniffing before she faced him, knowing it was probably futile to hide her fatigue-weary emotions from him.

"I'll let you settle in," Annalise said, patting her arm before passing by Grayson on the way to the door. "See you in the morning, my dear."

The shadows grew longer by the moment, and although Kipling knew it was barely mid-afternoon in Boston, the lack of sunlight dragged at her limbs. Grayson stood at the foot of the bed and rubbed his hands together. "Right, quick geography lesson, upon which I will improve tomorrow." He pointed toward the door and then to his left. "Next door down is the bathroom, only one on the first floor so I suggest you get into it before Shirl or it might be a bit. Across the hall is Shirl's room." He pointed toward the door again, but with a straighter arm, indicating the other side of the hallway. "Next door down from her is my room." He winked and grinned. "Mum and Dad are at the end of the hall at the front of the cottage."

With a wicked grin, Kipling headed for the door, catching his look of confusion as she passed. "Oh, please," she said, stopping at the door. "Do you think I'm waiting until tomorrow to see your room? Before you have a chance to hide anything you don't want me to see?"

She winked and bolted from the room, his laughter following her as she skirted around the top of the stairs and around the other side of the banister to the second doorway he'd indicated as his. Kipling paused, hand on the knob, intentionally waiting until he was nearly on her before she turned it and stepped inside.

The room was dim since the sun had set and he had heavier curtains on the one window facing her, his room bracketed on each interior wall by rooms. Kipling stopped short when she felt something near her foot and didn't want to trip, only making out the shapes of a bed, desk, bureau, and bookshelves. Grayson stepped into the room, then brushed past her to the desk by the window where he turned on a lamp, casting the room only partially in light. But it was enough for her to see the young man he had once been.

Parents were the same everywhere, it seemed. Until their children insisted, she believed all parents left their bedrooms the same as the day they left home. Kipling's room was the same, even though she hadn't lived at home since finishing her undergraduate studies. Grayson's walls were painted a dusky blue rather than the floral wallpaper in Johanna's room, and while she had several area rugs covering the weathered wood floors, his were mostly bare, only a single braided rug beside his twin-sized bed. There wasn't any particular color theme other than he had a lot of blues and different hues. His bed cover was dark navy, the curtain somewhere between the blanket and the walls, and a Union flag pillow sat at the head of the bed. The room was tucked into an angle of the roof, with the window set into a dormer and the desk in front of the window. Bookshelves took up most of one of the interior walls, and at first glance, she saw a solid mix of textbooks, literature, and fiction. Eclectic. The other wall was covered with frames, everything from the periodic table to diplomas to a variety of family photos.

Grayson stepped to the middle of the room, hands in his pockets, and turned one hundred eighty degrees. "Nothing too embarrassing, I suppose."

Kipling smiled in his direction, then walked to the picture wall, taking her time to look at each. She suspected deep down Grayson was a very nostalgic man, and she already knew he let his roots grow deep in his family. Photos ranged from him at a young age — or at least she suspected it was him based on the mass of curls on his head and the unusual shading of the eyes of the boy in the photos — all the way through university. There were common connections in all. Him. His parents. His sisters. And another man of the same age with hair, though darker and more definitely brown, nearly as wild with the Holmes curls. Grayson was taller, but not by much; his mate was heftier, broader. They shared angular features — strong jaws and cheekbones, long noses — but the other seemed less sharp, more heavy. Kipling stepped closer to look at one in particular of Grayson and this repeating man, both in black graduation robes with velvet bands on the arm capes and white ties. They stood arms around each other in a vigorous hold, shoulder to shoulder, grinning wide at whoever took the photo.

A sense of familiarity niggled at her. Not that she had seen *this* man, but perhaps he reminded her of someone else.

"Is this your Cambridge graduation?" she asked, glancing at him.

Grayson nodded and crossed to her, hands still in his pockets. He stood behind her, his chest brushing her arm. "That's Greg."

Kipling smiled, feeling both happy and melancholy to finally have a face to the name. And sad she wouldn't ever know him. She leaned in, trying to see his face better. Something about him struck her like a strange sense of déjà vu, and she decided it was his familial look with Grayson. They were similar, though not quite the same. "He is here as much as your family," she said, encompassing all the photos with a swipe of her hand.

"That's because he is family."

Her breath caught and she looked at him. "Oh, I didn't mean—"

"No, it's okay," he said, taking a hand from his pocket to rest it on her shoulder. "I know what you meant, but truly, Greg was far more than a cousin. Possibly more than a brother could have been. The Holmes line made us family, but he truly was a best mate."

Kipling turned to wrap her arms around him, resting her cheek against his chest so she could still see the wall of photos. Grayson slid his arm around her shoulders and held her there.

"I wish I could know him," she said, careful not to make Greg's life in the past tense.

"I wish you could, too." Grayson kissed her brow. "So very much."

Chapter Four

Grayson tapped Agent Flannery's call icon as soon as he felt confident he was clear of earshot from the house.

Kipling had retired, so there was no risk of her hearing, but he wanted to avoid serious conversations as long as possible, at least until after the wedding. He brought the phone to his ear and glanced at his watch. It was late in Boston, but still within the parameters of Patrick's usual workday. As he recently entered bachelorhood again, Patrick kept longer hours.

"Flannery," the FBI agent said as he answered.

"It's Grayson." He glanced back toward the house, assuring everyone was inside.

"Got the email?"

Grayson nodded habitually and leaned against the side of his father's Jeep. "I did. I will review the files more thoroughly later this evening."

"Yeah, let me know if anything jumps out at you."

"No need to continue your attempts to reach Kipling. I know where she is, and she will not be available for a bit for interviews."

"Where is she?"

"She's here. In England," Grayson explained. "I was unaware of her impending arrival when we last spoke. I wanted to make you aware of the situation, and also inquire whether you were able to make any progress on the other unnamed customer Kipling described prior to my departure from Boston."

"Interesting how you jump right past the fact she showed up in England without you knowing about it. No problem, chief, we can ignore that for now. On the other guy, nah, we got nuthin'. Not enough to go on, and since the bookstore didn't have any security cameras or anything, we got no visual. He didn't buy anything, or if he did your girlfriend didn't cash him out, so no name. "

"That's unfortunate. It's an angle worth pursuing."

"I'll leave the pursuing to you," Agent Flannery said with a chuckle.

"Send me the information and I will be in touch." Not waiting for anything further from the American agent, Grayson disconnected the call and slipped his phone back into his pocket as he walked toward the kitchen door.

Just before he reached the door, it opened and his father came out, pipe and lit match in hand as he ignited the tobacco in the pipe. Mum had restricted his father from smoking inside the cottage when they moved back to the cottage from London, and even on the coldest of winter nights, his father respected her wishes and stood outside to enjoy his pipe. The sweet, tangy aroma of his father's Oriental blend drifted in the air as Grayson approached.

"BBC News at Ten must be on the telly," Grayson said as he stepped up to his father. Ever since Grayson was old enough to be awake at ten, he remembered his father slipping outside for a pipe during the news.

Emerson Holmes made a small sound akin to a chuckle, quite near to a full-out laugh for the quiet man. "Trouble?" he asked, pointing off the way Grayson had come.

Understanding all the things his father meant, and filling in the words he didn't say, was something Grayson and his sisters had learned to do naturally from the time they learned to speak.

"Unfortunately, I am unable to fully escape my duties as much as I would like to from time to time. It's nothing pressing."

His father nodded and puffed on the pipe, sending fragrant smoke into the evening air.

Grayson stepped away from the circle of light cast through the cottage windows, looking out into the wildflower field lit by the silver moonlight. He glanced over his shoulder toward the back of the cottage, confirming Johanna's bedroom light was not on; Kipling was likely in bed and hopefully resting. The fatigue he saw in her eyes, and even in the way she moved, concerned him. He hoped a solid night's sleep would do her well, but he feared her exhaustion went beyond a long flight from the States.

"She's a special woman," his father said, and Grayson turned on the balls of his feet to look back at the house.

His father was now cast in shadows with the light of the house behind him, the red glow of his tobacco flaring with his breath. Grayson smiled. Of course, his father summed Kipling in four words.

"Yes, she is," Grayson agreed, his smile widening unbidden. "She's amazing. Do you remember her?"

His father bobbed his head, and Grayson wished he could see his father's face. "Difficult to forget."

Grayson let out a small chuckle. "No truer words, Dad."

Emerson Holmes cleared his throat and stepped away from the shadow of the cottage, moving into the light so Grayson could easily see his face. He lowered his pipe and released a billow of fragrant smoke. "She knows the truth." He didn't ask.

"You're either trusting me to know exactly what you're commenting on, or you're setting me up to reveal something I wouldn't want to otherwise," Grayson said, clicking in his cheek. He looked up to the window again, then took a step toward his father. "Does she know about my position at Six? Yes. I've told her all she needs to know, and when she has questions, I will answer them as best I can." He shrugged up his shoulders and held them, his hands pushed into his pockets. "Is that what you mean."

"Mostly." His father nodded, taking a long draw from the pipe. "Did you tell her about Greg?"

Grayson drew in a slow breath through his nose, releasing it again before he could answer. Even now, he did not know his father's belief when it came to Greg, since his father was a man of so few words, and while he had no doubt his father felt deeply and wholly, he was not one to reveal the intensity of emotion for others to view. Grayson turned away and took a few steps into the dark yard, pausing to rub the side of his fingers across his upper lip, his skin scraping on the day's whisker growth.

With his back to his father, he gave his answer. "I told Kipling quite a bit about Greg before I ever told her what happened in Edinburgh, and before leaving Boston I told her the whole of it." He pivoted on his heels to face his father again. "And my belief he did not die in that explosion."

His father nodded. "Good," was his only response.

Grayson tipped back his head and took in the stars. The sky wasn't quite black, but more a deep, dark navy, and the stars pinholes of light. It was a beautiful night, the air fragrant and cool. He'd open his window to sleep and enjoy the country air. At the thought of sleep, his jaw unhinged and he yawned deep, laughing as he let it out.

He walked back to his father as he stretched. "I'm off to Bedfordshire."

His father chuckled and smiled around his pipe. As Grayson passed, he laid his hand on his father's shoulder, giving a squeeze. Before he lowered his arm, his father called his name and Grayson stopped beside him, looking him in the eyes. The light from the house let him see the details of his father's face easily. Emerson Holmes was probably the first person Grayson had learned to "read", quite possibly out of necessity. Even at a young age, he understood that which his father didn't vocalize was far more important than what he chose to say. In the shadows of his aged face, Grayson saw deep concern and a heavy heart. It was enough to make him pause and take a sideways step closer to his father, his hand still on the man's shoulder.

"What is it, Dad?"

His father frowned, the expression tugging at his brow as much as his lips. Grayson waited, realizing he held his breath. He let it out slowly, squeezing his father's shoulder again.

"Is it still what you want?" his father finally asked.

"It what still what I want, Dad?" It was a rare event when Grayson couldn't somehow devise his father's intended question in whole by a partial statement.

"Six," was his only clarification.

Grayson looked away and lowered his head, letting go a long breath before meeting his father's eyes again. Eyes similar to his in their mismatched color combination, a trait of the Holmes bloodline inherited from his great-grandmother Violet's family. "I'm not convinced in my heart Six is what I *ever* wanted. I knew I wanted to do something worthwhile, something…meaningful." He shrugged, an uncommon action for him, but one rooted in his youth and inspired again by conversation with his father. "In the last year or more, I have had my doubts whether this is the way."

"How does she feel about it?" Emerson jutted his chin over his shoulder toward the house.

"She has never stated, or even implied, she would prefer I not be an officer. That being said, I am well aware of how difficult it is for her. More aware than I have been in past relationships." Grayson squinted, tilting his head. "Did she say something to you or Mum?"

His father shook his head and brought his glowing pipe to his mouth again, the stem clacking against his teeth. "Doesn't need to."

Grayson pressed his lips together and smiled, squeezing then patting his father's shoulder before he let his arm drop. As he took a step toward the kitchen door, his father moved away to cross the garden.

"Your heart is true, my boy. Listen to it."

Grayson paused and looked over his shoulder at his father's retreating back. Emerson hadn't turned when he spoke, perhaps because speaking two sentences at once was a feat. When his father was outside the circle of light from the house, Grayson opened the cottage door and went inside, greeted in the kitchen by Watson who paced between him and the hall, apparently anxious to go upstairs but only with Grayson's company. The cottage still held all the enticing aromas from dinner, with the added scent of Earl Grey, his mother's favorite tea. Grayson walked slowly through the house, through the front hall to the staircase, taking a few extra moments to enjoy the stillness of the house. Even with news on the telly in the parlor, the house was calm and peaceful. After weeks and months of chaos and battles and heartbreak, he let it wrap around him and soak in to his ragged soul.

Watson mewled from the top of the stairs, and Grayson smiled, obeying his master's command. Half way up the stairs, he hit the seventh step and it creaked beneath his weight.

"Goodnight, sweetheart," his mother called from the parlor.

"Goodnight, Mum," he called back, smiling, convinced she had learned to recognize the slight variation in sound between her children on the same step. In the upstairs hall, he looked to Jo's closed bedroom door. No light showed at the bottom, so both Jo and Kipling were likely asleep. Watson paced in front of the door, but Grayson shushed him and motioned toward his own room. Watson stared for a moment, then bolted across the dark hall into Grayson's bedroom. Shirley's bedroom door was open, light spilling across the wooden hall floor, and Grayson went there before his own room, leaning against the jamb to watch his sister for a few moments before she noticed his presence.

She sat on her bed, her back to the headboard, her legs folded with a photo album open in her lap. A far away, happy smile bowed her lips. He watched as she turned the page, and her shoulders bounced in a quiet giggle. He still saw the little girl in long braids chasing after him and Greg in the yard, wanting to do whatever it was they were doing just to be with them. It was hard to believe she would be a married woman in two days.

"What are you looking at?" he asked, taking a step into the room.

She looked up with a wide smile. "This was the last Christmas you were home before you went to Cambridge." Shirley leaned forward and patted the bed beside her. "Come sit and look with me, Grayson."

He did, and for the next several minutes they went through the memories, laughing and retelling the stories they'd both heard a dozen times before, but didn't mind hearing again. At the end of the book, Shirl closed it and set it aside, linking her hands in her lap with a deep sigh. She looked at him, her eyes shifting to study him, and Grayson smiled back.

"What?" he asked.

"You look so happy," she answered, her smile widening more. She sighed and shrugged. "I thought I saw it when you came home in February, even though things went badly in Boston. I had hoped I didn't read you wrong, because if I had, bringing Kipling here might have been a disaster." She rolled her eyes and shook her head, then focused on him again. "But…I'm pretty sure I got it right. You're happy she's here, aren't you?" A slight tinge of apprehension lilted her voice.

"Happy is far too inadequate a word," he assured, reaching to squeeze her hand. "It is your wedding, and you have given me the greatest gift."

Shirley's eyes shined and her smile wavered, and she lunged forward on her knees to wrap her arms around him. Grayson teased with a grunt, but couldn't keep up the farce and hugged her back.

"I'm so happy for you, Grayson," Shirley said before setting back again, her eyes bright in contrast to her wide smile. She held his hands and squeezed, and sniffed her nose. "You deserve to be insanely happy, and I think Kipling might be the one to do that for you. You *do* love her, don't you?"

Grayson stood, but as he did he leaned down to kiss his sister's cheek. "Absolutely and completely. Goodnight, dear heart."

Having conceded to the fact he wouldn't be able to get past the barrier of Jo's closed door to sleep with the one he truly wanted, that being Kipling, Watson had found contentment in sprawling out across Grayson's bed to groom himself. He didn't acknowledge Grayson's entrance until Grayson reached the bed and nudged the cat to move. With a pompous, slow blink, Watson moved to the foot of the bed to continue his bath. Grayson sat on the edge of the small bed, already dreading his attempt at sleep. He'd outgrown the bed at sixteen, but the room couldn't accommodate anything larger. Such was the truth of small English cottages. He leaned over, tugged off his shoes, glanced at his desk and closed computer as he sat up again.

Knowing sleep was hours away yet, he decided to accomplish in the dark hours of the night what he wouldn't want to take time to do the next day when his time was best spent enjoying Kipling's presence. He changed into his night clothing, then opened his laptop and sat at the small desk to study the files sent by Agent Flannery.

Within the hour, the words blurred and his focus was gone. Knowing sleep was still outside his reach, Grayson sat back in the chair and scrubbed his palms over his face, groaning into his hands. With a rake of his fingers through his hair, he let his hands drop heavy into his lap. His attention wandered to a photo in a frame sitting on the back corner of the desk. From Sandra and David Sookoo's wedding reception a few years before, the photo was a candid shot of Grayson and Greg, late enough into the evening their ties had long since disappeared and their shirt collars loosened. Standing side by side, someone with a trained eye would see the familial ties they shared with the unusual coloring of their eyes to the wave of their hair. Beyond the subtle, Grayson and Greg were very different. Grayson was taller, by no more than an inch, but Greg was wider, built for strength.

With a deep inhale, Grayson reached for the photo and held it in front of him, studying the image. Although a few years old, it was one of the last photos Grayson had with his cousin. Not willing to dwell on Greg's absence, since he knew there would be more than sufficient reminders in the days to come as the family gathered for Shirl's wedding, Grayson set the photo back in its place.

A sound in the hall, the slow opening of a bedroom door, carried into the quiet house. Watson jerked up his head from slumber, and with a quick glance toward the hall, jumped from the bed and bolted to the door. It was unlikely Shirl or Jo would inspire such an enthusiastic response from the cat, and by the way he paced and mewled at the closed barrier, Grayson didn't have to wonder who wandered the house so late. With a smile, he pushed back from the desk and headed for the door, Watson's cries urging him on.

Chapter Five

Logically, Kipling knew the best way to get over jetlag was to force herself to immediately adjust to the local time, but her body and brain wasn't having it. She was still tired; fatigue had been a constant companion for the last month or more. But her biological clock said it was only mid-afternoon and the three hours of sleep she'd gotten was just a nap. It was time to be up and doing something.

Except the Holmes cottage was completely silent.

Kipling slipped from the extra bed in Johanna's room and put her hearing aids in place. She couldn't tell if she made too much noise if she couldn't hear the noise. With her attention on Jo's still form in the other bed, she took a BU sweatshirt from her suitcase and pulled it over her head, walking on tiptoes to the bedroom door.

The problem with trying to sneak around in an old house was that it was an old house, with squeaky floorboards and noisy hinges. Just a few steps up from main floor, one board let out a particularly loud creak and Kipling froze, wincing. She looked up the staircase, waited, listening. When no doors opened and no lights came on, she continued down the narrow staircase to the front hall.

Where she was going she wasn't sure, just somewhere other than tossing and turning in the bed. As loud as the creaks and groans of the house seemed at midnight, the bed seemed just as loud and she feared she'd eventually wake Jo with her inability to sleep. She headed toward the kitchen at the back of the cottage once she made it down the stairs. No shades or curtains blocked the large, multi-paned windows, and silver-white light illuminated the small but spotless kitchen. The luscious smells from dinner still lingered in the air, and she tried her best to ignore the fact her stomach thought it was dinnertime.

Though, the fact she wanted to eat was probably a good thing.

Kipling took her phone from her pajama pants to check the time. Yep, midnight. There were two text alerts on the main screen. One from Mina, and one from John. Both asking if she'd landed okay, but Mina's had a distinct slant of sarcasm, asking how bad Grayson had freaked at her sudden and uninvited appearance. Not in the mood to talk to either of them, she huffed and set the phone on the small table set against the back windows. It was just big enough for two, maybe three, and Kipling imagined Annalise and Emerson sharing breakfast there, or the three children gathered around it when they were small. The image brought a smile to her lips.

"What caused that smile?"

She yelped and jumped, spinning to face Grayson, her hand pressed to her chest. "Grayson!"

He chuckled and walked toward her. "I guess that answers my question whether you are wearing your aids, or not."

Kipling's insides tumbling at the sight of him in dark blue cotton flannel pants and a basic blue tee shirt, and barefoot. She remembered back in Boston when he'd met her at his hotel suite door in bare feet, and it had made her tummy tumble then as well. Most might not consider it sexy, but it was enough to melt her toes. She swallowed and shook her head, trying to calm her frantic heart.

"I can't be quiet if I can't hear if I'm being quiet."

He crossed the room as she answered, and when the last word left her lips he kissed them, taking her face in his hands. Kipling hummed into the kiss, leaning into him to wrap her arms around his waist. After so long away from him, every kiss rushed through her veins and jumpstarted her pulse. When he parted their lips, he didn't move away, only enough she had to tip up her chin to look into his eyes, to see his slow, enticing smile.

"There is the kiss of welcome and of parting, the long, lingering, loving, present one; the stolen, or the mutual one; the kiss of love, of joy, of sorrow; the seal of promise and receipt of fulfillment."

Kipling smiled, her cheeks pressing into his warm palms. "Do you always seduce women in your mother's kitchen?"

Grayson chuckled, the low rumble in his chest resonating through her. "I can say without hesitation I have never seduced a woman in this kitchen. Oh, that I could now." He leaned down to speak over her open lips before kissing her again. "I long to say hello properly."

Kipling toed up to seek out a deeper kiss, his words and promise as much fire to her blood as his kiss and touch. For weeks, the promise of an intimate "hello" had kept her restless at night and thinking of Grayson by day. They had yet to be intimate, at least with their bodies, but he already knew how to bring her alive.

"Perhaps I didn't fully think through the limitations of seeing you again in your parents' home," she admitted as she eased out of the kiss again.

"Which begs the question…" Grayson motioned for her to sit at the table, which she did, tucking her heels on the edge of the chair seat with her knees under her chin. "How long are you able to stay in England?"

He moved away and went to the stove, turning on the flame before he took a small saucepan from the strainer beside the sink. Kipling rested her chin on her knee, watching him, trying to look as calm as possible despite the desire tumbling in her stomach already waging war against the apprehension of what to say and when. As a distraction, either intentionally or not, Watson rubbed his head and side along the edge of the chair, bumping her bare toes with his nose. He purred so loud she could hear him. She extended one hand and rubbed between his ears, and he pressed into her fingertips.

"Um, I don't actually have a return date."

He looked over his shoulder at her, a long and if she interpreted it correctly, pleased smile on his lips as he took a glass bottle of milk from the refrigerator, then went to the stove to pour some into the pan. Kipling swallowed and pushed her fingers through her loose hair. She felt the distinct crawl of heat up her throat to her face.

"When do you go back to London?" she asked, trying to hide the squeak in her voice.

"I return to work a week from Monday, so I had planned to stay here a few days, then head back for a few days of quiet." He smiled at her over his shoulder. "However, I am inclined to return to London on Monday. I can give you a proper tour, not the tourist version."

Going back to London on Monday was great timing since she needed to be there by Wednesday. She curled her lips between her teeth to keep from saying so. She would, just not yet. "You don't have other plans? I know this was a complete surprise, so if you have—"

"Nothing is more important or more delightful than spending nearly a full, *uninterrupted* week with you." He winked as he opened a cupboard and took out a glass honey pot, drizzling some into the warming milk. "So, are you going to tell me what you were smiling about when I interrupted?"

Kipling leaned back so her shoulders set against the windowsill, and she looked at the other chairs from her vantage point. "I was picturing you, with a wild mop of unruly curls, sitting here with Shirley and Johanna, having an after-school snack."

Without looking his way again, she heard him turn off the stove, pour the milk out, and set the pot in the sink before he crossed to her and sat down in the chair across from her, opposite the window. He set a ceramic mug in front of her, steam rolling up from the warm milk.

"Warm milk and honey," he explained. "Mum's secret to help us sleep when we couldn't. It will take more than a day for you to reset, so this might help in the interim."

"It would be nice not to fall asleep during your sister's wedding."

Kipling lowered her feet to sit properly in the chair, and wrapped her fingers around the warm mug, inhaling the steam. As soon as her lap was available, Watson jumped into it. "Milk and honey tonight, and coffee tomorrow. Or tea? Smells wonderful. I'm sorry if I woke you."

"You didn't, actually. I'd yet to attempt sleep. I heard someone moving about, but didn't initially check to see if it might be you." He pointed toward her lap. "It was that maddening beast. He must have heard you, or sensed your accessibility because he quite ardently insisted I come investigate." He smiled, and her insides warmed. "I do believe Watson intends to compete with me for your undying affection."

Kipling brought the cup to her lips and took a tentative sip. It was delicious. The richness of whole milk laced with the sweet zing of honey. The warmth spread down her throat and into her chest, and she hummed. "Oh, this is heavenly."

"Holmes honey, and fresh milk from Guillaney's farm."

Kipling raised her brows, looking at him over the edge of the mug as she took another sip. Licking the sweetness from her lips, she set down the mug. "Holmes honey?"

He grinned and winked. "Of course. Four generations." He tipped his head toward the window, implying the property beyond. "The hives are along the back away from the garden."

She wasn't sure why she was surprised each time Grayson revealed some tidbit or detail about himself or his family that linked him once again to his infamous great-grandfather Sherlock. It still amazed her that the stories were true, and just how true, and how fate or coincidence had brought Grayson into her life. Or her into his, depending on the perspective.

Kipling took another soothing sip of the milk, closing her eyes as the natural calmative eased through her. She hummed her pleasure as she set the cup on the table again. When she opened her eyes, a different warmth skimmed just beneath the surface of her skin when she caught Grayson staring at her. Blatantly, and without apology, studying her. She licked her lips and canted her head.

"You are so beautiful," Grayson said and drew in a slow breath.

"So beautiful you both steal my tongue and inspire the few words I can manage to be saturated in poeticism."

Kipling chuckled and shook her head. "That's you with a stolen tongue?"

Grayson cleared his throat, a self-conscious sound that struck her odd since there had been so few times she'd seen him uneasy, and he sat back, dropping his hands in his lap. "Speaking of stolen tongues, I am going to attempt this and hope I don't muddle it up too badly."

"Attempt what?"

He huffed a quick breath, met her gaze, then raised his hands. His movements were jaunty and amateur, and he hadn't quite mastered the idea that signing was more about concepts than actual words, so she inferred what he intended, but the fact he tried was one of the most beautiful and considerate things Kipling had ever seen.

"*The first signs I learned were you're beautiful.*" He waved his fingers in front of his face, pinching them together near his chin. "*...and I love you.*"

He didn't use the more common sign of holding the palm forward with the index and ring fingers curled down, but instead pointed first to himself, then crossed his arms with curled hands over his chest, and pointed to her. Kipling reached for his hand, wrapping both hers around his and leaned forward until she could kiss his knuckles. Then let go to sign in return.

"*Very good, Grayson.*" She touched her "g" positioned fingers to her temple beside her right eye, then brought the same hand to her heart, holding the letter sign. At his puzzled look, she signed slowly, knowing if he'd learned enough he'd still take time to process. "*This is your name sign.*" She repeated the motion.

"Ah, yes," he spoke, nodding. "My instructor explained name signs are very personal, and can vary based on the person signing, or speaking, however you wish to define it." He paused, smiling as he stared at her so long heat crawled up her throat to her cheeks. His smile ticked, and he dropped his hands below the side of the table. "I considered what symbol could encompass the value of your name for me."

"Did you find one?" she asked.

He parted his lips and canted his head slightly. "Only enough to consider it sufficient." Taking a deep breath, he put his left hand to his chest, his fingers cupped so his thumb and fingertips touched his body, but his palm rounded away as if making a cup or vessel of his hands. With his right hand, he made a "k" to symbolize her name and lowered a portion of his hand into the space made by the left, then drew it upward along his breastbone.

"It's a variation of the sign for—"

"Soul," she said with a hoarse whisper, his consideration for her enough to make her throat tighten.

Before he could confirm, her phone buzzed across the table. She hadn't opened the text messages from Mina and John, so either they had sent new messages or the alert was a reminder to her to check. Since she didn't always notice the vibration when she didn't wear her hearing aids, she had the phone set to vibrate until acknowledged.

Annoyed at the interruption, she picked up the phone and slid her thumb across the screen to unlock it. "Sorry," she mumbled. "Mina. I texted her earlier after I called Mom and Dad, to say I was here. She wants—" Kipling pressed her lips together to keep from commenting on what seemed to be Mina's intent. She read the curt message.

Did he pretend to be pleased?

"What's wrong?"

Kipling slapped the phone down on the table, screen down, with a huff. "I'd love to know. Mina has had an attitude since I made plans to come for the wedding. She warned me you wouldn't find it nearly as nice a surprise as Shirl assumed. And John isn't helping. He's convinced—" She bit off the explanation and shook her head, shoving the phone away from her. "Never mind Mina and John. They are in Boston, and I am here." Kipling poked the tabletop with the tip of her finger. She smiled, leaning on her hand. "With you."

Grayson nudged the side of her phone with a single, long finger. "John. You've mentioned him." He winked and grinned. "Should I be worried?"

She smirked, teasing. "Maybe. If I liked the bulky, broad, linebacker type." She wanted to say something flirty and sexy, but whatever she might have managed was lost in a jaw-popping yawn.

Grayson chuckled and stood, holding out his hand to her. "Come along, Miss Branson. Big day tomorrow, and unfortunately, it's likely to begin early. Off to bed with you. "

"Sounds like an offer," she said, with a wink that earned her a laugh from him.

She took his hand and unfolded her legs and he drew her to her feet but didn't fall into step beside him to leave the kitchen. Instead, she indulged her need to feel him close, wrapped her arms around him, and pressed her cheek to his chest. She had to tilt her head away enough to keep the aids from feeding back, but still pressed close enough she felt the steady rhythm of his heart. He hummed, a low rumble through his chest, and wrapped his arms around her.

"I'm really here, aren't I?" she asked, closing her eyes.

"I've asked myself the same question more than once since I walked into the parlor and saw you." Grayson pressed a kiss to the top of her head. "I am inclined to go buy my sister a much bigger wedding gift, as my Waterford crystal wine glasses seem rather pathetic in comparison to the gift she has given me."

Chapter Six

"Are you ready for the Holmes Introductory Course?" Grayson asked, drawing Kipling with him to the back of the rows of chairs set up in the garden.

Young boys who served in the local parish arrived at dawn in a truck loaded with white chairs, and went to work immediately with setting them up. The vicar of the parish would be performing the ceremony, and already stood at the far end of the set up speaking with Emerson Holmes.

"I don't know. Will there be a quiz?"

"Oral, yes."

Kipling couldn't help it. The burst of laughter hit her before she could slap her hand over her mouth. Grayson turned his head slowly, intentionally, with raised eyebrows mocking her. She managed to muffle her laughter, but her shoulders shook with it. Heat flushed her skin from hairline to toes, but it lost to the exhaustion-induced mirth his completely innocent answer spurred. Grayson slid his hand along her back to touch her far hip and drew her to his side, leaning in to whisper in her ear.

"You are a vixen, Doctor Branson." His low baritone hummed in her blood. "What a deliciously naughty mind."

Kipling wasn't sure what prevailed, the flash of heat his voice inspired or the silly, intoxicating giggle she couldn't stop. She had to fan her face with her hands and dab at tears before they ruined her makeup, still fighting the giggles. "I'm sorry," she finally managed to say. "I get punchy when I'm tired."

He chuckled again and planted a solid kiss on her cheek before sliding behind her, his arm wrapping around from behind so his hand rested on her stomach. Thus, when he spoke, his voice cut through the growing mingled conversations.

"Back to the lesson, shall we?" She nodded, her lips pressed together hard to withhold the laugher.

By the time he pointed out his cousin Petra, Greg's older sister, and her husband Steven Sebastian, Kipling had managed to find most of her composure. He then indicated each in turn Petra's three children. Erika was a teenager of about fifteen, sitting already in one of the rows typing at lightning speed on her smartphone. Steven and Petra had two younger children, Stevie at seven and Elinore at five. They weren't in the garden, but upstairs being prepped for their duties as bearer of the ring and flower girl.

With her giggles lessened, Grayson held her firmer against his chest, guiding her to see whomever he spoke of. Elton McQueen Jr. was there with his wife Lila, who was due to have their third child by the end of the summer. They already had twin boys, Peter and Patrick. Other than Johanna and Shirley, that was nearly the extent of the Holmes family line. Grayson's grandparents had passed years before, on both sides. His mother's family lived in the U.S., and mostly unavailable or not prepared to make the trip to the UK for the wedding.

"It's not that Mum doesn't have a close relationship with anyone," he explained, lowering his arm so both wrapped around her. "It's difficult being so far away."

"I imagine it would be," Kipling said, for a moment the lightness of the day gave way to a weight of thought. She was considering the same life as Annalise Holmes, thousands of miles and another continent away from her family.

Though right now, her only contemplation was for a job. As

much as her heart wanted to jump to a beautiful conclusion, her head — whose voice still sounded very much like Mina — warned her against assumptions. Then Grayson bent his neck and kissed her exposed shoulder, making her forget her apprehension. She was thankful she'd chosen the off-the-shoulder style dress. It fit snugly through the bodice, then flared into a loose tea-length skirt in a peach color she'd fallen in love with. He made his appreciation quite clear as soon as he saw her, and ran his fingertips along her clavicle and shoulders, sending a shiver through her.

He sighed, snuggling her into position again, and she rested her hands on his arms. "Other than that, everyone here would be family friends, and Daniel's side. Honestly, I can't introduce you there any further than his parents. They are the couple that just joined Dad with Reverend Anderson. Seem like good people."

"I doubt you'd allow your baby sister to marry anyone who wasn't," she said, tilting her head to look up at him.

His mouth quirked into a smile and he winked at her. "Quite right. There are sometimes advantages to my profession." He sucked in a breath and glanced around. "Speaking of which, only immediate family — anyone named Holmes and any McQueen over the age of thirty — know what I do. No one else."

Kipling nodded. "So, what do the others think you do?"

He pulled a face and tilted his head back and forth. "Commodities trader. It helps explain my frequent and lengthy times away from England, should the question arise. Which is how we met."

Kipling arched her eyebrows. "Oh?"

"I was in Boston on a business trip. We met, it was instant…" He tipped her to gain access to her lips. "…and undeniable love," and finished with a kiss.

She laughed into the kiss and pulled back to look at him again. "And what do I do?"

Grayson shook his head. "No reason to change anything. You recently earned your doctorate in literature and are here on holiday before seeking employment in your chosen field."

The truth stuck in her throat, but she wasn't ready. Not yet. She'd only been with him less than twenty-four hours. She smiled and nodded and he gave her a firm kiss before righting them both.

"Grayson, dear," said an aged female voice near them.

A petite woman of at least eighty, barely five feet tall if that, dressed entirely in purple stood beside them. Grayson shifted his hold on Kipling to come to her side, one hand on her back. He leaned forward, though his hand never left her, to kiss the cheek of the elderly lady who had greeted them. "How wonderful to see you, Mrs. Bertrand. You are absolutely radiant."

She pish-poshed and waved off his compliment, color blooming in her wrinkled, parchment cheeks. "Oh, you've always been the fresh one."

"Kipling, this is Mrs. Margaret Bertrand. Her mother was a dearest friend to my grandmother Amelia, who was married to Hamish Holmes and Mrs. Bertrand has long been a friend of the family. She taught Dad to play piano when he was young and often cared for him."

"How nice to meet you," Kipling said, extending her hand.

Mrs. Bertrand's gnarled, cool fingers delicately gripped Kipling's and she smiled wider. "Are you American, my dear?"

Kipling nodded, and Grayson cleared his throat. "Mrs. Bertrand, it is my utmost pleasure to introduce you to Doctor Kipling Branson. My—"

"Oh, no need to tell me what she is, Grayson. That was quite obvious," she said with another wave of her tiny hand, but quickly reached for Grayson, touching his arm. The smile slipped away, overtaken by deep sadness. "This is the first I've seen most of your family since Greg's death. How are you, my dear?"

Although he changed in no way Mrs. Bertrand was likely to see, Grayson worked his hand up and down her spine in a slow stroke. He smiled, but it was strained. "As well as can be expected, Mrs. Bertrand. Losing Greg hit all of us very hard."

"So sad to lose him in such a meaningless way as a car accident. Not that any other way would hurt any less."

Grayson tried to smile, and the attempt squeezed Kip's heart painfully. His hand slid up and down her back again. "No, it would not have made any difference how we lost him."

Mrs. Bertrand looked toward the far side of the garden, where a simple arbor had been built, rows of chairs between them and the structure. "Has someone seen to the chair?"

"I saw to it myself."

Kipling turned her head to look at him, but nothing in his expression gave her a hint about what they meant. Mrs. Bertrand sighed and patted his arm. "Good. I knew you would, I had no doubt, and you are the best for it. Dear, sweet, Grayson." Then she slowly shuffled away, leaning on her cane to stay steady on the grass.

Something had changed. Something had shifted in Grayson, and it resonated off him. Kipling turned into him and laid her hand on the lapel of his dark cream linen suit jacket and his hand pressed to her back, bringing her to him before he met her gaze. She tilted her head, studying the sudden lines barely disguising the frown he didn't want seen. After a moment, he smiled, but it was unconvincing.

"Walk with me," he said, taking her hand to lead her between the rows of chairs toward the front of the seating area.

The first row of chairs on the left was reserved for Emerson and Annalise Holmes and family, Kipling included. The second and third rows were reserved for the McQueens as being a larger contribution to the guest list. Resting on the third chair from the aisle was a bouquet of six dark crimson roses. They weren't tied, no embellishments like baby's breath, and they weren't in any type of vessel, simply set on the chair.

"The tradition of the empty chair has been in our family for more generations than we know," Grayson explained, his voice rough and low. So low she needed to focus on him to make sure she caught every word. "When a loved one is lost, at every important event when they would have normally been there, a chair is reserved for them for as long as those left behind need to acknowledge their absence. Shirl's wedding is the first major event since Greg—"

Kipling tightened her hold on his hand and stepped closer. He bent his arm, their hands still linked, to tuck it behind her and bring her against him, his focus still on the chair. He swallowed, and finally turned his head enough to look at her and the sadness in his eyes broke her heart.

"The task is never left to those in the greatest pain, in this case Greg's parents, but to their closest sibling or family member." By the time he reached the end of his sentence, his voice was nearly gone and she relied solely on the words playing on his lips. "Petra and Steven asked me to see to it, because although they were Greg's siblings, they knew he and I were closer than brothers."

Tears burned her eyes, but she tried to smile. When she knew she failed, she wrapped her arms around his neck and embraced him. Grayson pressed his face to her shoulder, a long shudder moving through him, and she held him tighter wishing it could be enough.

"So, here comes Grayson out of the water naked as the day he was born," Petra described between fits of laughter. Everyone around the table in the garden laughed, except for Grayson. He groaned, covering his eyes with his hand. "And without a bit of modesty. He marched right past all the other families, mothers covering their little girls' eyes and gasping."

"Please. Stop," Grayson begged. "Have mercy."

Kipling absolutely shook, her hand resting on his knee, tears streaming from her eyes. "Absolutely not," she said, shaking her head. "You can't stop now."

"Oh, I have no intention to," Petra said, grinning wickedly. "Grayson walks up the beach and stops at Aunt Annalise's chair, hands firmly planted on his hips. He declares, quite loudly, that a mermaid has stolen his swimming trunks."

"I was seven years old, " he cried in defense. "And I had recently completed reading Hans Christian Anderson's *The Little Mermaid*, so I was quite convinced they existed."

Kipling leaned sideways away from him. "You read *The Little Mermaid* when you were seven?"

"Grayson was always a bit of an overachiever," Steven said, taking a sip of his stout. "He was teased relentlessly once he began school. Couldn't just say two plus two is four, but the sum of the integers equals four."

Kipling smiled, leaning her head back on the arm he stretched behind her on the chairs. "I love that about him," she said.

Grayson kissed her shoulder, her skin cool in the evening air. As Petra continued her story without mercy, he moved away from her enough to shrug off his suit jacket and lay it across her shoulders, settling in again to voice protests against his cousins' need to tell every possible embarrassing story they could recall.

"Don't try to change the subject," Petra said with a finger wagged in his direction. "So there stands Grayson, hands on hips, I dare say quite proud of his state of undress. Aunt Annalise is rummaging frantically for something, *anything*, to put on him. Not to be outdone, Greg runs down the beach, sees Grayson, and promptly shoves his own trunks down his legs and tosses them in the sand."

Kipling burst out in laughter, covering her mouth, and despite himself Grayson chuckled as well.

"I'm not sure which one was prouder," his mother added. "Both standing there, matching stances, grinning like Cheshire cats. Emerson attempted to gather up the boys and get them covered, but they were having none of it. Side by side, they ran off again into the water, tiny little willies swinging in the breeze and all."

Grayson groaned again, heat rising in his cheeks despite the fact the story was well over twenty years old. Kipling rubbed her hand on his leg and leaned into his side. "Who encouraged who?" she asked his mother.

"Depended entirely on the day," his mother answered, taking a sip of her wine and ending with a laugh. "Hazel and I never knew what to expect from those two. They were like two halves of the same mischievous, brilliant mind."

"Right down to their matching birthmarks, and after that day, all of Sussex knew about them," Petra added. She winked at Kipling. "You know the one. On his bottom."

Kipling's slow, teasing grin shot straight down Grayson's spine as she looked up at him. "No, I don't actually. Is it a big one?" She feigned innocence, wide-eyed and teeth tugging at her lower lip.

"Well, no, but how could you have not seen—"

Grayson's glance toward his cousin silenced her, and her mouth hung open. Finally, after an hour of being tortured by his childhood being paraded in front of Kipling for their enjoyment, the bloom of color was in Petra's cheeks. She cleared her throat, though didn't look all that apologetic.

"Sorry. I just assumed."

"What kind of boy do you think I raised?" his mother asked, her voice just slightly slurred from the extra glass or two of wine she'd had since Shirley and Daniel departed to stay in the village until they departed for their honeymoon. "I've raised a gentleman."

Grayson cleared his throat, taking advantage of the change in song playing through the speakers set in the kitchen window to gain his feet and draw Kipling with him. "Dance with me."

Her grin was contagious, playful, and just naughty enough to inspire an array of thoughts he could not pursue. She left his jacket on the chairs and followed to a spot on the lawn now clear of the rows of seating. The beginning piano trills of "I'll Be Seeing You", the Billie Holiday version began to play as he raised their joined hands over her head, spinning her slowly so she ended in his embrace. Grayson rested her right palm over his heart and held it there while he wrapped his other arm around her and she laid her hand on his shoulder. The song was perfect for garnering a few moments alone with Kipling, as alone as allowed with most of his immediate family sitting nearby already back in conversation.

With Kipling in his arms, he rested cheek to cheek and kissed her jaw, closing his eyes as he swayed them slowly. She inhaled deeply, slowly, and let it go. Then she giggled, and even though he didn't know why, he chuckled as well.

"I love your family," she said by way of explanation. "I always looked in on families from the outside, even Mina's with four siblings and aunts and uncles. I was always visiting." She drew back enough to look up at him. "I don't feel like I'm visiting, and I've only been here a day. Is it foolish of me to feel like I belong?"

Grayson shook his head, swallowing at the sudden thickness in his throat. Whether he wished to fully acknowledge it or not, his emotions had run the gambit today, high and low, and he'd be a blind fool if he denied them. "No," he managed to say and brought his hand from behind her to lay his fingers on her cheek, his thumb on her chin beneath her lips. "I can't express how inexplicably happy such a simple statement makes me, Kipling."

She smiled, and he kissed the smile. Because he couldn't *not* kiss it.

Kipling sighed as he looked down at her, her eyes closed. "Once he drew, with one long kiss my whole soul thro' my lips, as sunlight drinketh dew." She opened her eyes and smiled. "Tennyson had it right."

They went back to their dancing position, cheek to cheek, her hand over his heart, swaying with the slow, hypnotic song. After a moment more, Kipling chuckled again.

"What are you laughing at," he asked, not changing their embrace.

"Your family is discussing us," she said softly, so only he would hear. "Petra thinks we are adorable, and apologized to your parents for assuming we are..." She cleared her throat. "Bonking. To which your mother gasped, feigning shock."

"I failed to warn them of your special skills," he said, changing their sway to turn her away from them.

"Uh uh." She held her spot, not letting him lead. "This is entertaining."

Grayson slid his cheek along hers until his lips brushed the side of her throat beneath her ear, and he spoke against her skin before kissing her pulse. "Must I distract you otherwise?"

She moaned, angling her head a few degrees to make it easier for him to nip at her throat. "I thought your mother said you were a gentleman. You are evil, Grayson Holmes."

"I am resourceful," he said low, mindful of his proximity to her hearing aids. "I didn't make Six officer by thirty by luck."

She laughed and moved into him, encouraging his kiss.

"Kipling, dear," his mother called from where they sat. "Your mobile is ringing. I believe it's your mum."

"I should talk to her. I haven't since yesterday when I landed, and they're leaving tomorrow for a two-week cruise."

Grayson kissed her cheek and walked with her back to the table, where she picked up the phone, tapped the screen to answer, and stepped away to speak, smiling at him as she went.

"Hi, Mom," he heard her say as she walked, her voice growing faint. "Oh, it was lovely."

She walked to the back of the garden, just outside the light cast by the house. With a sigh born of contentment he hadn't felt in months, if possibly ever, Grayson sat in the chair he had vacated for his dance with Kipling and draped his arm across the back of the chair beside him, setting one ankle on the opposite knee.

"She's lovely, Grayson," Petra said. "You do forgive us for telling tales, don't you?"

Grayson chuckled. In truth, he didn't mind at all.

"It's a low trick to get my mother to call because I won't answer your calls, Mina," Kipling said through clenched teeth, glancing back into the circle of light to where Grayson had rejoined his family. "There's a reason I didn't answer. Did you tell her I wouldn't talk to you, or did you just play innocent?"

"I was here saying goodbye before they left, she said she planned on calling, I said I'd say hello if she did. We've been friends our entire lives, Kip. What the hell?"

"That's what I'd like to know. You're the one who has given me nothing but grief for weeks about this trip. Even your texts last night had attitude. What do you have against Grayson?"

"Kip, you're my best friend and I don't want you to get hurt. From where I'm sitting, this relationship has disaster written all over it."

"Then you're in the wrong seat, and if you don't stop, you won't have any view at all."

"Are you willing to end our friendship over this?"

"Are you?" Kipling demanded. "I was willing to accept your concern at first, but you're getting petty and mean, Mina. I don't understand."

"I don't think you're thinking clearly about this relationship."

"That's *my* decision to make, not yours. When did you decide I was so incompetent I can't make my own decisions when it comes to who I am in a relationship with?"

"Please..." Mina took a deep breath. "Honey, please. Be completely honest with me. What was his first, instinctive, gut reaction when he saw you? *Before* he covered it up and acted happy at your little surprise."

"Do you even hear how cruel a question that is?"

A hand on her shoulder made her gasp and jump, and she turned to see Grayson standing behind her, his expression twisted into obvious concern. Of course, he had to have heard her side of the conversation.

"What happened?" Mina asked. "Are you okay?"

"I'm fine," she said through tense lips. "Grayson startled me." She licked her lips and rubbed them together before meeting his eyes so he knew she spoke to him. "It's Mina. She's at Mom and Dad's," she explained, turning the phone so he saw her mother's picture.

His scowl deepened. Kipling raised her hand and signed "*It's okay*", staying silent so Mina wouldn't hear.

"Does she still question my reaction?" he asked.

Before she could speak, Mina responded. "Wow, does he need to know everything?"

"Whether he needs to know, or not, I told him."

Grayson lifted his hand, revealing the reason he'd followed her; his jacket hanging off his fingers. Keeping his focus on her, he slid the jacket around her shoulders, then stepped close to her. "She can hear me, correct?"

Kipling nodded, and in her ear, Mina mumbled, "Yeah, I can hear him."

He slid his arm around her waist beneath the jacket and brought her to him, speaking near her ear so there would be no doubt Mina heard every word. "You wish to know how I truly felt when I saw Kipling yesterday." His tone was no question, and his voice sent warm shivers over her skin. "I cannot tell you because there are no adequate words to explain the joy. I couldn't speak, and all I could think to do was to kiss her." He pressed a kiss to her cheek, the distinctive sound no doubt reaching Mina. "I kiss her because I can't not kiss her."

He drew back and took Kip's face in his hands, the light of the moon and the lights from the house casting shadows on his angled features enough so she could see his smile. "Mina, I know your intentions are good because you care about your friend. And I appreciate your concern, but know this…I love Kipling. I love her wholly, completely, and to distraction. While she is with me, her heart is safe."

Tears burned Kipling's eyes, and he smoothed his thumb across her cheek before closing in to touch a soft, lingering kiss to her lips.

"Kip, we're just worried."

Kipling smiled because, despite the words in her ears, Grayson was focused on leaving a teasing trail of kisses along her jaw. "We? Is John there? Is he on speaker as well?"

Grayson drew back, watching her face to see the answer.

John cleared his throat. "Yeah, I'm here."

Grayson's arched eyebrow was his question, and she nodded. "John is on with Mina," she said softly.

"Then let's leave no question."

He took the phone from her hand, and poised with his thumb over the red disconnect button, but didn't end the call until her two friends got several seconds of the deep kinds of kisses that left Kipling's toes curled, her breath short, and her heart racing.

Chapter Seven

A soft breeze whispered through the trees, rustling like silk, skimming over Kipling's bare arms. It tugged gently at her hair, and filled her senses with the mingled aromas of wildflowers, lush trees, and the mild decay of the forest floor. Kipling leaned back on her hands, the dry forest floor covering crackling beneath her palm. It was so calm, so serene, here in Grayson's woods.

She already adored his family, although they were both loud and abundant. There were probably louder and larger families, but in comparison to Kipling's family of three — Mom, Dad, and her — the extra people in the back garden of the cottage seemed over-whelming. Yesterday had seen ten times the people, but she felt a bit overly stimulated even though the only additions today were Grayson's aunt and uncle from down the lane.

Grayson walked toward her, and with her eyes closed, she focused on the crunch of groundcover beneath his feet. She smiled, tipping her head back to angle her face toward him, not opening her eyes. "Could we live here forever?" she asked.

She opened her eyes as he crossed his ankles and lowered himself to the ground. Settled beside her, he brushed his hand across her legs, clearing away bits of leaves the wind had dropped in her lap.

"When I was a child," he said, his baritone voice seeming loud in the stillness of the forest, "I used to imagine living in my tree house. As long as I could run across the field whenever I caught the smell of Mum's cooking, I thought I might be happy anywhere."

Kipling smiled, imagining a young Grayson with wild curls streaked with red from a summer in the sun, dirt on his cheeks and knees, running through the trees. Grayson tilted his head, a slow grin tugging at his lips as he watched her.

"What are you thinking?"

"How adorable you must have been as a little boy, birthmark on your bum and all."

Grayson laughed and sighed, looking off across the field. "I had hoped after twenty or so years, they might let that story die. But no, they allowed it to lie in waiting."

She sat up and turned on her bottom to match his sitting position, legs crossed, knee-to-knee with him. When settled, she reached out to push her fingers into the crop of curls falling across his forehead, stirred by the wind and his constant inclination to push the waves back from his face. It was slightly longer than when he'd been in Boston, like he was perhaps a couple weeks overdue for a trim. He turned into the touch and kissed her palm.

"You're still smiling," he said.

"Is that bad?"

He shook his head. "No, not at all. You're beautiful, but even more beautiful when you smile."

"I keep thinking of this Longfellow poem I learned in elementary school. There was a little girl who had a little curl, right in the middle of her forehead." She smiled as she recited the elementary school poem. "And when she was good, she was very good indeed. And when she was bad she was horrid."

"But I'm not a little girl," he said with a baritone chuckle.

"No." She dropped her voice and leaned forward to close the distance between her lips and his. "You are most definitely *not* a girl."

He met her mid-way with a kiss, just skimming her jaw with his fingertips to draw her to him. A gentle kiss, a sip rather than a taste. Sitting back, Kipling sighed and looked around the forest and at the remains of Grayson's childhood playhouse. The roof had a hole where a branch had fallen through, and the house was full of dry leaves and bits of wood, but it still hummed with the love of two young boys who had spent most of their lifetime within its walls. There were still notebooks inside, curled and brittle from exposure to the elements, the words inside long since illegible, and toys in boxes left there to play with later but long since forgotten. Carved into the walls were the names Greg and Ollie, whom she knew Greg had called Grayson since their names were so similar.

From the distance, a single loud burst of laughter carried to them. "Are we going to be considered antisocial for sneaking away while your parents entertain?"

"Perhaps," he said with a bounce of his eyebrows and a lopsided grin. "But honestly I am quite convinced you can do no wrong in Mum and Dad's opinion. In fact, I'm quite sure that if I were to return to the cottage now and say we were over they would help me pack my bags and settle you solidly into my bedroom."

He said it with such conviction, Kipling couldn't help her laugh. It echoed back to her, and in the distance the bushes erupted with the rustle of birds as they flew away, startled by her outburst. Grayson rolled forward, pressing his finger to her lips to hush, bringing them both down onto the soft forest floor. He laughed with her, his low, baritone rumble that seemed to come from somewhere around his pelvis, shushing at the same time until he stretched out beside her with his arm behind her head to support her.

"You'll give us away," he whispered, lying beside her so she looked up at him.

She pressed her lips together, trying to stop, but the harder she tried the more she wanted to laugh. A lightness had filled her since she arrived in Sussex, and it had only grown since the moment Grayson arrived. As much as she had embraced the wonderfulness of falling in love with him in Boston, it had been tainted by the very danger that had brought them together. Here, there was nothing but Grayson Oliver Sherlock Holmes.

She forced her laugh into a giggle until it was just a silent shake in her chest threatening to push through her pressed lips. Grayson draped one arm across her body, supporting his weight over her with his palm pressed to the ground beside her ribs, leaning on the elbow of his other arm, and were it not for the trees over them and the ground beneath, she entertained the imagery of lying in bed with him and her stomach fluttered.

"Here's a poem about a boy and a girl." His voice rumbled through his chest to her where they touched, and her skin warmed. "Once upon a time there was a boy who loved a girl and her laughter was a question he wanted to spend his whole life answering."

The laughter eased away, replaced with a bloom of warm weight in her chest. She settled into his hold and ran her fingers along his jaw and the side of his neck. "I love you."

He shifted over her, covering her body with his body, and her mouth with his mouth, and in two beats of her heart she forgot everything but Grayson. He bundled her to him, his hand firm at her hip, the kiss leaping from simple and spontaneous to needy and consuming. She opened her lips to him and moaned when his tongue slid across hers. He'd already told his mother they were heading back to London tomorrow, and the anticipation of being alone with him — truly alone — made her body tingle and ache.

Just as quickly, her heart jumped when a sound cracked through the forest like a gunshot, piercing her ears for the half-second it took for her aids to compensate and muffle the high decibels. Kipling gasped, and Grayson was on his feet before she could scramble to her knees, fallen bark digging into her bare legs beneath the hem of her dress. His hands went for a weapon he didn't wear, and he turned a full three hundred sixty degrees, scanning the forest. Another crack sounded, and Grayson spun toward the road. Kipling slapped her hands over her mouth to keep from screaming out, a bitter swell of adrenaline burning her throat. She couldn't catch her breath.

A new sound, a deep rumble and chug, carried from the road. After what felt like an eternity, Grayson knelt in front of her. "Are you alright?" he asked.

She wanted to nod, but her body was frozen. Grayson tugged her trembling hands away from her mouth and held her face in his palms until she looked at him, unable to blink. "Kipling, it's nothing. It was Robert Ellison's old Jeep. The thing backfires if the wind changes direction."

He attempted a smile, but her heart pounded so hard in her chest it made her dizzy and she couldn't seem to make her lungs suck in air.

"Kipling," he said firmer.

Finally, her muscles released and her chest expanded, letting her take a breath but she swayed on her knees, his hold shifting to her shoulders to keep her from tumbling. He shifted to his knees and wrapped her in his arms, holding her until she could take another breath. Then another. Six months ago, the backfiring vehicle would have startled her, but it wouldn't have terrified her and she hated her visceral reaction to something so harmless. Grayson eventually released her enough to gain his feet, helping her to stand with him.

He stroked his thumb across her cheek. "Mum will refuse me dessert if she thinks I've made you cry."

She laughed, and his smile said her reaction was what he hoped, and wiped at her own cheeks. "I'm sorry. I didn't even realize—"

"Shush," he hushed and kissed her cheek. "Scared the bloody devil out of me too."

Grayson's phone toned, and he pulled it from his pocket, reading the screen. "It's Jo warning us Mum is looking for us, and we may want to come out of hiding," he read with a chuckle.

"Can we get back without them seeing where we went?"

Grayson winked and took her hand. "Of course. This spot hasn't remained a secret for over thirty years by me being sloppy."

She shoved aside the apprehension twisting somewhere just below her heart and focused on the feel of her hand in his as he led her back out of the forest.

"Sweetheart, is there something wrong with Kipling?"

Grayson turned his head enough to look at his mother, who sat beside him on one of the garden benches, then across the lawn to where Kipling stood talking with his cousin Petra and her eldest daughter Erika. They had come back to the house after tea to visit more before returning to Guildford, two hours away. By what Grayson had garnered in conversation, the trip back had been at Erika's plea. Erika was fifteen and enthralled with anything American, so Kipling was the sole focus of her attention. Though Kipling listened, her full attention on Erika, Grayson recognized the tension in her body. Her arms were crossed, her hands tucked at her sides, but her fingers were restless, rubbing together, bending, flexing. She didn't stand still but shifted back and forth.

Erika showed Kipling something on her phone, her smile wide, and Kipling smiled back. He thought he caught "Send those to me, will you?" to which Erika nodded.

"She had a fright, and I fear she hasn't been able to fully let it go."

His mother's scowl spoke the question she didn't say.

"You heard Mr. Ellison drive by, correct?" he asked, and his mother nodded. "The backfire startled her. Startled us both, in truth. But…" Grayson sighed and sat forward, resting his elbows on his knees to rub his palms together. "I suspect Kipling experiences lingering effects from the events in Boston. Post-Traumatic Stress Disorder." He shook his head. "Allow me to correct that statement. I don't suspect, I *know*, but as of yet I do not know to what severity as she hasn't confided in me."

"Oh, the poor dear," his mother gushed, pressing her hand to her bosom. When she looked at Grayson again, he felt like a schoolboy again, caught in a half-truth. "Grayson, what happened in Boston that you haven't told us?"

Grayson sighed and rubbed the back of his neck. He purposefully kept the most frightening of details from his mother, knowing his chosen profession caused her worry as it was, and while she knew of the bombing at the university that killed her uncle, and that it was at that event Grayson had first met Kipling, he had not told her of all the events following. Not in full.

"Grayson Oliver."

Yes, he definitely felt like a child again.

Grayson sat back and rested his arm across the bench behind his mother's shoulders, speaking low enough that the conversation would remain between them only. There was no need for his extended family to hear any part of it.

"You are aware Kipling was at the university," he began and she nodded. "I regret to admit that was not the only time her life was at risk in the course of the following weeks. An additional attempt was made on my life–" His mother gasped, and he rested his hand on her shoulder. "I believe it was more a show of force than an actual assassination attempt. She escaped only by minutes. Then the man orchestrating the events had her abducted—"

His mother gasped, covering her hand with her mouth. No one turned, lost in their own conversations.

Grayson swallowed, fighting the swell of anger he still felt at the memory of her abduction. "She was threatened and abused, and their ultimate goal was to see her die in an explosion. I — *we* — my team and the FBI, found her in time, but we barely escaped. It was within a few days of that event I returned to England. I know she already had trouble sleeping after the bombing, and had one particularly difficult night when the fears she had been denying finally overwhelmed her. Although she will not admit as much to me, I believe she has continued to have difficulty, perhaps more in the last few weeks. I see other signs as well. She's lost some weight, and her fatigue plays in her eyes."

"Why did you leave her there alone?" his mother accused.

He could have been angry at the question, but it was one he'd presented to himself more than once. "I was called back to Vauxhall, and Kipling was in the final weeks of her degree program. Believe me, Mum, when I say if I could have brought her with me I would have. She wasn't alone. She had her parents, her friend Mina, and I made a sub rosa request of Agent Flannery in Boston to do his best to keep an eye on her."

"It's not the same, Grayson," she said with a sigh.

"I am painfully aware, Mum. Circumstances worked against us on all sides. I hated leaving." He smiled and squeezed his mother's shoulders. "Which is one of the many reasons I am so pleased you and my sisters conspired to bring her here."

His mother looked him in the eyes. "But do you intend to keep her here?"

"She has a life in Boston, Mum. Yes, I want her with me, but—"

"Don't assume an answer until you've asked the question, sweetheart," she said gently and patted his knee.

She left him, using her hand on his leg as a leverage point to push herself up from the bench, heading toward the house likely to brew tea and serve sweets. Grayson linked his hands in his lap, looking again across the yard to Kipling. She looked away from his young family member, her lips bowing into a beautiful smile when she saw him. Grayson raised his hand and made the first sign he'd learned — *I love you* — and held it over his heart, then brought his fingertips to his lips and kissed them for her.

Her smile widened and he hoped the easing around her eyes was a sign she might be able to let go of some of the tension in her body. Holding her gaze, Grayson stood and pushed his hands into his pockets, walking across the yard to her.

She never looked away, even though Petra was talking. She nodded, acknowledging whatever his cousin said, but with each foot he moved closer her smile grew until it was full and honest and shining in her eyes.

"Excuse me, Petra," he said when he reached them, not waiting for her to say anything in return before he leaned in and kissed the brightest point in his life.

"Geesh," Erika mumbled. "Bit rude."

Grayson chuckled into the kiss and gave the teenager reprieve by placing his arm around Kipling's shoulders and turning into the conversation. "You have monopolized Kipling's attention quite long enough, and I felt peckish."

Erika pulled a face. "So get something to eat."

Petra laughed and patted her daughter's shoulder. "You'll understand one day."

Arms wrapped around Kipling from behind, and vice grips around her chest. No matter how much her throat hurt, no matter how she forced air from her constricted lungs, she heard no sound. She struggled against the hold, her blood going cold when a voice with the rasp of demon-spawn whispered in her ear.

"I've found what I'm looking for. The heart of the tin man."

"Howell!" Feet away stood Grayson, hands held up in compliance. "Let her go, Howell. It's me you want."

Her faceless abductor brought one arm around her throat, choking her, while raising his other to aim a gun at Grayson. She tried to scream, tried to call out, but his name was drowned by the gurgling sound in her throat. Two loud shots, and Grayson stumbled back, red blooming in his chest. She fought hard, and then everything exploded in red fire and boiling water engulfed her.

Her eyes burned with the heat of the water, her lungs ached for air. Kipling kicked and reached with her arms, trying desperately to break the surface of the water where the sky beyond glowed orange. Then Grayson's lifeless body floated in front of her, eyes open, the water tainted with his blood.

Kipling tried to scream, her lungs filling with water.

Rapid, desperate knocking at Grayson's bedroom door yanked him from sleep, and he was sitting on the edge of the bed before his eyes actually opened. It took a second for his mind to engage and remind him he was at home. He hobbled across the dark room, nearly tripping over Watson's frantic race to the door. Using the hall light shining around the door edge to guide him, he yanked the door open.

Jo stood, hand raised in her halted knock, eyes wide.

"What's wrong?" Grayson asked.

She shook her head. "It's Kipling. I tried to wake her but realized she couldn't hear me and I was afraid to shake her. She's having some kind of nightmare—"

Grayson pushed past his sister and jogged to her open bedroom door, hearing Kipling's muffled cries before he reached halfway. He bolted through the door, squinting as his eyes tried to adjust quickly from the dark of his room to the light of the hall, and back to the semi-darkness of Jo's bedroom. Kipling was on her side, tangled in the blanket, her arms drawn up around her head as she struggled against something or someone he couldn't see. Her cries sounded like someone unable to speak, unable to open their mouth to release the sound, a self-imposed gag.

Instinctively, he wanted to call her name, but intelligence won out and he went to her side instead. The bed was small, just like Jo's and the one in his bedroom. Jo stood in the doorway, her form a black shadow with the light behind her. Unwilling to allow Kipling to suffer for the sake of propriety, and quite sure his mother would forgive him considering the situation, Grayson did his best to untangle the bedding enough he could find space on the edge of the mattress to lie beside her, pulling her to his chest.

She pushed against him with her forearms, her crying still muffled, trapped in her dream. Knowing it might not be the sound that would sooth her, but some instinct telling her it was him, Grayson laid his cheek against hers and spoke her name. Spoke whatever he could think to say, what he might say if she could hear his voice. He held her firm, but without restraining her, with one arm beneath her and around her back. The other hand he cupped the back of her head, holding her in place so when he spoke she might feel the vibration.

His words were more for him than her. "Shush, darling. You're safe. You're safe." She calmed, but not fully; he kissed her cheek and smoothed her hair, closing his eyes. "Do you feel me, darling?" he whispered, rubbing his skin to hers. "Come back from wherever you are, come back to me."

A long, shuddered breath moved through her and she stilled with a tiny, whimpering sigh. Grayson bundled her to him and turned his face into her throat, swallowing hard against the mix of rage and sorrow choking him. Rage against the man responsible for the demons that haunted her sleep, and sorrow for her, that she had to struggle for peace. What had she done alone?

The blankets shifted and he raised his head to see Jo standing beside the bed, easing the covers over both of them. The light from the hall was enough to reflect off the trails on her cheeks. She covered them both, then crouched on the other side of the bed behind Kipling, so she faced him and rested her hand on his shoulder.

"She called your name," she said softly, despite the fact her voice wouldn't wake Kipling. "That's what woke me. She sounded so afraid."

"Thank you for coming for me," he whispered. "You heard nothing the last two nights from her?"

"No. She was restless the first night and went downstairs." She smiled. "You two weren't as quiet as you thought coming back up. But last night, I'm not sure she moved."

Grayson sighed and shifted just enough he could rest his head on her pillows, Kipling still curled against his chest. "I'm staying here for the night."

She shook her head. "Of course." Her chuckle carried in the stillness. "Mum might give you a naughty look, but I think she'll understand."

He knew she would. Jo rose from her crouch and went back to the hall, shutting off the light. Once the door was closed, the room was in full darkness, and his sister went back to bed. In the dark, Grayson kissed Kipling's cheek and closed his eyes, willing away the darkness in her dreams.

Chapter Eight

Grayson woke when Jo sat up and climbed out of bed, and he lifted his head to look her way as she walked around the foot of the beds.

"I'm using the bath," she mumbled and slipped from the room without saying much else, leaving the door open a crack.

He had a knot in his back, and part of his arm was falling asleep where Kipling's head rested on it, but he hadn't moved in several hours so she could sleep. The small bed was designed for a child, or at best a single person, not two grown adults one of which was over six feet. He often slept curled on his side in his own bed, so sharing had been a challenge.

But one he would accept every night if it meant holding her and waking to her tucked against his body. And if it meant his presence perhaps helped hold back the tide of whatever images haunted her sleep, her peace was well worth his discomfort. He was angry with himself for not pursuing his instincts sooner, and questioning her about his observations. He had resisted, instead choosing for the last two days to enjoy her presence in a way they had been denied while in Boston. Here, he had decided her fatigue was intercontinental jetlag and the days of activity and excitement before and since, but in the hours he'd held her before finding sleep himself, he'd analyzed all the details of the last three months he'd seen but not pursued. They were small details, but he was trained in the small details, and those details were often the threads that wove the greater tapestry.

He'd noted her weight loss even before she appeared in his mother's parlor. Nearly a stone, but Kipling was petite in stature and even that small quantity affected her appearance. He'd asked her questions about whether she'd eaten, and she appeased him with excuses of working late or studying so deeply she'd forgotten. He never actually commented on the weight loss.

He would sometimes receive texts from her during hours that were easily within his functional day, but in comparison would be late night or early morning hours for her. Even posts on social media, though she wasn't often active, might appear with time stamps indicating odd hours for posting.

She had said things in passing she probably had no idea meant anything, but he'd catalogued them. Mentions of headaches that were new, being uncommon in the past. She spoke of muscle aches on occasion, but dismissed them as a result of the self-defense class she'd decided to take. All small, but the sum of the whole painted a different picture.

A picture he would see changed.

Grayson rested his head on the pillow he'd managed to tuck between his shoulder and neck, allowing him to watch her sleep without permanently kinking his spine, studying the fine details of her resting expression. She was so beautiful to him it sometimes caught his breath. Free of any makeup, though even when she wore makeup it was subtle, he could commit to memory each small freckle dotting her nose and cheeks. Thick eyelashes, though not overly long, fanned on her cheeks. The scar remained near her hair-line from the butt of Isaac Sheldon's gun, pink against her fair skin, and the sight of it fueled a special rage he harbored deep in his chest, holding the anger until it served a purpose.

Instead, he found peace for the moment watching her sleep beside him. The action, though unfamiliar since the only time they had slept in the same bed he had been fully clothed, atop the coverlet, and so exhausted beyond definition he hadn't recalled falling asleep to begin with, felt natural. So much so he knew without question he wanted to wake like this every morning for the rest of his life.

Grayson brushed his thumb across her cheek, smiling at the kiss of color she'd garnered from being outside for most of the day prior. At his touch, she stirred and inhaled deeply. When he touched her lower lip, and her lips parted, he kissed her just before her eyes opened. Without hesitation, Kipling angled her head to allow him to deepen the kiss, her hand sliding from where she had it tucked between them to press her palm to his chest. She hummed softly against his mouth, encouraging the kiss. But with the bedroom door open, and both mindful of their location and in respect for his parents, Grayson reluctantly had to stop before his natural appetite for her was too much to ignore.

She smiled as he drew back enough she could see his face, running the tip of her tongue over her lips. "I could get very used to this," she said softly, her voice rough from sleep.

"As could I," he confessed, touching her jaw with the tips of his fingers. "Good morning."

"Good morning," she answered, then looked down the length of their bodies squeezed into the twin-size bed. "But I'm a bit confused. Did I miss something?"

Grayson touched her cheek, running his fingers to her temple to brush back her hair. "You don't remember anything? "

Kipling's brow pulled down between her eyes and she scowled, shaking her head. "No, not since I went to—"

Her scowl slipped into wide eyes and an open mouth and a blush flashed up her throat to her face. Her body tensed in his hold. Then she snapped her mouth closed, her jaw set, and she tried to push away from him, shifting her feet to free them from the blankets.

"No, Kipling," he said, trying to get her to look at him, having the disadvantage that without her attention on him, she could effectively ignore him.

He had the distinct impression avoidance was her goal.

Unwilling to forcibly keep her in the bed, he let her go and she scurried away out the other side of the bed, tugging her long tee shirt down over her hips where it nearly reached the bottom of the shorts she wore to bed, leaving her legs exposed from toe to upper thigh. She crossed the small space to the chest of drawers against the far wall, the small room cramped with furniture. Grayson tossed off the blankets and came around the foot of the bed as she placed her second hearing aid in her left ear.

"Kipling," he said, approaching her, but she didn't react. "Kipling, I know full well you can hear me now. Why are you running from me?"

She slapped her hand on the bureau, twisting to face him with her other hand set on her hip. "I'm not running. I'm getting out of bed," she said in a stiff, tight voice. "I respect your mother's wishes, and I don't want to insult her by—"

"By having a nightmare?" he cut off.

"That's not what I meant, and you know it."

"This isn't about worrying you'll get caught in bed with me," he said, shaking his head. "Kipling, have you been having nightmares since I left Boston?"

"I've been having *nightmares* since the explosion," she said with a toss of her head, and he didn't understand the anger bouncing off her like a force field demanding he stay back.

"But worse as of late." He considered when he first noted the difference and contemplated how long she may have had a resurgence of distress to cause them. His heart sank and he cursed himself in his mind. "Since I went silent a few weeks ago."

She glared at him. "Why bother asking if you're not actually *asking* a question? And if you already have the answer?"

"I'm sorry," he said on an expulsion of air. "Kipling, I'm so sorry. Why didn't you tell me?"

Before he finished, she snapped out, "It's under control."

"Is it?" he asked, trying to keep his voice calm. He couldn't suppress the tug of his eyebrow.

"I said it's under control, Grayson." She took a step back from him and crossed her arms over her body. "It barely happens anymore—"

"I highly doubt that. How often? Four? Five? Six nights a week?"

"—and when it does, I deal with it," she finished, ignoring his interruption.

"How?"

"How what?" She glared at him, tucking her arms tighter around her. He took a step closer, and she stepped back again, her backside bumping against the small bedside cabinet beside the bed she'd used the last three nights.

Grayson stopped and set his hands at his hips, pressing his lips together to avoid saying more than he wanted, more than he should. "How have you dealt with them alone? Do you even remember what you dreamt last night?"

Her lips pursed tight and she huffed several quick breaths through her nose, glaring at him. Finally, she shook her head, a tight jerk.

"So, you've only assumed, then, that the reason I came in here last night was because you were obviously in distress."

"Isn't it?"

"Yes," he said louder than he should have, thrusting his hand out to her in frustration, as if he held the answer in his palm. He looked away and closed his eyes for two beats of his pounding heart before focusing on her again. "Yes, and that is precisely my point. You have had enough of these episodes you know full well what I likely found when I came in here."

"Geez...*episodes*? You make me sound like some imbalanced mental patient. I'm not crazy," she snapped, tossing her arms away from her side, shaking her head to tousle her hair around her shoulders.

Grayson pressed his lips together, seeking calm before he said more. His walk was precarious at best around the minefield of Kipling's argument. "I neither believe nor intended to imply any such thing, Kipling. You experienced more than anyone ever should have. It is perfectly understandable it would linger. I'm not—" He huffed, closing his eyes for a moment before looking at her again. "I want, I *need* to help you, darling. I need to know—"

"I can't tell you," she shouted, her arms dropping straight to her side, her hands curled into fists. "I don't *know* what happens. I don't *know* what I do. All I know is I wake up sweating, sitting up in bed, with a sore throat like I've been screaming." With each point, her hands jerked, her fists tightening until her knuckles whitened. "So, what did you find last night, Grayson, hmm? A screaming lunatic? A frantic, weeping woman? Was I catatonic again? Talking nonsense? What did you find, Grayson?" Every question was an accusation.

He shook his head, moving toward her again with slow steps. "No, I didn't find any of those things. I found the woman I love."

"Who is so pathetic she can't deal with the crap that happened *months* ago," she said loud enough her voice bounced off the walls. "You want to know how I deal with them. I wake up." She shrugged up her shoulders, hands out with palms up, moving them as if illustrating some tableau in front of her. "I get out of bed. I watch television. I check Facebook. I study. I text *you*. I work on my dissertation. *Whatever*. I deal with it. I've done it alone since February, and I will continue to do it alone if I need to."

As soon as the words left her lips, she stilled, then gasped and looked at him. His heart sank, and for once, he had nothing to say. Nothing he could think to say. Grayson closed his eyes and let his head drop forward, a blanket of weariness settling on his shoulders. What argument was there to offer? Just as his mother said, he'd left her, even though he knew what the explosion and the kidnapping had left behind.

He knew.

"Bath is free," Jo said, coming through the bedroom door. "Better hurry. Mum is making a full English down there. Said Kipling needs a hearty meal because only the good Lord knows what Grayson will feed you in London." She finished with a laugh, but it died away. "Is everything okay?"

Grayson placed his hand over his mouth and snuffed, pinching his lips before he turned toward his sister and the door, unable to meet the eyes of the woman he'd failed. "I'll see you downstairs for breakfast."

The house smelled of bacon, fried eggs, roasted sausage, and toasted bread, and any other day it probably would have enticed Kipling, but her stomach revolted at the idea of eating. She'd felt sick since she'd let her mouth override her heart, and she saw the change in Grayson's eyes. If only she hadn't…

The list of "if only" things she wished she hadn't said or done was too long to categorize. Ultimately, there was one question. Why hadn't she confided in him?

She didn't answer the question, because to answer would be to admit how weak and helpless and inadequate she felt. How afraid she had been, how afraid she was now to admit all the opinions she held in herself and her inability to be the strong woman a man like Grayson deserved. How she thought she had a handle on the dreams, on the moments of swelling panic, and then he'd gone silent for three weeks and called her from a plane with a bullet wound in his side, and the nightmares had returned in full force.

It actually amazed her she'd slept without the dreams for the first two nights, and attributed it to pure exhaustion and the belief she could escape it all here.

She descended the stairs with slow steps, running her hand down the banister polished smooth from generations of Holmes children hanging on as they went up and down, listening to the conversation coming from the kitchen as they finished preparations for breakfast.

"Should I brew Kipling some coffee, sweetheart?" Grayson's mother asked, walking past the opening of the kitchen toward the dining room. "Or does she drink tea?"

"She drinks both, Mum," he answered, his deep voice a caress to

Kipling's frazzled nerves, even though his haunted eyes were the reason she couldn't take a deep breath.

"That doesn't answer my question, dear," she said, returning to the kitchen. "I'll just make both, and she can drink what she likes. I should have paid proper attention the last two days to see what she drank."

"She drank tea," Grayson said, walking past the same doorway with a plate of grilled sausages in his hands.

Kipling stopped one step short of the hallway floor, remembering the floor squeaked at the base, and gripped the banister with her lips pressed together hard in an attempt to push back the heavy sadness in her chest. Despite what she had said to him, she heard no derision in his voice, and that fact hurt almost as much as what she'd said.

Grayson crossed the kitchen doorway again, presumably returning for more food to take to the dining room, and glanced into the hall. She knew the moment he saw her because he stilled and shifted back in his step to look directly at her. Kipling sucked in a sharp breath, pressing her lips together to try to hide the frown twisting them, a sob twisting in her chest. He left the kitchen, walking with quick steps toward her. She wanted to say she was sorry, but she was afraid to speak, that the cry in her throat would escape. Before he came to the bottom of the stairs, she reached for him, arms open.

When he wrapped his arms around her, the cry escaped and she crumpled into him, clinging to his shoulders, pressing her face into his shoulder as she tried desperately to stay quiet to not draw his family's attention. "I'm sorry," she managed to choke past the grip on her throat. "I'm so sorry."

She barely heard herself speak, and hoped he did.

With his arms around her, Grayson lifted her feet from the bottom step and carried her the few steps to the library on the other side of the house she'd only glanced into when passing. With a tap of his foot on the door, he shut it, secluding them from everyone else. Even when he set her feet on the floor, she couldn't let go, the tears taking over. Her hearing aids whined the side of her head pressed too close to his shoulder, but she didn't care. Grayson cupped the back of her head with his hand, urging her arms down from their grip on his shoulders until he could take her jaw in his hands to push her away from him.

She let him, but couldn't open her eyes.

"Kipling, please. Look at me." When she didn't, he leaned closer, his breath warm on her face, but his voice lower. "Darling, please."

Sucking in sharp breaths, she opened her eyes and blinked to clear the tears. As soon as she met his gaze, he raised his chin and pressed a long kiss to the center of her forehead. "Forgive me," he said against her skin. "Please."

Kipling curled her fingers into the front of his shirt, pushing back the sob in her throat. She couldn't speak. Grayson smoothed his thumbs over her damp cheeks, his lips twisted into a frown that mirrored the ache in her chest. He shook his head, a slow movement, his gaze cast down but still on her face.

"I shouldn't have ignored what I knew was wrong," he said in a voice so rough she had to raise her hand and touch his cheek. "I shouldn't have left you alone. I shouldn't have—"

"I don't blame you," she said, touching her thumb to his lips, focusing on the point of contact. "I didn't mean what I said. I don't even know where it came from. I've never once even thought it, not for a second, it was just out of my mouth before I knew what I was saying. She raised her chin to look him in the eyes. "Promise me you believe me. I didn't mean it."

Grayson moved her hand from his cheek to scoop his other arm behind her and bring her to him for a kiss. Not a kiss of intent, of seduction, or even of pleasure; a kiss that felt like an apology and forgiveness. She wrapped her arms around his neck again, desperate for him to feel the same from her.

He held her head, his fingers spread to keep from pressing on her ears and touched his forehead to hers with their rapid breaths mingling between them. "Let's not do this again," he said, his voice still rough. "I don't want to do this ever again."

She sniffed, but gave a small laugh, wrapping her fingers around his wrists. "I don't want to do it again either."

Grayson looked her in the eyes, the tip of his nose a fraction of an inch from touching the tip of hers. "I promise, I *swear* to you, I will help you, Kipling. I swear with all my soul and heart. Will you let me?"

She nodded, tipping her chin up to encourage another kiss. When his lips smoothed over hers she tasted the salt of her tears, and possibly his. From the hall came Grayson's mother's voice, calling for both of them up the stairs since she likely didn't realize they'd disappeared behind the closed door. They slid out of the kiss, but only enough to part lips, their chins together.

"A few more hours, and I will be able to kiss you to my content without the fear my mother — or sister — or father — or *cousins* — might come looking," he whispered to keep their presence a secret. He smiled against her mouth, and the knot in her stomach eased, replaced with a warm tumble when he said, "And I can finally, *finally* say hello properly."

"Would it be rude to sneak out the back door?" she asked in an equal whisper, giggling.

His low baritone rumbled through him and both soothed her nerves and revitalized her. "She would chase us down, demanding we eat a banger and toast before we left."

"Where have they gone off to?" came his mother's voice again from the hall, and their laughter turned into shushing each other.

"Likely found a place to kiss and make up," Jo said, her voice passing the door as she walked past. "I think they had a row this morning."

"Oh, dear. Over what?"

"Don't know."

Anything else they said faded as they headed for the kitchen. Taking her hand, finger to his lips for silence, Grayson gingerly turned the doorknob, crept open the door, and peeked into the hall. Glancing left and right, he nodded to her. Swinging the door wide, they walked with purpose into the hall and kitchen to be greeted by the Holmes family and a breakfast feast like Kipling had never seen.

Chapter Nine

Grayson parked his car against the Baker Street curb, and opened his door to be out and around the front of the Bentley before Kipling had a chance to open her own door. In truth, taking in the details of Baker Street left her mesmerized. Before she met Grayson and later learned his address, when she visited London at eighteen, she'd visited Baker Street. She was on a literary point of interest tour. Of course they went to Baker Street, and they'd walked through the museum, but the idea that the true 221B was only a few doors away made her mind spin. Not just a number, but a home.

He grinned, opening the door to offer his hand. She took it, still looking more at the neighborhood than him, and brought up her hand to shield her eyes against the uncommonly bright early afternoon sun.

It would probably be raining in an hour.

Baker Street was narrow, just wide enough for cars to park and traffic to squeeze through, and the buildings on each side were typically four stories tall with brick facades and paned windows. The ground level of many buildings housed a variety of businesses, including a small deli restaurant and a variety gift shops likely geared toward tourists fascinated by the Holmes legend but not wanting to pay the higher prices within the museum. Kipling looked back the way they'd come, spotting the familiar and iconic green and gold sign of the Sherlock Holmes Museum. Memories of walking through the museum over a decade before came back with only bits of clarity. Had she had any idea what her future held…

"When did you move to Baker Street?" she asked, and realized it was probably a very random question since he wasn't privy to the jumble of thoughts.

"To live on my own?" he asked, and she nodded. "Shortly after graduation from Cambridge," he answered, drawing her away from the car so he could shut the door. "Both Greg and I moved in. Twelve years ago, roughly."

Kipling chuckled and shook her head. "Do you realize I could have been down this street, walking through that museum, with you just a few doors away…" She shook her head and blew through her lips. "…drinking tea."

Grayson laughed, and went to the back door of the car, opening it to retrieve Watson, who had been very vocal for the last twenty minutes in anticipation of making it home. "Darling, once I learned of your visit with Mum and Dad at the cottage, I became a full believer in both fate and destiny and have no doubt the universe has conspired to bring us together."

She met his gaze as he took the fretting cat from the back seat. "You say that even knowing all the planning Langdon Howell did to assure we met in Boston?"

His features tightened and she regretted bringing up the sore spot for both of them. "Langdon Howell may have engineered our meeting to advance whatever nefarious plans he contrived, but I cannot see any possible way he could have known of your chance meeting with Mum when you were eighteen, especially considering you had no idea whom you had actually met, and until recently your name had slipped from her memory. Thus, I stand by my statement." He punctuated his sentence by slamming closed the car door.

Before moving away from the car, he hooked his free hand

around her hip and slid her down the side of the car to be between him and the door. Kipling tucked her hands behind her back, the effect angling her against him and he smiled. "Love is our true destiny," he said, his voice dropping to an even lower baritone than usual. "We do not find the meaning of love by ourselves alone. We find it with another."

Kipling released a humming sigh, pulling her lower lip through her teeth. "We aren't even inside yet, Mr. Holmes, and you've begun your verbal seduction?"

His gaze settled on her lips, and she held her breath, wondering if he would kiss her, and did her best to hide her disappointment when he didn't. Instead, he winked, tugged her hand from behind her to lace their fingers together, and led her down the sidewalk away from the museum.

Logically, she knew there would be no sign over the day declaring, "This is the true 221B" over the basic brown door tucked within a stone archway. The entrance to his home was simple, understated, and less likely to draw attention, right down to the small, yet required designation of 221.

"No B?" she asked.

Grayson released her hand long enough to jangle his keys and find the right one to open the door. "The B designation is no longer required as the Holmes family acquired the entirety of the building decades ago, making it a single address." A brass doorknocker hung centered on the door, but tucked against the perpendicular alcove wall was an intercom system. Grayson paused after unlocking the door, his hand resting on the tarnished brass knob, looking at her over his shoulder.

"Is something wrong?"

His smile quirked, just enough to allow a crease to show along the sides of his mouth, then gone again. "I fear what lies beyond this door will not live up to your expectations." He went back to the lock and turned the key, the tumbler releasing. Pocketing the keys, he paused with his door on the knob. "Before you step through this door anticipating polished wainscot walls and bear skin rugs, realize the suite has long since been refurbished and expanded and may not hold the Victorian charm you might expect."

Kipling nudged him with her shoulder. "Just open the silly door and let me in, Grayson."

Grayson pushed open the door, motioning for her to step inside. A control panel on the wall just inside the door beeped in a rapid rhythm, and as soon as she passed him, he shut the door and punched a code into the keypad. The rhythm changed, three solid beeps, then went silent. The short entry led into a downstairs parlor with a coat rack and umbrella bucket just inside the parlor, out of the way of anyone coming inside. Two wingback chairs in an aqua blue and white print facing a white stone fireplace with an ornately framed antique mirror hanging on the wall above it. The walls were painted a complimentary blue and the trim was painted bright white.

"The entire property has been remodeled and redesigned to be brighter and more efficient over the years, modernized from gas lamps and backyard plumbing, retrofitted to the 20th Century, though possibly not quite the 21st yet," he finished with a single chuckle.

Kipling stepped into the parlor and laid her hand on the back of the chairs. The room held the faint scent of wood polish and bergamot, and possibly even the fading aroma of pipe tobacco. Or perhaps that was just her imagination taking over her senses.

A staircase began a few feet from the door on the left side of the foyer leading to the second floor. *First floor.* She mentally reminded herself Grayson would call it the first floor. Grayson set down Watson's carrier, opening the door. Watson bolted through the foyer to an open door at the back of the flat. Sunlight beyond made the space welcoming, drawing her toward it.

"Quick tour is likely in order," Grayson said, clapping his hands together before rubbing his palms against each other, and she smiled because he'd done the same thing prior to the 'quick tour' at his parents' home. "This is, quite clearly, the foyer and guest parlor. To put things into a more historical perspective, this level was for the most part Mrs. Hudson's realm and had a slightly different layout."

He motioned to a door tucked behind the entrance door. "That is the downstairs lavatory." Taking a few steps into the room, he walked toward the sunlit room. He pointed toward a closed door to the left of the fireplace. "Through the door there is a library, though I don't often use it as it has very little natural light. Though that is hardly the point."

Kipling followed him, the ornate Oriental rug protecting the wooden floor muffling her steps. Her heels clicked again when she stepped from rug to wood walking through the doorway into a small but serviceable, bright, and fairly modern kitchen, including a combined clothing washer/dryer tucked beneath the counter and stainless steel appliances. So perhaps this room was the most recent to be renovated.

The back wall of the house had several windows and a single door, with a nine-pane window inset, that opened to a bright. Surprisingly lush garden for the center of London behind the building. He walked her through the kitchen to a dining area tucked behind and around the foyer. The kitchen was the only entrance to the dining area, so he led her back to the foyer, taking her hand.

"The house footprint, as they say, is rather small, but the property has three living levels which gives me more space. The main living area, for television and such, is on the first floor." He explained as he led her to the bottom of the stairs.

She couldn't help it, but as soon as she took the first step she mentally took the first count. *One. Two. Three.* Halfway up the staircase, Grayson chuckled. "Yes, Kipling. There are seventeen steps from the stairs to the study."

She flushed and twisted her embarrassed grin. "Am I so obvious?"

He paused halfway up the flight of stairs, a step above her, and looked down at her. Kipling's heart did a funny, happy bounce behind her ribs at the way he looked at her. The way he always looked at her. "No, but I have no doubt you know well whatever details of Baker Street were relayed in the novels, and I know you would test the tale."

Grayson continued up the stairs to the landing of the first floor.

It wrapped around to run from the back of the building to the front, where twin windows overlooking Baker Street let in beams of natural light. The entire flat, thus far, was much brighter than she would have imagined. Perhaps that had been part of the remodeling Grayson alluded to when they arrived. Another flight of stairs led from the front of the landing to the second level. At the bottom of the next flight was a closed door, and a double door on her left was open and led into another room. Grayson pointed to the door at the far end of the hall.

"That is a guest bedroom with facilities. Initially, it was the sleeping chamber for Mrs. Hudson when she owned the property."

"But the Holmes family owns it now?" Kipling asked, giving in to the impulse to walk to the door and turn the knob, the decades-old hardware squeaking at the movement.

Beyond was a small, but not cramped, bedroom with a double bed, bureau, and desk. The room was long, but narrow, with only a single window at the front of the room once again overlooking Baker Street. A closed door at the back of the room presumably led to the bathroom. The room was clearly not used as much, the air a bit thicker and warm and dust motes danced in the streams of sunlight

"Yes," Grayson explained when she backed out of the doorway and shut the door again, turning to look at him. "In his advanced years, when Sherlock learned of Mrs. Hudson's passing, he contacted the family and offered to purchase the property. Outwardly, he often spoke against sentiment but his actions often said otherwise. Family rumor says he paid twice the fair cost to assure her family felt no financial burden." He motioned back the way they'd come to the double doors, resting his hand on the knob of the closed door of the two. "This is the common living space, I suppose you might say."

With a twist of his wrist, he opened the remaining door, giving her a full view of the room beyond. It was a substantial space, running from the front to the back of the flat, but wider than the bedroom on the other side, which helped her situate herself in the property. The staircase was left of center when she entered, so everything on the right was much larger.

She also knew instinctively this was the study referred to so often in the Sherlock Holmes novels. The hair on her arms tingled, and she couldn't deny the giddy bubble of literary joy in her chest. The room was clearly different now, more contemporary in its decoration and furnishings, though not modern or cold. Richly stained wood covered the walls amongst a dusty rose wallpaper, and a large hearth fireplace sat on the wall opposite the doorway. With a glance across the room, Kipling noted the space did seem a bit small in comparison to the same space downstairs. She crossed the room, Grayson behind her, to the fireplace and smiled when she ran her fingers along the scarred wooden mantel. Deep gauges marred the wood, like the tip of a knife. The Conan Doyle books spoke of Sherlock's habit of piercing any unanswered correspondence to his mantel with a knife.

"None of us could ever bring ourselves to have it repaired," Grayson said, and the weight of his tone drew her attention.

His gaze was on the mantel, where she rested her fingers. A small smile quirked the corner of his mouth. A wonderful feeling of warmth bloomed in Kipling's chest, spreading out into her limbs and settling in her belly. It wasn't the first time she'd felt a rush of love for Grayson, but sometimes the simplicity and completeness of it took her by surprise. Perhaps the universe had conspired to bring them together; who else could appreciate the treasure that was his family history than someone who loved it before it was real.

He sucked in a sharp breath, as if bringing himself back to reality, and took a sideways step toward a closed door. "Similarly, no one in three generations has sought fit to change this room. It stands as a sort of family-imposed museum. When Sherlock and Doctor Watson left Baker Street permanently, Mrs. Hudson no longer took in boarders. Not for the sake of sentiment, but for her advancing age. Thus, this remained."

Grayson opened the door and pushed his palm to the wood, making way for her to enter. The room explained why the study didn't seem large enough, and she knew immediately why they hadn't changed it. Here was the private chamber of Sherlock Holmes, before he was a father, a grandfather, a quite possibly before he was a legend. This was his private space.

"Some of the early books said Sherlock's bedroom was upstairs," she said, stepping into the room. This room, like the one across the hall, was narrow, requiring anyone in it to walk around the back of the brick chimney built on the backside of the fireplace in the sitting to reach the front of the room. A window looked down on Baker Street, with the headboard of the bed set near the window. A gramophone sat at the foot of the bed, then a secretary desk and a single chair.

"It was possible, but in his final years here in Baker Street, this was his room." He stepped back and motioned for her to come back into the common room. "One final floor. Up for the climb?" Grayson asked, his grin contagious.

"No wonder you're in such good shape," Kipling teased, running her hand over his chest as she moved past him. "Climbing stairs is good for the heart."

Grayson caught her wrist and brought her to him, wrapping his arm around her back to pull her to his chest, and she instinctively raised her chin to accept the kiss she knew would come. Grayson curled his fingers into the back of her sundress and his low moan vibrated against her mouth.

"Mmmm," he finished with a hum. "*You* are good for my heart."

Kipling drew back enough she could focus on his lips, the slick shine left by their kiss sending her heartbeat into a rhythm so fast it made her breath catch. She had purposefully avoided thinking of their long-anticipated situation. Since she arrived in London, this was the first time they were completely and entirely alone, with little to no risk of interruption of any kind. His kiss erased all ability to pretend she'd forgotten. But the kiss was short-lived, only accomplishing to create a hunger for more.

He took her hand, linking their fingers before he brought her back to the hall and led her upward again. Just as on the first floor, the staircase opened to a landing on the second floor, but on this floor, the landing was smaller, and the space had been remodeled more recently, she suspected, than the downstairs. There were four doors off the landing, one to her immediate left when she reached the top, one slightly to the right on the wall in front of her, with a door tucked between closer to the first, and one on the wall around the side of the railing leading into a room that would be directly over the common room one level down. That door was partially open, sunlight streaming into the hall.

"These two rooms," he said pointing to the door on the left and ahead, "were remodeled by my grandparents shortly after my parents married. At the time, my grandparents were living in Sussex, so Mum and Dad lived here. My grandparents had high hopes for many grandchildren," he said with a grin. "Each generation has added to the progeny. Sherlock had one child, Hamish two, each of his two children having three.

"Is that a glimpse into the future?" she said, intending to tease but the implications of her words immediately hit her.

When he looked at her, the slow, easy bow of his lips and warmth in his eyes was a jolt to her pulse and a pleasant bloom of hope behind her breast. Grayson cleared his throat and pointed to the middle door he'd skipped in his explanation. 'The door between is a common bath. Small, likely, in comparison to what you might expect in America, but serviceable, which was often the goal when Baker Street was remodeled. Do what is possible with the space available."

"Did you live here when you were little?" she asked.

Grayson nodded, glancing down as Watson made a loud, attention-seeking bolt up the stairs to skirt between them and around the banister to the open door. He chuckled, watching the cat's antics, before answering.

"We lived here until I was about ten. Shirl and Jo were still very little." He pointed to the bedroom to the left. "That was my bedroom, and the other was their nursery." He smiled at her and shook his head. "Don't bother rushing in to see if anything remains. For a time, Greg and I lived here together in our first years at Six and that was his room. Nothing of me remains, and Greg moved out nearly a decade ago, so all secrets you'd seek would be found in Sussex."

"I don't know why, but I assumed you'd always lived in the cottage," Kipling explained, stepping away from him to approach the door he'd called the nursery. If she had her orientation right, there would be a window overlooking the back garden and the room would be above the kitchen.

"It's my office," he said, and she stilled her hand, not opening the door. "My grandmother passed when I was ten, leaving my grandfather alone in Sussex. It was then we left Baker Street and moved into the cottage. Grandfather lived three more years before we lost him as well."

Kipling turned from the door, the weight in Grayson's voice pushing on her chest. "Were you close to him?"

"Hamish Holmes was a difficult man to be close to," Sherlock said with an upward push of his shoulders, one hand resting on the banister. "At least at first. I thought he was a grumpy old man who smelled of peppermint and didn't want children making too much noise. In time, I realized he was sad for losing my grandmother and was out of practice with children." He finished the story with a melancholy smile. "By the time we lost him, I'd learned to treasure his stories and miss him immensely. He was the last living member of the Holmes family who had any memory of Sherlock. Hamish was not out of his adolescence when Sherlock died, since Sherlock was nearly seventy when he fathered Hamish, but he still knew the man."

Kipling had never known anyone with such love, or more appropriately the reverence, for his family as Grayson. "That's beautiful, Grayson."

He cleared his throat and bounced his hand on the banister, then tilted his head toward the remaining door, following his own action by walking toward the entrance. "Last room. The master suite."

Kipling licked her lips and curled them together as she crossed the landing and brushed past him into the room. It was bright with sunlight, the drapes open with sheer curtains blocking the windows facing Baker Street. The entire room was bright, enhanced by the creamy yellow walls, white trim, blond furniture, and light yellow and cream bedding on the antique iron frame bed, the headboard set against the wall slightly overlapping the windows. The majority of a suit — trousers, a jacket, shirt, and tie — draped on the foot of the bed.

There was a hearth, built in the same chimney as the two downstairs, with a white carved mantel lined with various photos in different sizes and types of frames, with a large painting of the Sussex cottage in watercolor hanging on the wall. Like the room below, this room had more length than width but was much more spacious. At the back of the suite was a sitting area with a cream and yellow striped couch and two chairs in floral yellow and cream print. With windows at the front, and more windows looking down on the garden, the room was breathtaking.

Grayson moved past her, picking up the clothing from the bed with an embarrassed chuckle. "Sorry. I was in a hurry on Friday attempting to get out of the city. I don't usually leave dirty laundry lying about, but of course, on the rare occasion I do, I have company."

She smiled at him, walking further into the room. On each side of the mantel was a white wooden door, and Grayson pointed at each. "The one at the front of the house is the bathroom, the other a closet."

"This is a beautiful home," Kipling said, once the casual elegance of the room eased. It wasn't necessarily what she had imagined for Grayson's bedroom. The hotel suite he'd used in Boston was modern and cold, but she knew it wasn't any reflection of him. The bedroom in Sussex had been the room of a child and young man. This was a reflection of him, and it felt like home.

She meandered the room, stopping near the back of the couch set away from the sleeping area, and turned to look back at him. Grayson stood near the foot of his bed, hands pushed into his casual trousers, his buttoned short-sleeve shirt bunching at his wrists where it was untucked. He'd made no effort to tame the chunky waves in his hair, and curls hung across his sun-kissed forehead. Perhaps not the Hollywood definition of the epitome of sexy, Grayson Holmes stirred her, warmed her, and made her ache.

"I can go get our bags from the car," he said, glancing over his shoulder in the general direction of Baker Street, implying where the car was parked. "If you're hungry, we can go eat. Unfortunately, because I'd planned on being away, Mum was correct in assuming I have little to eat in the house, but we can remedy that in short order."

As he talked, she walked back to him, and with each step, her heart beat a little faster. She had never been the initiator in her past relationships, such as they were in low quantities, but perhaps because she had never been inspired to be. He watched her, his unique eyes never shifting away from her as she neared, dipping his chin to keep eye contact. When she stood in front of him, he smiled.

"Are you hungry?" he asked.

Kipling nodded, but instead of clarifying, she raised her hands and unbuttoned the top button of his shirt. He drew in a sharp, long breath, looking down at the work of her fingers. When she reached the third button, he drew his hands from his pockets and set them at her hips, his fingertips curling just enough to draw her closer. By the time she unfastened the last button, Grayson's breathing was rapid and hitched, and when she slid her hands over his warm skin to open the shirt, he made a low, pleased sound deep in his chest.

She looked up, holding his gaze as long as she could while she leaned in, then pressed a kiss to the center of his chest. "Hello," she said against his skin.

His abdominal muscles tensed beneath her hands as she explored his sides and stomach, then slid her hands up his chest to urge the shirt off his shoulders so it dropped to the floor, leaving him exposed to her. The scar on his side wasn't the only one marring his skin, but she chose not to focus on the few marks, but the man as a whole. Kipling kissed his chest again, moving over his heart.

"Hello," she said again.

Grayson took her face between his hands to tip back her chin and take her in the hardest, deepest, most arousing kiss they'd ever shared. Perhaps because now, more than ever, there was no reason to hold back everything a kiss could inspire. She raised her arms and he wrapped her in his, strong hands on her back, holding her impossibly close as his tongue slid over hers in a push and pull that had her tummy fluttering and her skin tickling to be free.

He lifted her, his hands behind her knees to draw her legs around him, and turned them both to set her on the bed, leaning her back without pause until she looked up at him and he moved over her, every point of contact a fire and spark. Agile fingers returned the favor of unbuttoning her dress until he moved it aside and revealed her stomach and bra, her ragged breathing pushing her ribs against the restraint. Then matching her idea, Grayson shifted down to press his hot mouth to her stomach. Kipling gasped and arched, suddenly so alive it made her ache.

"Hello, my darling," he said against her skin. "At long last, hello."

Chapter Ten

The nakedness of a woman is the work of God.

Never before now had Grayson more appreciated or understood William Blake's observation as lying in his bed studying the nude form of Kipling Branson sleeping beside him. She lay on her stomach, her head off the pillow with her cheek resting on the back of one hand, her arm above her head, tousled chestnut hair spread over her shoulders and sheets like a veil. Her other arm was tucked to her side, hiding her breast enough to entice him without giving him the view he wished for. The pearl strand of her spine flowed along her curved body, disappearing beneath the edge of the blanket where it draped low over her hips. They had arrived at Baker Street in the early hours of the afternoon, so now just a couple of hours later, sunlight still lit the room, shining in her hair and kissing her skin.

Serene features, relaxed form; she was beautiful.

Titian's *Venus of Urbino* was a child's finger painting in comparison.

Grayson shifted onto his side to face her, sliding closer to the foot of the bed so when she opened her eyes he would be level with her and pillowed his head on his arm. With his other hand, he embraced the temptation he'd denied himself since waking, and touched his fingertips to the back of her shoulder, sliding them along the curve of her back to the dip of her waist, and up again with the swell of her hips. Gooseflesh rose at his touch, and he smiled. Kipling inhaled deeply, blinking open her eyes as she exhaled again. Her smile grew, slow and enticing.

"Hello," he said, and her gaze shifted to his mouth.

"Hello," she said in return. "I think maybe that is how I want to say hello for the rest of my life."

Grayson chuckled and she unfolded her arm from her side to lay her palm against his chest, the vibration of his laugh translating through her touch to encourage a wider smile. There was something beautiful about Kipling, something undefinably beautiful when her world was effectively silent as he knew it was right now. She lingered longer in her glances, she focused with more detail, and at least with him, she sought a more tactile experience of her world. He leaned a bit toward her, waiting until her focus came back to his face again.

"I agree, as long as I am the only one you say hello to." He followed the path along her back again, smoothing over her skin with his whole palm. He leaned forward enough to press a kiss to her bare arm.

She smiled and pulled her lower lip through her teeth. "A promise I have no problem making." With her hand still pressed to his chest, she pushed up from the bed and slid across the sheets toward him, a beautifully mischievous glint in her eyes, and pushed on him until he lay on his back and she crawled over him. "I want to say hello," she said in a husky whisper, kissing his jaw. "And goodnight." Kissing his chin. "And good morning."

His body reacted immediately and instinctively and he moaned into her kiss as she moved over him. Her hair fell around them like a curtain, the fragrance floating in the air, and he brushed it back to draw her closer, deeper.

The loud chime of his doorbell broke through the moment, and he closed his eyes with a groan born of frustration rather than pleasure, letting his head drop back.

"What's wrong?" Kipling asked, supporting herself with her hands pressed into the bed near his shoulders.

"Someone is at the door."

She shifted enough to roll partially away, curling some hair behind her ears. "How does anyone even know you're back in London?"

"I informed my director, only because I am required to do so. I need to go see to it." He fought the petulant child in his head telling him to stay where he was, they could wait, knowing he couldn't ignore whomever it might be.

Kipling rolled away from him, holding the sheet to her breasts to stretch out on her back. The sight of her was a sore temptation, but he sat up and moved off the bed, grabbing his pants and trousers as he walked around the foot.

"If we are to be disturbed, why don't you get up and dressed. I'll take you to dinner, and then we'll stock the pantry," he said, standing at the foot of his bed to pull on his clothing, facing her so she could see his lips. "You might want something warmer. It is likely to cool down this evening."

"My suitcase is in the car," she teased, with an elegant, arched brow.

"Quite right. I'll loan you a cardigan," he said with a wink.

She smiled again, that sexy temptress grin with her lips drawn between her teeth. "Okay. I'll be down soon."

Zipping his trousers, he snatched his shirt off the floor and pulled it on, heading for the door as the doorbell chimed again. At the open door, Kipling called his name and he stopped to look back. She had sat up, one hand holding the sheet to her breasts, the other arm extended to the mattress for support.

"Petra was right, your birthmark isn't all that big." She tilted her head, a wicked grin on her lips. "Although, it does remind me a bit of Switzerland."

He laughed and bolted back to the bed, leaning over her for a quick, firm kiss, staying in front of her so she read "You are a vixen," on his lips before he finally left the bedroom, giving the sheet a good tug on his way out, and was rewarded with her indignant squeal.

The doorbell chimed a third time, and he jogged barefoot down the two flights of stairs, racing Watson for the door. Halfway down the final landing, a familiar female voice carried through the door and he nearly tumbled when his steps halted.

"Grayson, are you home? I saw the Bentley."

Steeling himself against the surprise, he finished taking the final steps and went to the door, shooing Watson out of the way with his bare foot. Giving him a glare of superiority, Watson padded away toward the kitchen so Grayson could open the door.

"Liz," he said, attempting pleasant surprise. "Sorry. I was upstairs."

Liz Pivens smiled brightly, taking off her sunglasses so he could see her brown eyes, her blond hair loose and straight around her shoulders. Feeling more than awkward, Grayson stepped back so she could enter the foyer and she walked through to the parlor before turning back to face him.

"I thought you'd be gone until later this week. How was the wedding?"

"Lovely," he said, pushing his hands into his pockets. "I hadn't planned on returning until mid-week, but circumstances changed." It took his full will not to look up the stairs.

"Nothing wrong, I hope."

He shook his head. "On the contrary. All is well. Did you need something?"

She laughed and raised her hand in a small wave. "Oh, no. I was just coming through here on my way back to Knightsbridge, and I saw the car. I thought you might be home. If you're free, I thought we'd go eat. It's been a bit since we talked. I'd love to hear about the wedding." Her smile eased a bit.

Grayson pressed his lips together, wincing at her impending disappointment. "I can't, Liz. Not tonight."

"We can still just have a chat, can't we, Grayson?"

"Yes, of course," he insisted quickly. "I've never considered you less than a friend, Liz—"

"Just never more than a friend," she said, her voice heavy. She smiled, but it was sad. Liz fortified her smile and walked back toward him. She laughed an uncomfortable sound and looked away with a huff. "Sorry. Been feeling a bit nostalgic as of late. Just me being silly."

From upstairs, he heard movement and the distinct creak of the floorboards; the blessing and curse of a home as old as Baker Street. Kipling would come downstairs soon. Though he doubted Kipling would be truly bothered by Liz's presence, as he'd made it clear the circumstances around and the ending of their relationship; he didn't think he could say the same for Liz. To see that he had found the happiness that eluded him when they were together might be a cruel twist, and he never wanted to be cruel. While he never loved Liz, not the way she deserved, he'd cared for her.

As much as he made a point of ignoring the sound, it didn't go unnoticed. Liz glanced toward the stairs, and her eyes widened. For the first time she looked down at his bare feet, the slight hue of color of moments before blooming into a full flush. She gasped and took a step backward. With her jaw working open and closed, working to say words she didn't have, she looked toward the stairs. Then she forced an uncomfortable smile and crossed her arms over her body.

"I'm sorry. I didn't realize you have a guest. I don't suppose it's Jo." She giggled, but it still sounded immensely uncomfortable.

"No, it's not Jo."

"Oh." She cleared her throat and licked her lips, snuffing her nose. "Do I know her by chance? Is she with Six?"

He shook his head, feeling the total arse. "No. I met her in Boston."

Liz's eyes widened. "This past winter?" He nodded. "Is she American?" He nodded again. "Does she know?" It was a simple question, but one every member of the intelligence community knew. Again, he nodded. "Well, she must be beyond amazing," she said, her voice now tainted.

"She is," he said honestly.

The distinct sound of Kipling's light steps on the stairs reached them, and Liz practically bolted for the door. Grayson took a side-ways step and blocked her, holding out his hand.

"You don't need to leave, Liz—"

"Oh, you think she's up for meeting the ex?" she snapped.

"I've told her about you," he admitted, and she blanched. Grayson smiled, shaking his head. "I also made it clear whose fault it was we ended. You were not lacking. I was."

"But you're not anymore," she said in a rough whisper.

Grayson shook his head but held her gaze. She stared back, but as Kipling's footsteps approached, she shook her head and stepped around him to the door. "I'm not ready to meet the woman who managed what I couldn't."

"Liz—"

She opened the door and was out, pulling it closed behind her as Kipling came down the final flight of stairs, her handbag hanging from her shoulder and his shoes in the other hand. Grayson sighed and scrubbed his hands over his face before turning toward her. The instant he saw her, the tension in his shoulders at Liz's unexpected visit eased.

He loved this woman.

Without measure.

Without limit.

Without boundaries.

Kipling reached the parlor, and set down his short boots at the bottom of the stairs, a small frown lining her brow as she watched him. "You left them in the bedroom. Thought I'd bring them down and save you the two flights. Is everything okay? Who was at the door?"

"Liz," he answered, pulling his lips back tight as he said her name.

Her eyes widened slightly and if anything, her expression was sympathetic. "I'm sorry," she said, her tone gentle. "That couldn't have been easy. What did she want?"

Grayson huffed and walked past her, indulging in a grazed touch across her body as he moved by to sit on one of the lower stairs steps to put on his socks and shoes. "She saw I was home, and wanted to have dinner. I don't think there was any other purpose." He squinted and looked to the door.

"What are you thinking?" Kipling asked, sitting down beside him.

"Something she said." He finished pulling on the second shoe and set his elbows on his knees. "She said she was on her way home to Knightsbridge and saw the car. This time of day she'd be heading home from work."

"You said she works at Six," Kipling confirmed.

He nodded. "She does. Support role. But, Six is in Vauxhall." She shrugged a shoulder and shook her head, and he chuckled. "Sorry, darling. Vauxhall is on the other side of the Thames. It's a ten-minute drive from there to Knightsbridge. Baker Street is fifteen minutes out of the way. Unless she wasn't coming from work, this is not on the way home."

"She lives in Knightsbridge, then?"

Grayson nodded and stood, offering his hand to draw her with him. "She was likely running an errand north of here. Ready for dinner?"

She nodded and he gave himself a quick review to assure everything was in its proper place, including wallet and property keys. He went to the coat closet by the front door and took out a blue knit cardigan, holding it out to her. "It will be overly large on you, but unless you'd like me to bring in the luggage first, it should do until we return."

"Thank you," she said, taking it. When she looked up at him, he recognized the look of question in her eyes before she spoke. "Is she okay? I hope she didn't leave because of me."

"She did," he answered truthfully, resting his hands on Kipling's arms. "I believe she was more surprised than any intention of avoiding you. Finding me here with someone was outside her expectations."

"You've been over for a long time, though, haven't you?"

"Almost a year exactly," he answered, realizing the truth of it only then, which partially helped him understand Liz's nostalgia.

"However, it was more than simply learning I am with someone else."

"What else," she asked, slipping on the cardigan. It hung off her like she wore her father's clothing, and yet, he found it intimately endearing to see her wearing it.

Grayson took both her hands so their fingers were linked between them, squeezing gently as he sighed, ending with a humorless chuckle. "Though I never made the conscious decision as such, my subconscious had a distinct inclination away from being with anyone here in Baker Street. I never actually realized the truth of it until Liz pointed it out to me during a particularly loud row prior to the end of our relationship. She told me later, after we were through, that when I stated I was leaving Knightsbridge, where we lived, and returning here she knew there was no hope for reconciliation."

Her brow furrowed and she canted her head slightly. "You mean, as in—"

"Intimately, yes. I suppose it stands as further testament to my prior need to keep elements of my life — Baker Street and my family, my heart — separate from relationships. Again, not any decision I clearly made. I'm quite sure, were I to submit to such an examination, a psychologist would have lengthy and poetic commentary on my state of mind."

"So us being here—"

He nodded and sighed, bringing her hands to his lips to kiss her knuckles. "Likely hurt her in ways I never intended. Beyond any conscious choice my head may make, my heart knows you belong here."

By the time they left the Indian restaurant a few blocks from the house, the sun had set and the streetlights were on. It had rained while they ate, so the sidewalks were wet and a cool dampness hung in the air. Kipling wrapped Grayson's borrowed cardigan around her body, holding it in place with one arm, while holding his hand as they walked.

"We'll pop in to Tesco's on the way home and grab what we might need for tomorrow morning," Grayson said, pointing toward the convenience store a bit further down the sidewalk. "They deliver, so I'll have it arranged for a full stocking to come to us."

"How very bachelor of you," she teased.

He grinned down at her, and she smiled wider at the heavy curl falling across his brow, the waves agitated by the mist. He might find the tendency frustrating, but she found it adorable.

"Perhaps, but no longer. If you wish to roam the aisles of the grocery with me, I am more than pleased to oblige."

As they neared the shop, the phone in her pocket buzzed and chimed in quick succession with both text and voicemail notifications. Letting go of her hold on the sweater, unwilling to release Grayson's hand to dig out the phone, she pulled it from the cardigan pocket. Several messages scrolled on the locked screen.

"Apparently I had no signal in the restaurant," she said, sliding her thumb across the screen to unlock it, and entering her code. "I'm getting everything at once." She read as she walked, and Grayson tugged her hand to pull her closer to the buildings to avoid people coming from the opposite direction. "Sorry," she mumbled. "Mom called. And texted. John. Oh, look." Kipling stopped walking as she opened one of the messages. "It's from your niece Erika. She told me she'd taken some photos at the wedding, and I asked her to share them. Looks like she shared in a group message, so you'll get them too."

Standing under an awning outside an office, dark and locked up for the evening, Kipling held out the phone to him so he could see. Erika had taken at least half a dozen photos of them when they were unaware. She really loved one in particular. If she had to recall, she thought it was after the ceremony and during the lawn party they held as reception. She and Grayson were seated beside each other, his arm draped across the back of her chair so she could sit close to him. Throughout the day, Grayson had found opportunities to lean in and kiss the exposed skin of her shoulders because of the off-the-shoulder straight neckline of her dress. In the photo, his lips were pressed to her skin, his eyes closed, and Erika had caught the exact moment when Kipling had looked down at him. It was beautiful.

"I would like that one framed," Grayson said, tapping on her screen as she held the phone, enlarging the detail. "You're beautiful."

"I think the whole photo is beautiful," she said softly as she went back to her main screens, seeing what else came through.

In addition to the notification that her mother had called, and hadn't left a message, she had a call and voicemail from a number in London. For a moment, her pulse jumped and her skin broke out in gooseflesh.

"Ready?" Grayson asked, squinting up at the sky. "We might get rain again. If we hurry, we might beat it home. I didn't bring a brolly, and would rather you not get soaked.

"Just a second," she said, tapping the voicemail message. "I just need to—"

She didn't finish as the message played through her hearing aids. "Good evening, Miss Branson. This is Jane Fischer at the University of Westminster calling to confirm your interview on Wednesday with President Rathborne. Please let me know if you require assistance with transportation to the campus and we can have it arranged. Otherwise, we will see you then."

"Anything wrong?" Grayson asked as they left the awning.

"No. I'll respond to everyone who needs responses when we get back home. It's one thing to read while I walk; I'm not nearly coordinated enough to type as well."

"What about the voicemail?"

He studied her even walking, and now Kipling had a clear understanding of what someone being interrogated by Grayson Holmes might feel. She'd been contemplating all through dinner how to tell him and hated her own indecision. He had made it abundantly clear, in more ways than just words, he was happy she was in London. But a niggling voice in her head — still sounding like Mina — told her a surprise visit was a far cry from her confession.

Kipling pocketed the phone and stepped closer to them as they walked, curling her free hand around the inside of his elbow. He tightened his grip on her hand, then released it. "I'll tell you when we get home." She raised her chin to smile at him as they reached the door of the small convenience store, and he opened it for her. "I promise."

"That seems fair." He had to let go of her hand to pick up one of the small baskets waiting by the door. "But before we get there, I would like you to know three things."

Kipling licked her lips and rolled them together, crossing her arms into the bunched yarn of the oversized cardigan. She fell into step with him as he navigated the aisles. "Okay."

"First, and quite possibly the most important point, I love you."

She smiled because he said it with the nonchalance of asking her if she preferred salted over unsalted butter. If someone saw them from another aisle, they'd likely have no idea what he said.

"I love you, too," she answered.

He grinned and winked at her, and put a package of chocolate digestives in his basket. "Second, it pleases me without limits when you refer to Baker Street as home, whether you realize you've done it or not."

Kipling shook her head, then immediately nodded when he held up a package of bagels. "I didn't realize I had."

"Precisely," he reiterated and also put a loaf of fresh wheat bread in the basket. "Third, you should be aware I have been waiting since Friday evening for you to tell me whatever secret it is you've held silent on."

Heat flared up her throat to her cheeks, and she had to blink to keep from staring at him wide-eyed. They rounded the endcap of the aisle and started down the next. Without confirming with her, he selected a package of breakfast tea.

"I've not said anything or asked specifically because as much as I know you have something you need to tell me, I've already eliminated all the worst possible bits of news." He continued walking and shopping, as casually as discussing the flavor of cream cheese he took from the cold display. "So, since you are hesitant to speak whatever it is, I can only surmise you are concerned about my response."

He stopped and turned to face her, and Kipling managed to meet his gaze. Grayson smiled and leaned in to kiss her. Short. Far too short.

"If you are truly concerned about my response, please refer to point one as previously stated," he said with a wink.

They reached the refrigerated section of the small grocery, and he quickly filled the basket with butter, yogurt, eggs, a small bottle of milk, and cream cheese. After bacon and a bottle of orange juice, they picked up a half dozen eggs on a shelf on their way to the cashier and Grayson laid out the supplies.

"Evenin', Mr. Holmes," the elderly gentleman behind the counter said, ringing up the items. He nodded to Kipling. "Evenin', ma'am."

"Good evening, Allan. Could you see to a delivery for me by early afternoon tomorrow? All the usual items, plus whatever your wife thinks should be added," he said with a friendly smile. He glanced at Kipling but pointed to Allan. "I have a general list of necessities, but Allan's wife has taken it upon herself to assure I eat well. I trust her implicitly."

"£20.80. Should I let her know you've a guest, Mr. Holmes?"

"Please do," Grayson said, opening his wallet to hand Allan a £20 and £5 note. Allan gave change, and Grayson pocketed it, along with his wallet. "Good evening."

"Good evenin' to you, Mr. Holmes. Miss."

Kipling offered to take one of the bags, but he shook his head, hanging them all from one hand while he took her other to walk again. They needed only to cross one intersection before reaching the stretch of Baker Street where Grayson lived, but even that short walk took forever. With each step, Kipling tried to formulate what to say and how to say it. It wasn't about finding the courage to tell him, or resolve, but the right words.

Once back in the house, Kipling took some of the bags from him and dodged Watson to make her way to the kitchen, taking out each item as Grayson put it away. She watched, making note for later. When all was away, Grayson turned in the corner of the kitchen, where two sections of counter came together, and set his hands on the counter edge, honing in on her.

He didn't have to say a word.

Shrugging off the cardigan, Kipling lumped it on the counter and focused hard on not fidgeting. "The voicemail was about an interview for a teaching position," she finally said, meeting his silently demanding gaze.

Grayson nodded, slow, and crossed his arms, settling into a relaxed stance with his feet extended, ankles crossed. "That's good. Your goal was to teach. I'm not surprised you already have an offer."

"The thing is," she continued, cupping one hand in the other in front of her. "I applied for this position months ago. Well before Christmas. My advisor said to start then, even before I had my degree because many schools take a very long time to act on applicants."

"Seems prudent."

She moved to stand near him, tapping her hand on the counter. "Do you remember when you said you believed in both fate and destiny and that the universe has contrived all along to bring us together?"

"Of course," he answered, the rough weight of his voice pulling at her until she drew back her shoulders, took a deep breath, and found in his eyes the confidence to speak.

She smiled, feeling at that moment foolish because she'd worried for so long. "I applied to this school on a whim. I knew it was silly, and probably without any hope, and yet..." She chuckled and shook her head, then took in a breath. "The day after tomorrow I have an interview with Peter Rathborne at the University of Westminster to fill a position in their English department."

Her assurance faltered for a few excruciatingly long beats of her heart while Grayson said nothing, just staring at her, his expression unreadable. She was a breath shy of stepping away with the hope of finding a way to minimalize her hope when Grayson moved from the counter, hands cupping her face in the same second his mouth — open and warm — covered hers, stealing her breath.

For a moment, Kipling was so lost in the devouring intensity she couldn't move, but when he shifted the angle of the kiss and his tongue caressed hers, Kipling moaned a purr and wrapped her arms around him. Her hips hit the edge of the counter, and without breaking the kiss, Grayson scooped her up and set her on the counter edge, a firm pull of her hips bringing her hard against him.

Panting for breath, and aching for him, Kipling closed her eyes when he paused the kiss, his forehead pressed to hers, their breath mingling in hard bursts between them.

"Don't you dare ask me if I'm pleased," he said and kissed her again.

Chapter Eleven

"God forbid I actually plan some sort of life without the express permission of MI6," Grayson snarled, kicking the front door of the house shut with a resounding thud, balancing his takeaway tray and bag in his hands. Without the Bluetooth piece in his ear, he wouldn't have had enough hands to manage. He immediately winced. "This is a courtesy contact only, Jeffrey. I have done what was demanded of me with regards to Kipling, and you informed me yourself she was without concern on all fronts."

"Yet, it is indisputable — even by you — that Howell used her—"

"*Used* her, yes. Without her knowledge. I'll not have this discussion again." Grayson stormed through the parlor to the kitchen, glancing toward the eating area to see if Kipling had come down yet. He'd left a note for her before he ran out.

"You would do well to remember just who is the superior officer in this conversation, Holmes."

It took all his control to set down the tray without slamming it. He placed his hands on the counter and hung his head, bracing himself on his straight arms. For the first time in his adult life, since accepting the position at Six, he considered the real option of just quitting. Just telling the whole lot of them to sod off.

"Finish your holiday," Jeffrey said after several moments of strained silence. "Enjoy a few days with your American. Come back next week and we will continue this conversation when level heads are more likely to prevail."

Before Grayson either consented or told Jeffrey his true opinion, the call closed. He pushed angry fingers into his hair and laced them behind his neck, groaning in frustration as he paced toward the garden door. It had been with extreme reluctance he'd sent an email to his superior, informing Jeffrey Cooper both of his earlier return to London and of Kipling's presence. In retrospect, informing his employer of his whereabouts and his companion's had not bothered him previously, but despite the fact he'd met Kipling as a direct result of his position, he resented the requirement to share her existence. Even if in no greater capacity than stating she was here.

In the last few months, and even more so in the last few days, Grayson found Six's intrusion into his life to be an open wound, into which Jeffrey and other in the command structure poured salt. Kipling's news from the night before had instantly filled him with hope for a beautiful future, but lying in the dark with her beside him, he had stared at the ceiling and cursed reality. She might be here, but how often would he not? Was it so insane, so unjustified, for him to wish for a life that had him waking to her every morning, and falling asleep with her every night without the risk that one day he might leave and never come home. Yes, tragedy happened, but his profession of choice nearly demanded it.

His frustration had only been amplified upon looking again through the photos his niece had sent to both him and Kipling. The images were beautiful, for the greatest part because neither of them was aware the photos were being taken, and in their ignorance, he recognized their love. Even on his own part, he saw in his eyes what he felt in his heart. Then he had looked deeper, his investigative mind unwilling to stop at the surface, and a single face emerged several times in the photos. Always in the background, and always with his focus on them. Grayson did not specifically recognize the face, but recognized in the man's expression and stance that he did not belong and was not there by any connection the man had to either his new brother-in-law's family or his. In every image, this man's attention was on both him and Kipling, far more than what would be nonchalant.

His interest concerned Grayson.

Feeling at least a fraction calmer, Grayson went back to the kitchen counter and unlocked his phone, this time taking the Bluetooth earpiece out of his ear. After tapping on his contacts, he dialed, and put the call on speaker so he could move around the small kitchen. It took only seconds for Sandra to answer.

"Hey, Boss," she said with a cheerful hello. "What could possibly induce you to call while on holiday?"

"Unfortunately, despite my best efforts it would seem work has followed me home."

"Is there a problem?"

"That is what I need you for," he answered, navigating screens on the phone to the text program, sending the photos to Sandra. "I am sending several photos to you. Before I explain, I feel I shall also be required to apologize for lack of information—"

Grayson laughed at Sandra's uncharacteristic, and very Lynne Connolly-esque verbal outburst, finally feeling a slight waning of his tension. Kipling had told him she hadn't even dared tell Sandra Sookoo of her impending visit, since Sandra had said at some point keeping a secret from him was near impossible. A reality Kipling now fully understood.

"Is Kip in London now?" Sandra shrilled.

"She is, and if you keep speaking as such, you're likely to wake her even without her aids."

"You dirty bastard." Despite her words, he easily heard the smile in her voice. "How long is she staying?"

Grayson cleared his throat and braced his hands on the counter again, so he spoke downward to the phone. "I fear I might jinx the situation if I speak out of turn."

"Aaaaah," she said, and he easily imagined her smug grin. "I insist you two come for dinner tonight. I don't care if you're my boss, I won't hear you turn me down."

Grayson chuckled again. "Can we first discuss the reason I've called before we move on to more pleasant conversations?" Not knowing the identity of either the unknown man in Boston or this intruder at his sister's wedding — clearly not the same man, which only doubled the danger — irritated him. Not knowing always irritated him.

"Oh, fine. Tell me what I'm really looking for."

With a sigh, he turned away to take the bacon from the refrigerator, and a pan from the cupboard. As he lit the gas on the cooker grill and set down the pan to heat, he spoke over his shoulder in the general direction of his phone. "In each photograph, you will note a man in the background. Dark hair, slight widow's peak."

"Okay, I see him."

"I don't believe he had any business at my sister's wedding, and based on his interest in Kipling and myself, I have concerns."

"Got it. I'll build a composite from the various photos and set up a face recognition scan. Should have an answer by tonight when you come for dinner. Say six?"

"I won't say yes until I speak to Kipling, but consider us as attending unless you hear otherwise. Fair?"

"Fair."

Something jolted Kipling awake, but once she opened her eyes, she had no idea what it might have been. Morning sunlight made the bedroom bright, and the sheers shifted slowly in the breeze coming through the open windows. She stretched, inhaling deep, and rolled to look at Grayson's side of the bed.

It was empty, except for a note on his pillow. His penmanship was masculine, but definitive and careful, and she suspected his mother had a hand in assuring he wasn't sloppy.

*For you see, each day I love you more today more than
yesterday and less than tomorrow.*
~Rosemonde Gerard

*Come down when you are ready. I had to leave very
briefly, but when I return it will be with a surprise.
So, if I should still be gone when you come, know I
will not be long.
You are beautiful, but when you sleep you leave me
mesmerized.*
Grayson

Kipling sighed, set the note on the table beside the bed, and picked up her phone to check the time. It was well after nine, and she couldn't recall the last time she'd slept so late. Or so well. Whether it was being beside Grayson, or maybe because he'd left her sated and sleepy, she wanted to sleep so well every night.

She tossed back the blankets and rounded the foot of the bed for the bathroom. Grayson's bath had a distinctive vintage feel, with white tiles on the floor and walls, a claw foot tub with the shower-head coming from the wall, and a shower curtain that would wrap around the whole of the tub, but it was deceptively modern and clearly remodeled in the last ten to fifteen years. She showered but promised herself someday soon a long soak in the deep tub. With her hair still damp, she dressed in jeans and a light, long-sleeved shirt, put in and turned on her aids, and headed downstairs, escorted by Watson.

When she hit the first landing, she smiled at the enticing aroma of bacon being cooked, and not the "streaky bacon" she was used to, but hearty, meaty English bacon. Walking on her toes, she eased her way through the parlor to peek into the kitchen. The counter ran along a portion of the back wall, with the sink facing the garden, then along the interior wall where the stove was positioned, and then extended into the kitchen to form a "U" with seating at the counter with high stools. Grayson stood at the stove, his back effectively to her, with a dishtowel draped over his shoulder, seeing to the bacon.

"Is that my surprise?" she asked, crossing the short space from the parlor entrance to the counter.

He twisted at the waist but didn't step away from the stove while flipping the thick-cut bacon, and smiled wide. "Good morning," he said, shifting his tongs into his left hand to motion to her with his right to have her move closer. When she did, he took a step back with one leg to wrap his arm around her waist and kiss her a safe distance from the pan. "This is not the surprise, but I thought you might be hungry—"

"Starving."

He grinned wider, and it was infectious. "So, I thought I'd make breakfast."

"If you're trying to encourage me to stay with your mad cooking skills, it's not necessary," she said with raised eyebrows and a shake of her head. "You've convinced me with your mad love-making skills."

His laugh was deep, rumbling up from his chest. "If that should prove to be insufficient, perhaps your surprise will be the final bit of incentive you need."

He set down his tongs, but without releasing her, twisted enough to reach toward the counter space behind him where she couldn't see. When he came back, in his hand he held a white to-go cup with pink and brown lettering that immediately struck a gleefully familiar cord. Kipling gasped and took the Dunkin' Donuts cup, staring in disbelief.

"Oh, don't tell me this is just a tease and you've put tea in a cup you managed to smuggle back from Boston," she said as she took it from him. The cup was warm, and she brought it beneath her nose to inhale the steam rising through the small sip opening.

Grayson laughed again. "It is not a tease; however, it would have been a brilliant plan had I thought of it. Take a sip and tell me."

She instinctively blew into the small opening, then brought it to her lips and tentatively sipped. There were plenty of places to get a hot cup of coffee, but for her none compared to the drink she'd been raised on. Sweet, rich, smooth, she sighed her pleasure. "How did you manage this?"

"There is a small deli just down the street in the opposite direction from our walk last evening. Their menu is limited, but the proprietors brought in the franchise option last month to appeal to visiting American tourists. As an Englishman, I'm embarrassed to say how pleased I was."

She took another sip. "Well, if I harbored any doubt about moving to London, it was because I would have to give up my Dunks."

"Then it's settled," he said before kissing her cheek and letting her go so he could return to cooking. "Breakfast will be done in short order. Not my mother's Full English, but satisfying. Sit and I'll bring it to you."

Kipling went to the table, taking a seat along one long side so she could watch him. A laptop computer sat open at the end of the table, but the screen was black.

"Should I forget again," he said, though his back was to her as he transferred bacon to a plate. He buttered bread and set it in the pan to toast. The enticing aroma mingled with the lingering bacon and made her stomach rumble. "Agent Patrick Flannery would like to speak to you at your convenience. He attempted to reach you last week."

"Did he call you looking for me?"

"Not directly, no. He'd called me on another subject, and during the course of the call, he mentioned he wished to speak to you."

Butter sizzled, and while the bread toasted, he opened a carton of eggs. Kipling chose to focus on the simple, domestic act of him cooking breakfast rather than the impending conversation. Not that it made any difference here, but she preferred not to relive it whenever possible.

"I never heard from him," she said and took another sip.

"No, because apparently you were winging your way across the Atlantic to surprise me in Sussex," he said, winking at her as he took the bread from the pan. "At the time, I told Agent Flannery I suspected you were busy with family. Later, when I knew you'd arrived, I told him I would inform you once the excitement of the wedding had passed."

"Does he need me there? In Boston?"

"Perhaps eventually. They are preparing their prosecution against Isaac Sheldon." At the name, Kipling's stomach twisted, but she chose to push aside the visceral reaction. She was in London, Grayson was with her, and Isaac Sheldon held no power over her. He cracked eggs into the pan and picked up another Dunkin' cup she had missed along with hers, drinking from it. "It is general procedure to interview again all witnesses, prepare them for the process, and such. While nothing you and I discuss would be considered part of the official process, I will help you."

Kipling sighed and set her chin in her hand. "I'd hoped to ignore all those things and just, you know, *be*."

"Speaking of not being able to ignore things, we have been invited to Sandra and David's home this evening for dinner." He glanced back at her as he flipped the eggs. "Would you like to go?"

Kipling perked up and grinned. "Oh, that's wonderful. Of course, unless you had plans."

"My only plans thus far are to spend as much time with you as possible before Monday, and then, to only be parted as much as is required."

With the plates full, he came to the table and set hers in front of her, his plate at the chair adjacent, then went back for his coffee before sitting. The table would easily seat six, two on each long side and one at each end, and she'd selected a side chair so he sat at the head of the table.

"You aren't going to cook like this every day, are you?" she asked, picking up one of the slices of thick bread. "My waistline couldn't afford food like this every day."

The smoldering look he gave her made her skin flush. "You must allow me sufficient time to impress you."

"If you insist." She worked together a bite of food but looked at him before taking it. She pointed to the laptop once she was done. "Were you working?"

Grayson sighed, casting a glance at the computer. "Sadly, yes. It would seem no matter how I wish to escape it, I cannot. Agent Flannery sent me some files to review, but until today had only attempted to view them on my phone."

"More about what happened in Boston?"

"Yes," he said simply before eating more of the eggs and toast, but his features pulled.

Kipling cleared her throat, then drank the last swallow of her coffee. She made sure he saw her vain attempt at getting out the last drop, tapping the bottle of the cup until he grinned. Mission accomplished, she smiled and set her chin on her hand to look at him. "Now, tell me what you're not telling me." At his single arched eyebrow, she shook her head and pointed a finger. "You aren't the only one who can read people, Grayson."

He held her gaze and took a deep breath before conceding with a small smile. "I'm reluctant to speak too much of it, I suppose because I don't wish to spoil the day."

"We can't avoid it forever."

Pushing aside his empty plate, Grayson pulled the laptop toward him and tapped a key to wake up the computer, and typed in a security code to unlock the screen. Several photos, grainy and in a variety of either black and white or sepia tones, overlapped each other on the screen. Different angles, and different places, but the man in each photo was similar enough that Kipling suspected he was the same man in all the shots.

"Who is this?" she asked.

"That is the question everyone would like the answer to," Grayson said, sighing with his arms crossed on the table between the edge and the laptop. "Apparently, in the FBI's review of all the CCTV footage they found of Langdon Howell in and around Boston, specifically the university and other key locations in the case, they repeatedly found this man in general proximity. At least, they suspect it to be the same man. Recognition programs have determined the man in each image is of the same height, same build, but since most of the footage was taken in the winter months, he is often bundled with hats hiding his face."

"How convenient," she mumbled. "Could I?" she asked, pointing at the computer.

He turned the laptop toward her, and she tapped between the images. Familiarity niggled at her, especially between two particular images. There was something…

"What do you see?" Grayson asked, pulling her out of her thoughts.

She took a sharp breath and looked at him, then back to the screen, pointing at the two photos. "I agree they're all the same man, or at least, by what I can see. But these two photos, there's something about them poking at me."

"Do you know why?"

Kipling shook her head. "No, I don't." She sighed. "It's like I should know this person, but I can't say who or how or from where. Just that niggling in the back of your head, you know?" She squinted and tapped her temple, and he nodded in agreement. Kipling sighed. "Maybe it'll come to me eventually."

"Perhaps." He closed the laptop, pushed back his chair, and picked up both their empty plates. "I am going to go shave as I didn't this morning before going for your coffee."

"Thank you for the sacrifice," she teased.

He winked at her as he rinsed the plates. "Once I come back down, we should go out and begin your formal education of your new home city of London."

Kipling smiled wide, a lightness filling her chest. "But what if I don't get the job? There's no guarantee—"

"Darling, they asked you to cross an ocean to meet you. I would say you have a far better chance than you believe." Drying his hands on a dishtowel, he tossed it on the counter and headed for the parlor. "I'll be back down shortly."

When she heard his footsteps reach the first landing, she stood and went to the sink, intending to wash the dishes he'd left, but Mina's ringtone stopped her. She glanced back at the phone, still on the table, and contemplated not answering. Since Saturday, Mina had texted three times with apologies, and asking forgiveness, and left one tearful voicemail. They'd been friends forever, but Mina's attitude had not just angered Kipling, it had hurt. It bothered her how her best friend would not only be so hard, but ultimately question her intelligence and ability to make a sound decision.

But, she missed her friend.

With a huff, Kipling went back to the table and tapped the screen to answer just before the call went to voicemail. She waited for the Bluetooth to connect before saying, "Hello."

"You answered!" Mina exclaimed and sniffed. "I was afraid you'd let me go to voicemail again."

"It's like two in the morning in Boston," she said, walking to the garden door. The sun shined down through the tall building walls on each side, but the garden was lush and filled with flowering plants. "Why are you still awake?"

"I haven't been able to sleep since Saturday. Kip, I'm such a bitch. I'm so sorry. I just—" She sniffed again, the wet sound carrying through the phone. "No, I'm not going to try to make any excuse. Especially after what I said on Saturday. If you had seen John's face when I said it, I think I knew right then I was an idiot."

"The problem wasn't that you were an idiot, Mina," she said, opening the garden door. The air was fresh, and a soft breeze brushed her face. "It's that you thought I was. I know my own heart."

"I know. I *know*." Another firm sniff. "I knew he loved you before he left Boston, I didn't need you to tell me. And I knew you loved him. I mean, who the hell am I to dictate to you about love?"

"Mina, have you been drinking?"

"No, but I've considered it. Kip, please…" This time, the sniff was a sob and Kipling stopped a few steps into the garden and closed her eyes, bowing her head. "Please tell me you'll forgive me?"

Kipling swallowed and raised her head again, looking up to the blue sky, just the edges of clouds sliding through the patch of visible sky. "Of course," she finally said.

"Good," Mina gushed. "I'm so glad." She sniffed again and seemed to gain her composure. "Are you having a good time?"

Kipling had to laugh at the left turn in conversation as if nothing had happened. "Yes," she admitted. "I'm having an amazing time. We are going to go around London today, and we're having dinner with Sandi and her husband tonight." She paused for a moment before adding, "And I have my interview tomorrow."

Mina sighed. "You know, I think that's been the hardest part of all of this, Kip. I mean, I know I was being a pain in the neck before but once you said you were going to interview — I just — I realized I might lose you." Her last words were a whisper.

Kipling's throat tightened and she had to blink to clear her eyes, a tear escaping despite her trying not to let it. "You'll just have to come to London, that's all."

"Will Grayson be okay with that?"

"Of course," she said without thinking anything different. Clearing her throat, she pressed the home button on her phone and returned to the main screen, opening the text program. "Would you like to see some photos from the wedding?"

"I'd love it."

As she spoke, she attached some of the photos Erika had sent and hit send. "They're probably coming by way of Shanghai or something, but you should get them soon." With the photos off, she walked further into the garden and smiled at a small stone cherub statue hidden amongst a flowering bush she couldn't name. Watson followed her out and rubbed against her leg before bolting off into the shrubs. "How is John?"

"Fine," Mina said with a sigh. " Oh, just got the text. Oh, my god! Kip, these are beautiful." She sighed, long and heavy. "God, he really does love you, doesn't he."

"I certainly hope so."

"Hope what?" Grayson's voice came from behind her.

Kipling turned and smiled wider to see him standing in the open doorway, hands pushed into his pockets. She had appreciated him in a suit in Boston, but there was something so sexy about Grayson Oliver Sherlock Holmes in a pair of jeans faded at all the right spots, a short-sleeved, button-up shirt, and low boots.

"I'm talking to Mina," she confessed and smiled at his slight surprise. "She said she believes you really do love me."

"More than that," he said, walking toward her. "You are my world."

Kipling raised her chin as he neared to hold his gaze, her heart pounding faster, her skin flushing. "Mina, I promise to talk soon. But right now, I feel a kiss coming on."

Mina laughed, and said, "Love you, Kip," before the line closed.

Just in time for Grayson to touch his fingertips to her cheeks and whisper, "I love you," before kissing her.

Chapter Twelve

"The Marylbone campus is less than a ten minute walk from Baker Street," Grayson said as they turned the corner from Marylbone Lane to Wigmore Street, "But I think you'll find the route to the Regent Street campus a lovelier walk."

"Either way, I can't complain about a twenty minute walk to work every day. Should I actually—"

"Ah ah," Grayson interrupted with a squeeze of her hand. "None of that. I highly doubt the university would ask you to come to London if they hadn't fully made up their minds about you."

Kipling sighed, and tipped her chin toward the sun as they walked through a patch between buildings. "I am trying to be as confident as you, but if this doesn't happen, I have some decisions to make."

Grayson stopped walking, and she stopped with him, turning so they faced each other. He still held her hand, but reached for her sunglasses so he could meet her eyes. "Amend that," he said, with a smile he hoped projected the full confidence he felt. "*We* will have decisions to make."

She smiled back. "Okay. *We* will have decisions to make."

Grayson kissed her forehead and handed her glasses back to her.

As she put them back on, he took a moment — not the first of the morning — to admire the woman he'd awoken beside once again. She wore a knee length tailored sheath dress in heather gray and a three-quarter-sleeve jacket in matching tones. He loved her hair down and loose around her shoulders, but for today's interview she'd twisted it into what seemed to him as a precarious roll from her nape to her crown, with tendrils framing her face. She looked every bit the university professor, which enticed him in a way he wouldn't have contemplated before.

Then again, everything about Kipling always enticed him.

They headed down Wigmore for another five minutes, reaching the Regent Street campus of the University of Westminster, a multi-story building of gray with large windows and University of West-minster along the first-floor marquee. While the outside was plain and blended into the city, the interior lobby was bright and ornate, with vaulted ceilings and gold marble walls and pillars.

"Oh, this is beautiful," Kipling said in a hushed voice, with even that carrying in the open space. "There are parts of Boston that are so much like London, it's hard to believe they are different places."

Two steps to the left of the entrance, Grayson took another moment to press a kiss to her brow. "I shall wait here whilst you go off to procure gainful employment."

Kipling chuckled at his elaboration, then sighed and nodded her head. "Thank you."

"For what?"

She smiled, slow and honest. "For walking me here. For waiting for me. For giving me a pep talk. For the coffee on the way. For..." She smiled wider. "For everything."

"And when you come back, offer in hand, you may thank me for the celebratory lunch we'll have on the way home."

While she walked, confident and tall, to the reception desk her heels clicking on the marble floor, Grayson walked to one of the sitting areas and settled into a leather upholstered wingback chair in a position he could see all angles of the lobby, no matter which way Kipling left or returned from. She spoke to the receptionist, and within minutes a middle-aged woman with graying hair twisted at her crown came down the steps at the back of the lobby to greet Kipling. With only a final glance back his way, when he offered another assuring smile, she followed the woman out of the lobby.

Since she'd told him of the interview, Grayson had fought the urge to give Peter Rathborne a ring. Likely just mentioning to the man who Kipling was, and her connection to the Holmes family, would most definitely have assured her position, but she might always wonder if she were at the university based on her own merits. He would tell her later, when she knew she had the professorship because there was no doubt in his mind she would be made an offer. He meant it when he told her they wouldn't have asked her to come from Boston for any other reason than final preparations.

Instead, he took his phone from his jacket breast pocket, having opted for a suit himself that morning so he didn't look shabby beside her elegance, and tapped Sandra's direct line. He unbuttoned his jacket and crossed his legs as he waited. Dinner the night before had been wonderful for Kipling to see Sandra again and to have the opportunity to meet David, but unfortunately, Sandra's investigation hadn't yielded any fruit by the time they arrived in Greenwich.

"Good morning," Sandra cheered when she answered. "Did she get the position?"

"She's just now gone back for the interview," he said, keeping his tone low in the echoing space. "I'll likely not see her for a bit."

"Oh, the suspense is killing me."

"One might think *you* are the one most excited at the possibility of Kipling remaining in London."

"You don't think we'd all benefit from her staying? Trust me, we'd all benefit from your better mood, Boss."

"You sound more like Lynne today. Am I such a tyrant?"

Sandra's laugh was contagious enough to make him smile. "Tyrant, no. But I've no doubt you'll be in a better mood. Regardless, sorry I didn't have information for you last night," Sandra apologized again. "This guy didn't want to be found out."

"Have you made progress this morning?"

"Of a sort, yes. His name is Victor Barriero of Portugal."

Grayson shook his head, switching his phone to the other hand so he could retrieve a small notebook and pen from his jacket. Several tables were situated amongst the chairs, and he shifted to the edge of the chair to utilize the nearest. He recited what he assumed to be the correct spelling of the last name, and Sandra confirmed. "I've not heard of him," he said, staring at the name again as if the answer would spring from the page.

"For good reason. He's practically a ghost, but I dug deep enough to find connections. You're not going to like it."

"I hardly suspected I would be overjoyed by whatever information you discovered."

Sandra chuckled. "There's the boss man we know and love. No, I mean you truly will not be happy. He's an associate of the Howell crime family, with original connections linking him to Nelson and now Langdon."

Grayson clenched his jaw and closed his eyes. Howell had dared touch his family, even if no one had come to harm. To realize what could have happened made Grayson's stomach twist and his blood heat.

"You still there, Boss?"

"Yes," he managed through his tight jaw. "Email me all the details you have on Barriero."

"You're on holiday—"

"And he was in Sussex," he snapped out.

She didn't counter, and all he heard was the click of her computer keys before she said, "On their way. For what it's worth, Grayson, I'm sorry."

"No one will be as sorry as Langdon Howell when next we meet."

"It's a pleasure to meet you, sir," Kipling said, extending her hand to the august man who greeted her as she stepped into his office.

He was tall in a nearly unnatural way, solid, and of perfect stature despite the fact he had to be approaching seventy. His hair was thick, and his face shaved smooth, and he wore a finely tailored gray suit.

"The pleasure is all mine, Miss Branson. Do have a seat." He motioned toward one of the chairs facing his desk and walked around to the back and to his own seat. "Though, if I'm not mistaken, the proper title would now be Doctor Branson. Am I correct?"

"Yes, sir. I completed my studies just last week."

President Rathborne settled in his chair, the leather and workings squeaking at his formidable size. On his burgundy leather blotter was a folder, with her name written on a label on the front. He opened it, placing a pair of reading glasses on his nose. Kipling took a brief moment to glance around the office. It was everything she would imagine of the president of a prestigious school. Books of varying sizes and ages filled shelves from floor to ceiling on two walls, with a window facing the street on the third. The office smelled of leather, old pages, and cigars.

"I hope making the trip didn't prove to be too troublesome," he said, still looking down at the file.

"Oh, not at all. In truth, I had already planned a trip for this week to attend a wedding."

He looked at her over the top of his glasses. "Do you have family in London, Doctor Branson?"

"No, but good friends," she answered, attempting to keep her smile in check. "This isn't the first time I've been to England."

President Rathborne spent the next half hour describing the exact position, one professor of many teaching in the English department. The school offered a variety of English programs, with a focus on literature, creative writing, and comparative languages. While she would be considered a full-time professor, she would likely teach six to eight classes a week, with the schedule varying based on day. By the time he rounded out the description, Kipling hoped she didn't look as giddy as she felt. Excitement bubbled in her veins like the sparkling wine they'd drank at the Sookoo's the night before, and she felt nearly as light-headed now as she did then.

"In truth, Doctor Branson, we have learned all we needed about your qualifications and character through the numerous conversations you'd had with myself and other members of the English department. I have spoken at length with several of your professors, and I've even had the pleasure of reading your doctorate thesis. An intriguing subject."

"Thank you, sir."

"Short of something drastic changing our mind upon your arrival, because I do believe in the authenticity of a face-to-face meeting, we had long since decided you would be our chosen candidate for the position. We are enthused at the idea of bringing some new culture to the university, and wonder if perhaps having an American professor on staff might entice more international students."

It was all she could do not to bounce in her chair. "That's wonderful to hear, sir. I'm thrilled."

President Rathborne took from beneath the folder a small stack of papers. "This is your compensation and contract offer. You are free to take it with you and review it carefully before committing to the position. Perhaps more than any other candidate, your choice comes with the longest list of ramifications."

Kipling took the papers, smiling at the University of Westminster stationary, but forced herself not to begin reading here. While she would probably call President Rathborne within five minutes of making it home, she didn't want to project any kind of unprofessionalism. "Of course. Thank you. I will."

"The position opens for our winter term, at which time the departing professor intends to retire to the country." He chuckled and shook his head. "Lucky bastard. We will assist you in the process of gaining a work visa, and I have no doubt all will be in order by then. We are also happy to offer several housing options to you."

"Actually, I don't believe that will be necessary," Kipling interjected, pausing to take a metered breath. The rapid pounding of her heart made it hard not to stutter. "I am all set in that regard."

"An easy commute to the campus, I hope."

"Quite. It took less than twenty minutes to walk here."

"Splendid. While I feel our meeting might seem short in comparison to the distance you've traveled, I believe our business today is concluded, Doctor Branson. Should you have any questions regarding the offer, be sure to reach out to Jane. She will either assist you or direct your inquiry to me."

He stood, and she stood with him, but rather than extending his hand, he motioned for her to walk with him to the door of his office. "Allow me to see you out. Until you are acquainted with the halls, you are likely to get turned around a bit."

She felt like a hobbit walking beside the giant of a man, having to take three steps for each of his long strides. He was correct in that after two hallways, she did feel like a rat in a maze until the familiar steps leading down to the lobby came into view. Though she kept her attention on taking the steps, she glanced quickly around the lobby until she spotted Grayson seated in one of the large chairs. He looked up when her heels clicked on the marble floor, and with a wide grin, stood. President Rathborne walked her to the entrance side of the reception desk, then extended his hand.

"It was quite the pleasure to meet you, Doctor Branson. I do look forward to working with you."

"Thank you, sir."

President Rathborne looked past her and his smile broadened. "Holmes," he boomed. "What brought you here? Finally willing to take me up on my offer?"

Kipling turned at the sound of Grayson's approaching footsteps, then back to the president. Grayson winked at her when he reached them and stood at her side so he could extend his hand in greeting to President Rathborne, his other hand skimming the small of her back.

"Not yet, sir," Grayson said, pumping the large man's hand. Even with Grayson's height, President Rathborne stood several inches taller. "I'm waiting for you to finish your interview, so I can take this beautiful woman to a celebratory lunch. Are we celebrating?" he asked, looking at Kipling.

She felt like a fish, drowning in air, and could only manage to blink before closing her mouth.

"I certainly hope so," President Rathborne said. "It would be a privilege." He patted a heavy hand on Grayson's shoulder. "Might we be so lucky as to gain two professors?"

Kipling knew she was scowling, but couldn't help it. She had been dropped into the middle of a story and she didn't know the plot. Grayson laughed, taking a half step closer to her so his hand wrapped over her far hip. "Peter has been attempting to entice me to the university since I graduated from Cambridge. This is where Mum taught when I was young before we moved to Sussex."

"Oh," was all Kipling managed to say.

"I remember you sitting under her desk, reading whatever book you could reach. Didn't matter if it was an encyclopedia." He bounced a finger toward Grayson. "I knew then you'd be a brilliant young man. And I was correct. The university would be thrilled to have another Holmes on the academic staff."

"Perhaps one day, Peter." He extended his hand again, and President Rathborne took it. "I have not excluded the idea."

"Your mind is wasted on whatever commodities rubbish you pretend to enjoy," the older man said, leaning toward Grayson. "Think hard on it, son." He then focused again on Kipling. "It was an absolute pleasure to meet you, Doctor Branson. Even if we had met under different circumstances, any friend of the Holmes family is welcome here at the university."

With a final wave, President Rathborne returned the way he'd come and once out of sight, Grayson took her hand and led her a few feet away from the receptionist. "Am I to infer from the conversation he made you an offer?"

Still at a loss, Kipling nodded and managed to look him in the eyes. "Why didn't you say you knew President Rathborne?"

"Because I didn't want to put into your head the very thoughts you have now." He tapped a finger to the spot between and above her eyes. "Yes, I know him. I've known him my entire life. But no, I had no idea until the night before last that he had contacted you. And no, until just now he had no idea you might be affiliated with the family." Grayson curled his hands around her upper arms and crouched to look her level in the eyes. "I had no doubt you would be offered the position, and I wanted no doubt in *your* heart you were given it for any reason other than your own qualifications." He smiled wide and leaned closer. "Which he did, and unless you've suddenly changed your mind, I am about to kiss the next professor at the University of Westminster and the newest resident of London."

Kipling sighed, parting her lips to welcome his kiss. It might be too brief, and restrained for public consumption in a city where public displays of affection weren't all that public, but it warmed her soul and left her giddy. Not just the kiss, but the reality.

London could now be home.

Baker Street could now be home.

Grayson Holmes was now her home.

"Shall we have that celebratory lunch?" he asked when he drew back, running his thumb along her lip.

Kipling smiled and kissed the pad of his thumb. "Maybe later. I'd rather go *home* and celebrate first."

The darkening of his eyes, and the sexy tick of his just-kissed lips into a lopsided smile, left no question whether he understood. Hand in hand, they left the building and turned the way they had come to return to Baker Street. To fill the time, they discussed the process of her gaining a work visa, and Grayson assured her he would likely be able to push the process along should the normal agencies prove to be too slow. For a time, she would be fine simply as a visitor on her passport qualifications. She contemplated calling her parents, but it was still the small hours of the morning in Boston, so she would wait to share her news. They had been thrilled at the prospect, and although a slight glimmer of melancholy had danced through her mother's eyes, both her parents were excited. As it was, they had begun to travel and were outside Boston far more than they were there, and now they would have a strong excuse to visit London.

As they walked the last distance on Baker Street, ahead of them she spotted a young man knocking at the door of 221. He stepped back, making to leave, but Grayson called out to him.

"Charlie! Looking for me?"

The boy turned at his name, grinned wide, and holding his cap to his head jogged toward them. "G'day, Mr. Holmes. I've come to retrieve the car."

"I didn't schedule until Thursday," Grayson said, his expression pinching.

Charlie shrugged. "Mistah Balakrishnan said I was to come today."

"Hold up." Grayson released her hand to retrieve his phone. "I'll give him a call. I had intended to this afternoon. My plans have changed for the week, and I'd rather keep the car." He glanced at Kipling as he put the phone to his ear. "I don't have need for the car most days and keep it in storage. Charlie here—Hello!" He switched from speaking to her to whoever was on the phone. "Yes, this is Grayson Holmes."

Kipling took a couple of steps away from them toward the door, inhaling a deep breath. As she was about to pivot back, a clicking set off her left hearing aid and she flinched. It wasn't particularly loud, but the odd noises always startled her. Especially since Boston when the clicks foreshadowed the explosion that killed Grayson's uncle and changed her life. Grayson was still talking, and she headed for him. Stopping short when the click happened again.

She looked up and down the street, wondering if someone nearby had a high-end camera since they sometimes interfered with her aids. But she saw no one. Someone took photos down by the museum, but it was a smartphone, nothing that would bother her. She continued looking as she walked, reaching Grayson and Charlie again.

"No, I didn't call for retrieval today. It was scheduled for Thursday, and I've not changed it. Yes, of course." He tilted the phone away from his mouth as he apparently waited for Mr. Balakrishnan to come back on the line. "Something wrong?"

Charlie strolled away, hands in his pockets, whistling as he headed for Grayson's beautiful Bentley. It sat exactly where they had parked it the night before upon returning from Sandra's dinner party.

She shook her head and swirled her fingers near her ear,

flinching again at another click. "No, just something…" A cold flush hit her when she realized the clicks were evenly spaced. Not random like someone taking photos.

Grayson lowered his hand, letting the phone leave his ear, his expression pulling as he watched her. "Kipling…" he led.

"Something is—" *Click.*

Grayson grabbed her arm and pulled her away from the direction of the car and 221, putting her behind him as he bolted forward. "Charlie!"

The young man turned, wide grinned, and raised a hand to acknowledge Grayson.

"Get back!" Grayson shouted, motioning to Kipling but running toward the boy. "Charlie, get back! Get away from the car!"

Everything moved in slow motion, but far too quickly for Kipling to react. Panic welled in her throat, choking her, and she tried to shout for Grayson as another click sounded in her ears. She took a step forward, instinctively, as Grayson reached Charlie — who was wide-eyed and slack-jawed — and yanked the boy with him.

The explosion lifted the Bentley several feet off the ground in a fiery ball, and hot air blasted Kipling backward to slam her into the wrought iron fence that ran along the front of the buildings, sucking breath from her lungs. Screams filled the air and fiery chunks of car fell to the street, the air stinking of burning fuel and rubber.

Kipling fell forward on her hands and knees, momentarily unable to decipher any sounds as her hearing aids tried to compensate for the spiked decibels. Everything was muffled, dull. She searched the street, trying to see Grayson through the chaos. Her eyes burned with smoke and acidic air.

"Grayson!" she screamed.

The aids popped and adjusted, all the sounds crashing into her in a chaotic cacophony. Kipling pushed herself off the sidewalk, only momentarily registering the bloodstain on the front of her jacket. She shouted again. Then the ground tilted and came flying toward her as she collapsed into darkness.

Chapter Thirteen

"**W**here is Grayson Holmes!"

Her throat hurt, the only indicator she had that the words made it free. She knew the nurses holding her arms were telling her to calm down, but she wouldn't until someone gave her an answer. Pain stiffened her body; her head throbbed, her skin prickled and pulled tight along her brow, and her lungs felt like steel wool rubbing together, but none of it compared to the fist squeezing her heart. She kicked out, her foot making contact with the rolling table beside the bed, and it flew backward. The crash of trays and charts had to practically shake the walls because the sound actually was loud enough to break through her deaf silence.

A woman in a white doctor's lab coat came into view, a needle in her hand, and she headed for the IV pole beside the bed.

"No! Don't you dare!" Kipling screamed, not caring how it tore at her throat. The doctor made eye contact with her, needle held still. "I am fully aware and am perfectly capable of demanding you do *not* sedate me. Answer my question! Where. Is. Grayson. Holmes."

The woman turned her head with a sharp jerk toward the door, and Kipling followed her shift. MI6 Director Jeffrey Cooper, a portly, grayed man Kipling had met only once, led the way. Sandra Sookoo followed, with the giant of a man — Angus "Mac" Hennessey — and Lynne Connolly right behind her. The director barked out something and immediately the nurses holding Kipling's arms released her like she was on fire and the doctor moved away just as quickly.

"Sandi," Kipling called out.

Director Cooper went straight to the doctor, and Sandi came to her. IV lines and pulse oximeter lines tangled when they hugged, and when she pulled back, Kipling's friend took her face in her hand and looked her in the eyes.

"Bloody hell, Kip," was all she said.

"Where is Grayson?" Kipling asked again, her eyes burning with tears. "Please, tell me. Where is he? They won't tell me anything. They won't even *look* at me when they talk to me."

"Sweetie, that's because they don't know where Grayson is," she read on Sandi's lips, turned down in a frown. "We don't know where Grayson is."

"How could you not know?" She sought out one of the nurses, pointing to demand her attention. "Where are my hearing aids?"

She shook her head, and looked to the doctor, wide-eyed.

Everyone in the room seemed to scatter, bustling about until finally one of the frazzled nurses came toward her, hand out and palm open, with her hearing aids. As Kipling snatched them up, Sandi touched her arm, and she read the final sentence on her friend's lips before turning them on.

"The doctor doesn't recommend you wear them because of the blast. They might hurt."

"I know damn well they'll hurt," she said through clenched teeth, bracing herself against the shot of pain she knew would come as soon as they were in place and chimed on. The jolt was no surprise, but still brought burning tears to her eyes. Every part of her ear canal hurt, right down to the eardrum, likely a result of the sudden pressure and magnified sound at the blast.

Right now, pain was nothing.

Everything in the room snapped on like turning on a television. Voices. Beeping equipment. Every sound was a slice through her head. She didn't care.

"We will notify you if she requires any further medical intervention," Director Cooper said to the doctor and raised his arm to motion them out of the room.

Neither the doctor nor the nurses spoke as they left, leaving the door open. It took all the restraint Kipling had not to yank the IV from her hand. She did remove the O_2 monitor on her finger and tossed it away. With every moment another ache or pain moved to the forefront of her awareness. She hadn't hurt this badly after jumping into the frozen Charles River.

Her stomach twisted at the memory.

"Will someone *please* tell me where Grayson is?" she begged, and the question grabbed the attention of his team, bringing them all around her bed, Director Cooper taking his place at the foot.

"Was he with you prior to the explosion?" Director Cooper asked, and the levelness of his tone made her blood heat.

"Of course he was," she snapped. Just as quickly, her ribs squeezed around her lungs and she couldn't take a breath, her heart pounding hard enough to burst through her chest. "He pushed me back and ran toward the car — toward the young man — telling him to get down. Get away."

"Toward his own car?"

"Yes, the Bentley."

"What young man?" the director asked.

Kipling shook her head. "He called him Charlie. That's all I know. He worked for the garage where Grayson stores his car. There was some kind of mix-up about when the car was supposed to be picked up."

"Did Grayson know there was a bomb?" Mac asked, his deep, rumbling voice at least tinged with emotion. Why that soothed Kipling, she couldn't define.

She nodded but shrugged. "He suspected the same time I did—"

"Why did you think there was a bomb?" Cooper demanded.

"My hearing aids. They were clicking. Just like they did at the university before the bomb went off there."

"Had you driven the car today?" Lynne asked.

She shook her head and looked at Sandi. "No. We drove to Sandi's last night for dinner. When we left today, we walked."

"Where did you go today?" Director Cooper asked.

The questions came at her so rapidly, she felt like she was in a pinball machine. "The University of Westminster on Regent Street," she answered, wincing when a sharp stab of pain shot from one ear to the other. "We were just getting home—"

"Why were you there?"

"What does it matter," she snapped. "Grayson was *there*. I saw him run toward Charlie. Then the car—" The words choked her and she clamped her mouth shut with enough force her teeth clicked. Sandi laid a hand on Kipling's shoulder, but she jerked away. "He was there," she managed to whisper. "How can he not be there? What about Charlie?"

"Several bystanders were brought in for treatment," Director Cooper explained, his voice still annoyingly flat. "Only one dead, found near the car, but we've confirmed it's not Grayson."

"How did you know to come here?" she asked, looking away from the pompous jerk of a boss, focusing on Sandi.

"Something like this always draws attention, but when we heard it was on Baker Street..." She looked away from Kipling, to the other members of the team, and back. "Well, of course, we assumed."

"Once we pitched up," Mac said, and Kipling looked up at him. "We got names o some o the folk there, and somebody found yer ID."

"Have you talked to everyone? How can he *not* be here?"

"We don't know yet," Lynne said, for the first time her voice lacking any snarky edge. "Honestly, we'd hoped you would tell us he was off to Tesco's."

Kipling let herself drop back onto the raised head of the bed, suddenly her own body weight too much to bear. She pressed her lips together and swallowed hard, tears burning their way down her cheeks.

"Where are you, Grayson?" she whispered, as much a prayer as a question.

Every muscle ached, down to the bone. Ligaments felt short, tight, and strained to move. The pain was the first sensation to push through Grayson's haze, and before he even moved, a moan rolled from his heavy chest. The worst pain of a migraine he'd ever known squeezed his skull, and he dreaded opening his eyes.

But the need overrode the dread, and he blinked then squinted, trying to raise his arm to shield his eyes. White bandaging wrapped his left arm, spots of red seeping through, and the movement pulled at the skin beneath with a fiery burn. It took a few moments, but his vision adjusted to the room, and his first observation was the most disconcerting. He was not in hospital. And if he wasn't in hospital, where was he?

From his vantage point, he assessed his surroundings as far as he could see. He was in a sizeable bedroom, well appointed, almost opulent. Brocade wallpaper walls in a dusty blue matched the blue of the bedding and the heavy drapes framing the windows blocked with security bars.

His nerves prickled with awareness and apprehension.

Before attempting to move, he did a quick mental inventory from head to toe, noting areas with the most discomfort but with a few testing movements, he acknowledged nothing was broken. Likely bruised, and good, but no breaks. With careful movements, continuing to test his physical abilities, he eased back the bedding. Whoever his host might be, they had removed his suit and he wore basic pyjama pants. His sides were bound, and upon sitting up, he understood why, and reassessed his belief nothing was broken. With another deep breath — or as deep as he dared — he suspected one break and possibly three fractures.

He also realized it was likely whoever had seen to his medical needs weren't physicians, since binding broken ribs so tightly was a treatment no longer generally practiced. The plaster on the back of his hand implied an IV, but the bruising implied an unpracticed hand.

Sitting on the edge of the bed, trying not to slouch to irritate his ribcage, he catalogued the rest of the injuries he could see. The bandaging on his arm covered from mid-forearm to shoulder, and based on the edge of skin showing where the bandages stopped, he guessed burns. How severe, he wouldn't be able to determine without removing the bandages, but because there was pain probably no more than partial thickness second degree, at worst. The sting told him the burn wasn't deep enough to cause excessive nerve damage. At least there was that.

It wasn't until he stood that the sharp jab in his ankle added sprain to the list of injuries. He cursed and reached out to find balance with one of the foot posts of the four-poster bed, gingerly shifting his weight to his right foot until he determined he would be able to walk, albeit gingerly. And with slow progression, he reconnoitered the room. The windows were barred and locked, and the glass had steel mesh reinforcement. No escape route there, especially since he appeared to be on the first floor with no balcony or ledge from which to maneuver.

The door exiting the room was also locked.

The accommodations were comfortable, but the intent was clear.

Grayson worked his way around the room to an open door with bathroom attached; only then did he have a full view of himself. Whoever his host might be, they had taken great care in treating and bandaging the cuts and abrasions on the left side of his face. One large plaster ran the edge of his hairline, and the red stain said the cut below had been deep, and likely the cause of his headache as well.

They had even, apparently, cut his hair, which implied the

flames had done more than burn his skin. His hair had grown longer than he usually wore, but his attention as of late had not been on making time for the barber. Now, the rebellious waves had been trimmed back to a close, neat cut.

Kipling wouldn't be pleased.

It was that simple thought that thrust his calm analysis into heart-pounding panic. A sound from the bedroom, the distinct click of a lock being disengaged, had Grayson stumbling out of the bath to face his host.

Langdon Howell.

Though clearly younger than Nelson Howell whom Grayson had encountered in previous years, Langdon was no doubt family to the dead criminal. Dark blond hair hung over his tanned forehead, the golden tone of his skin a testament to his Portuguese ancestry, and although Kipling had described him as having a mustache while in Boston, he was now clean-shaven, his otherwise smooth skin marred in spots by old pock scars. Not enough to diminish his appearance, but enough to be noted. He was dressed like any proper English gentleman, in a light gray suit and polished shoes, his hands tucked behind his back.

He was not alone, for if he had been Grayson would have ignored the various pains and hindrances and would have attacked the man on the spot. Likely knowing this, Langdon had entered the room with the escort of two very large, obviously armed henchmen.

"I'm pleased to see you are able to leave your bed," he said, and if Grayson hadn't known the lengths to which this man had gone, he might actually be convinced of concern. "Do be careful and refrain from doing anything foolish."

"Where is Kipling?" he demanded, taking a disciplined step forward, refusing to allow any single point of pain to hinder his movements in any visible way.

Howell sighed, long and heavy, and had the audacity to smile. "It does my heart good to know I may hold some small bit of responsibility for the perfection of the match between you and Miss Branson. Oh, apologies." He quirked his smile. "Doctor Branson."

"Where is she?" Grayson demanded again.

"Not here," Howell said with a cant of his head. "Bringing her here didn't serve my purpose. But I assure you, she has been well cared for. At last report, she was adamantly demanding to be released from London Royal. Your team is with her. Would you like to see?"

Not waiting for Grayson's response, Howell walked past him to a flat television mounted on the wall. He turned it on, but it was clearly not set up for viewing the news but rather as an interface to a computer somewhere else. Howell proceeded to taunt Grayson with images that made his blood heat and his gut twist. He didn't begin with the events of the day, but rather Boston.

"Holmes, I believe that perhaps on some level you and I are very much alike. People are open books to me. I can predict their behaviors. I can read their unspoken language. But where you prefer to read the book given to you, I prefer to write it."

With each click on the small control Howell held and pointed at the screen, new images filled the screen. Images of Kipling on the campus of her university, bundled against the cold of winter. Kipling was seated in the emergency vehicle after the explosion at the school. Then the same evening Grayson spoke to her as she waited to be taken to hospital. The image taunted him by capturing the moment he had offered his scarf.

Grayson clenched his jaw and curled his fists, despite the pain the tension shot through him. "You have made your point, and in abundance, Howell."

"Oh, not yet, Holmes." He smiled, a strange, pleased, almost dreamy expression coupled with a sigh. "I cannot begin to express the satisfaction I feel to speak your name to you directly. It has taken us far too long to meet."

"I agree," Grayson said, not attempting to restrain the snarl tugging at his lips. "Wholeheartedly."

Howell's grin tugged at one corner, and he turned back to the screen. "It took me months to discover Kipling," he said, her name tainted with a false fondness that made Grayson's skin crawl. "You were quite the challenge, my perfect opponent. What kind of woman would wholly capture your attention?"

More photos of them in those short weeks. Outside Grayson's residence hotel while he stayed in Boston, the night she had left moments before shots were fired. She had heard the click, but they had passed it off as inconsequential.

"Do you think you have revealed something I didn't know?" Grayson seethed. "We are both aware you manipulated our meeting — you *killed* people — playing your game."

Howell didn't respond, but continued the slideshow. Photos chronicling the build of their relationship during Grayson's short stay in Massachusetts, right down to the moment he kissed her goodbye at the international terminal of Logan Airport.

"I am that obvious to you, I suppose." He turned away from the monitor, the image of Kipling alone, tears in her eyes, frozen on the screen. "You do recall what your great-grandfather said about obvious facts. There is nothing so deceptive."

Grayson didn't gift him with a response, remaining silent as he looked past Howell to the image, rage twisting in his chest. The pain of standing straight and unmoving approached near unbearable, but he wouldn't yet concede. He couldn't yet determine if Langdon Howell truly was an insane sociopath, or if his words and actions were merely playing a part, a game he wanted Grayson to participate in with him.

"I've been studying you, Mr. Holmes, in minute detail, and I learned something quite intriguing. Would you like to know what I've learned?"

Grayson still refused to answer.

Howell continued without need for acknowledgment. Perhaps Grayson's silence was the answer he needed. "I've learned truth and fiction often walk hand in hand. I've learned we are whom we are born from, and I've learned that with the right twist of fate, any man can be broken. Though sometimes his own breaking comes at the destruction of others."

Jaw clenched to the point of excruciating pain, Grayson cut his gaze from the monitor to Howell.

And saw the flicker of acknowledgment in the man's cold eyes.

With a sigh, Howell took three slow paces toward Grayson, stopping just outside his easy reach. The two heavyweights moved with him, staying within easy subduing distance. Grayson wouldn't have a chance to hurt Howell, not here and not now.

"I will admit disappointment when you didn't assume betrayal on the part of Kipling Branson; after all, I had laid out the pieces so well to lead you to that conclusion. That was my error. I revealed too much truth, until you believed it a lie." He pointed a finger at Grayson's face when he said it, nearly touching the end of Grayson's nose. "An error I shall not repeat. You see, in my study of you I learned that of all things you guard, your heart is the most untouchable prize. I had assumed you would appreciate Doctor Branson's mind, her wit, and her vulnerability." He canted his head, his eyes shifting as he studied Grayson with a depth that made his exposed skin crawl. "I had also assumed that while she might gain access to your life, she would not gain such unadulterated and unrestrained access to your heart."

He tapped Grayson's chest and turned away before acknowledging the flinch it inspired. "You did the unpredictable, Holmes. You actually fell in love." He laughed and looked back at Grayson. "How utterly serendipitous."

"What is your point?" Grayson hissed through clenched teeth.

"My point is that you have made the game all the more fulfilling for me. We're playing a game, aren't we, Holmes? You. Me. Holmes. Howell. As it has been for generations, except your bloodline gave up the game for a bit. Didn't they? The son of Sherlock Holmes a simple doctor. Grandson an engineer. But his great-grandson… therein lies the prize. The game begins again."

"Why?" Grayson demanded. "Because your entire family is nothing more than a long line of criminals?"

"There is something elegant to maintaining the family business." Langdon Howell walked to one of the two chairs in the room, sitting with a sigh as he crossed his legs. He motioned to the other chair. "Do sit, Holmes. You look absolutely ghostly."

Grayson stood in his place.

Howell arched his eyebrows and shook his head. "I can see you are resistant and unwilling to follow along. Explaining is so dull, but if I must."

He pointed his remote toward the monitor again, and the slideshow renewed. Apparently bored with the game, he flipped quickly through a series of photos, all of Kipling, and all taken in Boston in the last few weeks. The timeline was evident as the snow melted, and she exchanged heavy coats for lighter jackets, and eventually shirtsleeves and dresses. Photos ranged from the university campus to the bookstore where she worked, to outings with Mina and a man Grayson didn't immediately recognize but assumed was the John Allen of whom she had spoken. Kipling had described him as the linebacker type, referencing American football, and this man seemed to fit the bill. Tall and broad, solid. But with Howell's intent on moving quickly through the images to some future goal, nothing more registered other than a frustrated niggling.

The rage turned to fury, escalating to a dangerous point when the photos changed location. Changed continent completely.

Sussex.

Shirl's wedding. He had recently learned one of the guests was a Howell associate, but the images taunted Grayson with how close Howell's touch had been. Perhaps not as lovely as the photos Erika had shared, the stealthy photos made clear the focus of the images was Grayson and Kipling. The unwanted guest had managed to steal frozen in time the moments Grayson explained the empty chair. Greg's absence. He'd captured Grayson's pain.

"This is our game, Holmes. Tit for tat. Swings and roundabouts. Everything comes back to the same point. Howell hurts Holmes. Holmes hurts Howell, ad nauseam, ad infinitum. In perpetuity" He clicked through the images, moving from Sussex to London.

When he paused again, Grayson's stomach turned.

The image was grainer than the others, likely indicating it had been taken from a distance and magnified, but the moment was undeniable. Were it not for the placement of furniture and the privacy allotted by his window curtains, the intimate moment on Monday afternoon, when they had made love, would have been brazenly displayed. Only shadows and silhouettes, but his memory response was visceral.

"You sodding bastard."

Grayson lunged forward. Howell's guards did the same. Breath-stealing pain irradiated his body as he slammed into their formidable bodies, massive arms wrenching him away from the unfazed Howell. Grayson groaned, swallowing the scream, and the room wavered in a haze of black and red spots.

"Do have a seat, Holmes," Howell said with deathly calm, and without care, Grayson was deposited in the chair previously offered.

Sweat covered him, and he fought the waves of nausea, fought his mind's desire to slip into unconsciousness, and fought the urge to attack again despite it all. Sucking in air through a tight jaw, Grayson wrapped one arm around his own body, his other hand gripping hard the arm of the chair until the pain ebbed enough he could see.

Howell hadn't moved, calm and almost serene. When Grayson finally managed to raise his head, perspiration running in his eyes, Howell smiled. "I do appreciate your righteous enthusiasm, Holmes." He sighed and shifted in his seat, smoothing a hand over the front of his suit. "I fear, however, your constitution won't hold out much longer. Thus, I'll hurry this along so you might rest with some peace."

He changed the screen again, this time to the outside of Baker Street. Howell scrolled through the images in quick succession, so quickly it was almost equivalent to watching a flipbook. Grayson pushed Kipling back, in the opposite direction of the car, and ran forward. Kipling screamed. The entire monitor was consumed with the blazing fire of the explosion, and his heart pounded viciously, scanning the screen. Then an image of Kipling lying on the side-walk. He couldn't breathe, his thoughts floating in a haze induced by rage, pain, and panic.

"I assure you, she is fine. Here is proof."

One final photo was taken through the doorway of a crowded hospital room. Grayson catalogued the inhabitants. Jeffery. Mac. Lynne. Sandra.

And Kipling.

She was bandaged, clearly bruised, but enraged. For a moment, for only the briefest moment, Grayson calmed.

"She will be sent home soon, though it stands to be proven where *home* will be," Howell said. "My money is on Baker Street, of course." He clicked off the monitor, and when it went black, focused on Grayson. "I told you I spent a great deal of time carefully selecting her as a diversion for you. The absolute poetic plunge into love you've experiences is just…as the Americans might say…frosting." Howell uncrossed his legs and sat forward, resting his elbows on his knees but looking at Grayson. "Now, I must know if she is worthy of the game."

Grayson sucked in several breaths through his nose, seeking strength as unconsciousness taunted him. "What game?"

"Our game, Holmes. A game is no fun if the players aren't worthy." He sat back and tugged at his trouser leg to smooth a wrinkle. "I selected Doctor Branson for her intelligence, her subtle beauty, and her even more subtle personality. I intend to put Doctor Branson to the test. If she passes, then you live on to continue the game. If she isn't as clever as we believe." He sighed and shrugged. "Then you both die. On this you have my word."

Chapter Fourteen

"**A**car bomb in London let alone on historical Baker Street, gets some wicked attention. Your parents are going to flip, probably jump overboard, and swim home when they see this."

Kipling kept her eyes closed, her head leaning against the back window of the Sookoo's car, her phone in her lap as she tried to talk down her best friend. It felt like days since she'd been home, not twelve hours. The hospital wanted her to stay overnight, but she'd argued until they conceded as long as someone stayed with her. Sandra volunteered, and David had come for them both. Beyond having someone to stay with her, Director Cooper stated — with a tone as level and cold as a frozen river — it was best she be in the company of someone who might be able to protect her should another attempt be made.

Should another attempt be made…

How cold.

Exhaustion sat heavy on her shoulders, and every part of her body hurt, but nothing ached worse than her heart.

"I know," she said, barely able to whisper. Her throat was raw, her soul was worse. "I talked to Grayson's mother this afternoon. She's devastated." The memory of Annalise's tears and strained prayers still squeezed her chest and made her heart ache. She had to swallow in an attempt to hold back the choking swell. "She called me when she couldn't reach Grayson."

Silence lingered until Mina sighed, sad and long. "I'm sorry, sweetie."

What could she say?

"Tell me what the doctor said," Mina urged.

Kipling opened her eyes to see where they were, but not knowing London, she couldn't really tell. Sandra had said it would take nearly half an hour to get home to Baker Street from Royal Hospital, but because that was the hospital favored by MI6, once she was identified, she'd been sent there.

"No long-term injuries," she tried to say, but her voice cracked. Sandi looked over her shoulder from the front seat and swung her arm back with a takeaway paper cup, holding it out to Kipling. "Tea," she mouthed, and Kipling took it with a nod and silent "Thank you." After taking a sip, the warmth soothing her throat, she tried again. "They said if I had been closer, it would have been worse."

Closer…like Grayson.

She had to suck in a sharp breath and swallow hard to keep the sob at bay, but the tears still ran down her cheeks.

"Oh, sweetie…" Mina whispered. "I'm so sorry. I don't know what to say or do—"

"There's nothing," Kipling whispered, her voice nearly gone. "They don't know what happened to him, Mina. He's just…*gone*."

"But, that's a good thing, right? I mean, it's better than the alternative that they found him and…" Thankfully, she didn't finish. "What's happening now?"

It took her a few moments to be able to speak, and when she finally did, it was on the end of a deep breath. "Sandra and David are taking me home. His director still has people searching for him, but they have nothing to go on. The director said it's likely whoever did this also took him, and until they make a move, we're at a stalemate."

"Do they have any ideas?"

"Considering who he is and what he does..." she answered, leaving the obvious rest of the statement unsaid. She slid a look toward Sandi, who staunchly kept her focus forward. "Though I suspect some might have ideas they're not sharing."

She gave Sandi credit. She didn't even flinch.

Didn't mean Kipling didn't suspect.

Giving her a reprieve from speaking for a few minutes, Mina provided her best long-distance medical opinion, asking Kipling a series of specific questions about her injuries. She relayed what she remembered that the doctors had said, in the most basic terms she could recall. Her throat was raw from the heat and chemicals blasted into the air; her lungs had been compressed, like having the wind knocked out of her from a fall. Her ears still hurt. Just like she'd experienced after the explosion in Boston, the aids had protected her ears, and yet the pressure of the blast had still done damage. Unlike then, she refused to go without the aids. She wanted to be sure to hear everything.

Her cuts and scrapes were from debris, but nothing requiring anything more than a plaster or gauze bandage, as the doctor had said. The overall pain she felt was from the sudden tensing of her body when it braced against impact, comparable to the aches and pains after an accident. Sometimes it was nice to have a doctor as a best friend, sometimes not so much. Right now, Kipling fell somewhere in between. Ultimately, Mina's best advice was to rest. Let her body heal. Sleep, eat, drink, and take the prescribed medications...

The idea of eating turned her stomach, and sleep seemed impossible, despite her exhaustion. She made no promises, especially since she'd quickly looked up the name of the drug on one of the bottles, and it was a sedative. She'd had to demand three times they didn't sedate her and didn't appreciate their continued efforts. Sedation was the last thing she needed.

She needed Grayson.

Finally, the neighborhood looked familiar and she believed they were on Marylbone Road, which meant they were nearing Baker Street. Every muscle tightened, her heart preparing herself for what she might see. It was late, nearing midnight, so the street would be dark; didn't mean she wouldn't see the destruction left by the explosion.

"We're almost home," she said, shifting with a wince and groan to sit up straighter. "I'll call you tomorrow."

"Hey, before you go," Mina said, and Kipling paused her thumb over the red disconnect button. "By chance, before all this, had you talked to John?"

"John? No. I haven't talked to him since he was in the call with you over the weekend. He texted me Monday, just a hello. But nothing since. Why?"

Mina sighed. "I haven't seen or heard from him since Tuesday. I sent him the pictures you sent me, and nothing since. Not your problem right now. I was just curious. Promise me you'll rest, Kip."

"Gotta go. We're home," she said as David pulled up along the curb across the street and down a bit from Baker Street. She didn't wait for Mina to argue the lack of her promise and disconnected.

"Hang on, love," David said from behind the wheel, his soft voice and smooth Trinidad accent both comforting and stern. "Let me help."

Kipling waited obediently. Both he and his wife exited the car, and he came to her door, opening it to offer his arm. Moving was slow and painful, every major muscle group protesting the smallest action. She was thankful the hospital had let her leave in soft cotton, loose-fitting scrubs and slippers rather than having to wear home the skirt suit and heels she'd been wearing. Not that the suit was ever wearable again. Bloodstains and rips ruined it. David gently eased an arm behind her and supported her as she stood, and as soon as she was clear of the door, Sandra shut it and took up her place on Kipling's other side.

Once in the street, Kipling took a fortifying breath and looked toward the place where Grayson's Bentley had been parked just hours before. Blue and white "Police Line Do Not Cross" tape segregated a section of the street, with danger signs and cones set up to divert vehicles. The car was gone, or what might have remained of it. MI6, no doubt, had taken over the investigation and clean-up and wanted all evidence secure and removed. It was difficult to determine in the dark, even with the few streetlights, but Kipling thought she saw charred black spots around the whole area. Some of the buildings nearest the explosion area had tarps or boards over their broken windows.

"Come on, Kip," Sandra said, urging her forward. "There will be plenty to agonize over tomorrow. Let's get you inside."

Non-movement seemed the worst thing for her because after sitting in the car for half an hour the first few steps to cross Baker Street were the most painful. But by the time they reached the door, the stiffness had already eased enough she could move without feeling like a zombie. The light over the door, apparently a motion-detecting light, came on when they approached. The light let her see that, unlike the other windows on Baker Street, Grayson's windows weren't broken. One had a mild crack in the glass, but none were shattered. She paused, scowled, and looked to the next building further away from the blast, and the windows were broken.

"Shatterproof glass," Sandra said, apparently reading the question on Kipling's face. "Can't be too careful."

Sandra took from her pocketbook a set of keys and flipped them until she found the one she wanted, and Kipling pushed aside the brief pinch of embarrassment that a member of his team had a key she herself didn't. But in truth, she'd only been there a couple of days and while Grayson had specifically said he would go to a locksmith for a duplicate, their time had been occupied with other things. Namely each other. Since they were together, the need didn't seem pressing.

"Do you know the code?" Sandra asked just before opening the door. "He changes it frequently."

At least in this Kipling could help. She nodded, and once Sandra opened the door and they stepped in, Kipling went to the security pad and disarmed the alarm. As soon as the door closed, Watson ran down the stairs sounding more like an elephant than a cat, wailing his discontent at being left alone for so long. Albeit only hours.

"Do we need to see to anything before getting you to bed?" Sandra asked.

Kipling shook her head and stepped free of the couple, taking stiff but steady steps to the bottom of the stairs. Right now, she absolutely hated the two flights of stairs to Grayson's second-floor bedroom. She had no illusion of sleeping but knew they would insist she try. "No. I don't think so." She paused before taking the first step, suddenly feeling like a complete stranger in the house, and her chest tightened. "Um…" she managed, then swallowed and looked back at them. "There's a guest room on the first floor at the front, or on the second floor at the top of the stairs. Honestly, I don't know if it's made up or not. I—"

Sandra crossed to her and laid a comforting hand on her arm. "We'll figure it out. Do you want help going upstairs?"

She shook her head and sucked in a shaky breath. "No. The more I move the better I am. I'll be fine." She looked from Sandra to David, his perpetual smile actually making her feel a degree better. "Thank you, both of you."

"Nonsense, love," David said, then took off his newsboy hat to reveal his smooth scalp — save for the short, dark hair that circle from ear to ear along the back of his head — and crouched to pet Watson, who was making friends. "Off to bed with you. We'll make a round of the place, make sure all is locked up."

She nodded and gripped the banister, using her arms as much as her legs to climb the steps. At the first landing, she thought she'd need to stop, but the movement felt good and she kept going. It wasn't until the second landing that the pressure in her throat threatened to choke her; not of effort, but of sorrow. The house felt empty, far too quiet, without Grayson. How would she do this when he went away? She refused to accept he wasn't coming back now, but he was an MI6 officer, and his profession demanded absence. The house was hollow without him now; how would she stand it?

She swallowed and walked the short distance to the bedroom door. She would because the alternative was to not be here at all, and her heart already knew this place was home. Weary beyond just the fatigue saturating her bones, she pushed open the door and stepped into the shadowed room. Moonlight and streetlights came through the sheer curtains, casting lines of light across the bed and floor.

The creak of floorboards might have been lost in the day, with traffic and life outside, but in the midnight stillness, the sound was as loud as a freight train. Kipling gasped and turned, a cold rush of fear washing over her when she caught movement in the shadows. She stumbled back, bumping into the closed bedroom door.

"Where is Ollie?" demanded a completely unfamiliar male voice, only the slightest lilt of an accent lacing the words. "Kip…"

She gasped at her name and turned, fumbling for the doorknob as the shadow moved closer, the floor creaking again beneath his weight. Her mind told her to scream for Sandra, but the croak that came from her raw, abused throat wouldn't have drawn their attention if they were at the end of the hall, never mind two stories down.

His hand came down on her shoulder and she tried to scream again, reacting instinctively with the lessons drilled into her head in her self-defense classes. She cupped her right hand over her left fist and used her elbow as a ram, shoving backward, coming in contact with a solid torso and pain ricocheted through her from her abused limbs. She lifted a foot to slam down on his arch, but a massive arm wrapped around her, both pinning her to him and lifting her off the floor so she lost any leverage. A large hand covered her mouth, but with only enough pressure to hold her still, not hard or rough. He eased her down again, but didn't release his restraining hold.

"Kip, I'm not going to hurt you," he said beside her ear. The accent was gone, replaced with a completely familiar voice.

She gasped and stilled. It couldn't be.

"Will you listen if I let go?"

She nodded, if for no other reason than to be free. Promises made to a stranger who had broken into her home and into her bedroom meant absolutely nothing as far as she was concerned. He set her down and released his hold. Kipling bolted away, flipped the light switch on the wall, and spun around to slam her back against the wall, her hand on the knob ready to run.

Then froze in her place.

And stared.

Shocked into silence.

John Allen.

He raised his hands, holding them palms out, and took a step back from her. Kipling stared so long her eyes burned and she had to blink, freeing tears to run down her cheeks. John's gaze shifted, scanning her from her hospital-provided slippers likely to the bandages on her forehead, and his features pinched.

"Jeezus, Kip, I'm sorry. I didn't realize — did I hurt you?"

The accent was back again, subtle and barely there, but certainly not the Boston "born and raised" accent she'd known for weeks from the man standing in her London bedroom. She sucked in a hard breath that pinched pain through her bruised sides. Blinking hard, she wondered for a moment if she'd somehow made it to the bedroom and actually fallen asleep, and this was some kind of bizarre, trauma-induced dream.

"Kip," he said again, shifting his stance to be square in her line of sight. "Kip, I'm sorry. This isn't...it wasn't supposed to happen like this."

"Why are you here?" she croaked out.

"Mina showed me the pictures from the wedding," he explained, taking a tentative step toward her. "There was a man in the background. Did Ollie say anything to you about him?"

She squinted, staring at him, trying desperately to think straight. "No. He didn't — why did you—"

Kipling slapped her hand over her own mouth, a realization she both fully understood but couldn't accept slamming hard into her, as hard as the explosion that had knocked her down. She heard herself mumble "Oh, my god..." even though her brain couldn't process the reality.

"Kip, honey, come sit. You've got me worried."

He reached for her, but she shoved away his hand, moving free of the space between him and the wall. Kipling stumbled back until her hips bumped the side of the bed and she used the mattress as support. Her legs wanted to give out beneath her, but she refused to give in. She stared at him, shaking her head, and finally dared voice her conclusion.

"Greg?"

He straightened, drawing back his shoulders, a melancholy smile pulling at his lips. "No one has called me that in a very, very long time."

She finally gave in to the weight of a realization she wasn't entirely sure she was ready to accept, sinking onto the edge of the bed. A prickling sensation danced up her spine, bubbling in her blood, a contradiction between fear that still gripped her chest and an acceptance of something so beautiful, but so impossible, it made her dizzy. "How?" She shook her head. "I don't understand. Why were you in Boston?"

He crossed the space to her, but Kipling felt no urge to move away, and he crouched in front of her so she had to look down at him. Only then did she note the slightest difference between the man she'd known in Boston and this one. The hair was the same, the face — including the small, almost indiscernible scars — but his eyes had changed. They were no longer blue, but reminiscent of the twist of heredity Grayson had said followed the Holmes line. Blues and greys mingled in an unbalanced swirl of color, not disturbing, and possibly not even noticeable to someone who didn't bother to look close enough to see, but they were the eyes of a Holmes.

She didn't realize she was crying until he raised a hand and brushed his thumb across her cheek. "I was there because Ollie asked me to protect you. Take care of you."

Kipling shook her head, trying to piece it all together. She had to be dreaming, or she was just so tired her brain wouldn't put together the pieces laid out in front of her. "How could he have done that? You're supposed to be—"

"Dead?" He nodded, and smiled, but it was without emotion. "I'm supposed to be. Nearly was. Six made a choice when I was unable to argue against it, and by the time I could, the lie had become truth. But I knew Ollie wasn't ever convinced. I couldn't contact him, couldn't tell him." When his smile hitched this time, it spread to his eyes. "When he took a blind chance and sent a message to what should have been the equivalent of a black hole, I couldn't…I had to do what he asked. Even if he didn't know." He cleared his throat and rubbed his thumb across his lower lip. "And even if I pissed off everyone in the upper levels of MI6."

"Why?" she demanded. "Do you have any idea what it did to him? I didn't know him then, but I know him *now*, and I know it's tearing him apart. How could you let him—"

"I had no choice," he said sharply, then closed his eyes and turned away for a moment, his lips pressed together. A deep breath tugged at his shoulders, and he looked at her again. "I've hated lying to you," he said, his voice heavy. "More than that, I've hated lying to Ollie. But, it was necessary, and I swear I will explain. But when I can explain to him as well." He pressed his lips together, studying her. "Kip, where is he?"

In one hard breath, the tears of shock and realization turned into sorrow and she sucked in a hard sob, shaking her head. "I don't know," she cried. "The car — he ran toward the car—" Every word choked her until she couldn't breathe. "They can't find him."

John — Greg — shifted to the bed beside her, wrapping her in his arms. She hadn't let it smother her, hadn't let it be real, not until that moment and she drowned in the reality.

"We'll find him," Greg said, rubbing his palm up and down her arm. "I'm sick of this game, sick of hiding. I'm done. We're going to find him, and we're going to end this."

Kipling only had a second to react when Sandra knocked three times on the door and called her name before opening the door. "We're about to go to bed—" Before Kipling could speak or move, a gun she didn't even know Sandra had was in her hand and trained on Greg.

Greg pulled back from her, hands in the air. "Hey, Sandi."

"Get up," Sandi snapped, motioning with the muzzle of her gun. "Get up! Get away from her!"

He complied, standing, and took a step away from the bed.

"Sandi, it's okay," Kipling said, snuffing her nose. "It's—"

"No, Kip," Greg said, holding his palm toward her to stop. "She's going to need to figure it out. And you will, won't you, Sandi." It wasn't a question, but a statement of fact.

"How did you get in here," Sandi demanded, moving to put herself between Kipling and Greg.

He grinned, a crooked smirk that once again tugged at Kipling's heart because it was so reminiscent of Grayson. So much so it made her heart hurt. "Through a hidden entrance beneath the back garden that opens behind a bookshelf in the library. It's the only entrance into Baker Street that doesn't set off the security system."

"Bollocks," Sandi said with a humorless chuckle. "Try again."

Greg pressed his lips together and shook his head. "Oh, come on, Sandi. You know it's there. Ollie told you about it, or at least that he'd found it. He didn't tell you we made it workable again." His smile was soft, reminiscent. "How perfect that Baker Street should have its own bolt-hole."

Sandi shifted her stance, loosening and tightening her grip on the gun, but she never lowered it. Kipling looked past her to Greg, waiting until he met her gaze, and nodded once.

Greg chuckled and grinned wider. "I remember when we found it. All cobwebs and dust, tucked away behind Mrs. Hudson's wall. Near we figure, Sherlock had it built when he and Doctor Watson lived here, and it was tucked away until we found it a few years ago. We joked about how we would have loved to know about it as kids. Imagine the adventures we could have had, sneaking in and out without anyone knowing whenever the family came to Baker Street."

He took a step toward them, and Sandi's arms came up, leveraging the weapon at the center of his chest, but he didn't stop. "I'm sorry, Sandi," he said softer, and stopped to swallow. "I swear, it wasn't my choice or my call."

Sandi sucked in a breath. Kipling held hers.

"You don't suppose Grayson has the ingredients for your internationally famous homemade jammie dodgers downstairs? I've sure missed them."

Sandi dropped both arms to her sides and the gun dropped to

the floor with a clatter. Kipling sank onto the bed's edge as Sandi and Greg embraced; in a heartbeat, the emotion, the exhaustion, and the revelations too much to fight any longer. She managed to slip her hearing aids from her ear canals and set them on the bedside table, silencing the reunion between teammates, and curled into a ball on the cold, too empty, bed.

Chapter Fifteen

Each time the click echoed in her ear canal it was the equivalent of someone jabbing a pin to the base of her skull. Her heart jumped with it. Her nerves tingled and burned, and her stomach twisted with anxiety. She was trapped in the memory, like walking through a vivid dream, knowing what was to come but unable to change the course of events. Kipling turned a full circle, searching Baker Street for any sign of watchers, of someone ready to strike. Seeing nothing unusual, she took two steps backward then turned to hurry toward Grayson.

"No, I didn't call for retrieval today. It was scheduled for Thursday, and I've not changed it. Yes, of course." He tilting the phone away from his mouth as he apparently waited for Mr. Balakrishnan to come back on the line. "Something wrong?"

Charlie strolled away, hands in his pockets, whistling as he headed for Grayson's beautiful Bentley. It sat exactly where they had parked it the night before upon returning from Sandra's dinner party.

In her mind, she told him there was danger. In her mind, she demanded they all get back. In her mind, she went to Grayson and pushed him away from the Bentley. But she was trapped in the moment, destined to relive the memory just as it happened. Unable to change anything. She shook her head and swirled her fingers near her ear, flinching again at another click. "No, just something..." The familiar cold flush hit her just as it had when she realized the clicks were evenly spaced. Not random like someone taking photos.

Grayson lowered his hand, letting the phone leave his ear, his expression pulling as he watched her. "Kipling..." he led.

"Something is—" Click.

Grayson grabbed her arm and pulled her away from the direction of the car and 221, putting her behind him as he bolted forward. "Charlie!"

She demanded her hands to reach for him, to grip him and hold on so he didn't go near the car. She struggled against her own uselessness, but regardless, Grayson stepped away. The young man turned, wide-eyed and wide grinned, and raised a hand to acknowledge Grayson.

"Get back!" Grayson shouted, motioning to Kipling but running toward the boy. "Charlie, get back! Get away from the car!"

Everything moved in slow motion, but far too quickly for Kipling to react, even though she'd lived this moment and she knew exactly what the next second would bring. Panic welled in her throat, choking her, and she tried to shout for Grayson as another click sounded in her ears. She took a step forward, instinctively, as Grayson reached Charlie — who was wide eyed and slack jawed — and yanked the boy with him.

The explosion lifted the Bentley several feet off the ground in a fiery ball, and hot air blasted Kipling backward to slam her into the wrought iron fence that ran along the front of the buildings, sucking breath from her lungs. Screams filled the air and fiery chunks of car fell to the street, the air stinking of burning fuel and rubber.

Kipling sat up, gasping, scrambling not to fall off the edge of the bed as she lost her balance. She twisted and braced her arms on the rumpled duvet, her hair falling across her face, clinging to her clammy skin. The bedroom was in complete darkness except for the patches of moonlight slipping through small gaps in the drapes.

The bed was still empty beside her.

As the memory dream released her from its terrifying hold, her body reminded her with painful acuity of her injuries. Her arms shook with the simple exertion of holding up her own weight, and parts of her body throbbed with a deep, tense pain with each beat of her heart. Knowing she had stolen all the sleep she was likely to find that night, she left the bed and walked with stiff limbs to the attached bath. Gingerly, she removed the bandages the hospital had sent her home with, turned the water on in the shower to a near-scalding level until steam curled above the curtain, and then stepped beneath the pounding pellets. The water pelted against her shoulder blades, and she hissed at the scorching temperature, but she needed it. She needed the heat and the sensation.

With her skin glowing red minutes later, she toweled off and eased a brush through her hair, conscious of the cut at her brow. She examined it quickly in the streaked center of the steamed mirror and chose to leave it unbandaged again. Before opening the door to the bedroom, she closed her eyes and said a quick prayer he would be lying in the bed, sleeping or awake waiting for her to return, she didn't care which as long as he was there. But the room was dark, the bed still empty, and her heart still broken.

She pulled on jeans and a camisole while standing in the small but serviceable walk-in closet, her clothing taking up space as if she'd always lived there, but paused as she reached for a blouse. Tucked in the corner of the closet was a wicker hamper, and draped on the side was the short-sleeved, button-down summer shirt in deep blue Grayson had worn Tuesday as he took her around the city. Tuesday seemed months in the past. Her throat tightened when she lifted the shirt from the hamper and brought it to her nose, inhaling. Grayson's scent clung to the material, a blend of his soap, his subtle cologne of sandalwood and citrus, and she swore she could smell the warmth of his skin. As small a comfort as it might be, Kipling slid her arms into the sleeves and buttoned the shirt, despite the fact it hung on her, the hem well past her hips.

Only once she was dressed did she bother to look at the time. It didn't matter what hour the clock read, she was awake and would manage no further sleep. Nearly half past four in the morning. The sun wouldn't rise for another hour, at least. As she walked past the bed to the door, she picked up her aids and reluctantly set them in place. At home, she didn't wear them as much as she had since arriving in the UK, but the idea of not being as aware as possible left her anxious and chilled to the bone.

With no clear destination, Kipling left the bedroom and walked toward the top of the stairs, leaving the lights off. Enough light came through the windows facing Baker Street to give her a guide until her hand found the railing. A small bit of light from the ground floor hinted through the stairwells, implying someone was awake downstairs. She rested her hand on the newel at the corner of the rail but stopped before completing the turn to take her down the steps. Across from the staircase was the closed door to what Grayson had indicated as his office, though he hadn't shown her inside. At the time, her focus had been on the next room in the tour — the bedroom — and suspected his thoughts had been similar. Two steps and she stood at the door, her hand on the knob. And she turned her wrist.

Why she had assumed the door would be locked, she wasn't sure, other than a man like Grayson would likely want to protect secrets; but this door was not locked, and it opened to her yet another faction of Grayson's life.

A single window looked out onto the back garden, and the lay of the room made it clear the room had been designed to be a bedroom, not an office. The pre-dawn light allowed her to see the long chain hanging from a domed, frosted glass light on the ceiling, and she tugged on it, bathing the room in a soft glow, diffused by the antique, smoky glass.

The room was decidedly masculine, a marriage between modern and antiquity. The desk was large and thick, dark wood with carved accents along the corners and legs, with leather inlay on the top and contrasting wood accents. It had to be an antique, which made the sleek, top-of-the-line computer atop the desk seem out of place. The walls were a rich burgundy in a velvety matte, giving the ambiance a heavy feeling, though not oppressive.

Sitting on the desk in front of the keyboard was a stack of leather and case-bound books. The antiquarian in her enjoyed a brief moment of excitement as she stepped to the desk and tilted her head to read the dark leather and gilded bindings. In a band near the top of each binding was the simple name BYRON, and each book indicated VOL 1, VOL II, through VOL IV. Kipling held her breath as she picked up the top book with VOL I on the spine, and gingerly opened dark green morocco, marbled paper cover. Foxing softened the edges of the first few pages, and a sketch of Lord Byron was on one of the left pages. The copyright read London, 1828. She let the pages brush past her fingertips until the first fell into place.

Written in a sharply angled hand, precise and carefully executed, was the name SHERLOCK HOLMES.

She set the book atop the stack, and picked up a folded piece of linen parchment beside the books. As she unfolded it, she immediately recognized Grayson's elegant, carefully schooled penmanship. For a heartbeat she couldn't blink, couldn't take a breath, when she read the first line.

My Darling Kipling

A sob nearly overtook her, but she sucked in a hard breath and pressed her fingertips to her lips, blinking against hot tears to clear her vision so she could read.

It has been my inclination since the moment we met to seek the best means to express myself by way of the words of other men. Yet, as I consider this note I wish to enclose in your birthday gift, a gift I wish more than anything I could give you myself, I find no adequate ramblings from men long dead. How could any of them have the words to properly tell you how I feel, and what I wish you to know, when none of them knew you?

So, for once I must rely on my own pathetic attempt at poeticism — though without the rhyme — to tell you what I wish you to know. To tell you what I truly hope you already know.

I love you. And while those three words are believed to be so all encompassing as to span the depth and breadth of the emotion, in my mind they only begin to touch upon my thoughts. To say you are my life, you are the air I breathe, and you are the blood in my veins is to allow this dedication to be mired in the sludge of trope and cliché.

I adore you. I cherish you. You are a treasure, a gift from God I do not deserve, and a sweet balm to my heart.

Happy birthday, my darling.
Grayson

By the time she reached the final words, Kipling couldn't bear the weight of her own heart and sank into the deep, soft leather desk chair, the note pressed to her chest. The chair was oversized, and she felt swallowed up by it. She drew her legs into the seat, tucked her knees to her chest, and curled up as small as she could, letting the scent of his shirt and the leather wrap around her. She was drained, so drained she couldn't cry anymore.

"Kip?"

She startled at John's — No, *Greg's* — voice and shifted her weight so the chair pivoted slightly, letting her see the doorway. Greg still wore the jeans and long-sleeved tee he'd worn when she found him, his hands pushed into his pockets, his eyes pinched and tired. In a blink, the tired twisted to concern and he crossed the office to crouch beside the chair, resting his hands on the arms to keep it still.

More than heartbroken, more than terrified, Kipling felt disconnected. Floating. She stared at the face of a man she'd called a friend for months, and in one moment he was John Allen, the next someone she only knew through Grayson's eyes. Yet, it made sense.

In the mess of moments and details, truth and lies, it made sense.

"Are you okay, Kip? You should be resting."

"He's going to be so happy you're alive," she said barely above a rough whisper, ignoring his question and suggestion. She wasn't okay, and resting was impossible. "You have no idea how he's missed you."

His smile was small and sad. "I acknowledge I know only a small bit, but I've felt his absence profoundly. I know it's not the same because I knew he was alive but I couldn't tell him."

Kipling rested her head against the chair back. "You speak of him the same way he speaks of you." She smiled, the action feeling foreign. "Every once in a while, you say something and you sound like him."

"We are both a product of the same upbringing, but I'm far more accustomed to changing who I am than Grayson." His brow creased and he frowned. "I know it's going to take time for anyone to believe me, but I didn't want this."

Kipling raised her hand instinctively to push back his hair from his temple, wanting to see the scars she'd noted there before but stopped short of touching him. John Allen wouldn't have cared, but she had no idea how much of the man she knew was Greg McQueen behind a different name and face, and how much was pretend.

"It's okay," he assured.

Without the heavier set of the Boston accent he'd put on, there was a familiarity to the weight and ease of his words, a hint at the similar background and education he shared with Grayson. It calmed her although it was entirely unfamiliar. She straightened her elbow and slid her fingertips into the light hair at his temples. It was soft, like Grayson's, and the act revealed the darker roots beneath. This color was not his, but all part of the pretense.

"What happened?" she asked.

Greg heaved a deep sigh and sank from his crouch to sit on the floor, crossing his legs at his ankles with his knees slightly raised to rest his arms. In that position, Kipling looked down at him. He raked his fingers over his short hair, ruffling it, then let his arm drop. "What has Grayson told you?"

She had to swallow, a sudden and choking wave of emotion squeezing her throat at the recollection of Grayson telling her the story. He had been so broken, so sad, and so worried about her reaction. "He told me about Edinburgh, that you were in a building wired to blow and you found the bomb. He said you did your job, but never told him you knew you did it with full knowledge the bomb was on a timer." She stopped, the first tear since she'd woken sliding free, and smeared it from her cheek. "You said goodbye, and the bomb exploded."

Greg let his head drop forward, clearing his throat. When he raised his chin to look at her, his eyes shined. "I woke up several weeks later, with the healing remains of a new face and a new assignment from my superior officers." He paused, his expression tightening. "And non-negotiable orders to not make contact with Grayson, any member of my family, or my team."

"Did your orders change?"

He chuckled, a single, humorless noise that bounced his shoulders. "No," was his simple, and non-committal, answer. Instead of elaborating, he pushed a hand to the floor and leveraged himself up to stand, offering his hand to her. "Come on. If you aren't going to rest, you might as well come downstairs. Sandi was scavenging in Ollie's pantry for something decent for breakfast."

She took his hand and unfolded from the chair, her body protesting the motion after being still. Aches and pains would likely manifest themselves for the next several days, but in a strange way, she welcomed them because the pain kept her grounded. By the time they reached the ground level, what should have been the enticing aromas of fresh bread and sausage filled the air, but made her stomach turn. The idea of eating held no appeal.

"The kettle is on," Sandi said, looking their way when they came in from the foyer. "By the time David gets up, the bread will be ready. Do you want a cuppa, Kip?"

She tried to hide her grimace but doubted she did. Greg leaned his hands against the edge of the kitchen peninsula and winked at her. For a moment, he was undeniably John Allen. "I'm betting you'd like a Dunks, hmm?"

It was meant to lighten the moment, and she attempted a smile. "Actually, there's a deli around the corner where you can get some," she said, sliding into one of the chairs at the table. "Grayson—" She choked on his name.

Greg pushed away from the counter, heading for the foyer. "That's all I need to hear. I'll be back in ten. Don't worry, I know how you like it."

He jogged from the kitchen, and Kipling looked to Sandi, who worked at washing a large mixing bowl. "He's trying to make it easier for me," she said. "Accepting he's Greg, and not the John Allen I've known for weeks."

"I have a feeling for the most part the two are one and the same," Sandi said, drying the bowl. "Greg is good at maintaining a legend, but we all know if it's long term it's sometimes easier to hide behind exactly who you are. He cares about you, about what this is doing to you, nearly as much as he's concerned for Grayson. His actions are genuine, Kip."

Before Kipling could reply, Greg jogged back into the kitchen from the sitting room. "I didn't make it far." He carried a paper-wrapped parcel in his hand. "Did anyone see this last night when you came home? Looks like it was too big to go through the mail slot, so the postman left it leaning against the alcove."

"No, I didn't see it," Sandi confirmed as Kipling shook her head.

Greg set the package on the table in front of Kipling and turned it so the address read properly. The return address was incomplete, only reading Great Russell Street, London, and was addressed to her.

DR. KIPLING BRANSON
FAO: GRAYSON HOLMES
221 BAKER STREET
WESTMINSTER
LONDON NW1 6XE

Kipling lifted the package. She'd picked up and opened enough packages containing books in her time at Dog-Eared Pages to immediately suspect the package content was a book. But who would send her a book, unless it was something Grayson had ordered? She'd only been there a couple of days, it didn't seem plausible he would have ordered something so quickly to have it delivered to her attention. And when would he have done it?

Sandi came to the table with a cup of tea, sitting at the corner nearest Kipling as she tore the wrapping off a white box, and opened the box.

Inside was a book so familiar an immediate cold sweat prickled Kipling's skin and she couldn't take a breath for two heartbeats. A red bound book, with the title *The Hound of the Baskerville* in gold foil, had been carefully set in the box, wrapped with great care on all sides in red velvet. It was a rare first edition she'd only seen twice. Here, in Grayson's own library…and in Boston months before.

"Are you a fan of Holmes?"

Kip looked up from the open book in her hands and smiled at the customer standing beside her, his decidedly British accent catching her attention.

He was in his mid-thirties, perhaps late to possibly forty, with dirty blond hair and a mustache covering his upper lip, his skin fair and marred by some pock marks along his cheeks, but they all but disappeared when he smiled.

She closed the copy of The Hound of the Baskervilles *and set it back on the display table. "Yes, I've always enjoyed Conan Doyle, but I've developed a greater appreciation for the Sherlock Holmes books as of late."*

"Who hasn't? With all the movie and television adaptations."

"Oh, I have other reasons for my interest," she said.

The customer shifted his coat to drape it over one arm, the interior of the bookstore being warm, to put his hands in his pockets. "I've been a long time appreciator. Who is your favorite villain?

"Hmm, that's not a question I've been asked before. Usually it's just which story I prefer." Kip pursed up her lips and tapped her fingers on the book cover. "I think most people automatically say James Moriarty because he's the one popular media focuses on the most. And he was the villain notorious for supposedly killing Holmes."

The customer nodded, arching his eyebrows like he might appreciate her answer. "But…"

"But, he wasn't the one Holmes despised the most. That was Charles Augustus Milverton. Holmes thought he was far more insidious."

"Quite true. You know your literature well."

Kip chuckled. "I hope so. I'm earning my doctorate in literature in a few months."

"Well done..." He made an obvious point of looking at her name badge. "Kip. What an unusual name. Possibly short for Kipling?" Kip winced and nodded. "Ah. Your parents were fans?"

"Unfortunately. Was there anything I can help you find?"

"Actually, I've found it already." Her stepped closer to her, invading her personal space more than she would prefer, and slid the copy of The Hound of the Baskervilles *from beneath her hand. "You've inspired me to renew my interest."*

Kip took a step back and moved around him. "Are you ready to check out, then?"

"I do believe I'd like to find something of Kipling's, if you have anything."

He'd been pleasant enough when he'd first spoken to her, but now the hairs on the back of her neck bristled and an uneasy twist curled in her stomach. She didn't like the way he watched her, the way he blatantly appraised her, and there was something uncomfortably familiar about him, though she couldn't place it.

Looking away from him, Kip motioned toward one of the rows of books. "Right over here is our classics section. We have several editions of The Jungle Book, *but we have a sizeable collection of his short stories, poetry, and one very rare copy of* The Second Jungle Book *if you're willing to pay the price." She smiled, or attempted to smile, over her shoulder as he followed her. "Since you're interested in that particular edition of* The Hound of the Baskervilles, *it seems price isn't your concern."*

"The greatest treasures are always worth the price."

She didn't respond, but showed him to the designated area. "I'll be out front when you're ready."

"Thank you ever so much, Kipling."

Had she known, had she any idea the man who taunted her with his words and made her skin crawl was the man responsible for the explosion at the university, responsible later for her abduction, responsible for more than she could catalog...had she known he was Langdon Howell...what could she have done?

"Is something wrong?" Sandi asked.

"I recognize that book—" Greg said low, stepping closer.

"This is from Langdon Howell," she managed to explain. "He

bought this from me in Boston." Sandi lunged for the box, but Kipling blocked her with a raised arm. "No. This is intentional—"

"Exactly, Kip. We have no idea what he's done to Grayson—"

"At least you'll finally admit it's him," Kipling snapped out, leveling a glare on Sandi.

The Six officer sighed so deep and long it pushed down her shoulders, and she shook her head. "We really have no doubt this is Langdon Howell. He's taunting you."

"And if taunting me finds Grayson, then so be it."

Before Sandi or Greg could stop her again, she lifted the book from the box. Beneath it, nestled in the velvet, was a folded piece of stationary. She held her breath as she unfolded it, squinting to read the aggressive, angled print, a drastic contrast to Grayson's neat hand. More than the angry writing, the words made no sense.

And yet, something niggled at her.

I NEVER REARED A YOUNG WOMBAT
TO GLAD ME WITH HIS PIN-HOLE EYE,
BUT WHEN HE WAS MOST SWEET AND FAT
AND TAIL-LESS HE WAS SURE TO DIE

"What the hell…" Greg mumbled.

Kipling shook her head, reading the verse again. "It's practically gibberish. Nonsense."

In her pocket, her phone vibrated for half a second before Grayson's ringtone sounded and she gasped, scrambling to free the phone to answer. The second it took for the call to connect to her hearing aids seemed an eternity. "Grayson?"

"Ah, if it were so simple, hmm?"

Langdon Howell's smooth, deceptive voice turned Kipling's blood to ice and she met Sandi's wide stare, shaking her head. "Howell," she mouthed. Sandi asked if she could go to speakerphone, but she shook her head. The Bluetooth setup didn't work that way.

"How are you, Kipling?" he asked, and his use of her name turned her stomach. He said it with an unearned intimacy. "I've been assured you were left relatively unscathed in comparison to… some."

Tears burned her eyes and she clenched her fists. A sudden realization made her scramble with the phone, thankful once again she had the upgraded device that allowed multiple tasks at once and turned on the recorder. "What have you done with Grayson?" she demanded, ignoring his question.

"No fear, Kipling. He is doing as well as can be expected considering the circumstances. It would do me little good to let my greatest opponent die."

"How do I know you're not lying?" She hated the crack in her voice, but it only hinted at the pain in her chest.

Howell laughed, a booming sound that made her flinch. "I wonder if we should credit your perceptive questions to your relationship with an officer of MI6, or your overexposure to American crime drama. Well played, Doctor Branson, and for that I shall indulge your curiosity."

The distinctive click of a phone camera carried through the line. If her phone could multitask, Grayson's could do more. Moments later, an alert appeared on her screen for a text message, photo attached. Her hand trembled so viciously that she had a difficult time tapping on the screen. Sandi had moved from her chair to stand beside her, reading over her shoulder. She couldn't hear the conversation, but Kipling had no doubt the woman could infer the gist of it.

The photo made her choke and she covered her mouth with her hand, the contact slick from tears she'd let slip. Grayson stared, his mouth set in an angry line, his eyes pinched, at the camera, his rage apparent at his circumstance. He was reclined on a bed, but clearly not in a hospital, his upper body bare except for white gauze bandaging wrapping most of his left arm and compression bandaging wrapped multiple times around his ribs. Red skin along the edges of the bandaging made her believe they covered burns, and abrasions and red surface marks marred his face. Bruises darkened his jawline, neck, shoulders, and abdomen where she could see. His hair had been cut in ragged chunks. Not to the scalp, but considerably shorter.

"As you see, my dear, he is alive though not pleased with the situation. I hope you believe me when I say it is my earnest hope you are up to the challenge; I believe he would heal much more efficiently under your loving ministrations."

"What do you mean by challenge?" she asked, her heated cheeks going cold again.

Howell sighed heavily, the almost pleased sound a scrape on her frazzled nerves. "My family has waited generations to once again meet the challenge only a Holmes can attempt, and in manifesting that challenge, I unwittingly chose far too well when I chose you, Kipling."

She closed her eyes, a tremor twisting her shoulders. Howell continued without interruption.

"I thought you a ploy, a means to an end. I chose you as a possible distraction for Grayson, but his history — his psychology — said you would be no more. I never imagined I could so effectively choose not just a distraction, but the one woman who could break through the hard shell of Sherlock Holmes' heart?"

The slip went unnoticed by Howell, but not by Kipling.

"Instead of finding distraction, our dear Holmes found love. How utterly poetic. Perhaps I should change my profession."

"You're not telling me anything I don't already know."

Howell laughed again. "Words spoken by Holmes himself. You two truly are two halves of a whole. A truth I intend to test." His last sentence came through cold and hard.

Kipling forced open her eyes, both Greg and Sandi watching her with intense anticipation. They heard none of these words, but would when the call finished.

"Do you believe you are worthy of him?" Howell asked.

"How can I answer that will satisfy you?"

"You cannot, thus, you must prove your worthiness. Either you are, or this day ends with his death."

She bit down on her tongue until it hurt to steady herself, refusing to let him hear her fear or her tears. "What do you want?"

"Three sets of clues, my dear. Sherlock Holmes holds the gift to see the connections few others see. Now I challenge you to do the same. I have provided you two parts of your first set, and to them I add this…You are his match and his downfall, but this fate is not owned by Holmes alone. May history never repeat itself."

"What do you want me to do with this?"

"The clues will lead you to a new destination, one you cannot reach until ten this morning. I give you until eleven, and then the chance at the next set is lost. But, decipher my riddle and find the next set, and Grayson stays alive. Fail anywhere along the way, and I doubt I need to repeat the outcome."

She wanted to call him a bastard, but the words in her mind couldn't force their way past her tight throat. Probably for the best, because Langdon Howell wasn't a man who took well to disrespect, that much she felt safe in assuming.

"One last stipulation, Kipling," he said with a dismissive, off-handed tone. "I know you're there with one of Grayson's team. This task is for you and you alone. Once you leave Baker Street, if you are not alone, the game is over. I sincerely hope to see you at the end of this day, Kipling. I enjoy the game more than you know."

Then the line went silent.

Chapter Sixteen

"I fear our dear Kipling might be so distraught she will be unable to think clearly." Howell sighed with excessive drama, sliding his phone into his jacket breast pocket. "Would be such a shame if she fails to save you for fear of not saving you."

Grayson wanted nothing more in that moment than to beat the smug, psychotic smirk off Langdon Howell's face. If he thought he had a chance to dole out a substantial measure of damage before either of Howell's bodyguards pulled him off or his weakened state did him in, he'd be off his convalescent bed and on the bastard. He tamped down the bitter taste of rage and instead focused on the sting in the skin of his left arm as Howell's pseudo-nurse unwrapped his bandages.

Since it was not the first time the bandages had been removed, Grayson had previously assessed most of his burns were either first degree or mild second, not requiring the excessive bandaging the aged woman had applied along with copious smears of Germolene. One rather long laceration on his upper arm required stitches, which the thick-fingered, shaky-handed woman had thankfully applied prior to his initial waking, but it would likely leave a permanent and ugly reminder of the days.

"I suspect you are ignoring me, Holmes."

Grayson angled his stare away from the female brute's treatments, glaring at Howell. "Your brilliance is blinding."

Howell barked a laugh and pushed his hands into his trouser pockets. "I also suspect you do not appreciate my efforts to make our day more interesting. Do you fear your American is not up to the challenge?"

Grayson leveled his gaze on Howell, channeling his anger into his voice, an effect intended to intimidate and mislead. "Are you more concerned because you doubt her ability, and you might be required to carry through with your threat to kill me, thus ending the game, or that I have no doubt whatsoever in her intelligence and you will be forced to concede and let us go free without harm?"

His effort was rewarded, and he wondered if Howell knew how transparent he could be; his truth often played in his eyes and the pinch of his face. A tight muscle beneath Howell's right eye twitched, and his smile slipped, yet never fully disappeared.

"Which outcome do you prefer, Howell?" Grayson pushed, maintaining a level, calm, stern pitch to his voice. "Do you intend to keep your word at all?"

"I am a man of my word, Holmes." His voice was so low, his expression so tight, his lips barely moved. "I gave my word to my family that my brother's death would be avenged."

"After the *death* and destruction the Howell family has perpetrated in the last hundred years, are you such a div you believe you have justification to seek vengeance?" Grayson demanded, raising his voice just enough as to imply he bordered on the edge of snapping himself.

"Were you justified?" Howell demanded back. "When you took my brother's life with your own hands, were *you* justified, Holmes?"

Grayson clenched his jaw, his lip twitching, and looked away from Howell. "No, I was not."

Howell sighed, and in Grayson's peripheral, he observed the man as he wiped a hand over his lips and jaw, erasing a fine sheen of perspiration, and looked toward the window. He'd shaken Howell more in the last two minutes than he had since awakening the day before, and he wondered if Howell had any idea how much he'd given up to Grayson. He was mentally unstable, though Grayson wouldn't quite define him as psychotic. Not yet. His fascination with the Charles Augustus Howell/Sherlock Holmes feud slipped into his contemporary thinking, so much so he directly referred to Grayson as Sherlock during the conversation with Kipling, and implied as much again later. He perpetrated the ruse in his own mind that they were, in fact, Sherlock Holmes and Charles Augustus Howell, enemies once again. If literary legend was to be believed, Sherlock allowed Howell's murder though he held no direct responsibility for Howell's death. In reality, Howell had been murdered and the case had never been resolved.

Likely, just as in the story penned by Conan Doyle, no one was sorry for the man's death, and likely many wished they had found the courage themselves to complete the deed.

The problem with the insane was their extreme unpredictability.

The pseudo-nurse finished her unnecessary wrapping of his arm — he had finally convinced her to leave his cracked ribs wrapped more loosely so he could properly breathe — and picked up a bottle from the bedside table, dumping two Paracetamol into her hand.

Grayson shook his head. "I don't need them."

Wordless, she looked to Howell, who sighed and shook his head, apparently having found his composure again. "Our guest is concerned his comfort is not at the forefront of our intentions. I assure you, Holmes, it is nothing more than something to ease the pain."

"I don't need them," Grayson repeated.

Howell shrugged, and the nurse put the pills back in the bottle, frowning as she left the bedside. "It was worth a wound; it was worth many wounds; to know the depth and love which lay behind that cold mask," Howell said with a nostalgic lilt as the puss-faced matron left them.

It irritated Grayson to have this man assume the audacity to quote a verse from the Sherlock Holmes stories to prove his twisted point, but he hid his annoyance so as to not play his hand. "Do you speak of your wounds, or mine?" Grayson asked, shifting his position. He tested Howell's wariness by swinging his legs over the side of the bed to sit on the edge. While one of Howell's thugs made a move to step forward, Howell waved him back.

"Our guest is hardly in a position to cause bodily harm to anyone here," he justified, then focused on Grayson and returned to their previous subject. "I suppose in this case, I speak of yours. How else could I truly judge Doctor Branson's willingness to meet my challenge if the consequences weren't substantial enough to convince?"

"Your words are those of John Watson. Are you sure you have straight the players in your game?" Grayson challenged with an arch of one eyebrow and a finishing hum.

"I may refer to this as a game, but I assure you, it is far more. We have waited generations for this chance."

"We?" Grayson questioned. "Or you, Langdon?"

He avoided the answer outright, turning away on the heels of his polished shoes to stride toward the door. "Breakfast will arrive within the hour, Holmes. I do encourage you to eat. You must maintain your strength, after all. By eleven one of two things will happen." He paused at the door, his hand on the knob, half twisted. "Either preparations for this evening will be underway, or I shall have to return for the distasteful activity of overseeing your death."

With just enough flourish to encourage the idea he bordered on insane, Howell yanked open the bedroom door and exited, his guards following. The door closed, and the lock engaged immediately. Aware his actions were under constant observation, Grayson denied himself the heavy sigh he wished to release, or the urge to let his shoulders drop in concern. Instead, he pushed himself to his feet and gingerly walked the circumference of the room to exercise his still-tender ankle and burn a tiny fraction of the nervous energy bubbling beneath the surface of his scorched skin.

He was fully truthful with Howell when he confirmed his confidence in Kipling, but his confidence didn't assuage his concern in Howell's commitment to simply release him when she met the challenge. More than that, he despised the fact the task was put upon her at all. Loving him should not require life or death challenges, and despite the reality of his life, he thought he could possibly keep her untainted by it.

The truth was more enraging than Howell's game.

"I've gone through the whole book. There are no other clues unless the book itself is a clue—"

"What about the poem? That must be something—"

"His fate isn't owned by Holmes alone. Howell said that—"

"He's got to mean Kip. She's holding his fate."

"But he said there were two parts before that. What else—"

"Shut up!" Kipling shouted with her fists clenched at her side, spinning back to face the kitchen table where Sandi and Greg bickered, hunched over the book and note. "I can't think with you two!"

Both of her friends stilled, staring at her with wide eyes. Then Sandi stood, the chair legs scraping across the floor with the same effect as nails on a chalkboard. She crossed to Kipling and reached out a hand, but Kipling flinched away, crossing her arms over her body in an attempt to keep from getting sick. An hour and a half had passed, ticking down to her deadline, and she couldn't think with the two super-minded Six officers chopping up and regurgitating all the facts. Sandi had the intelligence to lower her hand and not push the issue.

"Could you give me some space?" she asked. "I know the connection is here, I just need to see it."

"We've already got headquarters going over what we've got," Sandi started to counter, but Kipling shot up her hand.

"All due respect, Sandi, but I don't have time to wait for a computer to figure this out. Howell put this on me. I'm the one who will see it."

"Unless it's impossible," Greg offered.

Sandi shot him a glare. "Greg—"

"No, he wants the game. It's not a game if he cheats," Kipling countered and stepped around Sandi to go back to the table, sitting in the chair she'd vacated, the book still mocking her. "It's here."

Spurred on by her desperate need to figure out the puzzle, Kipling bolted from the chair again and ran through the foyer and up two flights of stairs. It was possible Grayson kept paper and pen somewhere else in the house, but she didn't want to spend needless time hunting where she didn't know to look when she could go straight to a known source. She shoved open the door to his office and studiously ignored the books and note on the desktop, not ready for the onslaught of emotion reading the letter would bring back down on her, and yanked open the thin drawer centered beneath the desk.

Just as she suspected, inside the drawer was a small stack of fine stationary as well as a lined notepad. She grabbed the notepad and a pen from the cup beside the keyboard and ran downstairs again. In the short time she'd been upstairs David had risen, and his worried expression indicated Sandi had told him at least some of the events over the last two hours or so. Kipling didn't know how much a spouse would confide in her non-Six-affiliated husband, and at that moment didn't much care. She went past them, not acknowledging Greg, and sat again with pen in hand and paper ready.

And began to write. Randomly. Any thought that came to mind. Something to help her connect the fragments and pieces. By the time she paused, she'd filled two solid pages and tore them off the tablet to lay them out side by side. The barely-decipherable chicken scratch would appall her mother, but penmanship wasn't her concern. Some of the notes were single words. Some questions. Some statements. She stared at them — waiting — hoping — the answer would come visible.

"Where is Great Russell Street?" she asked the room.

"A couple of miles southeast of here," David answered, his smooth, calming accent enough of a surprise to Kipling that she looked up. He stood within the horseshoe of the kitchen, Sandi beside him, a cup in his hand. "The British Museum is there. Some historical spots. Not much memorable other than the museum."

"Museum..." Kipling mumbled, writing the word in capital

letters and with a heavy hand beside the address on her paper. She tapped the pen on the paper, leaving blue dots. *Museum…*"I need to know what they have on exhibit," she said more to herself.

"I'll find out," Sandi said, drawing Kipling's attention for only a moment while the woman went for the laptop she'd left on the counter. Kipling didn't recognize it as Grayson's, so it had to be Sandi's. "Give me two. Anything in particular I need to look for?"

"I don't know yet."

She stared again at the list, and picked up the note from Langdon Howell, reading the words again.

> *I never reared a young wombat*
> *To glad me with his pin-hole eye,*
> *But when he was most sweet and fat*
> *And tail-less he was sure to die*

"Dante Gabriel Rossetti!" she cried, coming up out of her chair, the note still in hand. She shook the paper at Sandi, taking a step away from the table. "Is he on display anywhere at the museum?"

Sandi scowled as she typed, her eyes shifting as she read the screen. "Yes." Her scowl deepened. "Their search engine is horrendous. They have four pieces on display, by the looks of it. *Arthur's Tomb. Paolo and Francesca, The M's and Ems,* and *Rosetti Lamenting the Death of His Wombat.*" As she read the last art piece, she raised her head to look to Kipling. "Death of his wombat?"

"This—" Kipling declared, slapping the back of her fingers against the stationary. "This is inscribed on that drawing."

"What does Rossetti have to do with Howell?" Greg asked.

"I don't know," Kipling said with a shake of her head, staring at the words again. "I don't — Wait. Maybe I do."

She wondered if this was what it felt like for Grayson, when all the pieces tumbled together to make a whole painting. Of course, she was light years away from the level of processing his mind was capable of — she knew that — but seeing the threads form was a rush, making her heart pound and her skin raise in gooseflesh. She nodded, each bob of her head firmer as she convinced herself she was right.

"I'm so thankful part of my education included a class on art and literature history," she said more to herself, then looked at the three anxiously awaiting her response, eyes widened and bodies tense. "Charles Augustus Howell was a blackmailer, just like Milverton in the Conan Doyle books. His mistress, Rose…No, Rosa…" She snapped her fingers, trying to pull the name from the recesses of her memory. "Corder!" she cried, pointing toward them. "Rosa Corder was an art forger and was suspected to have forged several pieces by Rossetti. They had been friends before that, Howell and Rossetti, but not once Corder forged the drawings. The poem connects to Rosetti, which connects to Howell."

"So, what about the third clue? About you being his match and his downfall?"

"You are his match and his downfall, but this fate is not owned by Holmes alone. May history never repeat itself," Kipling recited from memory, then shrugged. "Perhaps he's comparing Howell and Corder to Grayson and myself. She was his match in that she aided him in his crimes, but the discovery of her forgeries was the beginning of his social downfall. Before then, he was suspected but nothing was ever proven. Not that anything was *proven* after that, but his victims weren't as silent. Some histories say Rosetti decided to have his dead wife's body exhumed well after her death so he could retrieve a bundle of poems he'd buried with her; others believe he did it because Howell forced him."

"So, what does this all mean?" Sandi asked with a frustrated flip of her hand toward the table and the array of clues and notes. "What does he want you to do?"

Kipling released a long, slow breath through her nose and focused on Greg, thankful when she met determination in his eyes and not doubt. "I go to the Rosetti display at the British Museum at ten when they open, and once there, hope I find the next clue before eleven."

"This is crazy!" Sandi declared. "And what if he's there and hurts you? There is *no* way I'm facing Grayson if you get hurt."

"If she doesn't go, you won't have to face Grayson," Greg countered, his voice cold and calm. "I have been dogging Langdon Howell for nearly two years. I have no doubt he will do what he says. If Kipling doesn't solve his puzzles, Grayson is dead."

"And if we just let her walk out of here alone, even if this works, we're all dead when Grayson finds out."

"You have to let me leave alone," Kipling said, looking first at Sandi and then Greg. "But we have a secret weapon Howell doesn't know about. He doesn't know Greg McQueen is alive, what he looks like, or that he's here in London. You got into this house undetected. I assume you can get back out?"

Greg grinned. "Have you ever considered a job in intelligence?"

"You're not the first to ask me that." She looked at the clock on the wall, a strange calm settling over her. She would do this. She *had to* do this. There was no option for failure, and with the lack of option, she found her focus. "We have an hour and a half before the museum opens. I need a crash course in the clandestine arts."

Chapter Seventeen

"That'll be £8.80," the cabbie said over his shoulder as the car rocked to a stop outside the British Museum.

Kipling handed the £10 note through the space between the seats and held out her hand palm up for the £1 and 20p coins as her change. "Thank you," she managed to say before stepping free of the black vehicle.

Her insides couldn't decide if they wanted to knot, twist, or turn inside out, and had been attempting to do all three since she left Baker Street. Muscles and joints joined in the protest by reminding her she'd been tossed several feet just the day before, and her first few steps across the sidewalk were jaunty and stiff until the movement limbered up her muscles again.

On any other day she might have paused at the bottom of the steps leading to the entrance and enjoyed the Greek-inspired architecture, but today enjoyment was the furthest thing from her mind. She took the steps as quickly as her body allowed, and moved with the early morning visitors into the main entrance, skirting around a group of schoolchildren likely there on a field trip. On any other day, the bright foyer would have given her a moment's pause. Any other day, she would have grabbed a floor plan and taken her time moving from room to room. Any other day, she might have walked with her head perpetually tipped up and her lips bowed in a smile. Any other day, and perhaps another day, she'd walk hand-in-hand with Grayson.

Today time and distraction were her enemies.

She headed directly to the information desk, and inquired where she would find the Dante Gabriel Rossetti art on display, and silently cursed the distance when the clerk circled the room on her map and drew lines for the most direct route. Since running through the museum might draw too much attention, a steady walk would take her several minutes.

Time ticked away with every second.

"I see you," came Greg's voice through her aids.

She crossed her arms over her body, the silent signal she heard him.

Smuggled through the same tunnel Greg had used to enter Baker Street, Mac had made his own way and spent the better part of an hour and a half finagling some fancy jiggery-pokery Kipling was quite sure would void any and all warranty she had remaining on her hearing aids, ultimately making them two-way communication devices without the need of connection to her smartphone. Neither Grayson nor the minds at Six had yet determined how Langdon Howell had found a way to manipulate her hearing aids in Boston to pull her into the web of his machinations. Mac had no doubt Howell likely had a way to monitor any communications through her phone, but by removing the aids from that method of connection, he felt confident they could stay in contact without Howell being any the wiser. While in public view, they'd worked out a means of silent communication on Kipling's part so she could know they were with her without clueing in anyone — and they also had no doubt Howell had eyes on her — who might be watching.

She didn't dare look around for Greg but embraced the slight wave of calm at knowing he was near. Mac, Sandra, and David waited back at Baker Street since Howell knew their faces.

Kipling marched along as quickly as her hurting body allowed without drawing attention to herself. She dodged several slower-moving museum patrons and finally reached the room circled on her map, pausing to catch her breath once inside, glancing left and right. Her heart jerked so tangibly in her chest when she spotted *Rossetti Lamenting The Death of His Wombat.* Her gut told her this was the piece of art Howell wanted her to focus on, the ridiculousness of it in comparison to Rossetti's other work some sort of guffaw at her expense.

"Excuse me," she mumbled, nearly running into an elderly woman leaning on a cane, a massive purse hanging off her other arm.

She finally made it to the small drawing, and stopped, staring. "Now what," she mumbled to herself. It was no bigger than 4" by 7", with the artist's handwritten poem at the bottom. The majority of the real estate hanging on the wall was framed and matted. When no revelation made itself immediately known, Kipling looked around the gallery, turning a slow circle as she sought anything to lead her to her next destination.

Having completed a full circle, she faced the drawing again and looked up to the ceiling. Then down. On the floor beyond the rope forcing her to keep her distance from the art was a folded brochure. Unwilling to overlook anything, she crouched and winced as her back muscles pulled, and angled herself beneath the rope enough to retrieve the brochure. When she opened it, a cardstock insert fluttered free but she managed to catch it, turning it over to read the calligraphy print.

When you come to London Town,
(Grieving-grieving!)
Bow your head and mourn your own,
With the others grieving.
For those minutes, let it wake
(Grieving-grieving!)
All the empty-heart and ache
That is not cured by grieving.
For those minutes, tell no lie:
(Grieving-grieving!)

> *'Grave, this is thy victory;*
> *And the sting of death is grieving.'*
> *Where is our help from Earth or Heaven*
> *(Grieving-grieving!)*
> *To comfort us for what we're given,*
> *And only gained the grieving.*
> *Heaven's too far and earth too near,*
> *(Grieving-grieving!)*
> *But our neighbour's standing here,*
> *Grieving as we're grieving.*
> *What's his burden every day?*
> *(Grieving-grieving!)*
> *Nothing man can count or weight,*
> *But loss and love's own grieving.*
> *What is the tie betwixt us two*
> *(Grieving-grieving!)*
> *That must last our whole lives through?*
> *'As I suffer, so do you.'*
> *That may ease the grieving.*

There was no title to the poem and no attribution; but, then again, Langdon Howell would assume she wouldn't need to be told. Especially this particular poet.

Rudyard Kipling.

Just like the book he'd sent to Baker Street, which was not in and of itself a "hint", this poem was Howell's way to let her know the message was truly from him. Tucking the card behind the brochure, she closed it to look at the front. It was a generic brochure geared toward tourists, with a photo of Big Ben and Parliament and a call to action not to miss these "must-see" attractions in London. She opened the brochure again and unfolded it. It was a multi-panel flyer, each section highlighting some tourist hotspots. Big Ben. The Tower of London. Parliament. Buckingham Palace. Westminster Abbey. The London Eye. The Temple Church. London Bridge. The London Zoo. And Shakespeare's Globe Theater. There were no markings on the brochure, nothing to provide a hint. Ten locations. Nine chances to be wrong.

She jumped and gasped when her phone simultaneously vibrated in her pocket, and Grayson's ringtone sounded in the otherwise quiet room. The few other patrons near her slid annoyed glares in her direction, one woman shaking her head with a haughty huff. Heart pounding, she fumbled to silence the sound and answer, taking the two seconds the Bluetooth needed to connect to the hearing aids to close her eyes and catch her breath. A small glimmer of hope flared that it might actually be Grayson on the other side of the connection.

"Hello," she said as calmly as she could.

"Good morning, Doctor Branson."

Langdon Howell's voice slid over her like cold grease, and she twisted her lips in a disgusted grimace, tamping it back a second later. "I would hardly call any part of this morning good."

"You fail to see the positive," Howell chided. "It isn't half past ten and you have not only proven you solved the first puzzle, but you hold in your hand part of the next."

Kipling raised her head and glanced around the room, a cold chill settling at her nape. Outside the room and in the hall she caught sight of Greg, but didn't allow her attention to pause even for a moment. It didn't surprise her at all that Howell also had eyes on her. How else would he know she'd solved his puzzle and Grayson stayed alive a little longer? Nausea twisted her nearly empty stomach.

"Part," she repeated. "Where is the rest?"

"In due time, Doctor. You have proven yourself in this first stage, and you have done so before the deadline. Well done. I am sure Grayson will be relieved he has at least a few more hours."

Kipling moved away from the drawing to an empty spot near the wall so she was out of any obvious line of traffic. She knew Greg heard everything both she and Howell said, and took the opportunity to relay information she couldn't otherwise.

"You made it clear the brochure was from you. A poem from Kipling. Nice touch." She made sure sarcasm laced her words. She refused to let him hear any hint of her fear. Such had been her gut instinct from his first contact, but Greg had provided her a brief lesson on Langdon Howell's twisted psychology. At least to the extent that Greg understood it.

"I am pleased you were amused," he said with a chuckle that reverberated through her head like a jackhammer. "Your first clues provided the answer by the sum of their worth. Now, you must find your next location through the process of elimination."

Kipling opened the brochure again, scanning the stock images of the London tourist spots. "Fine," she said through tight lips. "Where do I find my next clue?"

"I can tell you where to go, but it will be your job to see. I have no doubt you likely skipped breakfast this morning, so you might wish to visit the museum's café before heading into the city again. It's nearly eleven now, time for brunch. You have until half one to arrive at your next location; plenty of time to grab a tuck and revive your energies."

"I'm not hungry," she snapped out.

"Don't argue, Doctor," Howell said with a condescending sigh. "It is far from ladylike. Oh, and my dear, I commend you for honoring my instructions. It must be of no surprise you are under constant observation, so be advised my instructions still remain. If you seek assistance any further from any member of Grayson's team, he will die."

The line disconnected and a moment later, her aids chimed to indicate their return to normal use. Kipling drew in a shaky breath and leaned against the wall, fighting the urge to be sick.

"You're doing great," Greg assured, his calm voice a comfort, even if only a small degree. "I am already on my way to the café. Take a couple of minutes. Let his watchers believe you are composing yourself. Then follow. I'm with you, Kip."

She swallowed hard, and after a respectable pause, opened her eyes and pushed away from the wall, opening the museum map to find her way to the eateries. The idea of food made her stomach revolt, but the idea of losing Grayson threatened to stop her heart.

"She is a treasure. Wouldn't you agree, Holmes?"

Grayson didn't look toward the bedroom door when it opened, and didn't turn to acknowledge Howell when he spoke. He had watched the time for the last hour, and had fully expected Howell at eleven; Howell had acted as expected. The question remained was he here to taunt, or to see to Grayson's death?

"I doubt you need my validation," Grayson said, keeping his attention out the window, through the mesh and bars, to the garden below. No one had been in the garden all day, nor had he noted signs of anyone outside the house walls at all. He was not so foolish as to believe eyes were not abundant and ever watchful.

"I would expect more enthusiasm, Holmes. After all, your American has spared your life." As he spoke, Grayson turned from the window, his right arm across his torso in a useless attempt at fending off the ache in his ribs. Howell stood near the foot of the bed, his hands pushed into the pockets of his trousers, an uncomfortably pleased grin tugging his lips away from his teeth. "She showed no hesitation, rather marched to her destination with the confidence of a military general."

"Yet again, I wonder if you are pleased at her intelligence or disappointed at your own admitted error of misjudging her," Grayson said, lowering the tone of his voice to a level of condescension. Every word he said, every action, was a carefully calculated move to both judge Howell's reaction and elicit a response for Grayson to evaluate.

"I have decided I did not misjudge Doctor Branson in the least," Howell said, bobbing a finger in Grayson's direction before bringing it to his own lips. "While my forward intent had been a means of temporary distraction, my subconscious mind saw the potential such a woman might inspire. Her selection was not an error at all." Howell smiled like a sadistic Cheshire cat. "Perhaps I have the gift of precognition, Holmes."

"If that is the case, then save us both the time and end this. If you see the future, you know how this day will end."

"Ah, but the enjoyment is in the journey." Howell extended his arm to reveal his wristwatch and bent his elbow to look at the face. "I have given your Doctor Branson until half past one to both determine and reach her next destination. Would you prefer I stay and keep you updated?"

"Not necessary," Grayson answered, though his chest ached at the thought of knowing where she was. "We both know what will happen at one-thirty."

"Do we?" Howell arched a single brow, then smirked and chuckled. "I shall see you then, Holmes, one way or the other."

Despite Howell's instructions, Kipling fought to get down the few sips of tea and perhaps three pinches off bites of berry crumpet before her throat closed and her stomach made it quite clear nothing else would be allowed. She had found one of the small, round, two-person maximum tables to sit at along the edge of the café, a vantage point to allow her to see most of the space. It was not yet noon, but the café seating area had slowly begun to fill with people, varying in age to toddlers with parents or grandparents, to adults in small groups, to people apparently alone like herself.

Everything and everyone was suspect. Her next hint could come in any form, from the blatantly obvious to the obscurely benign. She studied everyone and everything: posters on the walls advertising exhibits within the museum, commemorating past exhibits, and advertising exhibits to come. A rack was full of brochures for other tourist hot spots around London; she took one of each. Nearly every one of the tourist attractions on the brochure from the gallery had at least two to three corresponding mentions in the café flyers. Nothing stood out as unique or significant. Even the descriptions from brochure to brochure read nearly exactly the same.

She even listened with great intent to every conversation within earshot, not doubting Howell might do something so subtle as to plant people near her to either guide *or* mislead.

Greg sat at one of the long, family-style seating tables designed to let people sit together either as large groups or small groups to mingle. He had ordered a sandwich and ate it with enthusiasm while flipping through a newspaper. Kipling struggled to keep her attention off him even as she scanned the room for something.

Anything.

A young man, college age, sat at the communal table with an open photo book spread out above his plate, one elbow on the table with a cup of something hot held aloft as he studied the pictures and turned the pages. She watched him surreptitiously when he turned one of the large, glossy pages and she caught a glimpse of what looked like city photos. Unfortunately, she couldn't tell if they were in London or another city. He turned another page, and she managed to identify the distinct silhouette of Big Ben.

A clue?

Or just a kid looking at a book?

He looked up to reach for his mug and caught her watching him. Heat infused her face when he smirked, winked, and pursed his lips in an inviting kiss.

"Hardly," she mumbled and looked away.

Immediate questions rolled around in her head. Just how rehearsed are the events in the café? Did that man situate himself there knowing she'd be watching? Did he look up when he turned to Big Ben? She dug into every obscure corner of her Holmes knowledge — every book, every report, every pastiche — to try to recall any mention of Big Ben at all, let alone in connection to Howell. After Grayson had identified Langdon Howell to her, just before he left Boston, she had researched Charles Augustus Howell; and found history severely lacking. There was more supposition and assumption than anything that rose to the top as clear fact. Even his death was questionable, with one conspiracy theorist saying Sherlock Holmes had witnessed his murder just as Holmes had witnessed the murder of Milverton...and did nothing to stop it.

An elderly couple sat at one of the lower tables with a little girl, probably no more than four. Leaning against her chair on the floor was a backpack with the London Bridge on it, what might have been lights replaced with sparkling sequins. She swung her legs with such enthusiasm she bounced in her chair and chattered relentlessly to the two Kipling suspected might be grandparents. They beamed with every word. The family unit was too far away for Kipling to catch anything they said, but she instinctively hoped they would not – could not – be a part of Howell's machinations.

A tall man of slight build, with a bald pate, and deep wrinkles in his rich, tropical skin tone, dressed in the traditional black cassock of a Catholic priest walked past her table. He smiled when she briefly made eye contact, his hands tucked behind his back. Hanging from a chain and only partially visible from the folds of his cassock was a red cross and the beads of his Rosary. The cross flashed when the overhead light glinted off its edge, making Kipling squint and look past him.

A couple sat together in the most secluded corner of the café, though the open-air concept didn't allow for discreet moments. They didn't seem to care. In comparison to some "public displays of affection" Kipling had witnessed on her university campus, these two were subdued, but they gripped her attention all the same. It was the way he looked at her, especially when she looked away. The softening of his eyes and the awestruck tilt of his smile made Kipling's heart ache for missing Grayson. Worrying for Grayson.

Kipling glanced at her watch. It was approaching noon. Howell had given her until half past one to reach the next destination, and she still had no idea where she was to go. The only place she had managed to eliminate as a likely destination was the London Eye, narrowing her options to nine. Howell held on to history and antiquity with iron fists, and the London Eye wasn't nearly old enough to hold his interest. Every other site was ancient in comparison, each in existence in some capacity during the life of Charles Augustus Howell, Conan Doyle, and Sherlock Holmes.

What if there was nothing at all? The book with Big Ben meant nothing. The couple discussing going to the zoo meant nothing. The priest meant nothing. The old couple meant nothing. The poster of Westminster meant nothing. What if Howell fully expected her to sit here, stare at the brochure, and just pick a best guess and risk Grayson's life on a hunch?

"Might as well be playing Russian Roulette," Kipling mumbled.

"Can I get you anything else, miss?"

Kipling jumped, so engrossed in her thoughts she hadn't noticed the woman approach her table. Trying to regain her composure, she shook her head and forced a smile. "No, I'm just picking now."

"Looking for a spot to visit?" she asked, pointing toward Kipling's stacks of brochures. "Been in London long?"

She shook her head. "Just a few days. I'm trying to narrow my options," she answered, skimming the truth.

"I'd skip 'em all was I you," the waitress said with a toss of her hand. "Tourist traps, all. You can buy a souvenir for any one of them at any shop in London and no one would be the wiser. Most you could get right here at the museum. What you come to London for?"

A chill, like a ghost breathing on her neck. Kipling glanced past the waitress to find the priest she'd made note of earlier watching her from across the space. She had made her way for most of her life by reading people, and while he wore the vestments and collar, his eyes lacked the comforting peace she usually recognized in someone truly invested in their faith. Rather, they were penetrating. Leering.

Blinking, she forced herself to stay in the conversation. "I came for a job interview, actually."

"Then you've got plenty of time to see that stuff. Hell, you'd be surprised how many Londoners never been to Parliament or the Tower of London. Guess we don't appreciate what's right in front of us."

"Sometimes it's the hardest to see," Kipling managed to mumble, feeling the priest's stare.

"If you go to Buckingham Palace, I'll let you in on a secret," the waitress said, leaning forward to whisper, temporarily blocking Kipling's view of the priest. "Ask the guards for a candy. They're legally obliged to give you a Werther's if you ask." She winked and grinned. When she straightened, she picked up Kipling's empty mug and stepped away, clearing Kipling's line of sight.

The priest's lip tipped in the illusion of a smirk, and then he took a step backward and turned away, walking through the tables and crowd.

"That was odd," said a woman at the table behind Kipling, her voice carrying a lyrical tilt of a British accent, yet not as robust as Kipling would expect from a Londoner.

Kipling looked over her shoulder at the solitary woman who had paused with a fork of salad halfway to her mouth, her elbow on the table. She was probably a few years older than Kipling with rich brown hair clipped at her crown in a haphazard twist, and dark-rimmed glasses accentuated her hazel eyes. She wore a purple tee shirt with a large bone and the phrase "I FOUND THIS HUMERUS" in white letters. On the inside of the wrist holding the fork was an elaborately designed Celtic scrollwork tattoo. She stared after the priest, then seemed to realize Kipling was looking at her and tipped her shoulder in a casual shrug.

"Was she lying about the candy?" Kipling asked.

"Soz?" She shook her head and set down the fork. "Complete cack. Making gits of tourists on hols is the done thing. I was watching the priest." She chuckled. "Sounds like the punch line to a bad joke."

If he's a priest, I'm a nun. Instead of voicing her thoughts, she turned in her chair to face the woman more directly. The tables were small and close together, and with the shift, she practically sat across from the woman. "What did you find odd?"

She shook her head. "S'probably nothing."

"No, I'm curious."

"American?" the woman asked, and Kipling nodded, inspiring a wide smile. "My dad's from Pennsylvania." She extended her hand, her jewelry sparkling in the sunlight; an emerald ring on her center finger connected with a golden chain to a cuff bracelet with Egyptian designs. "Esther Mitchell."

She wasn't completely sure, because there was plenty of ambient sound in the café to be distracting, but she thought she caught a mumbled word from Greg in her aids. Not enough to be clear, but enough to distract her for a split second. She fought the urge to look in his direction.

"Kipling Branson," she said, taking the woman's hand, not at all surprised by the arched eyebrows at her name. "Yes, I am."

"You are what?" Esther asked.

"Named after Rudyard Kipling. That's usually the next question."

Esther laughed and adjusted her glasses on her nose. "Obvs, hmm?"

Kipling nodded and pointed in the direction the "priest" had departed. "I got a weird vibe from him. Is that what you found odd?"

"Well, that, too. But no. It was the cross hanging from his cassock. It's the symbol of the Knights of Templar. Since it's no longer an order of the Catholic Church, it seemed odd he'd wear it." She shrugged.

Awareness and realization skittered over Kipling's skin, and she silently cursed herself for missing the forest by staring so long at the trees. The realization had to have played across her features because Esther leaned forward, her brow pulled.

"Is something wrong?" she asked.

Kipling shook her head and rattled off her theory as much to get it out as to relay to Greg. "No, just remembering something. Charles Augustus Howell — he's the man Conan Doyle based the villain Milverton in the Sherlock Holmes novels. I read somewhere once that Howell claimed to be a descendant of the Knights of Templar."

Esther smiled, and it was almost whimsical. She licked her lips and brushed at some of the stray hair around her temple. "Yes, I've heard that, too. A friend of mine really knew his onions on Sherlock Holmes."

Kipling snatched up the brochure she'd been staring at for the last three-quarters of an hour, her heartbeat jumping to a giddy pace. "The Temple Church. That—"

"Was built by the Knights of the Templar."

Before Esther could finish, Kipling stood so quickly the chair scraped across the floor and threatened to tip. Her bruised body protested, but she only acknowledged it with a groan and hitch.

"I'm sorry, I don't mean to be rude, but I've got to go. Thank you."

"For what?" Esther said, looking at her like she might be crazy.

"For more than I can say." She snatched up her purse and headed toward the nearest exit. "The Temple Church," she said as she jogged. "I'm going to catch a cab."

"I'll be a few minutes behind you," Greg said in her ear. "I may have an idea how to fill in some gaps in our plan. I'll explain later if it works."

She didn't acknowledge, didn't nod, just ran for the exit.

Chapter Eighteen

A cab ride that should have taken fifteen minutes took nearly half an hour, and Kipling cursed every extra minute. Even though it wasn't quarter until one yet when the cab stopped down the street from the ancient church, her skin was clammy and cold with anxiety. The fare came to £16.90, and she was tempted to bolt as soon as the £20 note was in the cabbie's hand, but clenched her teeth and pressed her lips together as he dug in his cashbox for her change.

She had taken a portion of the drive to research the church as much as possible, to see if there was anything useful. Everything on the church was saturated in history, and while the history was beautiful and might otherwise be fascinating, she didn't find anything of use. Or seemingly of use. Any Web search on her phone was slow and tedious, and information about the link between the Knights of Templar and Charles Augustus Howell didn't extend any further than Howell believing himself to be a descendant. So much so that he insisted on wearing a red cross, the symbol of the Templar, to acknowledge his ancestry.

That morsel, which she already knew, got her to the church.

That was all.

Her head swam a little when she stepped free of the cab, a mix of her fatigue, injuries, and overall lack of food, but she swallowed and refused to acknowledge the potential slowdown. Rain had dampened the city during the ride, and dark areas made a patchwork of the cobblestone surrounding the centuries-old building. Despite her reason for being there, the beauty of the structure made her pause for a moment as she crossed the yard toward the gated garden and entrance. Very few people were in either the garden or the vestibule, but a woman stood just inside, the name Gladys on her lapel.

Kipling paid the £5 admission fee to enter the main church and followed a young couple into the chancel. They walked hand-in-hand, heads tipped up as they pointed and spoke to each other in what Kipling thought might be Portuguese. She didn't know the words, but the lyricism of the language struck her as familiar. The interior of the chancel was cool, every sound echoing in the vast space, with arched buttresses, great pillars, and elaborate stained glass. If she dug deep into her years of education, she could probably think of all the names of the bits and pieces of architecture, but right now her mind didn't focus much further than pew, recital, and hymnals.

She passed through the sanctuary to the nave, which had been the original portion of the church, built round to replicate a church in Jerusalem. Here were several stone effigies of Templar Knights, laid out on the floor as if for presentation. They were roped off to prevent anyone from molesting or damaging the old sculptures. Every sound carried resonance, even the smallest scuff of her shoes on the stone. She circled the nave, studying and watching just like everyone else, fighting the crawl up her spine because she knew, without question, that someone in the building with her watched her. She took out her phone and touched the screen to reveal the time. Approaching one o'clock. If she was wrong, she'd know soon, and there would be no time to get anywhere else; not that she had a second location in mind. If she was right, she might be able to breathe until the next stage of the game began.

With no guidance, no end destination, and an emptiness in her soul, Kipling returned to the sanctuary and walked along the walls to reach the row of pews nearest the altar and organ, nestled beneath a series of beautiful stained glass windows. Sunlight streamed through the glass, dancing like ethereal fairies over the polished, aged wood of the long bench pews. Kipling slipped into one and sat on the red velvet cushion, setting her bag beside her. Along the back of each pew was a level surface, much like a desk, for the pew behind, and on the desk were hymnals laid out – she assumed – for the parishioners during services.

She ran her hand over the deep blue cover, opening the book with a creak of the spine that seemed painfully loud in the revered and still space. The pages within were thin, like tissue paper, and fluttered past her fingertips before she closed the book again. Perhaps it was the stillness, perhaps it was the concept of sanctified ground, but the weight of Kipling's fear and worry pushed down on her with a sudden, smothering intensity. She closed her eyes and let her head fall back in exhaustion, pressing free a tear to trail down her cheek.

"Please…" was all she could find to say.

"I'm here," came Greg's voice, low and slightly out of breath. "I'm outside in the courtyard. I don't want to risk coming in quite yet. If you need me to, just say the word."

She raised her head and opened her eyes again, swiping her finger across her cheeks. Using her hand to hide her mouth, she said quickly, "I don't know what to do," before dropping her hands into her lap.

"He may be running the board, but Howell has underestimated you from the beginning. You'll do what needs to be done when you need to do it. I have no doubt, and I know Grayson has no doubt."

"But what if I doubt myself," she whispered, her head bowed, so any observer might think she prayed. In a way, it was a prayer. She said them to Greg but hoped someone heard them with greater power and confidence than she could find in herself.

"Doubt is a good thing. I know you won't believe this, but Grayson questions himself all the time." She couldn't help her small snort, and he chuckled, the sound soothing. "He never shows it, because his confidence is what throws off those trying to trick him, but he always doubts. Especially when lives matter. The fact you're worried will bring you focus. You have too much at stake to let Howell win. Now, focus and I'm here if you need me. Whenever you need me."

Kipling drew in a long, slow breath through her nose and released it through pursed lips, blinking against the heated mist blurring her vision. Across the sanctuary, someone's cell phone rang, a non-descript and standard ringtone. Habitually, Kipling watched to see who answered. A man pulled the phone free from his pocket and brought it to his ear, turning his back on her. He spoke too low for her to hear any of his words, just the low tone indicative of speaking. But when he twisted and looked back in her direction, she caught "she's here" on his lips, and a cold chill sent gooseflesh over her skin.

Trying not to stare, Kipling lowered her chin and watched him. With her head down, he seemed to relax his reticent stance and turned with the intent to watch her as much as she intended to watch him; but, she was better at it. Or, at least, she hoped she was.

"No sign she brought any of Holmes' team," the man said, and tipped his chin toward a woman standing a few feet away, then angled his head toward the exit. "I'm sending Edith to take another walk."

To cover her speaking, Kipling threaded her fingers together and laid her hands on the back of the pew in front of her, duplicating prayer. She hoped God would forgive her deception, considering the circumstances. "Woman heading your way," she said softly. "Looking for anyone with me. Blond. Middle-aged. Jeans and a red sweater."

"Got her," Greg replied. "Don't let them see you talking—"

"They think I'm praying," she said, cutting him off. "Which isn't far from the truth."

The man on the phone with who she assumed to be Howell stood with his back slightly away from Kipling so he didn't obviously face her, but didn't face away either. With her head down, she watched him, the angle making her eyes ache but she ignored it. He stayed silent until the woman returned, shaking her head.

"No sign of anyone with her. She's vulnerable," the man Kipling had decided to think of as Stooge One said into the phone. He listened and nodded. "Yes, sir. She appears to be praying." A smirk twisted Stooge One's lips. "You might have her on the hook now, sir."

"Like most clever criminals, he may be too confident in his own cleverness and imagine that he has completely deceived us."

The words were Sherlock's, but the voice that whispered them in her mind was Grayson's. With the same effect as a bucket of ice water on her insides, a realization struck her and she gasped. She had been playing the game all wrong. The more competent she proved herself to be, the more Howell would extend the game, and the more he would test her. If he thought he had the upper hand…

Kipling sucked in a sharp breath, with enough dramatic flair several heads turned her way, and covered her face with her hands, giving in for the briefest moment to the well of terror she'd tamped back all day. She was rewarded within moments when her phone vibrated in her hand and Grayson's avatar appeared on the screen. Taking in air, she swiped at her cheeks and answered the phone, more aware than ever of the eyes watching her. Now they had faces.

"H-hello?" she said and sniffed.

"Oh, my dear doctor. Why the tears? You've met your next challenge," Howell scoffed, mocking her with the condescending tone one might use on a misbehaving child.

"I was afraid," Kipling said, letting her voice tremor. "I was afraid I was wrong and too late."

Howell tsked her. "Don't tell me you have lost confidence. How distressing. You are nearly there, my dear. Nearly there."

"Please," she begged, perhaps the most honest she had yet been in the conversation. "Please tell me where to go." She shielded her eyes with her hand, playing the part of a weeping wreck, using the position to watch her watchers. They still stood where they had been, but faced each other in a way the Stooge One could also watch Kipling.

"You've done well, Doctor. For this challenge, I am going to give you the names of three places. With only one statement from me, you must decide where I wish to meet you for tea. Do you have a pen?"

Kipling sniffed and swallowed, pulling in her focus. "I'll remember."

"Ever the confident one, aren't we?" He laughed, and the sound was like nails on a chalkboard. "First, the rules."

"I've done everything you've asked," Kipling argued.

"Of that, I am assured," Howell said, then sighed heavily. "Due to the nature of this last step, I am forced to clarify. If I suspect at any time you have somehow contacted or received help from Holmes' team, the game is done and Sherlock is dead. Do you understand, Doctor Branson?"

By the time he finished speaking, his voice was as cold as stone, any merriment gone. The fact he'd slipped again, and referred to Grayson as Sherlock, concerned Kipling more than anything else. The man walked a razor's edge of insanity.

"I understand," she managed to say.

"I will give you the three possible locations. You have until four o'clock to arrive, and do dress for the occasion. That being said, you are forbidden from returning to Baker Street since I am aware you left Sookoo there this morning, and I have maintained eyes on Hennessey and Connolly. This is for you, and you alone, Kipling. Any interference and we are done."

"I understand," she repeated.

"This gifts you with the opportunity to shop," he teased, his voice seamlessly sliding back to the almost cordial, jovial taunt. When she said nothing in response, her mind blank, he continued. "The King's Sovereign. Edinburgh Pub. Porto's. Your only pointer to the right location is this: Your beginning, his end. I hope to see you in three hours, Doctor."

Without salutation, the line clicked off.

"But it doesn't change anything. We haven't solved anything, have we? You are still going back to London whenever, and I'm still going to be here in Boston."

Grayson smiled when his response came to mind, accepting not for the first time how engrained the words and antics of his ancestor had become in his life, true or not. "My great-grandfather was once quoted as saying that nothing clears up a case so much as stating it to another person."

Her lips quirked into a small, slow smile and she ticked up her chin. "Well, if we're quoting, Richard Bach asked can miles truly separate you from friends? If you want to be with someone you love, aren't you already there?" Even though she kept her voice level, slow color crept up her throat to her cheeks.

Grayson hummed in appreciation, and added, "Francois del a Rouchefou-cauld said 'Absence diminishes small love and increases great ones, as the wind blows out a candle and blows up the bonfire'."

"There you go again," she said on a heavy breath. "Foreplay for a bibliophile."

Grayson groaned but grinned. With a reluctant sigh, he said, "As much as the idea of verbal foreplay appeals to me to no end, I must go. For now. I must return to my hotel, wash and shave, and report to the Bureau."

"Tonight?" she asked.

"I cannot say. I am resolved to find answers."

Kipling nodded, tapping her fingertips on his chest. "I know."

Grayson knew he tempted fate, but he'd decided some time during the night he didn't much care. He slid his hands up her neck to lay his palms along her jaw and leaned down to kiss her cheek. His honest intent was to give as much as he dared, but realized in a hard thump of his heart, he had dared too much. Her breath hitched, warming his skin, and Grayson closed his eyes, holding his lips to her cheek, unable to withdraw. Kipling slid her hand from its place over his heart to his shoulder, her fingertips skimming his throat at the open collar of his shirt. She tipped her head back a degree and turned into his cheek, her lips brushing the corner of his.

He was lost.

Each shift, each touch, was careful…hesitant, for at least on his part, to give in too quickly would be to lose whatever barely existing control he had remaining. Grayson slid his cheek along hers until his parted lips held over hers, her breath mingling with his, rapid and warm. She trembled in his hold. He rolled his tongue forward, tentatively seeking until he moved past her lips and tasted her soft moan. They sealed the kiss, the cautious exploration immediately shifting to an intensity that snapped through him. Grayson released her jaw to wrap his arms around her, pulling her firm against him and her arms raised to circle his neck and shoulders.

Her tongue met his, and he tasted peppermint. His only thought was to be closer. Hold her closer. He needed her. Desperately.

He had asked her once if the danger he faced was too much for her to be with him, and she had answered no. Would she say the same now?

The opening of the bedroom/cell door forced Grayson to blink and bring into focus the misty garden beyond his barred window, a foggy rain having started while he let his thoughts wander. His chest ached, as much from the torture of the memory as the cracks in his ribs. His skin prickled and itched with healing. But most, his heart and mind hurt for Kipling at the soul level.

"It speaks poorly of you as an officer of the Royal Majesty's Secret Service, if your enemy can so easily approach without you being aware, Holmes."

Grayson drew in a long, slow breath through his nose to calm his murderous, impotent rage. "Hardly," he said, keeping his tone low and level. He braced his hands on the sill of the window, looking at Langdon Howell over his shoulder. While he kept his voice level, he didn't attempt to disguise whatever contempt the man might see in his face. "What would you expect me to do? Hmm? Hide under the bed? In the cupboard?" He tossed a glance toward the bed, then glared at Howell. "I am hardly in a position to attempt stealth, and not jumping to greet you is in no way a representation of my awareness." Grayson looked out the window again.

"I don't believe you've spoken so many words in the sum of your stay, Holmes," he said with a chuckle. "I thought perhaps you would like word of whether you live or die."

"I need no assurance from you."

"You are far more sure of Doctor Branson than she is of herself, I dare say. She was quite shaken in our most recent conversation."

Grayson pressed his lips together and closed his eyes, trying with all his willpower not to imagine her distressed. "Fine," he forced, then straightened and turned to his captor. "Which is it?"

It was then he saw the man at the door, holding aloft from the hook of a hanger on his fingers, a slate grey suit with a light gray shirt. Howell motioned toward the man, then clasped his hands in front of him. "I felt the grey was more appropriate for tea than an execution."

"I suppose it would have been black otherwise," Grayson mumbled, intentionally condescending.

Howell chuckled and nodded at the man, who stepped forward and draped the suit on the foot of the bed, setting a Gieves and Hawkes bag beside it. "I took some liberties in selecting certain items for you, Holmes. I do hope everything is to your liking."

"Does it matter?" Grayson said on a huff, pulling back the edge of the shop bag to look inside: black leather shoes and matching belt, a package of vests and pants, and socks. Since he'd awoken without his clothing, based on his physical state, he assumed most if not all had been ruined.

Howell sucked in a sharp breath through his nose and pivoted away, striding toward the door. "Our reservation is at four. If your doctor arrives, we'll have a lovely dinner. If not, it will be your last meal."

"Promises. Promises," Grayson said low, but not so low Howell wouldn't hear him.

Howell chuckled, waved a hand at his man, and the two quit the room leaving Grayson alone with the distinctive click of the lock. With a roar curling in a fiery ball in his chest, Grayson took one of the shoes from the bag and threw it across the room to bounce off the locked door.

Chapter Nineteen

Howell sent Grayson a smug look as he slid his phone into the inside breast pocket of his jacket. "Breathe easy, Holmes. Your doctor has arrived. Neither of you will die today."

"How reassuring," Grayson practically growled.

One thing, and one thing alone, had prevented Grayson from killing this putrid-souled arse in the days since he'd awoken in the man's custody. He'd had moments when he saw one, two, sometimes three opportunities of vulnerability in which Langdon Howell would cease to be a scourge on the world. In some instances, he knew he himself might not have survived. In some, the risk was manageable despite Grayson's injuries. He could have killed the man in the back of the limousine on the way here, and escaped the car before any of Howell's men could react. Even now, if it were only his life, he could use the knife beside his plate to kill the man — with either little or great attention, depending on his attack — but it was not his life alone at risk.

The one thought that had kept him impotent and complacent had been Kipling. If he attacked, if he escaped, he had no doubt Kipling would be dead within moments. It was not a risk he was willing to take until he also had the power to protect her. And to escape. He held no faith in Howell's promise the two of them could walk away if only she showed up on time.

From behind him, likely seated at the bar, came a raucous laugh and cheer for the football game playing on a screen mounted on the wall, calling for another pint. He'd heard the same patron twice before, the man growing loud enough to draw the attention of other diners.

"You are poor dinner company, Holmes."

Grayson risked a look at Howell, doubting he could hide the murder in his eyes even if he attempted it. "I don't care for Portuguese cuisine," he said with a snarled smirk.

A prickly awareness skimmed the back of Grayson's neck and he looked to the door, his chest tightening painfully. Led into the dining room by her elbow by one of Howell's men, Kipling paused and looked around until her wide-eyed gaze found them. Rage, unadulterated and raw, slammed into Grayson and he had to put his hands beneath the table edge, in tightly clenched fists, to keep from snatching up the knife and completing the fantasy. She wore a demure, dark blue cocktail dress that left her arms bare but covered to the base of her throat. Her hair was swept up into a twist, exposing the bruises mottling her right cheek and an abrasion along her brow, visible even in the dim light of the restaurant. Logically, Grayson had assumed she'd been hurt in some way during the explosion, but seeing the marks birthed a primitive, visceral demand for justice from the man who had hurt her.

The man seated beside him.

Her steps faltered when she met his gaze, her lips pressed together, and her throat tightening as she swallowed. Howell pushed back his chair to stand, and Grayson followed suit, wanting more than anything to round the table and meet her.

"Hold your ground, Holmes," Howell warned as she approached, weaving through the tables. "What a pleasure to see you again," Howell said in greeting, reaching for Kipling's hand.

Her shining eyed held on Grayson even as Howell lifted her hand to his lips and kissed her knuckles. The jealous troglodyte in

Grayson wanted to growl and snatch her away from the enemy's touch, and perspiration tickled down the back of his neck at the exertion of not lashing out. Howell released her hand and motioned for her to sit, which she did as a member of the staff came to the table and pushed in her chair. Her wide eyes still focused on him, Grayson sat, and refused to look away even when Howell cleared his throat.

"I certainly hope you will be better dinner company than Mr. Holmes," Howell said, his tone already condescending. "I took the liberty of ordering for us." He raised his hand and motioned to their waiter to bring the entrees.

"I'm not hungry," Kipling said so softly Grayson barely heard her, but her gaze held on him.

"Do you also have an aversion to Portuguese?"

With an unnatural jerk to the movement that spoke to the tension drawing her body taut, Kipling turned her head and finally settled her wide stare on Howell. "You required I be here. Considering the circumstances, you can't expect me to be eager to eat."

"The circumstances are you and Grayson will live another day," Howell said, leaning toward her by a few degrees, and Kipling reclined away. "That is worth celebrating, don't you think?"

On cue, the sommelier came to the table with a bottle of *Cartuxa Alentego* white wine, presenting the bottle label first to Howell. He had ordered the 2008 vintage upon being seated, and gave the sommelier a nod of approval. Any other time, the inspection of the cork and sniffing of the wine wouldn't have bothered Grayson at all, and would have been expected, but tonight it felt pretentious and grated his nerves. Upon his second approval, the glasses were filled. Kipling looked outright ill as she stared at the glass.

"Drink," Howell said with a smile, bringing the glass to his lips. Before sipping, the smile slipped and his tone turned menacing. "I insist."

Grayson held her gaze as he reached for the glass, and with his lead she followed suit, her hands trembling enough the wine sloshed slightly in the bowl of the glass before touching her lips. Grayson couldn't look away from her, because if he lost his focus, he feared he would lose his battle to restrain himself.

"I require you indulge me, Doctor." Howell set down the wine glass, focusing on Kipling.

"Hasn't she indulged you enough for one day, Howell?" Grayson demanded.

His enemy didn't acknowledge he'd spoken. "You left the church twenty minutes after our call, and did exactly as I asked. You didn't return to Baker Street, and spoke to no one, instead going straightway to purchase your dress and came here directly with what appeared to be little to no hesitation in your choice. Do tell me, Doctor, how did you choose to come to Porto's?"

Kipling licked her lips and pressed them together, fighting a visible battle to find calm. "We're in Chelsea," was her simple answer.

Howell's smile widened. "And why is that significant, Doctor?"

She cleared her throat and pushed shaking hands beneath the edge of the table. "My beginning, his end. Him being Charles Augustus." She seemed to gain confidence as she spoke, raising her chin to meet Howell's scrutiny. "He was found dead outside a drink house here in Chelsea. I was raised in Chelsea, Massachusetts."

"Ah, but my other choices could have also eluded to that event."

Kipling nodded; a single motion. "The King's Sovereign was a reference to the coin found in his mouth."

"Why did you rule out that location?"

"It was in Westminster."

"Wouldn't that imply the beginning of this adventure?"

She shrugged one shoulder, but her voice belied the confident gesture. "Seemed rather pedestrian for you to take me back to the same part of the city I'd begun in despite the association."

"And the Edinburgh Pub? Why did I give that as a choice?" When a deep line formed between her brows, Howell chuckled. "Indulge me, Kipling. I have no doubt you analyzed my reasons for choosing the other locations as much as you analyzed your final choice."

Her shining gaze shifted and held on Grayson when she

explained. "Edinburgh was a reference — more like a jab — at Grayson because that's where you—" She choked on the words, pausing to press her lips together again before she continued, and Grayson's rage boiled. "Where your brother killed Greg McQueen, Grayson's cousin."

"His end."

She looked back to Howell. "But not my beginning. I have no direct link to Edinburgh other than knowing how you broke Grayson's heart."

Howell sighed, his pleased expression acid in Grayson's veins. "So touching." He looked to Grayson. "She is so outspoken with regards to her heart. How refreshing."

"How can I not be?" she spoke up, surprising them both. Kipling waited until Howell looked at her again. "I witnessed first-hand the pain of the entire Holmes family as they all acknowledged, and yet tried to avoid thinking about, the empty chair left behind in Greg's absence." She motioned toward the fourth, empty, chair at the table. "Can an empty spot like that be filled again?"

When her gaze settled and stayed on Grayson as she asked her damning question, the knot in his stomach flipped, twisted. Her question wasn't for Howell; it was for him.

"You would do well not to attempt seeking sympathy in that regard, Doctor Branson," Howell said, his voice as cold as a Boston winter. "Has Sherlock shared with you his own crimes?"

She pressed her lips together in an act of self-fortification and looked to Howell with absolutely no hesitance or insecurity. The trembling woman of moments — seconds — before was gone, vaporized the moment she'd asked her question. Grayson's heart-beat jumped, his skin tingled in an awareness and preparedness he didn't yet understand.

"Do you really want to line up his crimes against yours? He who has no sin shall cast the first stone, and your hands are empty, Langdon Howell."

The sound of scraping chair legs and cursing behind him forced Grayson to turn away from the suddenly confident woman who had taken the place of the uncharacteristically shaken female who had first walked into the pub. The patron who'd been getting pissed for the last hour at the bar was attempting to walk to the door, with little success. The noise had apparently been him bumping into a couple as they dined. He swayed one way, nearly falling into the lap of a man at a table, managing to keep himself upright only well enough to step back, turn, and fall against Langdon Howell.

Howell scowled and shoved the man away. "Bugger off, you drunken sod."

In answer, the man belched. Bits of food clung to his thick, red beard and red hair stuck out at odd angles beneath his cap. Swaying, he set his hand on his head, perhaps to keep the cap from falling, which seemed the least of his concerns.

"No' nearly drunk enough, chappie," he slurred, swaying again. He slapped his big, beefy hand down on Howell's shoulder, leaving it there. "Apologies for the incon-incon—" He belched again. "For the trouble."

Grayson looked to Kipling to assure she wasn't in the pissed fool's path and caught his breath when he recognized the small, but distinct, sign she made in front of her body. Fingers intertwined on each hand to make the letter "R", she slid them across the space in front of her body.

"*Be ready.*"

Again, his senses sparked like electrical wires.

Two members of staff stepped in and each took the drunk by the arm, leading him toward the door. Just shy of it, he shook them off, flicking the v, and stumbled his way into the street.

Howell huffed and tugged his suit jacket into place, dusting the lapels with his fingers. "It would seem I am destined not to enjoy dinner."

"More's the pity." Grayson made no attempt to suppress the angry curl of his lip.

Their waiter arrived, setting the same meal before each of them. Chicken Piri Piri with spicy Portuguese rice and grilled vegetables. Despite himself, the smell was enticing and his stomach argued the benefit of eating. He'd taken in little food since his initial waking, unwilling to risk a drugging despite Howell's assurances he would be sedative-free. He would rather be a cautious fool than an overly accepting prisoner. Howell retrieved his utensils, laid his napkin in his lap, and motioned with the end of his knife that each of them should begin as he cut into his own meal. Kipling met Grayson's gaze across the table and offered a small smile – one that did more than anything in two days could to lift his soul. It was a smile without fear.

He knew not her plans, only that she had them, and having come this far he had no doubt in the outcome.

"It troubles me greatly that neither of you believe me to be a man of my word," Howell said, cutting through the chicken. "Doctor Branson has succeeded, and as stated in our negotiations, you both will leave here alive."

"Negotiations?" Kipling cried, her voice lifting upward in pitch.

A new sensation crawled up the back of Grayson's neck and he focused his full attention on Howell. The man was smug, far more so than when they'd arrived. While his promise had been made, since it was his game, the end result was fully to his interpretation. They may leave here alive, but would they leave alone?

"You bloody bastard—" Grayson began, but Howell's choked cough interrupted him.

Suddenly red in the face, perspiration bloomed in large beads on Howell's forehead and he slapped a hand against his chest. He swayed but gripped the edge of the table with his other hand to keep from tipping over. His jaw worked in an attempt at speech, but nothing more than a gargled sound came out.

"Oh, God," Kipling cried, jumping to her feet with such force her chair fell backward and banged on the floor. "He's having a heart attack. Someone help!"

The restaurant erupted in chaos as people scrambled forward, someone saying he was a doctor. Grayson stood his place, his attention on Howell. With his face quickly approaching purple, he glared hard at Grayson and took his hand from his chest to point, but his trembling arm barely lifted above the tabletop.

"Come on, Grayson," Kipling urged, pushing through the crowd to stand beside him, her hand wrapping around his. "Come on."

Kipling shoved open the back kitchen door with enough force it bounced off the exterior wall, shouts in Portuguese following her and Grayson into the alley behind the restaurant. She squinted against the afternoon sun, wishing their plan could have been implemented after dark, but since Howell had set the time they had no choice. She looked left and right to orientate herself, then started left toward the street, but stopped short when Grayson didn't follow, his hand around hers keeping her from moving away.

"Kipling—"

She spun back to him, breathing hard from their run. Every time she looked at him, her chest ached and she had to fight tears. What she saw of his injuries only inspired dark images of what she couldn't see. Mottled bruises on his brow and jaw, angry splotches of red indicating surface skin burns and abrasions. His hair had been chopped shorter, with the remaining spots still appearing dry and singed. His movements weren't fluid, and his features pinched. He had been so close to the explosion…

What she saw in his eyes now were questions.

Kipling closed the space between them, wrapping his hand in both of hers. "We don't have time, Grayson. You have to trust me. Please."

He only paused long enough to take in a hitched breath and squeeze her fingers. "Lead the way."

She nodded, and gripped his hand again, running down the alley where it opened into the street on the opposite side from the front entrance. Rounding the corner, a truck with the name of what she assumed to be a completely made-up produce company painted on the side, sat parked along the curb with the back doors open. Boxes of vegetables and fruit-filled a portion of the container, giving the appearance of a purpose outside the restaurant. Greg stood by the open doors, his red wig and scruffy beard gone – along with his stumbling drunk act – watching the street. He still wore a wide-brimmed hat and glasses that shielded his face. When he spotted them, he waved them forward.

"Come on. Show a leg!"

For half a step, Grayson faltered, and when she looked at him she found him staring — stunned and perplexed — at Greg. Had part of him already recognized his cousin and best friend? This wasn't anywhere near an ideal way for him to learn the truth, but if they made it out alive, they would apologize for lack of finesse later.

"Compartments are open," Greg said, hopping with ease into the back of the truck amongst the produce. He reached for Kipling's hand and helped her in. As she stood beside him inside the stuffy box, he extended his hand to Grayson.

Kipling held her breath, wishing she could calm the vicious pounding of her heart as easily. Grayson stared, his eyes shifting in tiny degrees as she was quite sure his mind processed what it saw, what it recognized beyond the changes to Greg's features, and what he had to accept as real. Greg leaned over further, extending his hand.

"Later," was all Greg said.

Just as he'd laid his trust in her in the alley, Grayson's expression firmed and he slapped his hand against the inside of Greg's forearm. They gripped each other as cousin pulled cousin into the truck. Two small openings in the floor, like trap doors, opened to single person sized compartments extending below the bed of the truck nestled amongst the axles and undercarriage of the truck. From any normal approach or angle, the compartments weren't visible from anywhere around the truck, but easily spotted if someone took the time to crawl under the vehicle. The goal was to avoid suspicion so no one considered the need to check that closely. Greg had explained the setup to Kipling while she prepared for the meeting, but seeing the small spaces sent an unjustified tremor of nausea through her. It looked like a coffin. Greg had laid out heavy, padded moving blankets to provide some cushion, but once inside she would be alone until they reached the safe house.

"I hear people coming. Lie down," Greg urged.

With only a second to find her near-depleted store of strength,

Kipling looked to Grayson one final time before she stepped into the sunken compartment and stretched out as Greg lowered the plywood that created the floor of the truck bed, and the top to her coffin. Darkness engulfed her, and she closed her eyes, preferring the darkness in her own head over the smothering lack of light in the compartment. She focused on the sounds beyond her coffin, hearing Grayson climb into his own compartment just a couple of feet away. So close, but so far away.

Her heart pounded viciously in her throat, threatening to choke her, and even with her eyes squeezed shut tight the tears leaked through and ran hot along her temple to her hair. She sucked in the ball of bitter fear and held her breath, refusing to give life to it. Her panic wouldn't be the reason they failed.

She tried to visualize instead the action of each sound that managed to reach her through the insulating floor. Grayson shifted in the compartment that was likely a little too small for him, followed by Greg dropping into place the same type of board that covered her. Then Greg's heavy footsteps as he crossed the truck compartment, then a scrape and thunk. Was he moving boxes of produce to both hide their presence and continue the charade of his presence?

One of the heavy double doors slammed into place with a clank, metal against metal. The second didn't follow.

Voices — loud and angry — reached through the floor, but with the thick wood and the running of the truck engine, she only heard tone. No words, just volume. If she focused hard, she could differentiate Greg's pitch and bass from the other voices. With heavy thumps, she envisioned the pursuers stepping up into the truck, their footfalls echoing on the wood.

She held her breath as the steps neared, covering her mouth with her trembling hands, afraid that somehow her shaky breath might be heard through the wood and the engine.

Two heavy feet thumped on top of her, and she sucked in a sharp breath. This close, their words were still muffled, but she understood, and Greg was the first clear voice she recognized.

"Just delivered two cases of beetroot and courgette," he said, his accent now rough and northern. He truly was a master of accents. "Lest you be wanting a case of tomatoes or spring onions, I've go' nothin' here for you."

"We're wasting our time," came an unfamiliar voice. "Howell'll go ballistic if we lose them."

"Lookin' for someone in partic'lar?" Greg asked.

"Man and woman," a different voice answered. "Would have come from the restaurant alley."

"Can't say as I *saw* anyone," Greg answered, the boots above her shifting, and she realized he stood on the board. "Heard someone, though, bit of a commotion. Looked down the alley there, didn't see anyone so they likely ran the other direction. Can't speak to whether there was one or six, man or woman, though."

"Let's go. This is a waste of time," came male voice one, and their heavy steps hurried to the door, with Greg's more casual steps following.

Not until the heavy truck doors closed, the engine revved, and the truck jostled into motion did Kipling dare take a deep breath. Even then, she didn't dare open her eyes. The noise was overwhelming, so much so her hearing aids couldn't compensate enough to dampen the sound, and she yanked the aids from her ears, finding a small degree of peace in the silence.

After a few minutes of rambling through the streets of Chelsea, speeding up and slowing, she felt sick. Motion sickness hadn't ever been a problem, but this was far beyond just motion. Her heart pounded so hard she doubted she'd be able to stand, she'd be so lightheaded, and her mouth was dry. She crossed her arms over her chest, like a corpse in a coffin, with her fists clenched so hard her nails dug into her palms and her joints ached, squeezing the aids, but it kept her from pounding on the floorboard. Kept her from giving in.

Greg had warned her it would be a long trip. The intent was to "work a theme", he'd said, and at her confused silence he'd explained it was an anti-surveillance maneuver. He would drive around the city, pretending to be a produce truck driver, long enough to assure no one was following them before actually heading to the safe house. If he felt confident they'd fooled Howell's men, the trip would be shorter. If he suspected anything, it would be longer…depending on what needed to be done to assure their safety.

Every time the truck slowed, she tried not to imagine Howell's men finding them. She held her breath and focused on the vibrations of the truck. The door felt different, was distinctive. The engines felt different when idling at an intersection from when they'd been sitting.

She just had to stay focused…

Chapter Twenty

Grayson had his hands and one foot braced against the wood above him as soon as the lorry came to a full stop, wincing at the pull in his side, in anticipation that this might be their final destination. The ride had been a low level of torture, jostling and jolting him despite the cushions laid out by the driver.

The driver…

He wasn't ready — not yet — to put a name to the man, even though every fact before him said he knew the truth. *There is nothing more deceptive than an obvious fact.* If his mind wanted to argue his point with infamous familial quotes, he mentally tossed one back at his own psyche. *Once you eliminate the impossible, whatever remains, no matter how improbable must be the truth.* Everything fact, every action, every moment since the restaurant told him to accept the niggling whisper in the back of his mind — nudging at his heart — but his heart wasn't ready for the ramifications if he was wrong.

How could he be wrong about this?

For well over a year, he had been told it was impossible. At the least, improbable. But…was it the truth? He'd argued with Jeffrey Cooper more than once he didn't believe it. Where was the proof?

Cooper and Six had argued lack of proof of death — especially in an explosion — didn't equate to proof of life; but his gut, his *heart*, screamed otherwise again and again and again.

Why was he here now? How did Kipling know to trust him? *If* he was who Grayson believed...The onslaught of "Why?" and "How?" questions was too massive for him to split, define, or categorize and he was unaccustomed to being so doubtful of his own mind.

The lorry stilled and the engine died, and Grayson pushed up with all the strength he could leverage in the cramped confinement. The board cleared the edge of the space, and he shoved it away, using the edge of the compartment to push himself free. His side pinched, squeezing his lungs, and the ragged stitches in his shoulder pulled. The shirt clung to his skin, confirming his suspicion that the wound had at least partially opened. It didn't matter. None of it mattered.

Wounds healed.

If a man could come back from the dead, a shoulder stitch was inconsequential.

If...

Every time he let himself think it, if even for a moment, his heart expanded painfully in his chest. The pain of hope.

Kipling's sounds of struggle escaped through the wood, no longer smothered by the sound of the engine, and they pushed him harder to shove aside the cases of food and find the pry point. "Kipling?" he called out. "Kipling!"

He found purchase at the edge of the board when it popped upward from Kipling's kick from beneath. Grayson used his right hand only, his left hugged to his side in an attempt to minimize the pain, but couldn't help the grunt of exertion when he shoved aside the wood, freeing her. He stepped down with one foot into the compartment and reached for her as she scrambled free and into his arms, his name hoarse from her throat. Holding her, he managed to shift them so he sat on the edge of the box, and she was in his lap, her arms around his shoulders, her face pressed to the curve of his neck to shoulder.

For two days, he clung to the memory of holding her to keep his rational mind in control, to keep his rage from taking over and pushing him to take his vengeance on Howell for hurting her. Because he knew Howell had hurt her, and knew he only saw the surface. He closed his eyes, cupped the back of her head with one hand, and held the palm of the other to her back so he could feel the pound of her heart. A high-pitched whine came from her clenched hands from her aids. He had found the noise in the cramped box loud and grating and knew it would have been worse for her.

Her arms tightened, her chin on his shoulder and the comforting scent of her hair filled his senses. He was thankful she didn't hear his groan when she held on tighter. "I've wanted to do this since I saw you in that pub," she cried, her voice rough, raw, and louder than her natural tone. "I don't think I've ever been so afraid, not even with kidnappers and exploding warehouses in Boston." Panicked laughter laced her words and she hung on tighter.

Grayson kissed her cheek and gently forced her away from him so she would see his lips, and took her face between his hands. Her cheeks were slick with tears, but a genuine smile tugged her lips. "Are you okay?" he asked, and her focus shifted to his mouth as she nodded. "I know you were in hospital."

"I'm fine," she said on a long expulsion of breath, a tear slipping from her eye to fill the seam between his skin and hers. "Bruises don't matter. I'm better now that I'm with you." Her gaze shifted, and he knew she took in the bruising and abrasions on his face, and the hack job of a haircut they'd give him. She slid an arm between them to barely brush her fingers along his chin. "

Knowing she wouldn't hear the conviction in his voice, he hoped she felt the conviction in his kiss as he drew her to him. He desperately needed Kipling's ability to ground him, and desperately needed affirmation all this was real. She hummed against his lips, her cold fingers curling into the cropped hair above his nape and he let himself drown in her. If nothing else was real — if he was wrong — this was right and true.

With a clank and creak, the large doors of the box container opened, letting in the waning sunlight, and reluctantly Grayson let her draw away from him. Sunset approached; they had driven around for nearly two hours. Kipling hurried to put her aids back into place, a shuddered breath moving through her as she stiffened, her gaze sliding from him to the door.

His heart lodged in his throat as he did the same.

Their ally stood on the street, his torso visible above the tailgate, the dimming sunlight behind him leaving his face in shadow beneath the brim of his hat. But when he spoke, his voice slammed into Grayson's chest with the power of a train car. "We have to keep moving. We're leaving the lorry here, and taking a car the rest of the way to Southpark."

Kipling sniffed, wiped at her bruised cheeks, and stood from his lap, letting him stand as she stepped out of the compartment, her grip hard on his hand. Grayson followed but felt he moved through concrete. That same battling bundle of emotions in his chest kept him from moving forward. Hope warred with denial.

The woman he loved and trusted with his life looked up at him and squeezed his hand. "You know it's true, Grayson," Kipling said softly. Bright eyes met his, and she smiled, a small tick at the corner of her lips. "You've known all along. You told me. You were right."

"But how do you know—"

"You asked him to protect me," she answered before he could finish the question. Her lips bowed in a strained but honest smile and she blinked rapidly. "He said you sent a message into what should have been a void if he were really gone, but he read it and did as you asked." Kipling tipped her head toward the man. "I've known him as John Allen."

"John Allen…" Grayson knew he scowled, but that and the name of her newest friend 'from Boston' was all he could manage.

"Come on out, Ollie."

Grayson's chest tightened around his heart. Before he made the conscious choice, his wooden legs propelled him to the truck tailgate. The brim of the man's hat hid his features, with the sun behind him, but Grayson recognized his shape. The width of his shoulders. The way he moved. Greg McQueen had been closer than a brother, a constant companion, and Grayson could pick out his shadowed form in a dark building during a raid. Greg raised his arms to reach for Kipling, helping her down from the truck as Grayson crouched to set his hand on the wooden floor and jump down to the street. The jolt shot pain through him, making him sway and groan.

His cousin reached for him, steadying him. There was no doubt left. No fear of disappointment, only the heady rush of realization. With both of them outside the truck, Greg took off the cap he'd worn to shade his face and tossed it past Grayson into the truck, then did the same with his sunglasses, revealing a face Grayson didn't recognize but eyes he did. Holmes eyes.

"I've a medic of sorts waiting," Greg explained, assessing Grayson with a quick glance. "You're doing a hell of a job keeping your feet. Am I right?"

"Howell ensured I received medical attention," he said through clenched teeth. "Such as it was." With his jaw set and his fisted hand resting on Greg's shoulder, he forced himself to stand upright. Kipling watched him from behind Greg, arms crossed over her body and her eyes wide. "I'll be fine, darling," he tried to assure. "It's as you said. Bruises don't matter."

"But a punctured lung might," Greg interjected and shook his head. "I'm sorry, Ollie." His voice was raw, heavy.

Grayson had to force a hard swallow, his lips in a pressed line. "Where have you been?" he managed to ask. "Other than in Boston."

The moment the question passed his lips, Grayson realized he didn't give a damn and didn't allow Greg to answer. In a sudden step forward, Grayson embraced Greg with such ferocity both men swayed and grunted with the impact. Greg's fists thumped his back. "Shut up, you stupid bastard. I don't bloody care."

Kipling sniffed and watched them, amazed and thankful for the wave of joy she both felt in herself and saw in Grayson's face. The last few hours had been a non-stop onslaught of emotional punches, from realizing Grayson was missing, to Greg's revelation, Howell's challenge, and the moment she saw Grayson in the pub bruised, battered, and alive. Each had beaten her to the point of crumbling, but witnessing the reunion between these two amazing men made up for every bruise – both physically and emotionally.

They talked, but the way they held each other, she only heard the low timbre of their voices and not the words behind them and wasn't sure she wanted or needed to hear them. She wiped at her cheeks and took a step back until she reached the corner of the truck, turning her back to them to give them all the privacy she could without being out of sight, and she looked up and down the street. She had no idea where they were, but they were away from the main bustle of downtown London. The side of the street they parked on seemed residential, with four-story complexes showing their age. An open field behind a chain link fence was across the street, with buildings in the distance. The road needed repair, but she'd seen far worse in Massachusetts after the spring thaw. No traffic drove past, and except for a car parked a few yards behind them, the only other vehicle she saw was far enough down the road all she could determine was it was white. And that was only because there was a streetlamp near it. Darkness was settling quickly.

She jumped and gasped when Grayson's arm came around her waist, his other across her chest, in an embrace from behind. Were it not for his deep voice near her ear, she might not have tamped down the sudden and intense urge to fight. He tightened his hold, resting his cheek against her temple, and the warm contact was an almost instant sedative.

"I called your name," he said.

Hoping he didn't feel the pounding of her heart or the cold sweat chilling her skin, Kipling leaned back into his chest and wrapped her hands over his where they rested. "I was trying not to listen. You deserved a few moments."

"We've said what needs to be said here, but we need to leave.

Best to be off the streets as soon as possible until I can make contact with Director Cooper and move in on Howell while he is out of sorts."

Kipling tilted and turned her head so she could see his profile. "Tonight?"

"Perhaps not tonight, but it should be quickly, and tonight is my preference. I'm familiar with the drug Greg used on him — yes, I've concluded that was Greg," he added with a smile. "It will mimic physical distress, but unless Howell already had some dire medical condition exacerbated by it, the effects will wear off on their own. Though he will be weak for up to seventy-two hours. If he was at all able to communicate, I'm quite sure he would have told his men not to call for emergency services, and if they arrived, he would have refused. He is probably as familiar with the drug as we are, and knew full well he'd been injected the moment it affected him."

"He'll be angry."

"Quite." Grayson ended the statement with a long kiss to her cheek before he turned her to face him. "Enough talk of him." He kept his arms around her, holding her near him, and bent at the knee to be closer to eye level with her. "I need you to know how very proud I am of you."

Kipling shook her head, breaking eye contact. "I did what needed to be done."

"As much as I hate you were required to act as such, don't belittle your accomplishments." Grayson lowered his arms, leaving her feeling cold, and took her hand to lead her away from the truck as Greg shut the back door. "I want to hear all of it."

Kipling sighed and wrapped both her hands around his, feeling the rough abrasions on his knuckles. The thought of reliving the last two days, especially the last few hours, even if only verbally left her exhausted to her soul. At that moment, all she wanted – all she cared about — was to curl up in bed, in his arms, feeling his heart-beat beneath her cheek, and sleep for two days.

"I'm not even sure I remember it all," she said with a tired sigh.

"Which is why I will likely leave the telling to Greg," he said with a smile. "I doubt you see yourself with the same clarity."

"I've always seen Kip's brilliance," Greg said, stepping to Grayson's side. "I must say, though, despite the way she spoke about you I still held doubts even she could change you, Ollie." He winked at Kipling. "No more doubts. You're a changed man."

"For the better," Grayson added before pressing a kiss to her forehead. Kipling leaned into the touch and closed her eyes. Just hours before, she feared she'd never feel his touch again. She immediately had to tamp down the choking lump in her throat.

Logically, and if she stepped away from herself and looked in, Kipling knew the exhaustion and the smothering mingle of relief and grief was a delayed reaction to the day's events. She'd tried the therapist route after the bombings and near misses in Boston, and it all sounded so textbook, that she'd stopped. Textbooks didn't fix this and didn't change anything. She wanted to weep, to let it go, but refused because it was over and they had succeeded. There was nothing to cry about now.

The words she'd said more than once in Boston replayed in her mind. "*I'm fine. I'm here. I'm alive. And I'm fine.*" She would fight with stubborn tenacity to make sure the words were true.

"Kipling," Grayson said, his voice heavy enough to draw her gaze up. "What are you thinking?"

"Trying not to," she answered as honestly as she could.

"Come on." Greg ticked his head toward the car parked behind the truck, and they fell in step behind him. He spoke over his shoulder as he walked. "We're only ten minutes from Southpark."

"Southpark," Grayson said, his brow pulling down. "The only person I believe we know in Southpark is—"

"Esther." Greg winked. "You can thank Kip for the idea."

"Esther…" Kipling looked between Greg and Grayson. "I talked to a woman today at the museum. She said her name was Esther." Her step slowed as part of their conversation — part that seemed irrelevant at the time — came back to her.

"Is something wrong?" she asked.

Kipling shook her head, and rattled off her theory as much to get it out as to relay to Greg. "No, just remembering something. Charles Augustus Howell — he's the man Conan Doyle based the villain Milverton in the Sherlock Holmes novels. I read somewhere once that Howell claimed to be a descendant of the Knights of Templar."

Esther smiled, and it was almost whimsical. She licked her lips and brushed at some of the stray hair around her temple. "Yes, I've heard that, too. A friend of mine was a Holmes aficionado."

"Esther Mitchell," Grayson said, a wide smile spreading his lips. "Darling, you certainly know how to make the absolute best of a bad situation." He brought her hand to his lips and kissed her knuckles. "Esther is a dear friend I — *we* — have known for years. In fact, she and Greg—"

"Yeah, okay. Can we just move along?"

Grayson laughed and Greg walked a little faster.

When they were close enough for her to see the make and model, Kipling chuckled and shook her head. At Grayson's inquisitive expression, she answered, "Seven thousand miles from the United States, and our getaway car is a Ford Fiesta."

Chapter Twenty-One

"I was about to go looking for you in all the lay-bys between Chelsea and Southpark," Esther gushed, motioning them through the open door into the narrow foyer of her flat, giving a quick glance up and down the residential street. Once through the door, she quickly hugged Greg and moved on to Grayson.

He brought Esther to his side opposite where Kipling stood, unwilling to let go of her hand to fully embrace Esther. Grayson winced and grunted when she squeezed, and she immediately pulled back.

"Sorry." She jerked a thumb over her shoulder toward the interior of the flat. "My best mate Juds is in the parlor, ready to check you over since Greg didn't know what to expect." She eyed him up and down, focusing on his face. "Geez, Ollie, you look terrible." She looked to Greg. "Should we take him to A&E?"

"No," Grayson answered before Greg had a chance to respond. "I'm much further from death than I look." Kipling's shift to stand closer to him, close enough he felt her warmth against his back and arm. Her cool fingers tightened their hold between his, her other hand wrapping around his wrist, and she squeezed. "I've some stitches she may need to see to, but all else is healing and *will* heal with time. Hardly the worse for wear."

"I'm not sure you're the proper judge of that," she said with a soft laugh, arching a thin eyebrow. "Have you seen yourself in the mirror?"

Esther looked just as lovely as she always had, haphazard and messy enough to avoid conformity, but with a gentle smile and welcoming eyes that spoke of her heart. When she and Greg had dated, Grayson had been thrilled, and he'd called Greg an idiot when he let her go. Especially since his cousin had gone so far as to have her vetted, and when she was cleared, told her who he was — who Grayson was — and what they were. She had been surprised, having not suspected at all as far as she confessed, but had taken it all in stride. Within three weeks, Greg had gotten pissed, showed up at Baker Street at two in the morning, and told Grayson it was over without another word of explanation. Though her gaze lingered for a moment longer on Greg than himself, Grayson saw no contempt or anger on her part. The true story intrigued him.

She set her hands at her waist, making the "I FOUND THIS HUMERUS" statement on her shirt more obvious, and sent a wink and smile at Kipling around Grayson's arm. "Hello, Luv. Fancy meetin' you again. Had I known you were friends with this wanker, I might not have had a chat at the museum." Her grin and wink softened her insult.

Greg still groaned and gripped his chest. "Ouch."

She ticked her chin at Greg, still grinning. "Not quite used to the new face. Wouldn't have known it was you if you hadn't opened your mouth. Ran out of birds in London who didn't want to give you a bunch of fives whenever they saw the last one, huh?"

Grayson cleared his throat, hoping to save Greg at least some pride. Esther laughed, enjoying Greg's discomfiture far more than she should, and looked past Grayson again to Kipling. "You look like you could use a bevvy. Come on in and settle for a bit while Juds does her thing." She slid her gaze toward Grayson and said "No worries. She's out of Royal; knows all about you lot," before looking back to Kipling. "What's your pleasure?"

"Alcohol," Grayson said low, leaning over so Kipling heard him. She shook her head. "Oh, no. Thank you."

"Tea? No Brit can turn down tea. You may not be a Brit, but bonk one and you're required to convert," she said over her shoulder as she headed for the kitchen to their left, motioning for Kipling to follow.

"Same Esther," Greg said, a touch of melancholy in his voice.

Kipling didn't follow, didn't release her hold on Grayson's hand. Turning so his back was to the direction Esther had gone, and he could bring Kipling around to face him, he kept her hand in his and laid his free palm on her cheek, urging her with his touch to look at him. Before focusing on her, he took a second to glance at Greg, who immediately took the hint and silently quit the room, heading for the room where Juds waited. Holding her gaze, he lifted her hand and turned her wrist to him, pressing his lips to her pulse point. Her pulse was fast, not racing, but far from calm. They needed a few moments — no, they needed far more than a few moments — but a few moments was all he could conjure to assure both of them the danger had passed. Grayson was no stranger to having his life at risk, and no stranger to loss, and yet on this day he'd been given a gift of perspective. Greg was alive — *confirmed* — and Kipling was beside him. The value of life was different today.

"It's over now," he said against her skin before bringing the hand to his chest so her palm rested over his heart.

She nodded but said nothing.

"We need to go in the other room with Esther's friend, and Greg, so we can begin the final steps in resolving all of this." Grayson drew her to him and kissed her forehead; her skin was cool. "I would like her to give you a look over as well—" She shook her head before he got halfway through his request. He touched his thumb to her lips, and she stilled, meeting his gaze. "Then we will get some rest. I want nothing more than to hold you, Kipling."

His words brought a shuddered breath from her, and she leaned into him, her fingers curling so her knuckles rested on his lapel. She nodded and sniffed. "You aren't angry, are you?"

"At Howell?" he said, mimicking a smile as he pulled back so she'd see his face. "I'm bloody pissed off at him. Not likely to let that go any time soon."

Her lips ticked in the smallest of smiles. It was a start. "I meant, are you angry at Greg? Or me?"

He shook his head before she finished the question. "No. God, no," he said emphatically. "Absolutely not. I have just been given a gift very precious few will ever receive, someone they feared lost." He canted his head, left then right. "I will admit I have a great many questions for Greg, but I suspect I can already deduce some of the answers. Those answers lead to more questions from me, but not questions of Greg. Or you."

If what he suspected was true, it was Director Cooper and Six who would have questions to answer. He doubted he'd like any of the justifications.

"Why would I be angry with you?"

She shrugged, her eyes shifting away for only a moment before coming back to him. "For not realizing who he was. It all seems so obvious now—"

"In solving a problem of this sort, the grand thing is to be able to reason backward," he said, and her immediate smile lightened his heart. "There, I knew that smile was still there."

"Foreplay for a bibliophile…"

The weight of her voice was as tactile as a touch, and with his finger crooked beneath her chin, he tipped up her lips to kiss her. He had underestimated the chest-punch effect, and while their kiss at the lorry had been one of relief, this was one of confirmation. All intentions to assure them both with a brief intimacy were destroyed when she tipped her chin and parted her lips, and he willingly let himself be tempted. Only the awareness of their location and company made him force his lips from hers and press their cheeks together as he drew ragged breaths, her own breath warm on his neck.

"You are my world, Kipling."

The thought birthed in his mind the same moment it passed his lips, and not a moment of hesitation came over him at having said them. A shuddered, rough release of breath moved through Kipling and she leaned closer, her cheek to his chest.

"Let's see to what we must," he said softly before kissing her temple and sliding his palm down her arm to link their hands again.

Greg's voice carried from the parlor. It had been at least four years since he'd been to Esther's Southpark flat, but he still remembered the layout. She had changed little within the dwelling, other than her stacks of books on the tables were higher, and the bookshelves were at least two rows deep, some bowing dangerously and possibly only held up by the books in the shelf below. The house held the aroma of aged pages and leather, laced with sandalwood and exotic spices with a subtle underlay of lavender. There was nothing modern and sterile about Esther's home, furnished with carved wooden furniture from East India and rugs from the Orient, faded and worn but still beautiful. Old maps with torn edges hung in massive frames, pressed behind UV glass to protect them, and along with other carved reliefs and tapestries, not much exposed wall existed.

Grayson didn't attempt to hide his smile when Kipling's eyes widened and her lips parted as she took in the shelves and stacks of books. She let her fingers brush over a cover as they passed, and if they were here any length of time he was sure she wouldn't be able to resist cracking one open, if only to smell the pages and ink.

Greg sat on the cushion edge of a marigold chair, phone to his ear, and if Grayson had to guess the name of the person on the other end it would be Sandra. He was busy assuring the task was complete, Grayson was in their company, and Kipling had executed the plan without fault. At the mention of her name, Greg grinned and winked in her direction.

Sitting at one end of a red brocade settee was a woman for whom Grayson couldn't readily determine an age. With long hair, clearly dyed, almost fully black except for the last few inches, which were bright blue, she had a youthful air, but the medical bag beside her and the smile lines around her eyes spoke to more years. She had a stud in her nose, and heavily shadowed/mascaraed eyes, but when she looked up and smiled any preconceived notions of what to expect based on her appearance disappeared.

"Tell Director Cooper Grayson will be in contact soon," Greg said, looking his way with raised eyebrows. Grayson nodded, and mouthed "within the hour", which Greg repeated. "Still leave me out of it. I don't want you or Mac caught in the fallout from this. Just keep saying you helped Kipling from Baker Street." He nodded, still looking at Grayson, then smiled. "Of course. Until later." Then he took the phone from his ear and tapped off. "I promised we'd let her know when I'd secured you safely. It nearly killed her and Mac not to be on the ground on this one."

"I would imagine so."

Greg motioned with flat palm toward the woman who had sat silent during the conversation. "This is Juds — or Judith, if you prefer—"

"Which I don't," she interjected with a wink and wider smile.

"Or, today, she is Nurse Oswald."

"You make it sound so sexy. I can see why Esther fancied you," she flirted with another wink in Greg's direction, then jutted her pointed chin toward Grayson. "Plain enough to see you're the patient. Pardon my bluntness, love, and no disrespect to the missus but strip and tell me what I've got."

"Kip, let's—" Greg began, rising partially from his seat, but Grayson raised his free hand enough his cousin saw it, staying his suggestion. He meant well, Grayson knew, but he also knew Kipling and while this would be difficult to see, she needed to. At the deepest root of honesty, he didn't want her parted from him, but if he believed it would be better, he'd let her go.

He didn't believe it.

Grayson kissed the back of Kipling's fingers before releasing her hand so he could tug free the necktie he'd loosened while trapped in his traveling coffin. As Juds opened her bag, pulling out a gauze bandage, some plasters, ointment tubes, and a variety of implements, Grayson kept his attention wholly on Kipling, only observing Greg and Juds in his peripheral.

"This is going to look far worse than it is," he said low enough her gaze automatically shifted to his mouth. "I fully realize what I say may not help, but I need you to hear it. Kipling..." He waited until her eyes moved back up to look into his, and he spoke louder. "I am fine."

Shrugging off the jacket, his suspicion was confirmed when he revealed the sticky, stained fabric of his shirt stuck to his arm over the poorly executed and now pulled stitching. It had just begun to bleed through the shirt, leaving a dark crimson line.

Kipling gasped, her wide eyes quickly shining, and she brought shaking fingers to her lips. Juds swore, and dug deeper into her bag, drawing out a suture kit as well as suture plasters. With a wince, Greg stood and moved to help Grayson unbutton and peel off the shirt down to the white cotton vest beneath, exposing the wound again when the saturated gauze came away with the shirt. By the third button, Kipling's initial shock wore off − or she pushed through it − and she worked to unbutton his cuffs to drag the sleeves over his wrists. The final tear away shot tingling pain to his elbow and up his shoulder, making him hiss.

"Geezus, Ollie," Greg growled, balling the shirt to toss it in a plastic bag. "Who the hell patched you up? Doctor Frankenstein?"

"No, Howell had a thick-fingered woman who probably retired from medicine two decades ago. I woke with tightly bound ribs, crooked stitches, and my arm bound shoulder to elbow in gauze and Germolene for the surface burns."

He glanced away from Kipling long enough to assess his own physical state. The entirety of his left arm was a vicious red, spreading up his shoulder and chest beneath the vest, with the worst areas just inside the cuffs of his shirt and along the edge of his collar; both areas with the least amount of protection when the car exploded. His suit jacket and shirt had likely caught fire, but since the burns were not worse, he assumed Howell's people had been at the ready to put out the flames and carry him off before the chaos died and someone went looking for him. The blisters around the worst areas had broken earlier that day, and Nurse Frankenstein had wrapped his wrist and bandaged his collarbone, but had left the rest at his insistence. The rest of the burned area was merely a harsh red, radiating heat, and irritated from the shirt. In truth, removing it had immediately alleviated much of his discomfort.

"Dark ages," Juds said on a hiss and with a shake of her head. She motioned to the space beside her. "Nothing I can't fix. Have a seat."

Grayson sat beside her at an angle that allowed her to work on the worst damage on his left side but allowed him to speak with Greg and keep Kipling on his right. "Before I contact the director, I need to know how involved in today's…" He winced, searching for the proper word. "…activities Six might have been. If I properly interpret the side of the conversation with Sandra I heard, they are not aware you are here."

Although he didn't ask it as a question, Greg nodded, taking his seat again. He sat forward, elbows on his thighs, loosely linked hands hanging by his knees. "I'm not exactly on working terms with Six right now." Grayson waited, his silence his request to continue. Greg sighed and shook his head, a lopsided grin tipping his mouth. "We're going to get into it eventually, but I've been deep undercover for several months. Since I recovered from Edinburgh." He paused, focusing on his hands as he rubbed his palms together.

"We will leave that for another time," Grayson offered. Although he wanted to know it all, their time was limited, and it was clear the conversation would not be a pleasant one."

Greg nodded. "My assignment was to observe and report on Howell and his activities without connecting myself with them in any way Peripheral only. Connections to connections, that sort of thing."

"Was. Not is." Distracted by the conversation, the sudden jab of searing pain when Juds tugged free one of the remaining stitches dragged a hiss from him and he flinched.

"Sorry," Juds apologized, wincing. "She put them in a bit deeper than she should've. S'why they split. Too much strain."

Kipling's hold on his hand tightened as Juds swabbed away the stream of blood running in a dark rivulet down his arm. The smell of antiseptic tickled his nostrils and Kipling laid her cheek against the back of his shoulder, trying to hide her small sniff. Clenching his jaw, he turned his focus back to Greg.

"Yes. Was," Greg repeated. He shook his head and looked at Kipling, his smile shifting slightly. "I went offline from Six the day you left Boston." He met Grayson's gaze again. "And you asked me to take care of Kipling. Since Howell was the potential danger, I considered it a reinterpretation of my assignment."

"How did you know who she was?"

"I'd been in Boston. Followed Howell there. I didn't know you were in the city. Cooper didn't share that bit of information. Once I heard about the explosion at the university, and my contacts relayed details like an MI6 officer and the name Holmes, I stepped up my surveillance. I found you both."

"It was you, wasn't it…" Kipling said, her raspy voice drawing the attention of both of them, but her focus was on Greg. "In the bookstore the day Howell came in and bought *The Hounds of the Baskervilles*." Greg nodded, his smile slipping into a thin line. "And when Howell attacked me, you tried to stop him."

"I tried, but I couldn't. Not without risking your life even further." His honest conviction carried in the weight of his voice. He looked to Grayson. "I couldn't call the FBI. At that point, I still couldn't risk exposure. But I followed him as soon as I could." His grin twitched. "I was about ten seconds away from going into that warehouse when you arrived, Ollie. Geezus, but that was impressive."

For the first time since accepting the identity of the man with the stranger's face, a curl of anger rolled in his chest. "She could have died."

Before he finished, Greg was shaking his head and shifting closer to sit on the edge of the chair. He reached for Kipling, resting his hand on her bare forearm – mottled with bruises – and shook his head again. "No, I wouldn't have allowed it. I knew, I already *knew* she was important to you, Ollie. I'd…" His face flushed red and he sat back again, clenching his hands. "I'd seen you together enough already to know."

"You questioned me about him all the time. You even tried to get me to admit he'd—" Kipling cut herself off, a deep scowl digging between her eyes. "If you knew, why did you press me so hard? Why did you try to get me to tell you who Grayson was, *what* he was?"

Greg cleared his throat, rubbing his palms together again. A new habit he'd developed in the year and a half he'd been gone. "Okay, time to air all the laundry. I knew this was coming." He huffed before continuing. "Because I know my cousin as well as, if not better than, I know myself. Like I said, I already knew you were important to him. More important than anyone, *ever*. So important he sent a message to what should have been nothing to ask me to protect you." Greg had the good manners to look contrite when he said, "I needed to know you were worthy of him. So, I tested your loyalty."

"And did I pass?" she asked with a voice so small Grayson nearly didn't make out her question.

In a beat, Greg's smile returned. "Let's just say I now wonder if *he* is worthy of *you*."

Juds interrupted long enough to explain the wound required additional stitches. Grayson nodded his consent and clenched his jaw as she administered what anesthetic she could before setting to work. A whistle came from the kitchen, and after giving Grayson an antibiotic jab, excused herself to help Esther with the tea and what smelled like a meal. With the break in conversation, Grayson chose to focus for now on the immediate; he held no doubt the unanswered questions between him and Greg would be resolved in time.

"I need to determine where we will find Howell," he said as he stood and pulled on a clean shirt Esther had had the foresight to leave for him. "Greg, I need your assistance for that."

"You know where he kept you?"

Grayson shook his head and smiled at Esther and Juds as they came back into the room, carrying trays of steaming cups and bowls of soup. While much of the discussion they'd had since arriving in Southpark was probably arguably information not to be shared with anyone outside the intelligence community, but clandestine measures were far from viable anymore and they needed to do what needed to be done.

"Not precisely. The only view I had from my room was of a garden with a high wall, but it was well-maintained, and the house was spaced a respectable distance from the next home. I could only differentiate rooflines, but the properties were also sizeable. Affluent."

"Where are you thinking? Not right there in Chelsea…"

Grayson shook his head. "No, he wouldn't be so cocky as to arrange the final meet so close to where he resided, but I don't think we were far. He kept me blindfolded from the moment I stepped out of my cell/bedroom until we reached the restaurant. But I mentally mapped the route, and although I believe he likely suspected I might be able to follow the traverse of the car so he had his driver take a random route, I am confident I was able to still track sufficiently. We were not in Chelsea, but not far."

Greg scowled, his eyes shifting as he considered the possibilities. Then he sucked in a sharp, deep breath and looked to Grayson. "Knightsbridge?"

Grayson nodded, swallowing against the bitter dread forming in his throat. The possibilities had unfolded while he rattled and bounced his way through London in the lorry, and while the reality wasn't one he wanted to believe, he had accepted the conclusion easier than he'd accepted the truth of his cousin's presence. "There was also a familiarity to the view; perhaps in that I recognize it from a different angle."

"Do you think he is near where you lived with Liz?"

Rather than answering Greg's question directly, Grayson handed one of the cups to Kipling before taking a satisfying sip from his own. Only when the warmth spread through his chest did he explain. "Two days before the bombing, Liz came to Baker Street. She said she was on her way home from work and had seen the Bentley parked on the street, and wanted to have dinner."

Grayson raised his head and met Greg's inquiring look, and although they had not been in one another's company in well over a year, Grayson knew the moment Greg came to the same conclusion he had.

"Liz and Howell..."

Chapter Twenty-Two

Kipling woke with a jolt, the dream on the peripheral of her memory not enough for her to remember, but enough to have her pulse jumping. She was alone in the bed, but not alone in the dim room. Grayson sat hunched on the edge of a chair, facing the single window in the room, moonlight revealing the angular lines of his profile. His head was down, his elbows on his thighs seemingly the only thing holding him up.

On a desk within arm's reach of him was an open laptop, the screen lighting lowered to dim. On the screen was some type of app icon she didn't recognize, but a pop-up window stated "Congratulations! Your mobile has been remotely wiped. All data has been uploaded to your cloud server for future download." She vaguely recalled him talking on Greg's phone to Mac about accessing an application Mac had created to effectively kill the phone Howell still had in his possession. It would be nothing more than a paperweight.

She sat up and wrapped Grayson's shirt around her, the same she had taken from the closet what felt like a week past, swinging her legs over the side of the small bed in one of Esther's spare bedrooms where they had taken a couple of hours to rest. The night was far from over, and by dawn, the hope was to have

Langdon Howell in custody. The few hours of calm might be the last for days. Instinctively, she reached to the bedside table and found her aids, closing the battery doors as she set them in place, then stood and crossed the small space to Grayson as they chimed their activation. She hesitated for a moment before resting her hand on his bare right shoulder as lightly as she could; although the worst damage was on his left side, she didn't want to inadvertently hurt him. He crossed his arm over his body to lay his hand over hers, squeezing before he pulled her hand away and drew her to step in front of him. She couldn't define the emotion thickening the air around them, but it was heavy and tangible and squeezed her chest.

He raised his chin to look up at her and her heart lodged in her throat when she saw the shine of moisture on his cheeks, the moonlight making his eyes appear silver.

"Grayson," she said barely above a whisper, intuitively unwilling to disturb the stillness around him. She knelt on the embroidered rug in front of the chair, smoothing her thumb over his cheek and he turned into the touch, holding her firm to his cheek so he could kiss her palm. "What's wrong?"

He chuckled, but it was a humorless, heavy sound, and sniffed. Instead of answering, he took her face in his hands and she watched mesmerized as his gaze shifted — back and forth, and from her brow to her lips — and her lungs squeezed so tight she could barely breathe when a single tear slid from his unblinking eyes.

"Please," she begged. "Why are you crying?"

"Perhaps our eyes need to be washed by our tears once in a while so that we can see life with a clearer view again," he said in a voice so low she was thankful for the moonlight behind her to gift her with enough light to see the words on his lips.

"Alex Tan," she responded, their game of quote and speaker so natural now. "What is it you need to see clearer?"

"My life," he answered, so quickly she knew it was his heart that spoke, not his intellect. He sniffed again, his gaze cast down to her mouth as a focal point, his thumbs smoothing over her cheeks and chin. "It does something to a man's perspective to both nearly lose something soul-precious to him, and be given back a piece of himself he feared he'd lost, both in the same day."

Lost for what she might say, to either confirm or reassure, she moved closer and raised up on her knees to be nearer to him. He didn't take his hands from her, didn't lose his focus. She waited, watching the storm in his eyes. He drew in a breath, held it with lips parted, then released it again with a small shake of his head.

"I don't know how to begin."

"Don't try to start at the beginning. Just...start."

His smile was small, barely discernible, but honest. Then he sat back in an uncharacteristic slump in the high-backed wooden chair and snuffed at his nose. Needing to stay close, Kipling sat on the floor between his spread feet and folded her arms on his leg, looking up at him as he stared out the window. He rested a hand on her shoulder, stroking gently, absently. When he spoke, his deep voice resonated in the stillness of the room.

"I tried to rest," he began, then shook his head and twirled a long-fingered hand near his bruised temple. "My mind wouldn't allow it. So many questions, it was like an orchestra trying to tune itself in my mind. A cacophony with no adhesion. When I knew you were asleep, I slipped away and sought out Greg."

At the mention of Greg, his voice wavered and he paused, pressing his lips into a fine line, his chin dropping toward his chest. It was several moments before he tried again. "In a single breath, I am overwhelmed by the sudden filling of the hole from his absence, and yet, my nature has already adapted as if he never left."

"I noticed that," she said softly, drawing his attention down to her, and she smiled. "You two work like joined cogs in an intricate machine. You know each other instinctively."

"It was always as such. It's why we insisted if we were to join Six, we did so together." The smile of a moment before slid into an angry curl, bunching his lips. Pushing aside whatever flared his anger, he cleared his throat again. "He had no choice. They took his choice from him. To such a degree, if I did not know the extent of Nelson Howell's guilt, I might be inclined to believe Six machinated the entire series of events leading to the bomb explosion that supposedly left him dead. For the final purpose of bending him to their intentions."

"He didn't tell me everything, just that it wasn't his choice. None of it was his choice. I think…" She paused, wondering if her words were the right ones to use. "I think he's afraid you won't believe that fact."

"I believe him. Knowing my superiors lied to me, again and again, only cements my belief in their deception and my faith in his choices."

"His lack of choices," Kipling clarified.

Grayson nodded, touching her hair at her temple near where she knew was the worst of the abrasions along her hairline. "He willingly gave his life that day, a fact that birthed a great deal of anger in me for a long time. Until my suspicion he might have survived surpassed my anger at his decision. When he woke, they took everything away from him, convinced him in his broken mental, physical, and emotional state that it would somehow be worse for those he loved if he suddenly appeared alive, and leveraged whatever control they could until he did what they wanted. Until he couldn't any longer."

"When you reached out."

Grayson nodded again. "It had been a snap decision. Even now, I don't know what inspired me to send an email to what should have been nothing. All my previous messages had gone unanswered; I had no reason to believe this one would be different."

"Previous emails?"

"I've heard of people calling the voicemail of someone they lost, or sending texts to disconnected numbers. I sent emails to his private account, venting my rage and my sorrow. But—" He shrugged and stilled his hand on her shoulder. "Of course, there was never a response. It was in that sorrow and rage-filled period I found and killed Nelson Howell." The pain of speaking the words carried in his voice.

He sniffed and swiped a thumb across his cheek, though she hadn't seen the tear fall from her position. "When I sent the email as I left Boston, left you, I expected an immediate bounce notification.

Something to say the account was dead, or the mailbox was full. When it didn't come, I expected nothing more and felt foolish for my impulsiveness."

"You trusted your heart."

"Something I am quite unaccustomed to," he admitted, squeezing her shoulder. "Something I am working very hard at mastering."

Kipling rested her cheek on his hand. "What happens now? With Greg? And MI6?"

The air hissed as he sucked it in through his teeth, then huffed it out, shifting forward to lean over her and she had to tip back her head, resting it on his knee to keep eye contact. "First, I have a conversation with my director, one which I can guarantee he will not appreciate."

"And then?"

"And then we apprehend Howell." He paused, his eyes again studying her as if he looked for some detail he'd missed. "And then, I am going to return to Baker Street, with you, and…"

He trailed off, and she held her breath, waiting. When he didn't elaborate, she asked softly, "…and what?"

Instead of answering right away, he hooked his finger beneath her chin to tip her mouth toward him for a kiss. The first press was simple, giving, but when he opened his lips and his tongue requested entry, she moaned her pleasure and angled up to him, deepening the kiss. They kissed in a tug and pull limited by their positions, but the intensity left her warm and flustered. Ending the slide of lips on lips, Grayson opened his eyes and said against her mouth, "And discover my life."

"Don't you dare pull a Scarecrow on me, Grayson Holmes."

Grayson scowled when he looked up from the weapon in his hand. She didn't know what it was, didn't pretend to even try to guess. It was hefty for a handgun, dark gray, and intimidating. That's all she needed to know. "Pardon?" he asked.

"Don't think you can just tell me to stay in the car—"

"I'm not asking you to stay in the car. I'm asking you to stay *here*—"

"While you run off and fight the bad guys," she continued, ignoring his justification. She crossed her arms over her body, ignoring the pull of still sore muscles. "Amanda King never stayed in the car, and she darn well saved Lee Stetson's hide more than once for not listening, so neither am I."

"Who the bloody hell are you talking about?"

Greg barked a laugh behind her, and she glanced over her shoulder at him. He sat at the small kitchen table in Esther's flat, now crammed full with Grayson's team of Mac Hennessey, Sandra Sookoo, and Lynne Connolly, a similar weapon to Grayson's on the table in front of him. If Grayson had to go after Howell — which she knew he did – she felt some level of relief that he would be going in with people he trusted. And she trusted.

That didn't mean she intended to sit on her hands and wait for his safe return.

"Your American pop culture knowledge has failed you," Lynne said, her voice practically lilting with her teasing sarcasm, which was a sharp contrast to the image of a woman dressed in black from head to toe checking her own weapon. It was different than the boys', but still as menacing. She ticked her pointed chin toward Mac, who stood beside and just behind her. "You can manage a MacGyver nickname, but you don't know the legendary Scarecrow?"

"Legendary might be a stretch," Sandra mumbled.

"But still, a spy should know—" Greg began.

"We aren't bloody *spies*," Grayson cut off, casting a scathing glare at his cousin, who didn't seem the least bit bothered by it. "I don't care who this Scarecrow or King person is, and see no relevance to the situation. Kipling, you *cannot* go."

"I have spent the better part of the last three days worrying about you, and the better part of the last twenty-four hours doing what I had to do to get you back. I can't — I won't – just sit here and wonder—"

Despite his battered body, the agility at which Grayson came out of his chair and took her hand to pull her out of the kitchen and through the flat made her words catch in her throat. She didn't say anything until they were back in the bedroom they had used an hour before, and he firmly shut the door.

"I can't, Grayson," she said again, shaking her head as he pivoted them both to face each other. "I just can't. I'll go insane."

"And I can't have you there," he said just as insistently. "Kipling, this is what I *do*. *This* is the frightening side. The *dangerous* side."

"I thought I lost you!" She didn't mean to shout, but the storm in her chest wouldn't be released at any softer volume.

Grayson spun away from her, marching several steps across the dark room, hands set at his waist, his head down. He wore dark clothing like his team, and without the benefit of a light, he was nothing more than a shadow. This was the closest she'd ever seen to Grayson angry. Annoyed, yes. Concerned. Frustrated. Emotional. But not angry. She wasn't even sure if this *was* anger, but she knew she'd inspired it, and she knew it left a cold, hard knot in her gut.

Shaking with abject terror, not in fear of Grayson but for Grayson, she stepped sideways to the wall beside the door and turned on the light switch. The lights in the room were just two small lamps on either side of the bed, but it was enough to push aside the darkness and illuminate more than the room, but the violin-bow tension in Grayson's form.

She crossed her arms around her body, gripping her own sides despite the diminishing pull of aching muscles, and tried to will her heartbeat to slow. After what felt like an eternity, Grayson drew in a long, deep breath and raised his head. Another moment passed before he turned to face her. Frustration no longer pinched his features, but something akin to sadness dug into the lines around his eyes. Before, when she had found him with tears they hadn't been of sadness. But this was his heavy soul showing on his face.

"I asked you a question," he said, his voice so deep it almost vibrated in the air. "When we were in Boston. The night I sent Sandra to you to protect you."

She nodded, unsure yet of her voice.

"You asked me if that was what it was like to be with me. Attempts on my life. I was honest and said yes, and I asked you if it was too much."

She nodded again, trying to swallow but her throat was dry. "I said it wasn't."

"That night you *knew* of what happened, but you hadn't yet lived any part of it." He took a step toward her, his head tilted slightly as he studied her, and let his hands drop from his waist. "You've lived it now, probably in a capacity not many spouses ever would."

"Which is why I'm so afraid…"

"I know," he said, barely as she finished, and stepped close enough to lay his hands on her upper arms. "I know, Kipling. Please understand; I do not know how this night will end, but I know it will be dangerous. As much as you want to be there, and as much as every instinct I have practically demands I keep you near, I can't have you anywhere near it. If you really think on this, you'll see it just can't be."

She pressed her lips together and swallowed, looking away from him as heat infused her cheeks with such fierceness it made her eyes burn. "I know. I've known since I began the argument."

He took his hands from her arms and laid his warm palms against her cheeks, tipping her chin up until she relented and looked him in the eyes. "I will offer a compromise. Come with us to Knightsbridge, where I am meeting with Director Cooper and a team of additional agents. You will stay with an agent until I come back for you. I will know you are with someone who can protect you, and you will know when it is over before I can return for you." He tilted his chin to look her more square in the eyes. "Will you agree?"

She nodded in his hold and unfolded her arms from around her body to curl her fingers into the front of his dark, long-sleeved shirt. "I agree."

He sealed the promise with a kiss, and with his lips still on hers, reached between them to take her hand and lace their fingers together. With a heavy sigh, he leaned back from her and took a step toward the door. "When this night is done, I will ask you the same question."

She stood her place, and he stopped when she didn't move with him, turning to look at her again. "Ask me now."

"Kipling—"

"Ask me now, Grayson."

Squaring with her again, he stepped close but touched her no more than the hand he held, and searched her face. She stared back, confident in what she hoped he saw. "Is this too much?" he finally asked.

She shook her head, and pushed the fingers of her free hand into the short remains of his hair, drawing him down for a deeper, intention-filled kiss. She knew she'd made her point when his hand pressed into her back and brought her firm against him and the low sound in his chest shifted through both of them.

Left panting, held against him, their breath mingling between them, Kipling ran her thumb along his slick lower lip and focused on the contact. "No matter what happens, there is nothing that could be enough to make this too much." She chuckled. "And that was possibly the most poorly formed sentence I have ever spoken."

Grayson chuckled, a deep, short rumble she felt against her ribs. "Yet, I have never heard anything so eloquent."

The momentary lightness slid away when fear snuck back in and she pushed herself against him until she felt his heartbeat. "I love you, Grayson. Please don't forget that."

"Impossible."

Chapter Twenty-Three

"Ollie, I'm the only one in trouble right now with Cooper and Six for going off the grid. You don't need to be caught up in the shitestorm to come when they find out where I've been. I can just disappear again—"

"Not bloody happening," Grayson said as he stepped free of Mac's van they'd used to move across the city to the staging grounds in Knightsbridge where they'd meet Cooper and additional officers.

He looked to Kipling for a moment, winked to offer assurance he'd be back shortly, and slammed shut the door. When they turned to cross the lot toward the waiting team, Grayson set his hand on his cousin's shoulder. The contact was as much to affirm what he said to his cousin, as it was to steady his vision. He purposefully ignored the temporary dizziness from exiting the van, pushing it aside for the matter at hand. There would be time to rest later.

Side by side, they walked away from the van and across the lot to the rest of the waiting Six teams. It had rained in the last hour, leaving areas of wet, shallow puddles off which the overhead lights reflected. The air was chilled, petrichor heavy in the air, and the briskness revived Grayson as they walked, letting him shake off the weariness that had settled while they rode in the van from Southpark

"First, I sincerely doubt either Esther or Kipling will allow you to slip away. You are and have been Kipling's friend for months, and Esther let you be the berk once and cock up what the two of you had, but I doubt she'll allow it again. A few hours in the same flat as the two of you and I saw it plain."

Greg grinned a quick tug at his lips, at the mention of Doctor Esther Mitchell, anthropologist and impromptu clandestine rescue.

"Second, while I have been trained thoroughly to lie to just about anyone about just about anything, I can tell you now I would never be able to look into your mother's face – let alone *my* mother's – without confessing all knowledge like a five-year-old caught with his hand elbow deep in the cookie tin."

Greg chuckled

"My final reason is wholly personal. I'll not allow it."

Greg looked at him sideways, his lips curling down in a contrite frown. "Honestly, I don't know if I could do it again. Leave behind everyone I love. I didn't choose it before; it would be a choice this time. I wouldn't have made it the first time, can't now."

"I note you didn't contradict my observation regarding Esther."

Greg laughed, a deep rolling sound. "You told Kipling you had a new perspective. Well, so do I. Especially after being around the two of you for three minutes."

"Are you saying you are falling in love with Esther again, without actually saying it? You just reconnected with her today, out of either sheer coincidence or the machinations of the universe as a whole, and she has to adjust to the idea you aren't actually dead as much as the rest of us."

Across the lot, Grayson spotted Director Cooper exiting his vehicle, starting toward them. How close would Cooper need to be before he realized it was Greg beside him?

Greg shook his head, pressing his mouth into a thin line, before he spoke. "I'm not saying I'm falling in love *again*. I'm saying I never stopped loving her." He looked sideways to Grayson. "Don't pretend you hadn't assumed how I felt about her when we were together."

Grayson raised his hands in defense. "Of course, I knew. I'm the one who called you an idiot for letting her go. Though I have been curious as to what happened. It's obvious the two of you have no contention for each other. Quite the opposite."

"I *am* an idiot. You said as much." Greg shrugged and gave a humorous laugh. "When we aren't about to face down a sociopathic, possibly psychotic, criminal mastermind, I'll explain."

"Oh, Cooper isn't *that* bad…"

Greg's bark of a laugh echoed back to them, and Grayson chuckled. Cooper's steps slowed, but they continued their walk toward him. Another dozen feet and they would reach Cooper. Grayson tensed himself for the confrontation. At least Cooper approached them alone. Grayson preferred not to make the row fully public.

Grayson motioned with his hand down by his hip for Greg to hold back a few feet, and he stepped in line behind Grayson before stopping completely. He stayed far enough away his face wouldn't be clear, cast more in shadow than the lights from the overhead parking lamps. Let Cooper wonder. He closed the final few steps to reach his director. The man he had once considered a friend. A mentor. The next few seconds would prove if Grayson's faith had been grounded, or if the man was an outright liar.

"Good to see you're on your feet, Holmes," Cooper said when they came within conversation distance. Grayson watched, studied, and saw the first slight sign of nervous concern. It was nearly indiscernible, but then again, men like Cooper had been training men like him in the clandestine arts for decades. Perhaps he was concerned the student had finally surpassed the master. The fact he'd gone this long without Grayson realizing made Grayson both angry for being deceived and not seeing the signs, and doubtful he could ever trust this man again. In anything.

"You lied," Grayson said without preamble. He had no plan for confronting Cooper, other than it would happen. The few short hours since his rescue hadn't been long enough to form a plan. His words were the first that came to mind when he looked into Cooper's lying face.

"What the bloody hell are you talking about?" Cooper sputtered, but he'd already lost his hold on the lie.

He knew it.

Grayson knew it.

"Gregory McQueen," Grayson ground out through clenched teeth.

Cooper cursed under his breath and shook his head, turning partially away. Away from Greg. "You've lost the plot, Holmes." Cooper shook his head and took a step backward. "We aren't going down this bloody road right now. I certainly hope this whole thing hasn't scrambled your senses—"

"You *lied*," Grayson said firmer, louder, but not so loud his voice would carry. Loud enough to snap Director Cooper's attention back to him. Grayson pressed his lips together, breathing slow and steady through his nostrils to hold back his rage. He'd fought the waves of rage so often in the months following Greg's death, but after killing Nelson Howell, he'd forced himself to find new control. He forced himself into control now.

"Where is this coming from, Holmes?"

"Are you pretending to be blind? Or thick?"

Cooper's eyes rounded and his face blanched when Greg closed the space by stepping forward.

"Hello, Jeffrey," Greg said, as nonchalantly as if they'd just run into each other at the local.

Cooper flushed bright red, so much so Grayson had a passing moment of concern the man would have a heart attack. Grayson pushed his fisted hands into his pockets to keep from making anyone watching believe he might choke the man and took a step toward Director Cooper. When he was close enough the man had to adjust his stance to look Grayson in the eye if he had the nerve, Grayson leaned over him and could smell the perspiration of fear.

"You can't deny him," he said in a low, deep voice, the anger curling in his chest like smoke to roughen his tone. "He has told me what you required of him, and how you required it. Now, Director Cooper..." He let his contempt weigh his words. "I want to hear you defend your actions. I want to know how you could have justified the devastation, the heartbreak, and the lies. I want to know how much of your soul you had to sell to the devil himself to be able to look me in the eye and console me for his death."

"You've crossed a line, Holmes—"

"No!" Grayson didn't care now if anyone heard. He'd stopped the moment he'd seen the realization in Cooper's face. There was a moment, a second when Jeffrey Cooper might have convinced Grayson he didn't know. That the command came from higher levels. But the moment never came. Cooper was as guilty as any of them. "*You* crossed a line. We committed our loyalty and our lives to Six the day we walked into this building, but that *never* gave you the right to steal it. *Never.*"

Cooper stepped back and pivoted away, and for a moment Grayson thought he might bolt back to his vehicle, as much as the man was capable of bolting. He was far from a field officer, and even tonight would serve only as direction outside the action. When he turned, he looked past Grayson to Greg.

"Where the hell have you been? You have put my career, and the careers of everyone in this organization, who—"

"I don't really care," Greg said with a shrug and wing of his arms away from his sides.

Cooper sucked in air through his flared nostrils, looking between them. "The day we recruited the two of you, I knew — I *knew* — you would either be our greatest assets or our greatest pains in the arse!"

"We were your greatest assets, Director," Grayson pointed out, dropping his voice again. "When we were a team."

Cooper made a sound between a groan and a guffaw and shook his head. He wiped his hand across his bald, sweat-beaded brow. "Do we bloody well have to do this now? Here?"

"And give you a chance to write a new series of lies? I think not," Grayson bit out. "This is just the beginning of our *conversation,*" he stressed.

Cooper took several deep breaths, ending the last with a nod as he looked back to the cluster of vehicles. Some men had exited and stood watching. Even if they didn't hear the words, Grayson knew the tone had carried and they saw the animated conversation. His body language was obvious enough a blind man could read it.

"Fine. Fine. I realize you aren't going to give a shite about me saying this, but I wasn't in favor of this. Of *any* of this."

"You're right, I don't," Grayson said, cutting his hand through the air between them. "Means nothing."

Cooper shook his head and pounded his fist into his other hand. When he looked up, and met their hard stares, Grayson read the defeat in his eyes and believed whatever the man said from that point would likely be the truth, or at least the truth as he believed it to be.

"Honest to Jesus Christ, Holmes, on that day in Edinburgh I was gutted. Nearly as gutted as you. We all thought McQueen was—" He choked on his words, and swallowed hard. "Dead."

"I wasn't," Greg said.

Cooper shook his head. "No. You were found the next day in the rubble, and men very high in the SIS — people higher than any face or name you've seen at Six, even — decided to seize what they saw as an opportunity. As far as Howell and his organization would know, Officer Gregory McQueen was dead. He was given a new face, and when recovered..." Jeffrey sighed, so deep and heavy it dragged down his shoulders and made him slump. "A mandate."

"When did you know?" Grayson ground out through a jaw so clenched it shot pain down the side of his neck.

"Not right away."

"When did you *know*?" Grayson demanded again, making each word a punctuation.

Cooper looked away, but found enough pride — or courage — or both, to look Grayson in the eyes. "April. Last year. Weeks after the explosion. I never knew before that. I never knew during the memorial. I never knew when I offered my condolences to your family. I was sincere."

The rage that had ebbed slightly, doused by Cooper's lack of fight, swelled again and he had to turn his back on his director. Greg grabbed his arm, keeping him in place. His heart pounded so hard in his ears it muffled whatever one of them said after that.

"You bastard," he cursed and spun back, lunging at the director, only stopped again by Greg's grip. In his peripheral, he saw men move forward. "You knew. You *knew* when I went after Howell. You *knew* Greg was alive. You *knew* I wanted justice, and you *let me kill him*."

Cooper held up his hand so the approaching men stopped and released a long, tired sigh. "God help me, yes. I knew. But I had no idea you could—"

Greg's arm across Grayson's chest, pulling him back, was the only thing physically stopping Grayson from grabbing the bastard again. "Ollie. Ollie!" Greg shouted, dragging Grayson away until several feet separated them from the director. "Don't. He's not worth the possible retribution." Greg grabbed his arms, yanking him around so they faced each other. "We've heard the truth."

Grayson bit down hard, sucking in each breath through his nose, forcing it out again. "They stole your life, Greg. They devastated your mother. Your father. They—"

"They did. But, sod them. I'm not dead. We can fix everything else."

He dipped his head and turned to face Cooper again. Cooper looked defeated, and Grayson wondered if he were to run straight at the man, would he even try to escape.

"I expected more fight. More denial. More justification."

"Director Cooper is an intelligent man, Ollie." Greg made no attempt at masking his voice to keep Cooper from hearing. "Only a fool would attempt to argue a point he knows is already without worth. There is nothing he can say, no way he can explain, that will appease either of us. He's wiser for not trying."

Director Cooper cleared his throat and took two steps toward them, but no further. He kept his face tipped down, the fact he wouldn't look them in the eyes speaking more to his shame than his attempt at deceit. "My words mean nothing, and I accept that, but I am truly...truly sorry."

"This isn't done," Grayson promised, then turned and marched back to the van, knowing everyone else would fall in line.

"Grayson? Dear God!" Liz took a step toward him, hand raised to touch his face, but he leaned away, avoiding the contact.

Her hand stilled, and she looked past him to Officer Freya Contee, who stood behind him and to his right, then back to him. "What's going on? All of Six has wondered what happened to you. When I heard about the explosion on Baker Street..." She trailed off, clutching the front of her dressing gown over her night clothing.

"Allow us in, Liz," he said stern enough he hoped she would realize the weight of the situation. After the confrontation with Cooper, his patience was worn thin and threadbare. "This is not a conversation you want to have in the hallway. I've no doubt Mrs. Resen still enjoys a good chin-wag with the neighbors, and you really don't want to be the topic of discussion."

Eyes wide and blond hair disheveled from sleep, she stepped back and opened the door wide enough for the two of them to enter.

"Are you alone?" he asked, dropping his voice. Liz stared at him, wide-eyed, looking only briefly at Officer Contee as she moved past them both into the main part of the apartment, an **RF** signal detector in her hand. "Liz," he said firmly, drawing her attention. "Are you alone?" he asked again.

She nodded, watching Contee traverse the main room. The woman was rail thin, but nearly six feet tall, her silent presence commanding despite her slight figure. In her dark clothing, black hair, and rich skin she blended into the shadows with only minimal lighting in the room.

A moment of familiarity struck Grayson once he reached the main part of the flat, but at the same moment, he noted all the subtle changes she had made since he moved out a year earlier. The cream color on the walls had been replaced with a dusty mauve, and the cloying scent of fresh flowers from the large bouquet on the hall table filled the space. It was a gift bouquet, far more elaborate than Liz would ever purchase for herself, and a tented card sat on the glass top table beside the cut glass vase. She led the way to the open parlor, and Grayson noted the array of framed photographs on the fireplace mantle. A large watercolor hung on the wall.

"It's nearly midnight," she pointed out, wrapping her arms around her body. Officer Contee looked their way and nodded, indicating there were no listening devices in the main room, and left them to check the rest of the flat. Liz scowled, watching her go. "What could possibly have you showing up at my door at this hour, with an armed Six officer, that couldn't wait until morning? And why are you checking my home for surveillance?"

"Langdon Howell," Grayson said, and watched her face for any sign of recognition.

There was none.

She shook her head and scowled. "Who?"

He took from his pocket his new mobile, since Howell had confiscated his and he'd remotely wiped it clean and opened the photo album to the clearest image of Howell Grayson could obtain on short notice. Liz kept her attention on him as she took the phone, then looked down, and only then did he see the shift of recognition. Her eyes rounded and she gasped, her gaze snapping to him again.

"How do you know him?" he demanded.

Deep color flushed her cheeks, and his gut twisted in both empathy for her embarrassment and rage at Howell for using her. He wished he could be gentle, wished he could ease the information from her, but there was no time. "Liz, what is his name and how do you know him?"

She blinked rapidly, her mental shift from shock to resolution visible in the steeling of her expression. "Charlie Augustine. We have been seeing each other for six months."

Grayson nearly laughed at the name. *Pompous bastard.*

"Has he been here? To this apartment?"

She nodded, still wide-eyed.

"Have you been to his home?"

Again she nodded.

"Where does he live, Liz?" he asked, taking a step toward her.

"Here. In Knightsbridge. Just 'round the corner a bit. We met at the grocery. Grayson…you said Howell…is he—"

"Yes," he answered simply, convinced without question Liz Pivens had no knowledge of Howell's true identity. Most strangers couldn't lie to him, and most definitely not someone he knew as well as Liz.

"Oh, God," she gasped behind her hand.

Of course, perhaps he knew nothing at all about human nature. Jeffrey Cooper had managed to lie to him for months, and he'd never questioned the man's sincerity. He believed Cooper thought Greg was dead, never had he assumed Cooper was one of the ones hiding the truth and manipulating reality. The Great Holmes had been compromised by his own emotions.

Freya returned from her reconnoiter of the flat and offered another simple nod. There were no bugs. Howell had likely deemed Liz's flat not worth the time to hide surveillance equipment. He used her for what he needed, and once done, he was done with her. Grayson rubbed his fingers over his upper lip and set his hands at his waist, battling with his inner rage. Liz didn't deserve this, not because of her association with him. Once Six knew she'd been compromised, she might lose her job, as low level as it was at Six. She still helped a murderous criminal, even if unknowingly. Tempering his anger, he looked to Officer Contee.

"You can go get her," he said simply.

While he held confidence in Liz' innocence, Kipling would be his secret weapon. When Liz retreated from Baker Street before meeting Kipling, she had left open an avenue of discovery, as long as Howell did as he expected and played the unknowing new beau to the fullest. Freya nodded, remaining silent, and left the flat.

"I need you to answer questions for me, Liz. I need answers quickly, and as thoroughly as you can. Do you understand?" She nodded, and he hated the tears in her eyes. She understood far too well the ramifications. "Did you ever speak to him about me?"

Color bloomed high in her cheeks, spreading up from the open space in her dressing robe and up her throat. "Only that you were m-my past. We were over. Usual get-to-know-you conversation."

"The day you came to Baker Street, you said you were on your way home from work. But Baker Street is not a direct route from Vauxhall to Knightsbridge."

He left the statement as his only question. Liz' chin trembled and she looked away from him, swiping at a tear. She sniffed and slid her gaze to look at him though she kept her body angled away.

"Charlie encouraged me to talk to you," she said with a tremble in her voice. "He said he wanted us to move forward — him and me — and felt your ghost still lingering. He thought if I saw you, it would help me. I drove home by Baker Street on a whim, I had no idea you'd be there. I thought you'd still be at home for the wedding." She shook her head as she explained.

"But I was. Did you see him after that and tell him I was in London?"

Her face twisted with her tears, her body shaking. "I went straight to him."

"And you told him I had a woman with me." Not a question.

She nodded. "I was in such shock. You never — Grayson, I'm so sorry. Did he do this? Did he try to kill you?"

"He is responsible for the explosion, yes, but he had no intention of killing me. Or Kipling. Not yet."

The door to the flat opened, and Grayson raised his hand to keep Liz in her place, stepping to the edge of the hall to confirm it was Freya and Kipling. He motioned for Kipling to come to him, beginning the ruse. Officer Contee acknowledged his request, then stepped back into the hall, closing the door behind her. Such would be her post until he returned, or provided word to her to act otherwise.

Kipling was bundled in one of Esther's spare sweaters over her jeans and a shirt he recognized as his own. She'd confessed to procuring it from the laundry that morning. Her long hair was loose, falling around her face, shielding her ears from view. She looked from Grayson to Liz, and back to him. Grayson laid his hand on the back of her shoulder and guided her forward so he stood at one point of a conversation triangle and motioned between the two women. Then took his hand away from Kipling to struggle through his unskilled maneuvering of BSL.

"Kipling," he said aloud, but made his sign for her name — his left hand to his chest, his fingers cupped so his thumb and fingertips touched his body, and making a "k" to symbolize her name, lowered a portion of his hand into the space made by the left, then drew it upward along his breastbone. "This is Liz Pivens." For Liz, he spelled her name.

Liz looked from Kipling to Grayson. "Is this..." she asked, trailing off, keeping her voice low as if that would keep Kipling from hearing.

If Kipling were as disadvantaged as they wanted Liz to believe, the lowering of her voice would have been pointless completely, but their game played otherwise. As far as Liz was to know, Kipling was completely deaf and communicated purely by sign. Her hair disguised her aids, and if she feared discovery, she would discretely remove them and rely on her other communicative skills. Grayson maintained confidence in his belief Liz was a dupe in the game, but he didn't rule out the possibility of garnering further information when she believed she would be unheard or understood. Even Officer Contee believed Kipling to be fully without hearing, in order to maintain the deception.

Following his lead, Kipling waved, just a half-circle arc of her hand, but said nothing. Answering Liz's question, Grayson smiled at Kipling and signed. "Kipling is the woman I met in Boston, and the woman at Baker Street that day."

He pressed his hand over his heart but provided no translation. While he didn't glance to see if Liz understood, the sparkle in Kipling's eyes let him know she knew the truth in his gesture. He continued to sign, knowing full well it was terrible, but since Liz didn't know BSL she wouldn't recognize his ineptitude.

"We are going after Howell, or Charlie Augustine as you know him. Until he is in custody, Baker Street is not safe. Kipling is staying here under Officer Contee's protection while she also holds you in custody—"

"Custody? Grayson, you can't believe—"

"I don't, but you also know this cannot be ignored."

Liz pressed her lips together and nodded, avoiding looking directly at Kipling. "I'm so sorry for all this."

"We will discuss that later, but for now, I need you to tell me everything you can about his home. Everything. Grounds. Entrances. Everything."

"Of course." She nodded and met Kipling's gaze. "I'm sorry."

Ever the actress, Kipling made an expression of confusion and looked to Grayson, signing "*I don't understand.*"

"Kipling doesn't read lips," he explained to Liz, adding the signs with the words. "You can communicate by writing back and forth if needed. She said she's sorry for everything," he added, directing the statement to Kipling with sign.

Kipling nodded and smiled, and raised her hands to sign slowly for his benefit, and he noted she kept it simple. The most basic of vocabulary. "*Grayson told me he didn't believe you would be involved. He speaks highly of you.*"

He cleared his throat before interpreting, glancing only briefly at Liz. With the premise established he motioned for them to sit at the small round table situated on the edge of the open kitchen, collecting first a tablet and pencil from near the phone where Liz had always kept it. Seated with Kipling directly beside him and Liz across, he asked her again to tell him all she could. As she began, Kipling shifted closer and set her hand on his thigh, a contact that might have any other time been intended to arouse, but he felt and understood it was just a need for touch. He needed her touch as much as she needed to reach out.

He covered the details in five minutes, ever mindful that time was their enemy and the night their friend. It had only been hours since Howell had been drugged, and he would still be weak, even if he had been given a counterdrug. He wasn't without protection, but with the head at least disabled, the body might flail. With quick sketches, however rudimentary and limited to her knowledge, he stood and took Kipling's hand to draw her with him into the foyer.

Away from Liz, with his back in her direction and blocking Kipling from sight should Liz glance their way, Grayson steeled his final courage by holding her face in his hands and kissing her both deep and brief. He withdrew only far enough that she could see his lips because he didn't want to speak and give away their deception.

"I love you," he mouthed. "I will return for you as soon as possible, I promise you. Officer Contee is outside, and should an urgency arise, do not worry about breaking your guise. Do what must be done to keep yourself safe. Promise me."

She nodded, her eyes shining. "Promise me the same," she whispered. "Grayson, I'm worried. You don't look right. You're so pale, and your hands are cold."

"I'm fine," he promised and realized the irony in the statement since it was the one she had used again and again in Boston when she had been far from fine. But he had been in far worse physical states before, this was nothing more than fatigue. A handful of hours and he could sleep for a day. "I promise you."

He kissed her again to bind his promise, then squeezed her hand, opened the door, and stepped into the hall. With final instructions to Officer Contee, he left the flat behind and jogged through the building to meet his time. By the end of this night, Howell would either be dead or in his custody; Grayson cared not which.

Moving with training that had been ingrained in his subconscious, Grayson stepped behind the house guard and looped his arm around the man's neck, with his bent elbow under the chin. With the same hand gripping the man's bicep, he shoved his opponent's head forward with the other, applying pressure to the back of his head. He counted to three, and while the guy struggled for a second, the blood choke took him down like a rock, quickly, and he slumped in Grayson's grip. Easing him to the floor to avoid excess noise, Grayson motioned for one of the support team members to come to him and fasten a rip-tie around the man's hands to keep him secure.

He tipped his head for Greg to take point and move on to the next guard.

Mac and additional backup were in the lower level where they suspected the security system mainframe was housed, "clearing the obstacles" and accessing the system to shut it down and prevent any type of alarm from going off, alerting the security staff. Sandra and Lynne led a team through the back of the house from the garden Grayson had seen from his bedroom/cell window. Based on the rough floor plan Liz had provided, they would likely find Howell on the far end of the luxury home, but still facing the garden.

He enjoyed the view, apparently.

Grayson kept against the side of the house, catching up with Greg, who had taken down the guard stationed at the door. Standing on each side of the door to get them inside, Grayson looked through the window beside the door, finding the red light indicating the security beam.

"Mac," he said, his voice carrying through the conduction earpiece.

"Two seconds, Boss," came Mac's Scottish lilt.

Grayson looked across to Greg, not for the first time the sensation of both familiarity and astonishment hitting him. How many times had they done this together? How many times since that day had he waited for Mac to clear a system, allowing himself only the moment of melancholy at his cousin's absence, his teammate's absence. Greg looked at him, and while the face was different, the minimal light shining from inside the house hit familiar eyes.

"Clear, Boss," Mac said, and a second later, the red light blinked out.

Grayson tested the door, and it was locked, but with a solid twist and kick the latch gave way and they slipped inside. The outside was the easy part. His team ran point against the eight guards around the complex, and they had been easy enough to dispatch; inside would be different. Howell would keep his most trusted, most effective, deadliest men near him. Especially in his weakened state.

"We're inside," came Sandra through the conduction piece.

"Take the back staircase. Only rely on hand-to-hand when completely feasible. Shoot to incapacitate."

His team knew the process; he ordered for the benefit of those serving as their backup. Those not accustomed to Grayson's command.

"Got it, Boss."

They hit trouble on the first floor, and while *their* goal was to incapacitate, Howell's men had no such penchant. Grayson dropped to a crouch, his back to the wall, as shots splintered the thick wood-paneled walls. He held his breath against the pressure squeezing his pained ribs. Juds had pushed hard for binding, and highly recommending a shock-absorbing layer beneath his ballistics vest. The added layers restricted his movement, but he logically knew his movements would have been restricted by pain were he not bound. It didn't stop him from cursing his limitations. Or the occasional jab or pinch of pain that would steal his breath.

At a pause in the array, he took aim and squeezed off several shots with the satisfaction of seeing one fall. He and Greg alternated their attacks, each one bringing the other a few feet further down the hall toward their goal with two other officers serving as cover.

Shots came from the other end of the hall, indicating more of his team had arrived, dispatching the last of their obstacles; at least the ones in the hall and along the balcony. There would be more inside Howell's personal space.

Shots came from the open floor below as three more of Howell's men found them, leaving wood and plaster to spray and splinter around them. The house was surrounded by gardens and property, and they had assured their weapons were silenced, but the loud pop and burst of Howell's weapons echoed in the cavernous, luxury home. A bullet hit close to Lynne, and she dropped.

"Lynne!" Grayson shouted, and she raised her head, looking at him so he would know she was fine other than the gash along her cheek from flying fragments.

She brought her fingers to her cheek, taking it away wet with blood. "Sodding bastards," she cursed and pivoted on the balls of her feet to shoot through the carved spindles of the banister. One of the three fell back, but the other two stumbled forward, falling on their face when shots came from the hall behind them, heralding Mac's arrival.

Holes blew through the bedroom door when someone from beyond tried to end the fight, probably assuming either Grayson or someone else on the team held their ground in front of it. Grayson shifted on the balls of his feet, turning his back and hunching to avoid the shots and the splintered wood, the position catching his breath. By the time the spray ended, Mac had come up the side stairs, taking his position near Greg.

Grayson took a moment to drop the clip from his Glock 17, aware there were still two rounds left, but he'd rather go into the room with a full weapon rather than worrying about the waste of two bullets. He motioned with a jerk of his head for each of them to move into a position of advantage and tried to take a deep breath. Failing, he shifted his weight for quick action.

Lynne and Sandra flanked the frame, and Mac had his hand weapon trained on the door. Grayson didn't bother with subtlety. He stood, leaned back to maximize leverage with the shift of his center of gravity, and kicked in the door with a hard plant of his foot to the knob. The door cracked open, bouncing off the interior wall, and Grayson angled to his left as shots whizzed past him. He dropped to a crouch, taking advantage of Mac's height behind him, and the agility of the rest of the team, they fell into well-rehearsed positions and fired. Shots were exchanged back and forth, but in seconds the final guards were down, and all that remained was Howell lying pale and still in his bed, Nurse Frankenstein slumped, whimpering in the corner.

Her wails and begging for mercy were nearly as loud as the bullet array moments before. Grayson brought his finger to his lips, shushing her, and with wide eyes she fell silent, gasping for each breath as he moved around the foot of the bed to stand at Howell's side.

His eyes were open, but barely. Ashen pallor, lips parted in labored breath, the effects of the drugs still wreaking havoc on his body. He rasped a breath and tried to lift his hand to point at

Grayson, but no words left his white lips. The rest of his team worked to assure the men they'd taken down were either incapacitated by their injuries, dead, or restrained until they could be taken into official custody. Mac and Lynne left the room together to meet two officers in the hall, Mac already fussing over Lynne's scrape. With all Howell's people down, the clean up would begin. Everyone would be properly in custody within ten minutes. Sandra was on the phone with Cooper, telling him to send in the medical team for those who needed it.

Grayson leaned over Howell, waiting until weak eyes focused on him. "Part of me wished you met us armed, you bastard."

"This…" Howell rasped, and tried to take a breath, the oxygen cannula tubing line taped beneath his nose not much help. "Isn't." *Gasp.* "Over."

"No," Grayson confirmed. "No, it's not. Not by half."

He stepped away, walking toward Greg. Greg stood from strapping rip-ties to the wrists of one of the guards. The man was shot and bleeding, but the wound didn't appear fatal.

"You okay, Ollie?" Greg asked, squinting. Not that he'd ever been one for excessively formal language, but Greg's vernacular had definitely shifted in his time away. Relaxed. "You look pale."

Grayson tried to square his shoulders and take a breath, but his ribcage protested, catching his breath. He had doubts the multiple layers binding his torso, while each serving a purpose, actually did him good. "I'm fine," Grayson said, despite the blind spots dancing in his vision. "I want to call Kipling, though. I promised—"

Before he could finish, Lynne's shouts came from the hall, preceding the crack of bullets before another of Howell's men burst through the door, gun raised, and pulled the trigger. Greg lunged and they both hit the floor. Blinding pain sent Grayson into black.

Chapter Twenty-Four

A rhythmic buzz tugged at Grayson, pulling away the heavy blanket of sleep leaving him foggy headed and unwilling to move. He forced his eyes open, and immediately squinted at the sunlight coming through the partially open blinds on his room window. He had to blink several times, rolling his head on his pillow to shake the dregs of exhaustion. His brain slowly engaged, and he processed the room around him.

He was in a hospital room, private, and it was likely early morning based on the angle and level of light coming through the window. He'd been in the rooms at London Royal enough to recognize the space. An IV pole was to the right of his bed, dripping clear liquid into the needle taped to the back of his hand. The head of the bed was raised only slightly, enough he could see the full room without raising his head, but short of sitting up. He tested his ribs by taking a deep, slow breath. A dull ache accompanied the full expansion of his lungs, but minimal in comparison to the breath-stealing pain he'd fought through during the infiltration of Howell's complex.

The buzzing began again, and now fully awake, he sought out the source, realizing he hadn't been as awake or alert as he'd believed or he would have first noted Kipling slumped over in a chair she'd pulled to the side of his bed, her cheek resting on his blanket-covered leg, her face turned away from him. He raised and extended his left arm to reach for her, testing the pull of the sutures in his upper arm, finding only the slightest discomfort. Perhaps the bag hanging from the pole held more than saline.

Especially considering the ease by which he found himself distracted. He rolled his eyes and blinked in an attempt to find focus, again honing in on the buzz. The source was Kipling's mobile, lying near her shoulder on top of his blankets, face down. He picked it up and swiped his thumb across the screen when he saw the name Annalise and his mother's photo, a cropping of an image likely taken at the wedding.

Working his dry tongue within his mouth, he brought the phone to his ear, the change in angle causing a pinched tug on the back of his hand. "Hello, Mum."

"Grayson?" she cried, the upward pitch of her voice clearly indicative of her shock. "Dear god, my boy. I've been trying to reach Kipling to learn of your condition. Where is she?"

He chuckled, letting himself relax into the bed. A quick search around the immediate space found her hearing aids, battery cases open to leave them off, on the bedside table beside a water pitcher. "You are calling your only son's girlfriend to inquire about his health, and when he answers, your first question is why he has answered and not his girlfriend."

"Oh, pish. You shocked me. Sweetheart, you sound tired. Are you resting like the doctors have ordered?"

"I don't know yet what the doctors ordered, Mum. I've only just woken." He took the phone away from his cheek to glance at the display, a momentary flush of anxiety hitting him. Sunday. Two days gone.

And tomorrow was the 30th of the month. Something significant. Something important. He cursed the fog in his brain. His great-grandfather had long been known for using opiates to expand the capacity of his brain, but Grayson avoided them. He hated this muzzy, blurred view of the world.

"How are you?" his mother asked, and the fog lifted enough for him to hear the genuine concern tainting her usually uplifting voice. "We have been beside ourselves here, and I've debated for days whether to contact your sister to have her return early."

"No," he managed to say, focusing hard. "No need to bring her back early." He squinted, trying to find a path to follow. "When are Shirl and Daniel due back, Mum?"

"Saturday. They were going to come the night and head home Sunday."

Grayson closed his eyes and pinched the bridge of his nose, slowly edging his way toward full awareness. "I need you to do something for me, Mum."

"Of course, sweetheart."

"Kipling and I will be returning to Sussex on Saturday. I'd like to see as much of the immediate family as possible." And prayed by Saturday he could determine a way to share the news of Greg's condition without sending every family member over the age of twenty to hospital with a heart attack. "Uncle Elton and Aunt Hazel quite specifically, if no one else."

"I'll call straight away," she said, but her voice was confused. "Sweetheart, is there something wrong? Tell me in truth, are you okay? Is Kipling okay?"

At the mention of her name, Grayson looked down at the woman sleeping beside him, as near as she was able. Her chestnut hair cascaded over her shoulder to pool on the blanket and her ribs expanded and eased with deep, sleeping breaths.

"Nothing is wrong, Mum. I speak honestly, I swear to you." His throat tightened and he closed his eyes, once again pommeled by the overwhelming ramifications of the last few days. Had it only been just over a week since Shirl's wedding? Just a bit more since he'd walked into his mother's parlor and found Kipling?

So much in such a short period of time.

"I believe you, sweetheart. Please rest, and call often to let us know. Or have Kipling call. Tell her we love her."

He smiled, a slow pull of his lips that bloomed warm in his chest. "I shall, Mum. I promise." Like a switch being turned on, the importance of the date hit him. "Mum," he managed to say before she rang off.

"Yes?"

"Tomorrow is Kipling's birthday. It's not the purpose of the visit, but—"

"Enough said, sweetheart," she said, the smile audible in her voice. "Leave it to us. Does she like chocolate? Oh, silly question. Who doesn't like chocolate? However, our rhubarb patch is overflowing and the strawberries are coming in nicely. Perhaps a birthday cobbler?"

"She will love whatever you make, I've no doubt."

His mother was still mumbling, likely more to his father than anyone else when he hung up the phone. He set the mobile back where it had been left, and with only the slightest shift, was able to smooth his hand over Kipling's hair. It was cool, clinging still to a slight dampness likely from a shower she'd taken before trying to rest. At his touch, she inhaled deeply and raised her head, twisting to look at him, her eyes sleepy. As soon as she was awake enough to process the moment, she sat up straighter, and her eyes widened.

She stood, pushing the chair back with her movement, and leaned over the edge of the bed to press a long, warm kiss to his cheek, her fingers brushing his throat with undue caution. Before she could withdraw, Grayson snatched her hand despite the uncomfortable pressure of the IV in the back of his, and pressed her palm to his jaw. He waited until she looked directly at him.

"Kiss me," he demanded, and her attention shifted immediately, yet briefly, to his mouth to read his words.

Her lips curled, chasing away some of the concern shadowing her eyes. "Very brief for a recitation, Mr. Holmes. Who said it?"

"I did. Kiss me, Kipling. I need it."

Her gaze settled on his mouth and her touch shifted to ease, stroking his cheek as she leaned in as much as the restrictive bed would allow, and kissed him. Slow and intentional, for the sake of the kiss and no other purpose. For only the briefest second he tasted salt and felt the slick of a tear before she dropped her head to his chest and released a shuddered breath. Grayson kissed the top of her head and stroked her hair, holding her as best his position would allow.

"Well, it's quite obvious you're awake."

Grayson looked to the door, where Doctor Tish Shah stood, smiling at them. She shifted her focus more on Kipling. "I left clear instructions you were to go rest."

Rather than answer, whether she translated Dr. Shah's admonition or whether she didn't read the words across the room, Kipling stepped back from the bed and turned her back on the doctor while she retrieved her aids and set them in place. By the way she gave the doctor her back and didn't immediately turn, Grayson was inclined to believe she didn't want to acknowledge the woman's observation. Aids in place again, she faced the doctor with a smile and stepped close enough to the bed that she could lay her hand on Grayson's arm.

The cant of Doctor Shah's head and the concession in her smile implied if the conversation continued, it wouldn't be the first on the subject. She cleared her throat and came into the room, closing the door behind her. "When did you wake up?"

"Minutes ago," Grayson confirmed. "I've noted the day."

Doctor Shah hummed. "Yes, you've been asleep two days. Considering the fact that beyond pain relief medication and anti-inflammatories, you've not been given anything to forcibly induce sleep, you needed the rest to truly begin your recovery. You've had numerous guests, though none so persistent as Ms. Branson, and despite them all you never woke." Reaching the foot of the bed, the doctor glanced again between Grayson and Kipling, and he read in her expression her assessment of their relationship.

Grayson suspected she was pleased.

Yet another testament to the type of man he had been prior to Kipling, which had become his new timeline. Before Kipling and after Kipling. The four months that constituted "after Kipling" were far richer than anything before.

"I've relayed this information to Ms. Branson since it was made abundantly clear to me by your team that she was to be your proxy, no arguments. Your mother, whom I had the distinct pleasure —

and I do not mean that in any facetious way — in speaking with by phone, also informed me that in the absence of immediate family, Ms. Branson would stand in their place."

Kipling looked down and away from the doctor, gifting him with a brief, flushed glance. He lifted her hand from his arm and kissed her fingers. "As is correct, Doctor. You needn't fear me arguing against it. Tell me."

Doctor Shah sighed and pushed her hands into her white coat pockets. "I doubt I need to tell you that you should have been in hospital after the explosion, but I am aware of the circumstances, so don't hold you at fault there. Perhaps at another time, you might have fared better, though you're far from Superman, but considering the fact not three weeks ago you were shot and still recovering, your body was weakened. Not *weak*, mind you, but not to your normal strength and resistance.

"Add to this your wholly inadequate medical care, pushing yourself beyond your physical limit, multiple damaged ribs to various degrees, dehydration and mild malnutrition, exhaustion, and the early stages of infection, I'm quite surprised you managed to do what you did. I've seen officers run on adrenaline, and I've seen the effects later, but you—"

"—did what was required," he finished.

"Yes, well, one cannot argue against that." Doctor Shah sighed and smiled. "All that being said, I am recommending to your director a minimum of three weeks of full relaxation. *No* fieldwork. Not even deskwork. I don't want you near Vauxhall. You may argue—"

"No argument from me," Grayson said with a wink at Kipling. "For once, Doctor, I fully accept my diagnosis."

Kipling was surprised to go back to Grayson's room to find everyone gone. When she'd stepped out to make several phone calls — she hadn't spent so much time on the phone in, well, she didn't even know — the room had been overflowing. Mac, Lynne, Sandra and David, and Greg and Esther had arrived *en masse* within an hour of Nurse Judith's — no longer Juds — visit confirming Grayson was awake. Kipling suspected as soon as the woman left the room – looking radically different than she had at Esther's, now with the blue dyed tips of her hair hidden in a neat coiffure and her makeup drastically toned back — she'd contacted Esther, and from there the message had spread.

Grayson was awake.

"Where did everyone go?" she asked.

Grayson poked at the tray of food in front of him. "Stepped out to eat. They will return later." He grimaced. "Unfortunately, their discussion of Indian versus Italian has made my baked chicken seem rather unappetizing."

Kipling offered a sympathetic, but teasing, pout and came to the side of his bed opposite the IV pole. Once he'd woken, they'd taken out the IV since he could now take medications orally. They had restored his fluid levels to a point Doctor Shah was satisfied, but before he woke the IV drip provided an antibiotic solution to fight the infections that had begun to brew in some of the worst burned areas. He'd take a schedule of antibiotics from here on out.

"One more night, and you can come home. Tell me what you'd like for dinner and I'll make it. Whatever you like."

His grin was slow, beginning with a mischievous press of his lips together before one corner tipped up, a dimple forming on his cheek. He reached for her and shifted to the far side of the bed, giving her a place to sit, and she perched beside his hip to face him. Grayson laced his fingers through hers and held their joined hands on his thigh.

"Do you know how it pleases me to hear you call Baker Street home?"

"You've mentioned it," she said with a wink. "You should know, however, that Watson is highly put out. With both of us, likely."

"I've no doubt." His laugh was a deep rumble, low in his chest. "Did you finish your calls?"

Kipling sighed and rolled her eyes, focusing on the remains of a healing cut on the back of his knuckles. The skin was rough, a little too pink, but almost healed. Not all his wounds or abrasions, or hers, could be defined the same. Though her bruising had mottled to an ugly yellow-green in most spots.

"All done. For now."

She ticked off each of the call recipients as she listed them.

"Spoke to your mum. Assured her you are recovering fine and I'll take very good care until we drive back down Saturday. How are you going to handle that?"

He shook his head. "I don't know yet. I doubt I *will* know until the moment arrives."

She offered what she hoped was an encouraging smile, and moved on to her next finger. "Spoke with *my* parents. They are currently docked in Portugal and had only heard of the explosion yesterday. They couldn't get any cell service until today. I had to hang up with Mina to take their call, then called her back. They wanted to get off the boat and head for Heathrow, but I think I talked them out of it now that they know I'm fine." She pressed her lips together, and hated having to add, "Unfortunately, they have some misgivings about me staying in London."

"About you staying in London, or staying with me?" Before she could try to offer an answer that wouldn't sting, Grayson brought her hand to his lips and kissed it. "Not to worry. It is my responsibility to prove myself worthy to your parents, and I shall not fail." He finished with a wink. "You spoke to Mina."

Kipling groaned. That had been the most difficult call of them all because Mina was the most difficult to have a rational conversation with. Greg had accepted responsibility for telling Mina the truth since he had been the one deceiving them for months. Kipling only knew of the fallout from that call, which he apparently at least did by Skype so Mina would see the earnest apology in his face, but it had been brutal. Mina had been furious, raging against Grayson and Greg, and the storm of lies and deception they lived in. That had been yesterday; she was only moderately calmer today. The call had been short. Kipling ended it when Mina's tirade turned personal and cruel.

Grayson squeezed her hand. She had no doubt the full conversation played across her face. "She'll come round."

"Is it bad of me to wonder if I want her to?"

He arched an eyebrow, tilting his head, but said nothing. Kipling shrugged and curled her hair behind her ear. She'd left it down after showering early that morning, and now without any attempt at taming it, it had waved and curled into chaos. Grayson said it was sexy.

"I've known Mina my entire life, but I honestly don't know the woman she's been since February. At first, I believed she was just overly concerned, especially while you were still in Boston because everything happened all at once. But after you left…" She shook her head. "There were days she was almost cruel in her opinion. Spiteful. And then she would excuse it for worry. I understand worry. I don't understand her mean streak."

"Perhaps time and distance will tame her emotions."

Kipling shrugged again. "We'll see. Anyway, the last phone call was to the university. Since it's Sunday, I didn't actually reach President Rathborne, so I won't know the status of the job offer until tomorrow. Since only two business days have passed since the interview…" She shook her head because it all seemed like an eternity ago. "…I hope he thinks I was just considering the offer."

"I'm quite sure that will be the case, and he will be thrilled with your acceptance."

"We'll see." Kipling shifted to bring her feet onto the bed after toeing off her shoes so she could hug her knees to her chest, balancing on the edge of the narrow mattress. "Before everyone comes back, can I ask you a question?"

"Of course."

"It's about Liz."

"Liz…"

Kipling nodded. "What is going to happen to her? You said yourself you don't believe she's at fault. She didn't intentionally tell Howell anything to harm you. Or me."

"There will be an inquiry," he explained, shifting to recline into the pillows behind him. Despite the fact he'd slept for two days, he'd been up for four or five hours and looked tired. "She is still an employee of the Secret Intelligence Service, even if her capacity is far from higher levels, who provided information, even if unwittingly, to an enemy of Crown and Country. She may see no repercussions at all, save for those she condemns on herself, to redaction."

"I hope nothing happens to her. Despite it all, I like her." Kipling winced and looked toward the window. "I feel terrible about deceiving her that night. I know I was there to listen for anything that would prove her guilt or innocence, but..." She shook her head. "Honestly, most of those hours waiting to hear from you were in silence. Literally. She thought I wouldn't hear, and made little effort to talk other than writing me a note to offer me tea. But, after a couple of hours, she started talking."

"Talking?" he asked, and for some reason, the way his lips formed the word sent a pleasant shiver up her spine.

"Yes. She sat facing away from me, probably assuming if I didn't see her I wouldn't know, but then she began talking. She said how interesting our conversations would be if I could hear her. We'd have tea and talk about how we met the men we loved, and laugh about it being the same man. You."

Grayson pressed his lips together and rubbed his thumb across the top of her foot. "I apologize. That couldn't have been comfortable."

"No, it wasn't, but—" She paused when his attention shifted past her to the door just as she heard footsteps behind her. She twisted until her muscles, still a little tight, protested so she slid off the bed to face the doctor.

"Sorry to interrupt," Doctor Shah said with a pleasant smile. "I came by to see if you might like to go home today. You're awake, and I have Ms. Branson's assurance you will rest," she said with a wink at Kipling and a smile. "There is no reason you can't sleep in your own bed tonight."

"Doctor, there are very few things that would sound more appealing."

Chapter Twenty-Five

Kipling woke with a long, low purr to the sensation of firm lips and warm breath on her stomach. She stretched and hummed, arching her back into the touch as she opened her eyes. She smiled when Grayson grinned against her ribs, looking up her body at her over the bunched hem of her tee shirt he'd pushed out of his way.

"Good morning," she said, pushing her fingers into his thick hair, even though it was shorter.

He pressed a long, open-mouthed kiss to a spot between her breasts and her navel and shifted over her until they were skin-to-skin, belly-to-belly, warmth-to-warmth, and he leaned over her.

"Good morning," she read on his lips. He used his bent arms to brace himself over her, and took her mouth in a deep kiss that made her heart flutter at the base of her throat.

Grayson stretched out beside her, lying on his right side with his temple supported against his curled hand so he could look down on her and she could see his face. He rested his spread hand on her stomach where he had kissed her minutes before, stroking his thumb back and forth. "And happy birthday."

She smiled, pressing her palm to his bare chest. His left arm was still red from the healing burns, with the worst areas bandaged to keep the skin layers intact. Just the description made her cringe. For the most part, he'd been instructed to keep his exposed skin from drying out, so Kipling was assigned the responsibility of applying a healing moisturizer a few times a day. The stitches in his shoulder were covered with a large rectangle of gauze, but the sutures would be removed in a few days. At least the tired strain around his eyes was gone.

"Thank you," she said, wiggling closer to him. "I would have forgotten, but my mother reminded me of it yesterday when we spoke. Well, it was more of a 'not much of a happy birthday' comment."

"Not exactly the kind of birthday I would have given you had I been able to plan better." He stroked his fingers over her stomach, just above the elastic waistband of her pajama shorts. "In fact, once you were here I'd begun thinking about a proper way to celebrate. Until Howell threw a spanner in the works."

"I don't know. It's off to a promising start." Shifting her head on the pillow so she could look at him more squarely since she was at the disadvantage of not hearing his voice. "How do you feel?"

"Well rested," he said with a lopsided grin. "I've slept the better part of the last three days, and I have been lying here for the last twenty minutes waiting for you to wake up so I could say good morning properly."

"I like your idea of saying good morning properly. It's much like the way you say hello."

She barely finished the words when he cupped her cheek and kissed her again. Need set off in her veins like a wildfire and Kipling moaned against his tongue as it thrust along hers. He stopped kissing her only long enough to pull her tee shirt over her head and toss it aside. Urgent hands and desperate mouths shed their night-clothes, and Kipling let herself sink into the love of Grayson Holmes.

"Going to the office on your first official day of medical leave hardly seems like following the doctor's orders, Grayson."

He smiled over his shoulder at her as he adjusted his silk tie into place, and she remembered with a pleasant warmth beneath her skin the first few times she saw him in Boston; always impeccably dressed in a suit tailored to his lean, trim body that accentuated his height and frame. She still hadn't decided what she found sexier: suit and tie All Business Grayson, or Levis and boots Casual Grayson. Probably whichever Grayson she had at the time.

Of course, shirtless and making her breakfast Grayson was pretty tough to beat. Though since Greg was staying in Baker Street until things were settled with their superiors, the likelihood of Shirtless Chef Grayson probably lessened.

With the Windsor knot in place, he buttoned his jacket, adjusted his cuffs, shifted his shoulders, and smoothed the lapels before turning to face her. Yep, right now All Business Grayson had some definite appeal.

"Unfortunately, this matter is best dealt with quickly. Director Cooper has requested a conversation, and now that Howell has been processed, I would like to assure myself he is secure. I'll sleep better at night."

Kipling scooted further onto the mattress, rumpling the coverlet she'd tucked into place after they'd finally left the bed, and crossed her legs, her ankles tucked beneath her. "What do you think Director Cooper wants to talk about? Do you think he'll try to deny everything he said before you captured Howell?"

Grayson took a deep breath as he crossed the bedroom to stand at the foot of the bed, setting his hands on the elegant ironwork of the footboard in front of her. "Until a couple of years ago, I willingly accepted the fact I gave my life to Six, on many levels. My view has changed *drastically*, and I cannot abide their manipulation of me, of Greg, and of our entire family. I want them to look me in the eye — look *Greg* in the eye — and explain why they felt their only course of action was to steal his existence. The other night he admitted guilt, but he provided no justification."

He pressed his lips together, pursing his upper lip, and tapped the heel of his hand on the footboard. Kipling laid her hand over his and he stilled. He took another deep breath through his nose, releasing it before he met her gaze. "We have all accepted under-cover assignments, some requiring extended periods of time away from our lives. I want to know why they destroyed his life to complete an investigation."

"What if..." She shook her head and looked past him, then to him again. "What if Director Cooper refuses to answer? What if he says either accept that Greg's life, *your* life, is forfeit and you step back into line and follow orders or—"

"Leave?" he asked, cutting off her question, and she nodded. "Then perhaps I leave. Losing Greg was one of the first life-changing events that has made me question my choice." He leaned over the footboard and she stretched up to meet his kiss. "But he wasn't the last."

Then he came around to the side of the bed and offered his hand to her as she unfolded her legs and slid off the mattress. When they opened the bedroom door, Watson bolted in, zigzagged between their feet, and jumped on the bed in a sunny spot. His eyes were closed before his head settled on the duvet. The enticing aroma of coffee and toast drifted up from downstairs.

"Smells like Greg is up already," Grayson said, taking her hand as he led her to the stairs. "When we return, and once the details have been relayed, I intend to take you out for a proper birthday dinner."

"Just don't be gone too long."

Grayson stopped on the first floor landing before finishing the descent to the main level and slipped his arm around her to bring her to him, kissing her. "Trust me when I say I won't be away from you any longer than absolutely necessary."

"Do you remember Harry Wilson?"

"Of course." Grayson shut the back door of the cab, and handed the driver a £10 note, nodding a thanks when he was handed back a quid in change. His cousin had been uncharacteristically quiet during the cab ride from Westminster, only nodding an acknowledgment when Grayson asked if he would be seeing Esther later.

When he couldn't inspire conversation, he'd left his cousin to his thoughts. Only now, as they neared Six's headquarters did he decide to speak on anything. It seemed odd his first question would be whether Grayson remembered a fellow officer who had been killed in the line of duty three or four years previous. He had been a good officer, but not often directly working with Grayson or his team.

"Do you remember when he died?"

Grayson walked away from the kerb, Greg falling into step with him. It wasn't more than a five-minute walk to the office from the common drop-off spot. "Perhaps four years now? Just short of, I believe." Realization formed and Grayson's steps slowed. He recovered and caught up to his cousin in two quick steps. "He was killed not long after you revealed the truth to Esther. She accompanied you to the funeral."

Greg nodded. "I saw something in her eyes that day, and I never wanted to be the cause of it. She saw what could be our future. I loved her enough to spare her."

"That was your reason for ending it? The reason you didn't want to get into the other night?"

"Seemed to make sense at the time."

"You spared her nothing," Grayson said, practically stomping on Greg's words of justification. "You cannot imagine what she went through when she learned you'd died. She loved you always. Your death devastated her. At least if the two of you had been together, the family would have felt justified stepping in. Offering comfort."

Greg pushed his hands into his trouser pockets, his head down, regret lines digging in around his eyes and the corners of his frown as they neared the building. The sound of the Thames carried from the other side of the SIS, the air holding a more distinct chill here with the moisture carried on the breeze, cooling Grayson's skin and his ire.

He sighed and cleared his throat, rubbing his fingers across his brow. As much as he'd told Kipling he felt fine, he had a lingering headache. Nothing debilitating, or worrisome, just annoying. It made him short. "Apologies, Greg. You didn't deserve that. What happened wasn't your choice."

"In a way it was."

Greg's voice was low and rough, but enough to cause Grayson to stop and catch his cousin's elbow so Greg turned to face him. "What the hell are you saying?"

He tilted his head, back and to the side, not meeting Grayson's eyes but rather more to the multiple levels and green surface of the SIS building. The way he worried his lips together, then bunched them into a tight line, Grayson assumed he didn't want to say whatever he had to say. But he wouldn't have brought up the topic of conversation if the goal wasn't to confess.

Fortified, his gaze shifted to Grayson and held. "I chose to stay in that building, Ollie. I thought what I had to retrieve was more important than me. I knew going in I wasn't likely to come out the other side. I've wondered a few times – hell, more times than I can count – if Esther had been waiting for me at home if I wouldn't have tried harder to get out. If I'd gone in at all."

Rather than chastising, Grayson took his hand from Greg's arm and patted it down firmly on his shoulder. "She's been given a gift as much as I, or the family. And you've been given a gift, too." They fell into step again and reached the entrance to the public lobby and Grayson yanked open the door to allow Greg to enter. "Don't cock up again."

Not given the chance to argue further, Greg followed Grayson into the building. Some nodded to Grayson, and some expressed their pleasure he was still with them after the events of the week before — as even casual employees of the Secret Intelligence Service, they all could calculate the likelihood of an explosion on Baker Street as being an attempt on his life.

In the lift, Greg looked from the control panel to the ceiling and back to the door. "This feels painfully familiar."

"Don't look at your former office," Grayson said as the lift approached their level. "They gave it to Simmons."

"Simmons? Bloody hell, what a wanker."

The lift stopped and in the second before the door opened, Grayson pulled on the mental vestment of an SIS officer, something that after two weeks outside the walls felt foreign and uncomfortable. Like a poorly tailored suit, tight in the shoulders and restricting. When the doors opened, they stepped in synchronization with each other into the hall toward Grayson's office. No one gave Greg more than a passing glance as an unfamiliar face, and being accompanied by an officer required no further attention.

They reached Grayson's office door, and he entered the security code to unlock it. In just a week, he swore the air smelled stale. It lacked life and activity. "Have a seat," he said, pointing toward his office chair.

Greg sat, the leather hissing at the weight, and bounced in the seat. "Hmm, new chair. Comfy."

Taking the phone handset from its cradle, Grayson dialed an extension number he knew well and waited for Director Cooper's assistant to answer. When she answered, he took in the final breath needed to steel his resolve. "This is Grayson Holmes. Please inform Director Cooper I am in my office." The woman didn't deserve his ire, but he was far from letting go of his anger. It may have subsided enough to clear his thoughts, but if anything the time and separation from the revelation of Greg's existence only honed his focus and kept the fire of his anger and disappointment burning like glowing embers.

He hung up with nothing else said, and tucked his hands behind his back, looking to where Greg now sat in his chair. "Are you prepared for this?"

"I'm prepared to claim my life again. Whatever that means." He chuckled and smiled. "I might be applying for jobseeker's allowance by the end of the day. What do you think a former Six officer is qualified for?"

"Politics."

They both laughed, but it was short lived. The tension sat in the air like fog, still and cold. The final confrontation – or heated discussion, however it played — with Cooper would be the sun burning it off, but until then they waited. Grayson stood on the guest side of his desk, leaning with his hands curled around the edge, his ankles crossed. He kept his head bowed and his eyes closed, running possible scenarios through his mind like broken scenes of a film. Unfortunately, until he knew what justification Jeffrey Cooper attempted to provide, he had no clear line of dialogue for argument.

Not knowing how long they would wait, they fell into silence.

"I'm happy for you, Ollie," Greg said after a few minutes.

Grayson raised his head and looked over his shoulder at his cousin. "Quite likely surprised as well." When his cousin tried to look puzzled by his statement, Grayson shook his head. "No one is more surprised than I, Greg. She quite literally took over my life the moment she stepped into it. I have never imagined loving someone could be so complete."

Greg smiled, a tug upward at one corner of his mouth. "You're in deeper than I thought. I wouldn't have ever imagined you so poetic."

Grayson sighed, letting a chuckle bounce his shoulders. "Then you should read my letters."

Greg's brows pulled and he canted his head. "What letters?" Then he laughed and raised his hands in defense. "I have *no* interest in reading your love letters to Kip."

"Nor do I have interest in sharing," he countered, smiling. Then drew in a deep breath and released it through his nostrils. "When we are home, I'll show you since they were to you. Of course, I never knew with certainty you'd have the chance to read them—"

The doorknob turned, simultaneously accompanied by Director Cooper's triple knock before he pushed open the door and came in.

Grayson straightened but didn't stand away from the desk edge, and Cooper's gaze shifted from him to Greg, and back again.

"If this isn't déjà vu…"

Grayson fought the urge to cross his arms, instead resting the tips of his fingers of his left hand on the desk surface while easing his right into his trouser pockets. He'd railed against Cooper in the small hours of Friday morning; today, he'd be the calmer mind, but the non-relenting voice.

"How is Miss Branson weathering all this? She wasn't much for speaking with—"

"*Doctor* Branson is fine," he stressed. "As fine as one might expect given the circumstances. I am thankful for those on my team who stepped in and did what they were able in order to assist her."

"You know, Holmes, she may be glad to return to her quiet existence in Boston."

"She isn't returning to Boston." He defied Cooper to look away by staring him down. When he'd informed Jeffrey of Kipling's presence in London, he had no idea what opportunities were in store, what would transpire, and how absolutely he would want her to stay. He didn't feel the requirement to offer any further explanation, even when Cooper's eyebrows arched in inquisition. "She is not why we are here."

"Are we reduced to only hostile exchanges?" Jeffrey asked, sounding as fatigued as Grayson felt. "We have known each other for years."

Grayson took a step toward the man who had been his mentor, even his friend. "Time and again, you have chastised me for believing Greg might live, or more to the fact, for doubting the word of my superiors when you declared it wasn't possible. You've gone so far as to threaten my standing due to being emotionally compromised."

"Facts I will not deny, and do regret, though I assure you my options were nearly as limited as McQueen's."

"*Nearly* being the optimum word, Jeffrey. You looked me in the eye every day, you argued with me, and you questioned my mental stability so much I questioned it myself."

"Alright. Alright! I bloody well get it," Cooper snapped, taking a step back to move behind one of the guest chairs, his grip on the back tight enough to whiten his knuckles. "I can't and won't argue that I was somehow in the right. But I was *doing my job*. As was McQueen."

Greg snorted from where he still sat, elbows on the arms of the chair, fingers steeled together. "Slight difference, Director. You still have a pension. I don't even have that. Paid out to my mum." Greg sat forward, the chair squeaking with the shift, and pointed at Cooper. "She's not paying it back, by the way. Consider it compensation for heartbreak."

Jeffrey Cooper's eyes rounded and color drained from his face. "You're dead as far as they know. It would be cruel—"

"To allow them to continue to believe a lie," Greg finished and stood, coming around to stand beside Grayson. "I don't care what happens when I leave this building today, but by this weekend my family will know I'm alive."

Cooper let go with a string of profanities the likes of which Grayson had never heard from the man. Of course, he had also never seen Cooper as shaken to his foundation as he had been in the last few days. Perspiration ran from his flushed pate, and he swiped at his brow with a handkerchief from his pocket. Grayson looked to Greg, who arched an eyebrow as their director mumbled and cursed, his head down. Finally, with a huff, Cooper looked at them again.

"Answer me one bloody question, McQueen."

"Ask and I'll consider it."

"Where the hell have you been?"

"Exactly where you sent me. Boston."

If Director Jeffrey Cooper had been so slow and thick to have not seen the connective tissues before now, they all suddenly fell together and wove for him a picture he suddenly saw with wide-eyed clarity. His jaw fell slack and he looked to Grayson. Then he groaned low in his throat and shook his head. "Explosions. Death threats. You suddenly realize you've got a bloody libido. And losing a damn covert field agent. Sending you to Boston was the worst decision of my entire career."

"No, your worst decision was hiding the truth," Grayson said, keeping his voice level. "Now...where do we go from here?"

Kipling ran her fingertips along the aged, cracked, and worn spines of the dozens of books lined up in the century-old library, tilting her head to read the gold leaf titles. The library was made up of four walls, floor to ceiling with the exception of the front window and the door, filled with shelves, and shelves filled with books. She suddenly felt like Belle in the Disney version of *Beauty and the Beast* the first time she stepped into the Beast's library.

Except the owner of this library was no beast.

She'd spent the morning trying to find some way to keep herself busy and her mind occupied. The offer paperwork had survived the bombing because it was in her satchel, and she'd reviewed the position offer from the university but hadn't called. She wanted Grayson home first. She'd cleaned the kitchen and washed laundry after taking fifteen minutes to figure out the machine tucked under the counter in the kitchen. It both washed and dried the clothes, and she had to wonder why such a great idea hadn't made it to America yet. She'd even baked cookies and drank at least a gallon of tea. Then she'd tried the door to what Grayson had pointed out her first day at Baker Street equivalent to hidden treasure for a bibliophile.

She smiled when her gaze settled on a particular shelf. From one end of the shelf to the other were first editions of every Sherlock Holmes novel written by Sir Arthur Conan Doyle. On the shelf below were carefully sorted and stored copies of *The Strand*, the magazine that first introduced Sherlock Holmes to the world. She was tempted to draw one from its sealed back, but the antiquity lover in her held her back, and she only allowed herself to run her fingers over the clear plastic, examining the magazine from its sealed container.

She heard the front door open, the very reason she had stayed on the main floor, so she would hear Grayson and Greg as soon as they were home. Setting the magazine back in its place, she jogged across the antique Oriental rug to the door she'd left open.

"Kipling?" Grayson called and looked to the door as she exited the den. He smiled, but he looked tired. Worn. "I wondered how long it would take for you to explore."

"Did you find my bolt-hole entrance?" Greg asked, walking toward the kitchen. He inhaled deeply. "Wow, do I smell…snicker-doodles?"

"I needed something to do," she said but didn't follow Greg. Instead, she met Grayson halfway, raising her arms to wrap around his neck as he pulled her into his embrace and buried his face into her shoulder with a long, low moan.

His hold was firm, unrelenting, and she made no move to step free, feeling in the hug he needed her to just be still. She didn't ask him anything, didn't want to make him let go until he was ready. When she felt his arms relax a small degree, she drew back and smoothed her hands along the side of his neck and against his jaw.

"I don't know what to ask," she said with an attempt at a smile.

He attempted the same and rested his forehead against hers. "There is much to tell, but I confess I haven't the heart or the energy. Simply put, and the end result is, no absolute resolution was found today. A resolution may not come for weeks. Offers were made, in exchange for discretion on our part regarding the return of Greg McQueen to the SIS. Until such a time as Greg and I decide what to accept, I am here…recovering…and relishing in every moment I have with you."

Kipling stroked his cheek with her thumbs, studying his eyes. His gaze was cast down, deep lines at the corner. Something had bruised him today, not physically, but bruised his heart. She didn't push, knowing he would tell her when he had the energy and resolution to do so. He always told her. Kipling toed up and pressed her lips to his in a firm, simple kiss until the tension in his body eased some and his hands flattened against her back to hold her close.

With a shorter kiss to punctuate the first, Grayson rested his forehead against hers again and spoke with a sigh. "I love you, Kipling. I would be lost if it were not for you."

"You'll always have me," she promised, kissing his cheek. "I promise you." She smiled, slow and easy, hoping a return to their game would make him smile. "They do not love that do not show their love."

He smiled and laughed low, and she felt satisfaction in making him smile. "Seize the moments of happiness, love, and be loved. That is the only reality in the world, all else is folly."

Grayson kissed her again and didn't stop until Greg came out of the kitchen with his mouth full and a stack of cookies in his hand. "Oh, hell. Is this what I'm going to have to put up with?"

With her still in his hold, Grayson turned them to face his cousin. "Yes, most definitely so as long as you live beneath the roof of 221 Baker Street." He smirked. "Or move to Southpark."

Greg waved them off, walked past, and took the stairs two steps at a time. Alone again, Grayson looked down at her and the shadows had eased, replaced by the spark she loved so much. "I believe I promised you a birthday dinner."

"Mmmm," she hummed and glanced toward the grandfather clock in the corner of the foyer. "You did, but it's a bit early to go to dinner." She slid her gaze back to him with as much seduction as she could manage, being entirely out of practice. "Don't you think?"

Chapter Twenty-Six

"You know in the end it won't matter how you say it."

Grayson glanced to his left, diverting attention from the country road stretching out in front of them to look at Kipling. The hired car seatbelt crossed over her, but she had managed to twist in the seat to have her back more to the passenger door with her feet tucked into the seat beside her. The temporary vehicle was smaller than the Bentley, not affording nearly as much comfort. To avoid being distracted by her smile, he shifted his focus back to the road.

"Do you really believe that?" he asked.

"I'm not saying you should walk through the door, announce 'Oh, by the way, Greg is alive', but the moment reality sinks in, they aren't going to be anything but ecstatic." She leaned across the space of the car to smooth her knuckles across his cheek, scraping her fingers through his hair. "I know this has been eating you up all week."

"It has been, yes." He slowed at an intersection, checked the connective roads, and pulled through again. They would be at the cottage in a few minutes once they passed through the village. "And while I know you're right, I still would prefer not to induce a heart attack in the more elderly members of the family." He offered a quick smile.

A glance in his rearview mirror confirmed Greg and Esther still followed in Esther's car. The plan was they would not arrive at the cottage together, but Greg would wait until Grayson confirmed he should enter. It might be too harsh for them to walk in together. Grayson needed the family to understand he wouldn't look the same but was the same man before they saw him. Whether it was the right decision, Grayson had no idea, but he had to start somewhere.

A short distance from the cottage, at the edge of the Holmes land, Greg pulled off to the soft shoulder, where he would wait. Grayson watched in the rear mirror until the car disappeared from sight when they followed the curve of the road and the cottage came into view. His uncle's car was parked along the road, as was Steven and Portia's saloon and Elton and Lila's MVP. It would be a greater challenge with the young ones at the house. All the adults in the immediate family knew what Grayson and Greg were, who they worked for, and they all knew how Greg had died. The children only knew Uncle Greg was gone.

Grayson slowed and turned into the drive, parking the car behind his father's Jeep, Jo's yellow Mini Cooper to the right of the Jeep. He didn't see Shirl's red Mini Cooper, but Daniel's Hyundai was there.

"Hail, hail, the gang's all here," he mumbled as he pushed the gear lever to park. Turning off the car, he sighed, letting his hand holding the keys drop heavy on his lap. He looked toward the house, his heart in his throat. "You would assume one would not be so nervous about sharing good news."

Kipling took his hand not holding the keys and leaned across the console to kiss his cheek. He turned to her, and she kissed his lips, then set her hands on his shoulder and rested her chin on her hand. The bruises were gone, the scrapes almost completely healed, and her smile lifted his soul.

"I love you. In case you didn't know."

Grayson tipped his head to take another fortifying kiss before opening his door to exit the car. He walked around the boot end and reached her door as she opened it, offering his hand. His heart pounded hard, and he had to focus to keep his breathing steady. In truth, he was excited at the prospect of sharing the news he'd hoped he could share for the last year or more since the day he confessed to his family his heartfelt conviction Greg was somehow not dead. That he couldn't accept the fact without irrefutable proof Six could not provide.

With Kipling's hand in his, he led around to the back garden, where Shirl and Daniel had been married just two weeks before, and to the kitchen door. Voices carried from inside, filled with laughter and the squeal of the younger children, and the enticing aroma of roast pork loin with apples, one of his mother's specialties.

"We're home," Grayson called, and the voices coming from the parlor quieted for a second before being followed by the chorus of multiple footsteps coming their way. "Brace yourself," he said with a wink before his mother appeared first, followed by the combined Holmes and McQueen horde.

Hugs were exchanged, and a cursory inspection of both himself and Kipling to assure they were, indeed, fine, not near death, and still in possession of all their limbs. Apparently bored with the adult conversation, the children asked if they could go to the garden and Erika offered to go with them. Perhaps serendipity was on his side. Either that or Erika had been instructed before their arrival to keep the little ones occupied since he'd made it clear he had something to discuss. With the overall volume decreasing, someone suggested they move to the parlor. Dinner would be ready in another half hour.

Kipling walked close to his side, the fingers of one hand laced through his, with her other hand curled around his arm. His mother's watchful eye, looking from him to Kipling, and back didn't go unnoticed. With the amount of people squeezing into the parlor, several chairs had been brought in from around the table and a couple from his father's library. All squeezed into the parlor. Everyone found seats, doubling and tripling up on the couch, with Shirl sitting on the arm of the couch beside her new husband.

"Well, sweetheart, we're all here," his mother said with a false calm in her voice.

He wished he could have assured her, and the rest of the family, there was no need for concern with his visit. But even as he had assured her, he knew it wouldn't work until they were there and the words were spoken. Kipling sat in one of the wooden dining chairs, looking up at him with a reassuring smile.

Too much nervous energy refused to allow him to sit, and he set his hands on the high back of another of the dining chairs, looking down at it while he tried to remember *any* of the possible scenarios he'd run through his mind in the past week. Then like a whisper in his ear or a hand across his back, a starting point revealed itself to him. Swallowing and licking his lips, Grayson cleared his throat and looked around at his circle of family.

"I'm sure many in this room would find it quite surprising I am at a lack for words."

"Geezus, it's the end of the world," Elton said with a chuckle.

Many joined in, but the sound was strained. When it settled again, Grayson found himself looking into his father's face. Emerson Holmes was a man of few but powerful words. One of the many ways Grayson acknowledged he was not like his father. He often wished for his father's economy of speech, to be so sure of what he had to say he could say it with succinct eloquence and clarity. His father dipped his chin, holding Grayson's gaze, silently offering his strength.

He thought his strength would come from Kipling, but he had ruled out his source of strength since his childhood. She was his new life, his new home, built on the foundation Emerson Holmes had laid. The swell of emotion choked him, and he hoped to speak without losing his composure.

"An empty chair," he said, speaking to them all but holding his gaze on his father. "The Holmes family has maintained the tradition of an empty chair for a lost family member for more generations than we know. Two weeks ago, we had a wedding here — a happy, wonderful occasion — but amongst us was an empty chair."

He heard a sniffle from the direction of his aunt, and his heart squeezed. He wanted to be quick, but he wanted to be sincere. Breaking his stare at his father, he lowered his chin and closed his eyes, gripping tight on the back of the chair in front of him. "I have not held it a secret that I openly and adamantly questioned my employer about Greg's death." Even now, he felt odd mentioning Six directly despite the fact it was no mystery to anyone in the room. "I stopped speaking of it when I realized the pain I inflicted on the people who loved him."

Grayson raised his head and opened his eyes to find his aunt and uncle, the tears on his aunt's cheeks already a testament to the fact he needed to say what was required to end the heartache. "Please know I would have never spoken of my belief again if I didn't believe it warranted."

When no one spoke, only stared at him with anticipation, Grayson turned and took two steps away, taking a deep breath to fortify his resolve. A hard, burning moment of anger hit his chest. Anger at Six for their deception. He sucked in a deep breath through his nose and pushed his fingers into his hair, rubbing his scalp before turning back.

"Everything that I am," he said, pressing his hand to his chest. "Everything I've learned to do and understand, every naturally born skill passed down from Sherlock told me — again and again — it wasn't true." With each point, he thumped his hand over his heart. He shook his head. "Greg was *not* dead. My mind, my training, my *job* always demanded proof. Act on proof. Proof brought justice. Proof brought an end. And there was no proof."

"Your director told us—" began his uncle.

"Yes," Grayson said, his turmoil twisting harder and faster than his calm. "He did. He told you. He told me. Greg is dead."

"Grayson, why—"

"Greg isn't dead," he forced out, a mix of relief and dreaded anticipation slamming into him. In the face of every family member, he saw the doubt, the thoughts that he must finally be crazy. He shook his head. "I wish I could be more gentle, but if I continue to avoid the words this will take too long, and truly, you will be happier when I am done."

"You can't keep saying that," his aunt said softly. "Grayson, it breaks our heart all over again when you do."

"Which is why I swear to you I wouldn't do this if I wasn't absolutely sure in my words." Grayson skirted the chair and dropped to one knee in front of his aunt and uncle, taking his aunt's hand. "I swear to you, Aunt Hazel. Greg is not dead. He is alive."

"Grayson," Kipling said softly and he nodded, glancing for only a second in her direction as she took her phone from her pocket.

"This is cruel," Aunt Hazel whispered.

"Yes, it's cruel. It's cruel what we were made to believe. Cruel to break our hearts. Cruel to perpetuate the lie."

As soon as he heard the front door ease open, a sound seemingly lost by everyone else, he assumed Greg had already come to the house and waited at the door. As anxious as Grayson for the reunion. Grayson brought his aunt's trembling, cold hand to his lips and kissed it. Now was the moment of trust, of faith. If they would do as he asked so they could believe with their hearts before they were asked to believe with their eyes.

"Auntie, will you do something for me?"

She shook her head, more an act of confusion than negation, tears running down her cheeks. "What could you need me to do, Grayson?"

"Close your eyes," he asked, offering the most comforting smile he could. "Please. Close your eyes and listen. Listen and believe what you hear. Believe it over what you will see."

"I've never had a reason to distrust you, Grayson..." Her sad eyes said as much as her broken tone. She was on the edge of disbelief.

"You have no reason to now. Please, Auntie, close your eyes."

He held his breath under her scrutinizing gaze until she closed her eyes and dipped her chin. She released a long, shuddered, sad breath and her hold on his hand tightened. Grayson waited with all attention on him and his aunt.

"I love you, Mum," came Greg's voice from the hall. "I've missed you and I'm sorry."

His aunt gasped, her hand wrenching from Grayson to cover her mouth, a similar response from nearly everyone in the room who might know the voice of Gregory Sherlock Holmes McQueen.

Grayson stood and took his aunt's hand again, drawing her to her feet and his uncle followed. She swayed, looking ready to faint, but followed him to the archway leading to the hall. By the time they reached the arch, she wept openly and trembled.

"Greg," Grayson said. "She needs you."

Greg came around the wall and didn't give his mother time to study his face or look him over, wrapping her in his embrace. Like Grayson did with his own mother, Greg towered over her, their height a throwback to past generations. Aunt Hazel wept, saying her son's name again and again as her husband wrapped them both in his arms. Everyone rushed forward, and Grayson moved back, giving them all the moments they needed to accept the beautiful truth. There would be questions, and they would both be called on to answer, but for now the return of their prodigal son required no other words.

Kipling joined him, wrapping her arms around his body, and he held her against his side. "I knew you'd find the words."

"I fumbled and sounded like a fool," he said, looking down at her.

She smiled, her own eyes shining. "No, you spoke from your heart in the most sincere way you could. Sometimes sincerity requires the hardest words."

Grayson pressed a long kiss to her forehead, closing his eyes.

Kipling walked away from the Holmes and McQueen family cluster in the back garden of the Holmes cottage, the scene so reminiscent of two weeks prior, following Shirl's wedding. The atmosphere tonight was as celebratory, if not even more than it had been that evening. The wine was poured liberally, the food coming non-stop from a seemingly endless rotation of casserole dishes, and the laughter was constant. There had been questions, and both Greg and Grayson had answered what they could as much as they could without putting their loved ones at risk for the knowledge, but in the end all that mattered was that Greg was amongst them, alive, even if his face had changed.

That part had been the most difficult for Grayson to explain because he adamantly refused to justify the actions of their joint employer — his and Greg's — in any way. He had told her, in numerous ways, that he would never *ever* accept this had been the only way to accomplish what they wanted, especially since as it had always been, it was the joint effort of Grayson and Greg *together* that had brought Langdon Howell into custody.

Greg's mother swore as long as she looked into his eyes, the line of his jaw and the angle of his nose didn't matter.

While the revelation of Greg's life was monumental, as an observer Kipling found their reaction to Esther Mitchell even more enthusiastic. Greg had only allowed a few minutes before he introduced her. She was welcomed with open arms, without hesitation, much as they had welcomed Kipling. She still knew little of this woman other than the basics – British and American, much like Grayson, and a doctor of anthropology – but family and history were blank. Not that it mattered, and it all would come – whatever needed to be revealed – in time. There was no doubt Esther was in Greg's life to stay.

Now that assurances were firm, dinner was eaten, and evening wine poured the family had gathered together in the garden to reacquaint themselves. In the middle of a burst of laughter from everyone around her, Kipling had caught Grayson's back as he slipped beyond the light cast by the backyard lamps to the back fence. She watched him, wondering if she should follow. Even after the truth was known, and after his aunt and uncle had forgiven him his broken effort to share it, she had sensed a heaviness in his heart. Lost in thoughts she didn't know.

Annalise patted her knee, drawing her attention. "Go after him, sweetheart. I know my son, and he has much on his mind."

"Maybe he needs some time alone," Kipling said, looking to his mother. She smiled, but didn't think for a moment it was convincing. "I more or less thrust myself on him, and short of a rather unpleasant couple of days, he has had to put up with my presence twenty-four-seven."

"And you don't think he hasn't loved every moment?" Before Kipling tried to answer, Annalise nudged her and jutted her chin toward the direction her son had gone. "Go on."

Knowing no one would miss her amongst the stories and laughter and wine, Kipling stood and tugged her borrowed sweater around her. She hadn't yet acclimated to the idea that a day could be lovely, but once the sun was down, the air could take a drastic turn, so Emerson had give her one of his heavy wool sweaters that smelled of pipe tobacco and aftershave. She waited at the edge of the lawn until her eyes adjusted to the darkness beyond and saw Grayson's silhouette against the split rail fence, one foot on the lower rail, his arms folded on the top as he hunched over.

She made her way to him, and the voices behind her dimmed, providing some calm to her over-stimulated auditory nerves. She sometimes didn't know how normal-hearing people dealt with the constant, overwhelming noise. Her audiologist had told her she didn't hear like someone with normal hearing. A hearing aid, no matter how technologically advanced, couldn't match the delicate operation of the human ear. They could try, but it would never be perfect. She wondered, too, how different the sound of some things — like the deep timbre of Grayson's voice or the melodic tinkle of a piano being played — sounded to someone else.

Strange thoughts as she walked across the lawn toward him.

He turned his head toward her as she reached him, and straightened when she was within reach. Before she could ask him anything — Was he okay? What was on his mind? — Grayson curled his long fingers behind her neck at the base of her skull and drew her to him for a long, deep kiss that tasted of red wine and a future promise of more. Kipling hummed into the kiss, letting it wrap around her and make her dizzy. When he let her go, she tipped back her head and let the evening air cool her lips before she opened her eyes and smiled at him.

"Hello to you, too," she said with a smile.

He chuckled a low rumble that shifted through his chest and

into her. "It has been hours since I've been able to kiss you, and I was peckish."

"Is that why you came out here? Hoping I'd follow so you could steal a kiss?"

He winked and clicked his cheek. "Added bonus."

Kipling drew in a deep breath and settled against him, curling her arms between them while he wrapped her in his embrace. "Are you going to tell me what's been on your mind? All week I thought it was coming here, telling everyone. But everyone knows, everyone is overjoyed, and you are still thinking."

His mouth ticked at one corner, quickly there, and just as quickly gone. "I am not accustomed to having someone in my life who notes such things."

The same apprehension she'd just confessed to his mother tickled up her spine, but she refused to surrender to her insecurities, especially when she had far more evidence of his love than her concerns. Instead, she laid her cheek against his chest, angled just enough to prevent her aids from whining, but enough she could feel and hear the rhythmic beat of his heart.

"That doesn't answer my question," she said, enjoying the warmth of his arms around her. "What else have you been thinking on so hard?"

He chuckled, the rumble against her cheek and chest enough to make her smile, and firmed his hold. "I have said since our time in Boston that you are a very observant woman, Kipling."

"And I am currently observing your avoidance."

"Not avoiding." He smoothed his hand up and down her back. "Determining how to answer without cocking it up."

Kipling drew back enough she could see his face, but without taking her arms from around him, or leaving his hold. "You have always spoken clearly and succinctly, without beating around the bush, so why try anything different?"

He took in a slow, deep breath, studying her face as he released it again, the moonlight giving her just enough light to see the shift of his eyes, though the color was lost. "Because I have told you, all of this is unknown to me. Familiar in concept, perhaps, but not in practice."

"You mean me. Us." A cool chill skimmed her skin, and despite her promise to herself not to assume anything, a ball of lead hit her stomach.

He took his hand from her back and laid it against her cheek, his palm warm, stroking her skin with his thumb. "Yes, but do not think for even a moment I speak in any way of hesitance or regret. Never. Kipling, you have thoroughly destroyed the man I was, and I could not be more thankful. I knew my life changed when we met, but it has been Greg's return that has forced me into deep contemplation."

"What are you contemplating, Grayson?" she asked, hating the crack in her voice.

"The future. Kipling, do you remember the day at your parents' home when you were brave enough to tell me you loved me?"

She nodded.

"I told you I already knew I loved you, but being so unfamiliar with the idea I was terrified to speak. First time in my life I would confess to fear that didn't involve a ticking bomb or possible death." He finished his confession with a smile, but her stomach still wouldn't' relax. "My logic said a fortnight was too short a time to be so fully in love. And now, four months later, I feel I've loved you forever."

"You said I'm observant, Grayson, but right now I feel blind."

"If a fortnight is enough time to fall in love, is four months enough time to decide on the rest of my life? That is the question I've been contemplating all week."

"And what did you decide?"

"That it is more than enough time when the heart is sure. But, I decided that within moments of asking myself the question. The greater question has been how to ask you if you feel the same."

Kipling blinked, her eyes burning with tears she'd held back, and her vision cleared when they tracked her cheeks. Grayson's gaze shifted to her cheek and the point of contact between his thumb and her damp skin. "I'm pretty sure I just mucked up any attempt at a romantic proposal."

"Is that what you're doing?" she managed to croak.

"I'm trying, yes," he said with a self-deprecating chuckle. "No matter how I've tried, I couldn't find a way worthy of you. So, I fall upon my sword and will simply ask." His eyes shifted back to look into hers. "Kipling, would you consider accepting me as your husband?"

She sucked in a sharp, shaking breath, all ability to speak stolen from him. Her thoughts raced, her heart pounded, but her tongue was a dead weight in her mouth. All she could think to do was reach for him, wrapping her hands behind his head to bring him to her for an answering kiss. He met her open mouth kiss, his arms wrapping around her with enough strength she had to toe up to keep her feet on the ground. She tasted the salt of her kiss on their lips, but it took all she had not to laugh, the sensation in her chest like the bubbles in a bottle of champagne shaken to the point of explosion. When she couldn't kiss him for the laughter, she held him tighter as he pressed his face into the curve of her shoulder and kissed the side of her neck.

"I can only hope that is an acceptance," he said near her ear before kissing her cheek and pulling back to look her in the face.

Kipling nodded, swiping at her cheeks. "I'm sorry. I couldn't manage to speak, so, I did the next best thing."

Holding his attention on her face, which she was sure fairly well glistened in the moonlight with her tears, and reached into his pocket. He brought his hand between them, and uncurled his fingers to reveal a ring in his palm.

The moonlight glinted off an antique yellow gold ring with three oval opals, set side by side, accented with four brilliant diamonds, in an engraved band. Grayson took her left hand and slipped the ring onto her trembling index finger.

The ring was loose, but not overly, and he slid it over her knuckles to settle it in place. "This was the ring my great-grandfather gave my great-grandmother when they wed. It served not as an engagement ring, but as their wedding ring. If you'd like a different ring — providing you say yes — I'll get you whatever you would—"

"I can't imagine anything more perfect."

Grayson lifted her hand to his lips, kissing her finger above the ring. "Thank you," he said, his voice now the one to carry the rough weight of his emotions. "No matter how I was sure you would say yes, I must confess there was a small bit of my thinking — which seemed to shout much louder than the rest of my thoughts — warning me to guard my heart should you say no."

Kipling sniffed and rested her hand on his chest so she could see the facets of the opals and diamonds in the moonlight. She swallowed and licked her lips, looking up at him. "I accept, with one request."

"Name it," he said without hesitation.

She looked back toward the house, where she could easily see the rest of his family, and again she remembered the last time they were here. "I want to marry you here. In this garden." She looked back to him. "Can we do that?"

"Of course," he said with a smile that pushed aside any whispers of doubt that wanted to hang on. "Mum will be ecstatic. But, it's early June. By August, it wouldn't be advisable—"

"Then we get married before August," she cut him off, holding her breath through her smile — so wide it made her cheeks ache — to hear his response.

He stared at her, his own smile growing slowly until it crinkled the corners of his eyes and dimpled his chin. "Then we get married before August," he repeated. Then laughed and looked past her to the cottage. "She planned Shirl's wedding in four months; I've no doubt with the proper motivation she can plan another in less than two."

"She won't think we're rushing?"

Grayson hummed a negative and circled her shoulders with his arm, drawing her to his side to start back toward the cottage. "Are you kidding? She's been watching me with great intent since I asked her for this ring earlier tonight. She is already ecstatic. I told you, darling, you have made my family fall in love with you quite thoroughly."

"I should call my parents."

"In the morning. If you call now and wake them, they will think something has happened and will be on a plane before you can explain."

She laughed, curling into his side as close as she could and still walk. They hadn't fully forgiven Grayson yet, and she knew it would take time, but her father had already said he knew Grayson was a good man at his core. They would be happy. She knew it. She believed it.

As they stepped back into the light, all conversation ceased and all attention turned to them. His mother immediately moved to her feet, but his father touched her arm and she sank down again, but the smile on her face didn't waver.

Grayson laughed and kissed Kipling's hair before drawing her closer to the house. "How do you feel about a July wedding, Mum?"

Annalise squealed, hands in the air, and leaped from the bench to run to them and embrace them both in a hug. The rest of the Holmes and McQueen family followed.

Chapter Twenty-Seven

"Good to know you're alive, chief. Gotta say the talk around the water bubbler was wicked scary."

Grayson smiled, finding he'd missed Agent Flannery's slightly abrasive accent and unique word choices, though he supposed by Boston standards they weren't all that unique.

"Thank you. I appreciate the concern. We are both recovering well."

"So, it's true. I heard Miss Branson was on site. She get hurt bad?"

"Quite bruised," Grayson explained, glancing from the kitchen through the garden door to where Kipling was outside, in a telephone discussion of her own.

By the motions of her hands and shaking of her head, her conversation with Mina Russo was not going as well as his with FBI Agent Flannery.

"We have both been ordered to rest, and for the time being I am taking leave from MI6. Which is why I contacted you. Should you need to reach me regarding the upcoming Isaac Sheldon trial, please feel free to do so."

"You sure, chief? I wouldn't want to break in on your vacation. Must be nice with your lady there. Wink wink nudge nudge."

Grayson scowled, not failing to understand Flannery's reference, but shaking his head at the juvenile slant of it. He decided to ignore the implications. "Langdon Howell is currently in custody, should you find solid evidence to link him to Isaac Sheldon."

"Yeah, heard that, too. Your Director Cooper reached out to Stanton, let him know MI6 was open to cooperation if it meant putting Howell away for good."

Jeffrey Cooper had been highly accommodating since confronted about Greg's mortal state, and while Grayson appreciated the lack of argument when he informed Cooper he intended to take some additional time off past his doctor-ordered recuperation period, the director's overly-amendable behavior raked on his nerves nearly as much as a recalcitrant attitude. Though the fact he actually admitted his actions were deceitful and cruel gave Grayson some satisfaction.

"Did I lose you, chief?"

Grayson cleared his throat and turned to the kettle, which had just begun to boil, to pour tea. "Apologies. I admit my mind isn't focused. When do you anticipate the Sheldon trial to be underway?"

"It may be summer in Boston, but the wheels of justice roll as quick as molasses uphill in January, you know what I mean? They're talkin' probably August. You gonna be back on the clock by then?"

"It will depend on what part of August," Grayson said, glancing to the garden again when he heard Kipling's raised voice. Just as he looked, she flopped down onto one of the wooden benches, hunched forward with her head braced in one hand, and her phone in the other. "Early in the month may prove to be a challenge."

"So, you're planning on coming back to Beantown for the trial?"

"Yes."

From the garden, Kipling raised her head and their gazes met. She tried to smile but rolled her eyes and shook her head. She set the phone on the bench beside her and sighed *Not going well.* Grayson set his fist on his chest and circled it in a sign of apology.

He felt partially guilty she was in the difficult call, though the recipient was far more to blame.

"You probably don't need to be here for the whole of it."

"As long as Kipling is required in Boston, I will remain."

"She goin' back to London with you?" The uptick in Flannery's voice was amusing, and Grayson smiled at his attempt at casual information gathering.

"Most certainly. After all, by that point, she will be my wife."

Flannery sputtered and coughed, and it sounded much like he might have just taken a sip of coffee. "Geez! Warn a guy when you're gonna drop a bomb like that."

Enjoying Flannery's discomfiture probably more than he should, he chuckled and carried the tea to the table, catching Kipling's attention so she knew it was ready. The truth was he liked Agent Patrick Flannery, though the man seemed to go out of his way to hide his intelligence. He had proven himself a strong ally and peer. Someone Grayson wouldn't mind working with on a continuous basis, were it possible. He returned to the kitchen to retrieve the breakfast he'd left warming in the cooker once he realized her unscheduled telephone call was running long.

"Apologies, though I'm not sure how I might have properly prepared you."

"Geez, I don't know but you could've tried. Gonna try the whole marital bliss thing, huh? Course, I'm not one for advice."

Grayson had determined while they were still in Boston that Agent Flannery's marriage was at an end, though even in his tone Grayson believed the man was dealing well with the divorce.

"I am indeed," he said instead. "And on that note, I must go. While your day is winding down, ours is just beginning."

"Yeah, sure, chief. I'll be in touch."

Grayson disconnected and set the phone on the table as Kipling came through the garden door with a heavy sigh that visibly dragged at her shoulders. She set down her phone with more force than required and sank into the chair in front of her breakfast. Grayson leaned over to press a kiss to her cheek before taking his seat adjacent to her. He took her hand on the table and waited for her to look at him. When she did, she looked weary. Not physically tired, but soul weary.

"Where is Greg?" she asked, looking at the empty spot beside her.

"He opted instead to head to Southpark. He and Esther have made plans for the day."

Kipling smiled, and while he saw earnestness in it, the drain of the telephone call still sat heavily on her.

"I assume Mina didn't congratulate us," he said, offering a smile.

Kipling sighed again and took a sip of her tea, eyes closed, setting the cup down before answering. "Not congratulating us would be putting it mildly." She shook her head and looked at him, and the sadness in her eyes made his chest ache for the need to fix it, even though he knew it wasn't in his power. "I don't understand. Mina and I have had arguments – that's expected – but this is outright hostility toward you, toward my move, toward the new job, toward *everything*. Were all this new since she found out John wasn't John, but was Greg and your cousin, I would accept it to some degree and believe she would eventually understand. Maybe even be happy for me. But, she has been like this since February, shortly after you left."

"Other than the obvious, has anything changed for her? I'm wondering if all of this is the culmination of many events and circumstances."

"Nothing that stands out; at least nothing she mentioned specifically." She paused, her brow pulling, and canted her head.

"What have you recalled?" he asked.

Kipling shook her head, slowly, possibly still processing whatever had come to mind. "She has mentioned someone a few times, but I haven't met her. Someone named Patty, but I don't know what that would have to do with anything. Except..."

"Except what, darling?"

She blanched, her eyes widening. "I was so frustrated with the whole of the conversation, I missed something she said. It didn't register until just now. She was talking faster than I could get a word in edgewise, about how you and Greg are liars, and how could I possibly trust someone whose entire skill set is knowing how to deceive people. Then she said 'Patty warned me this could happen. That he'd keep pulling you deeper and deeper until you drown'." She blinked, focusing on Grayson. "I don't even know who this woman is, but it sounds like Mina has told her everything."

"Unfortunately, such is a risk we take when we allow others to know who we are and what we do. It is why usually a person is vetted like Esther was before they know. In our case, my position was part of our meeting and we skipped the clandestine part." He winked and smiled, attempting to put her at some kind of ease. "When you gained knowledge, so did those around you. I didn't believe it prudent to ask for secrecy. Nor would I now. It would be unfair to you to ask you to exclude those closest to you for a relationship with me."

"You mean marriage," she said with a slow grin that pushed aside the weary sadness.

Grayson hummed his approval and leaned toward her, meeting her for a kiss. "Yes, I do." He motioned toward her plate. "Now eat up. We have some shopping to do today."

"For what?" she asked before taking a bite of the omelet he'd made while she spoke to her estranged best friend. She rolled her eyes and hummed in approval. "Oh, this is so good."

"Thank you. Not all bachelors are rubbish in the kitchen. And for a car," he answered, smiling at her praise. "Seems I am in need of one."

They worked on breakfast, but the casual, comfortable lack of conversation eventually changed and Grayson knew she was again in deep thought. When her hand stilled, holding her fork over the remains of her eggs, he laid fingers over her wrist to draw her attention.

"Tell me," he said simply.

"Mina," she said, then sighed deeply again. "I'm not happy about her being so loose-tongued. Before we knew John was Greg, when he was just John Allen, she told him who you were and what you did as if it were nothing at all. I was annoyed, and intended to confront her about it, but it was the same day you called me from a plane somewhere and the university called me for the interview. In the chaos and excitement, I never revisited it. I wonder now how many people she's told."

"You can't dwell on it," he said, shaking his head. "If she has, she has. Perhaps when tensions lessen between you, you can speak to her about it. I doubt she would want to hear from me. She would see it as a reprimand."

"Maybe she deserves a reprimand," Kipling mumbled, shaking her head as she stabbed her breakfast.

Though he tried to make light of her concerns, Grayson already anticipated a telephone call or two to investigate the extent of her chin-wagging. "Is she coming to the wedding?"

"As of right now? No. Honestly, even if she changed her mind I'm not sure I would want her to come."

Grayson lifted her hand to his lips and kissed her fingers. "I'm sorry, darling. You have been friends for a very long time."

"Yes, but she's not proving to me it will last much longer." Tears glistened briefly in her eyes, but she sniffed and shook her head, and the tears were gone. "I would love her to be part of my life, but not if that is the way she's going to be. Things change." She smiled at him, and he knew she believed it. "All for the better."

"All for the better. So, do you have a particular type of car you would like?"

"What has it got to do with me? I can't even drive in the UK."

"But you'll learn."

Kipling laughed and shook her head, her chestnut hair falling around her shoulders. "One thing at a time."

9 June

I am leveraging the weak point to full potential. Have received confirmation Holmes and the woman are engaged. Plans progressing. Should I proceed with phase two?

10 June

Confirmed. Proceed.

CONTINUED IN BAKER STREET LEGACY
BOOK THREE: INDEFINITE DOUBT

About the Author

Gail R. Delaney is a multi-published, award-winning author of romance in multiple sub-genres, including contemporary romance, romantic suspense, and epic science fiction romance. She always wrote stories as a kid through her teens, but didn't decide to write 'for publication' until her early twenties after the death of her mother. While helping her father go through her mother's papers, she found a box her mother kept with everything Gail had ever written—from book reports to short stories. It was then she realized her mother saw her as a writer, and it was time to live up to her mother's vision.

You can find out more about Gail R. Delaney's body of work at:

http://www.GailDelaney.com

Also by Gail R. Delaney

Contemporary Romance

Something Better

Precious Things

Feel My Love

Fools Rush In

THE FUTURE POSSIBLE SAGA

BOOK ONE: REVOLUTION

BOOK TWO: OUTCASTS

BOOK THREE: GAINING GROUND

BOOK FOUR: END GAME

BOOK FIVE: JANUS

BOOK SIX: TRIAD

BOOK SEVEN: STASIS

BOOK EIGHT: LIBER